女

Empress

皇

SHAN SA

TRANSLATED BY ADRIANA HUNTER

HARPER  PERENNIAL

NEW YORK ● LONDON ● TORONTO ● SYDNEY

HARPER ● PERENNIAL

Originally published in France by Albin Michel in 2003.

A hardcover edition of this book was published in 2006 by HarperCollins Publishers.

FIRST PAPERBACK EDITION PUBLISHED 2007.

Designed by Paula Szafranski

The Library of Congress has catalogued the hardcover edition as follows:

Shan, Sa, 1972–
    [Impératrice. English]
    Empress : a novel / Shan Sa ; translated by Adriana Hunter.
      p. cm.
    ISBN 0-06-081758-5 (alk. paper)
    1. Wu hou, Empress of China, 624–705—Fiction. 2. China—History—Tang Dynasty, 618–907—Fiction. 3. Empresses—China—Fiction. I. Title.

PQ3979.2.S47I4713 2006
843'.92—dc22

                                    2006040845

ISBN: 978-0-06-114787-6 (pbk.)
ISBN-10: 0-06-114787-7 (pbk.)

07 08 09 10 11 WBC/RRD 10 9 8 7 6 5 4 3 2

PRAISE FOR *EMPRESS*

"As a story, *Empress* shocks and mesmerizes; as a piece of writing, it flows with undiluted poetry."
    —Michelle Lovric, author of *The Floating Book* and *The Remedy*

uch originality, lyricism, uncanny characters, and painstaking historic construction of court intrigue . . . *Empress* is a masterpiece."
    —Maurice Druon, L'Académie française

Dazzling. The reader hears the horses neighing during the imperialist ids, inhales the intoxicating scent of the royal apartments, and visits a st land of ever-changing scenery."   —*Paris Match*

" imbitious and intriguing . . . a sprawling fresco of blossoming r etaphors."   —*Elle* (France)

ALSO BY SHAN SA

The Poems of Yan Ni (poems)

The Red Dragonfly (poems)

Snow (poems)

May the Spring Return (essays)

Porte de la Paix Céleste (novel)

Les Quatre Vies du Saule (novel)

Le Vent Vif et le Glaive Rapide (poems)

The Girl Who Played Go (novel)

Le Miroir du Calligraphe (poems and paintings)

Les Conspirateurs (novel)

Alexandre et Alestria (novel)

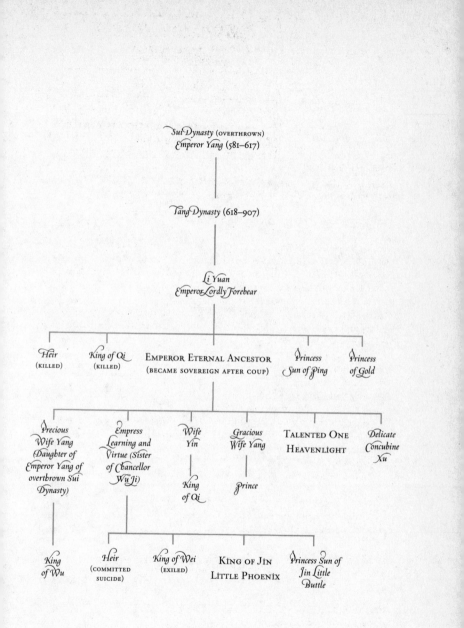

Sui Dynasty (OVERTHROWN)
Emperor Yang (581–617)

Tang Dynasty (618–907)

Li Yuan
Emperor Lordly Forebear

Heir
(KILLED)

King of Qi
(KILLED)

EMPEROR ETERNAL ANCESTOR
(BECAME SOVEREIGN AFTER COUP)

Princess
Sun of Ping

Princess
of Gold

Precious
Wife Yang
(Daughter of
Emperor Yang of
overthrown Sui
Dynasty)

Empress
Learning and
Virtue (Sister
of Chancellor
Wu Ji)

Wife
Yin

Gracious
Wife Yang

TALENTED ONE
HEAVENLIGHT

Delicate
Concubine
Xu

King
of Qi

Prince

King
of Wu

Heir
(COMMITTED
SUICIDE)

King of Wei
(EXILED)

KING OF JIN
LITTLE PHOENIX

Princess Sun of
Jin Little
Buttle

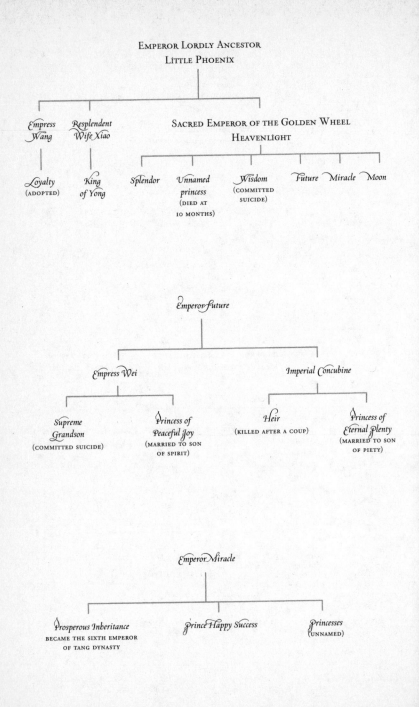

EMPEROR LORDLY ANCESTOR
LITTLE PHOENIX

Empress Wang — Resplendent Wife Xiao — SACRED EMPEROR OF THE GOLDEN WHEEL HEAVENLIGHT

Loyalty (ADOPTED) — King of Yong — Splendor — Unnamed princess (DIED AT 10 MONTHS) — Wisdom (COMMITTED SUICIDE) — Future — Miracle — Moon

Emperor Future

Empress Wei — Imperial Concubine

Supreme Grandson (COMMITTED SUICIDE) — Princess of Peaceful Joy (MARRIED TO SON OF SPIRIT) — Heir (KILLED AFTER A COUP) — Princess of Eternal Plenty (MARRIED TO SON OF PIETY)

Emperor Miracle

Prosperous Inheritance BECAME THE SIXTH EMPEROR OF TANG DYNASTY — Prince Happy Success — Princesses (UNNAMED)

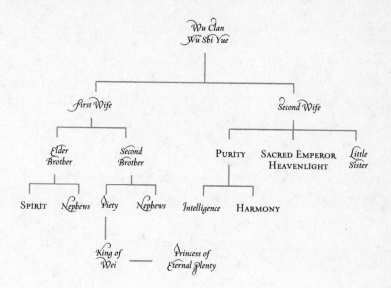

Wu Clan
Wu Shi Yue

First Wife — Second Wife

Elder Brother — Second Brother — Purity — SACRED EMPEROR HEAVENLIGHT — Little Sister

SPIRIT — Nephews — Piety — Nephews — Intelligence — HARMONY

King of Wei ——— Princess of Eternal Plenty

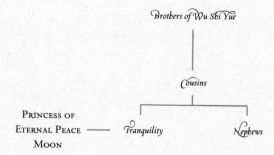

Brothers of Wu Shi Yue

Cousins

PRINCESS OF ETERNAL PEACE MOON ——— Tranquility — Nephews

The sharp wind and the swift dagger

The only blessings from my ancestors

—Shan Sa

Empress

ONE

*E*ndless moons, an opaque universe, thunder, tornadoes, the quaking earth. Rare moments of peace; forehead up against my knees, arms around my head, I thought, I listened, I longed not to exist. But life was there, a transparent pearl, a star revolving slowly on its own axis. I was blind. My eyes stared into that other world, that other existence that dwindled a little every day. Its colors were extinguished, its images blurred. I was still left with cries of astonishment and feeble sobbing. I was oppressed by the impotence of these vague recollections, burned by their melancholy. Who am I? I asked Death as it crouched at my feet. Death moaned and gave no reply.

Where am I? I could hear laughter, voices saying, "It will surely be a boy, my Lord. He is moving. He is full of life."

It mattered little who I would be. I was already weary of this vastness. I was weary of hoping, of waiting, of being myself—the center of the world.

I was soothed by the rustle of the wind. I listened to the trickle of rain. Across my sky in which the sun never rose, I could hear a little girl singing. I was lulled by her gentle, innocent voice. My sister, I foresaw

1

great sorrow for her. A hand tried to caress me. But a wall lay between us. Oh Mother, the shadow outlined against the screen of my thoughts, do you realize I am already old, condemned to live within the prison of your flesh?

IN THE DEPTHS of the lake, in the sepia-colored waters, I swiveled round, curled up into a ball, spread my limbs, turned circles. Day by day my body grew, weighing heavily on me, strangling me. I would have liked to be the prick of a needle, a grain of sand, the flash of sunlight in a drop of water; I was becoming flesh, an exploding flesh, a mountain of folds and blood, a marine monster. One breath raised me up and rocked me. I was irascible. I was furious with myself, with the woman who was my jailor, with Death—my only friend.

They waited for me. I heard someone whisper that the boy would be called Heavenlight. The rustle of preparations hampered my meditation. They spoke of clothes, celebrations, wet nurses: plump, white, and sturdy. They were forbidden to speak my name, for fear that demons would possess my soul. They were waiting for me to pick up where their own destinies had left off. I felt pity for these fervent creatures, so affable and eager. They did not yet know that I would destroy their world to build my own. They did not know that I would bring deliverance—but with fire and ice.

One night I awoke with a start. The waters were seething. Furious waves broke over me. I held myself tightly, struggling with my fear and concentrating on my breathing, on my gnawing pain. When the tide surged, I was launched into a narrow opening. I slid between the rocks. My body bled. My skin tore. My head imploded. I balled my fists to stop myself from screaming.

Someone pulled me by my feet and slapped my buttocks. With my head hanging down, my cries spewed from me. I was wrapped in a cloth that flayed me. I heard a man's anxious voice: "Boy or girl?"

No one replied. The man grabbed me and tried to tear open my swaddling.

2

He was interrupted by a woman's quiet wail:

"Another girl, my Lord."

"Ah!" he cried before dissolving in tears.

A dozen women watched over me as I grew. Three wet nurses took turns quenching my thirst. My appetite was frightening. I was already laughing. My eyes were great black pearls rolling in their sockets. I looked on the world day and night, never wanting to sleep. My mother was worried by my constant agitation; she called on a number of exorcist monks. But no one succeeded in expelling the demon from me.

I eventually grew weary of their fears. Behind the gauze of my mosquito net, I pretended to sleep to have some peace, while a woman sang as she rocked my cradle. Another waved a fan to waft away the odd fly that had strayed into the perfumed universe. With my eyelids closed, I let my thoughts fly away.

The kingdom that Father ruled as absolute master was divided into two parts. The Front Quarter was reserved for men. Stewards, secretaries, accountants, cooks, pages, valets, grooms, guards, and lackeys busied themselves from the first light of dawn. Government officials took their orders and set off on horseback. Troops of soldiers undertook training exercises all day long in the great courtyard to the side. This virile world ended before the vermillion gate where the gynaeceum began. Behind the high, snow-colored wall lived hundreds of women: old, young, and little girls. They wore their hair in topknots pinned with flowers and had jade rings threaded into their silk belts. It was the eighth year of Martial Virtue;[1] fashion favored the pallor of early spring: dresses were crocus yellow, the soft green of narcissus leaves, the pleasing pink of cherry blossom, and the crimson of the sun reflected in a lake. Sweepers, servants, seamstresses, embroiderers, bearers, wet nurses, cooks, governesses, stewards, gracious attendants, singers, dancers . . . all of them moved slowly, with composure, and spoke in hushed tones. They rose at dawn, bathed at dusk. They were the flowers

[1] A.D. 625

3

of my father's garden, blossoming to compete with the beauty of one person alone.

Mother dressed soberly. Her least little cough was a command, her every gaze an order. She was naturally elegant. Fashion changed, a flitting butterfly, Mother maintained an eternal springtime. She was of the Yang clan from the Hong Nong region; one of the thirty most noble families in the Empire. As a daughter, niece, and sister to eminent ministers, a cousin to imperial brides, and a close relation to the Emperor and the princesses, Mother wore her dignity like a jewel, a cloak, a crown. She gave alms in the monasteries and distributed food to beggars. She was a fervent Buddhist, observing a vegetarian diet and showing no interest in the turmoil of this lowly world. She copied out the sutras in her careful hand and dreamed of reaching the land of Extreme Joy, the kingdom of Buddha Amida, He who launches countless rays of light.

Mother was cold, delicate, soothing. Her gentleness was cutting and opaque and reminded me of the jade disc that hung over my cradle. I wanted her. I grew agitated waiting. She would appear from time to time after several days' absence. When she arrived, her long silk train and her endless muslin shawl set the curtains to my room aquiver. The ground kissed by her slippered feet whispered with pleasure. Her perfume went before her. It smelled of sunlight, snow, the East Wind, flowers laden with happiness.

She never took me in her arms, happy to contemplate me from a distance. My eyes consumed her hungrily. Her lips were two scarlet petals. Her face was as perfectly smooth as a mirror. Beneath her eyebrows, which had been shaved and redrawn in the shape of cicada wings, her eyes betrayed her disappointment. She had desired a boy.

THE POMEGRANATE TREES exploded into blossom and the summer arrived. My one hundredth day was grounds for a celebration. Mother had the pavilion in the middle of the lake opened up and gathered together her noble friends and relations for a sumptuous banquet.

In that room surrounded by the glittering water, I was passed from hand to hand. I was stroked and petted. Servants came up the steps to lay down gifts. One lady offered me a pair of emerald bracelets—she was convinced that my sparkling black eyes were a sign of intelligence. Another had nine gold ingots brought on a silver tray, saying that my wide forehead was an omen: I had been placed under the sign of a wealthy and happy marriage. Another bedecked me with nine rolls of brocade—she said that my straight nose, my chubby cheeks, and my round mouth foretold exceptional fertility: I would have many sons.

Mother was happy. With a nod of her head, she ordered for a carpet of silk to be unrolled in the middle of the banquet, for me to be freed of my swaddling and to be seated. The servants laid a dozen objects out around me. I forgot this gathering of pale women in all their finery, caught hold of an ice-cold toy and tried to lift it. There was a general murmuring and one woman said: "She chooses neither the makeup box of Beauty, nor the jade of Nobility, nor the flute of Music, nor the book of Wisdom, nor the quill of Poetry, nor the abacus of Commerce, nor the rosary of Spirituality. My dear cousin, your daughter's future will be singularly unusual. It is truly a shame that she is not a boy."

"Indeed, your Highness, it is a great shame," agreed another.

"Ah well, we must not let this distress us," exclaimed a sonorous voice, ringing with pride. "In our time women can demonstrate prowess in a thousand ways. Long ago the great Princess Sun of Ping fought for her father, the August Sovereign. At her funeral, His Majesty called for the trumpets and drums to be sounded, an honor reserved for men. Your daughter has a curved forehead to accept the celestial breath, she has luminous eyes, a strong jaw, generous lips; she has touched of her father's sword. Excellent! My dear, from this day you must dress her as a boy. Give her an education worthy of her own determination. The daughter of a general likes commandment. I can see her as the mistress of a noble warrior household!"

Soon I felt the need to venture out into the world rather than receiving it from my cradle. Unable to stand upright on my feet, I crawled.

One step toward the unknown meant coordinating all my muscles. Pinning my eyes on an object, keeping my ears alert and my mouth open to roar silently, I raised an arm, a leg, I crawled my way through the universe.

A bearded man leaned toward me. He was wrapped in a silk coat lined with sable, and seemed to have come from far, far away. When I saw him, I heard the thundering of hooves, the wailing of the wind, the unbridled moans of the courtesans. The bestial smell of him made me shiver. His gruff kisses tore my cheek.

There was a little girl watching me. I was fascinated by her pink complexion, fine features, sturdy legs, dark eyes, and the wooden duck she trailed behind her. After looking carefully up and down, she put a finger in my hand, and I squeezed it until she flushed red and began to cry. "You must not hurt your sister," my wet nurse told me. She did not know that later, as she had in those days of innocence, Elder Sister would beg me to be her torturer.

In the ninth year of Martial Virtue, the Emperor abdicated in favor of his son. Twelve moons later, the new sovereign recalled Father from the noble province of Yang where he had been sent on a quest, and named him Governor Delegate of the province of Li where an insurrection under Prince Li Xiao Chang had just been repressed.

I was two years old. I stumbled around among the wooden cases and the carriages covered in oiled drapes, unaware of the suffering of a father exiled from Court. The horses and the oxen trod the endless road that dissolved into the horizon. I devoured the world through an opening in the carriage door. Outside, the colors jostled and furrowed, spreading out and contorting. We shall see each other again, Long Peace, my native town!

The wheels' rattles over the stony track kept me awake. We crossed a vast plain where the arid soil had been cracked and crazed by the sun. Hordes of children in rags came and prostrated themselves as we passed by. I was astonished that such thin, dirty creatures existed at all. Mother asked for food to be handed out to them: biscuits, bread, and rice meal, which they swallowed while it was still scalding hot.

I was tormented by questions. I kept asking them all day long: "What is hunger? Why do the fields need to be cultivated? What is wheat? How is bread made?"

After a month of traveling, the caravan embarked into the misty mountains. The track was carved into the cliffs and, further down, the Jia Ling river roared as it hurled itself against the tormented rocks. Forts rose up from the peaks; military outposts opened their barriers for us. The imperial soldiers were brutish men who drank from chipped bowls and ate haunches of beef with their bare hands. In the evenings, around the camp fires, they beat their drums and sang. The moon rose, and I fell asleep listening to the roar of tigers. When the first hint of dawn appeared, birds launched themselves in pursuit of the sun, while monkeys fled the light, screeching as they swung from one strand of creeper to the next. "Why is the sky going red? Why are the trees so still? Why do the boatmen slash their own faces?" Streaming with blood, they raised anchor and threw themselves into the torrents.

I HUNG THE birdcages under the awnings. The robins, orioles, and canaries started to sing. I let the ducks out onto the pond, the cranes into the long grass, and the peacocks into the camellia bushes. Inside our new home, the furniture was taking root, the curtains were growing, and the cats and dogs scrapped over their territory.

Nurse dressed me as a Tartar boy. In my blue turban, leather boots, and emerald-green tunic with its fitted sleeves and cuffs embroidered in gold thread, I tottered like a drunken man, bellowing military songs.

Four years old, the age of diamonds. Free. There, with my arms in the air, I could fly. The new garden was a vast expanse of parkland, a whole continent. The summer was on its way: the hills oozed, the sky evaporated, life slowed down. I crouched down and watched the caravans of ants at the foot of trees. I shook off my servants by running through the bamboo forests. In the evenings, I would refuse to sleep and asked questions till the early hours: "Why does the frog have such a fat belly? Why do mosquitoes flee the herbs burning in bowls? Who do the stars play hide-and-seek with? Why is the moon sometimes round and sometimes thin? Who are the fireflies bearing their tiny lanterns for?"

Mother was afraid of my capacity to think. She called for a wandering monk known for the truth of his predictions. The man assured her there was absolutely no evil in my soul, praised my intelligence, and decreed that I had a spiritual vocation.

In the fourth year of Pure Contemplation, maternal Grandmother left this world. Mother asked me whether I would like to be the family delegate to observe mourning in a monastery and to pray for the salvation of the honorable deceased. I was five years old. I accepted the suggestion with joy: Father was my idol, so the word "delegate" filled my heart with pride, and I would at last have the same degree of importance as the governor of six districts and forty thousand souls.

The river flowed at the foot of the fortified town. The torrents propelled sailing boats toward the skies. From the harbor we could see the mountain of the Black Dragon. Along its sheer cliffs thousands of pavilions sheltered the entrances to Buddhist caves filled with statues and decorated with frescoes. After the boat crossing, I was carried on a servant woman's back up the steep steps and over the bridge of plaited rope that swung across the middle of the valley. I was engulfed by the Monastery of Pure Compassion, which hung between the earth and the sky.

I LOST MY family name and my own name, I was now known as Light of Emptiness. I did not even know how to untie my belt. I would wake in the night calling for my wet nurses. I missed their breasts. I would finger my bedclothes and suck on my blanket, but in these I found neither the satin of their skin nor the wrinkles of their nipples and I wept.

Mother did not come to see me. She had abandoned me to Buddha. Every day I watched and waited for a familiar face at the entrance to the monastery. On that gently rising path, the leaves fell with the dusk.

This monastery, which was famous throughout southern China, bustled with more than one thousand nuns. Pure Intelligence was responsible for my education. She was twenty, her muscled body smelled of green tea, and her impeccably shaved head was velvety soft as a white lotus. She gave me my bath, scrubbing my big tummy and my thin legs. She answered my questions and introduced me to reading. She taught me how to wash my face, dress, fold my blanket, and sing the songs of her homeland.

I swept the courtyard, shuffling back and forth with a bamboo broom taller than myself. I climbed onto the altars and dusted the faces of Buddhas and celestial kings. I crouched beside a waterfall and beat my clothes clean with a large pebble. I busied myself with the old women. For some of them, who were simply tired, I arranged their cushions and fetched pails; for others, who were already loosing their minds, I acted as a prompt for their memories. In the mornings, begging bowl in hand, I seduced rich visitors and made them open their purses. In the evening, after all the lights had been put out, I put on great performances at everyone's request: acting out the scenes I had witnessed during the day; I played wealthy, worldly townswomen as well as our obsequious superiors and an exasperated Buddha. I could hear their laughter and compliments buzzing from beneath their blankets. I savored this glory, but feigned modesty.

My greatest friend was called Law of Emptiness. She was a white goat who followed me everywhere in my feverish activities. When I wandered into a temple, I would tell her about the life of Prince Siddhartha and the wonders of the Pure World. Deep in the forest, I would take a twig from a tree and give her writing lessons. When I was thirsty, I would slip between her legs, and she would offer me her udder full of milk.

"Were you sent by Buddha to watch over me?" I asked her. In her golden eyes, Law of Emptiness had all the goodness that was lacking in humans. Her curly coat was a parchment scribbled with ineffable words. Her hooves, like cloven rocks, trampled over the history of the world. One day I fell asleep at the foot of a statue of Bodhisattva. She woke me by licking my face: darkness was creeping over the sky, and I was late for evening prayer. As I sat up I saw the twinkle of a smile on her muzzle.

"Law of Emptiness, are you an incarnation of Buddha?"

My family home disappeared like a dream.

The mountains seemed to breathe. The mountains were sad; the mountains were happy. The mountains flaunted their furry coats of snow, their brocade robes, their sumptuous and extravagant cloaks of mist. The sky opened up vertically when dusk fell, all ochre, yellow and black. When evening came up from the valleys, the heavenly bodies revealed themselves. I would lie down in the long grasses: red, blue, green, sparkling, evanescent. Every star was a mysterious writing on the sacred book of the sky. Seasons passed, clouds drifted away and never came back. On the other side of the valley, hanging from ropes in the void in front of a cliff face, workmen sculpted day and night. I was told that an imperial donation had been made to create the largest Buddha on Earth.

The moon waxed and waned. The days, those tiny dots and circles, changed into a flowing script whose meaning was now lost. I understood the passage of time by watching the Buddha gradually materializing under those iron picks. Gentle eyes, a mysterious smile, drooping ear lobes, the mountain revealed his face. The cliff lost its sheer exterior, and his body appeared. His draped robes started to flutter in the wind. Birds wheeled around his knees with terrified cries. His ankles came away from the rock. The curve of his toenails emerged. I was mute with awe: Divinity had risen from nothingness!

One morning, in the reception hall, I found Mother and her retinue. She had gained weight; her breasts bulged. I was dazzled by her carefully applied makeup, her hair piled high on her head, and her embroidered gown. She told me that Father had been named Governor Delegate of the distant province of Jing and asked whether I would like to go with him or stay in the monastery.

My feeling of joy shattered: She made it clear that if I left, I would never see the mountains again, and if I stayed, I would lose my family forever. That same evening the monastery shook in the grips of a violent storm; the thunder roared, and the earth trembled. A tree just outside our sleeping quarters was struck by lightning and collapsed. The girls were terrified and started to pray. Huddled in my cot, with my hands over my ears, I slipped into another world. The darkness was drawing me in; I had never felt so alone. The thought of gliding across the years without seeing Mother again frightened me. I cried all night.

Before I left, Pure Intelligence gave back the box of belongings I had entrusted to her when I arrived. I secured the necklace of pearls and jade about my neck, put earrings in my ears, and put on three gold bracelets. I was heartbroken to find that the pleated skirt, the silk shirt, and the scarlet tunic with the bird design had all shrunk. I had grown.

With one hand I held Law of Emptiness by a length of string attached round her neck, and with the other I shook hands with Pure Intelligence. My tears flowed on and on. She wiped her eyes with the sleeve of her tunic and stopped by the monastery gate.

"Buddha speaks through every moment of pain. Listen to his words. Your destiny lies elsewhere. Forget me."

She turned away and started to run. Her grey dress melted into the trees.

Farewell, monastery! Time will devour you, and you will be turned to dust. Farewell, Pure Intelligence! You will soon die, and we shall see each other again in another life. Farewell, my friends the monkeys, the tigers, and the pandas. You will become carrion, and only the mountains will remain.

They will watch over the Buddha's enigmatic smile.

HORSES WHINNYING.

Cartwheels rumbling.

Coachmen shouting.

Huddled on my cot, I drifted in and out of sleep. The endless earth unfurled as I traveled onward. In my dreams, I was straying through the belly of the mountains with a torch in my hand. A succession of frescoes: green, mauve, yellow, ochre, indigo, images of the gods, the celestial kings, and the bodhisattvas appeared and disappeared. Birds called, wild cats laughed, dancers tiptoed through the clouds scattering a shower of flowers. In the depths of the cave, I could see a statue of Buddha lying down, taking up the entire valley. He had one hand under his cheek but was not asleep. He was the only breath of life, his vast body weightless as a feather ready to fly away. Not the faintest rustle of wind, not one insect cry, not one drop of water falling. The world was silent before his state of bliss. Suddenly Buddha smiled at me. I woke with a start. I no longer knew where I was or what my name was.

I had lost Law of Emptiness. The little goat had disappeared without a trace; the mountains had reclaimed her from me. I had gone there almost naked, and now I was emerging with nothing.

"Everything is dreams and illusion," Pure Intelligence had told me.

WE ABANDONED THE earth path. The wind filled the sails, and the huge boat was like a whole town as it traveled down the River Long.

The banks stretched out, mountains loomed up and dispersed into the mist. Fishermen surrounded by cormorants, groups of little houses on stilts, villages clinging to the side of the cliffs and fortified towns glided past. We threw anchor in ports that smelled of grilled fish. Hundreds of boats buzzed around us, offering cloths, furniture, clothes, vegetables, and young girls. At night the reflection of the moon would scatter over the water, a myriad of silver flowers flutter away. There were black boats covered in oiled cloth and red lanterns at the top of their masts; they emitted the wail of musical instruments, women's laughter, and ugly voices of drunken men.

The river was growing wider. The torrents, no longer eager to rejoin the sea, were slowing down. There were countless vessels, still larger and more magnificent than ours, traveling in both directions.

The journey ended when the season of green plums began. The rain trickled and did not stop. Water streamed over the roofs in the town of Jing; it seeped down the walls and crawled over books, leaving its flower-shaped tracks. Servant women dried damp clothes over fires fed with sandalwood bark. I studied the Four Classics with a private tutor. The cook heaved me up onto her donkey's back and gladly brought me along on her trips to the market.

In the narrow streets paved with black stone, the servants' feet grew red in their wooden clogs. The whole town came together in the float-ing market on the river, their rain hats pulled down over coats woven from bamboo leaves. The boats bustled and nudged one another on the water. The cook bartered fiercely: She could feign anger or improvise with flattery. The fishermen, beaten back by her eloquence, would throw us fish that squirmed through the air.

To console me for the loss of Law of Emptiness, Father gave me a horse and permission to go through the gateway into the side court. I went into the exercise yard where soldiers trained for battle. The animal was as tall as a mountain, spewing hot breath through great nostrils that quivered. All of a sudden he sneezed: terrified, I backed away and fell flat on my backside. He shook his head up and down and laughed, showing off his yellow teeth.

I called him King of Tigers. Up on his back, the world was at my feet. When he went into a gallop, my body melted away, my thoughts scattered in the wind, and I became a warrior on his flying fortress, a goddess on her winged chariot. At last, days of happiness had arrived like the midday sun. Only a few sorrows flitted across the skies of a childhood that knew no suffering.

My sisters and I had private tutors who gave us lessons in painting, calligraphy, music, and dance. When she was twelve, Eldest Sister Pu-rity was as beautiful as the dawn breaking over the River Long. Having been forbidden any exposure to the sun by the doctors because her skin was so delicate, she preferred candlelight, and she would read and write all day long. Her poems already had the rhythm and resonance of a more mature mind. While I scratched my head trying to find obscure words, indispensable ornamentation for my prosaic compositions, sentences would flow from her swift hand in elegant pairs.

Little sister was the mirror image of me. She was seven years old, and she had the sparkling vitality of a young animal. When Father set out to inspect garrisons and other districts, Mother would shut herself away from us in prayer. We would slip away from the clouded gaze of our ancient governesses and explore the Front Quarters. The imposing pavilions seemed to reach the sky. The white walls bore calligraphy in black ink, spelling out the rules of conduct for imperial officials. The hall shimmered with gold. The pillars supported vast vaulted roofs. Father, who was responsible for the paddy-fields and trading and who meted out supreme justice, was the most powerful man in the region!

In the eighth year of Pure Contemplation, Father gave a party for my ninth birthday. The gifts accumulated into great hills of treasure in the pavilion where the reception was held. Father gave me an armor breastplate in red leather with black laces, a suede hat decorated with a goose head, and a small bow bound with rattan. A general sent me a young falcon and three pups. The dignitaries of the province paid me intoxicating compliments. Blushing and delighted, I made a pretense of shyness as I welcomed the last days of my innocence. The rustle of silk, the tumbling rhythms of music, laughter, shouts, whinnying horses . . . these were the crowning moments of the beautiful firework display that had been my childhood.

Our infant years are like cruising on a cloud: suspended on high, the celestial landscape seems to unfold so slowly, motionless and eternal, while we flit past a thousand plains and mountains on the ground below.

My journey was already coming to an end.

One morning a few months after this party that dazzled me still, a carriage came to collect Eldest Sister. She emerged weeping from the house, dressed like a goddess, and left forever.

The previous year she had been betrothed to a boy from the local nobility. I had admired her dowry with its crimson lacquered trunks that took up an entire pavilion. As I counted her dishes of jade, gold, and

Empress

silver; her sheets of velvet and satin; her countless dresses; and her embroidered shoes, I even felt a tinge of envy. I did not understand what marriage was. Only after she left did I realize that a harmonious world in which everything had its rightful place had just collapsed. Later Purity came back to the maternal home with her husband. Just as I had feared—with her fringe lifted off her face, her eyebrows completely plucked, her cheeks powdered, and her hair in a topknot—she was no longer my sister. She had become a woman!

In that ninth year of Pure Contemplation, there were weeds growing in the garden of my heart, and I was a melting pot of scorn and insolence. I had read *A History of the Han Dynasty* and *Poems of the Lands of Chu*. I had studied *The Virtue and Piety of Women*. I was well versed in arithmetic, calligraphy, painting, and playing the zither and the game of go. This image of a well-brought up young lady irritated me: I wanted to be like those barefoot adolescents with their trousers rolled up who hurled their nets into the river.

On the sixth day of the fifth moon, the retired emperor died. Imperial messengers spread the grim news to the four corners of the empire. Surprised by their mournful announcement, Father collapsed. When his officers rushed to support him, his eyes rolled back in their sockets, and he struggled as if possessed by some invisible demon. As his thrashing became calmer, he was taken into the inner quarters. Father never awoke. He had left this world.

Doctors could not diagnose the mysterious illness to which he had succumbed. They concluded that the late emperor had called up his warrior: He was to escort him as he ascended to the celestial kingdom. The imperial Court soon confirmed this theory, and, touched by this proof of loyalty to his master, the reigning emperor conferred on Father the posthumous title of Minister of Rites.

I wandered from one room to another in that unreal world, understanding nothing. Father's body lay on a bed of ice. With his smooth features and half-closed eyes, he looked deep in thought. Mother wept as she took off all her jewelry. Behind her, men and women could be

15

heard wailing. The house was draped with linen and white hemp, transforming it into an immaculate temple.

A few days later, two officials arrived from the Capital borne by exhausted horses. The servants knelt as they passed. The officials wept as they climbed the stairs, then threw themselves before the funeral bed and howled with pain. I watched these black-bearded strangers through a window and recognized my half-brothers, the sons of Father's late wife.

Tears, cries, and wails. We observed the ceremonial procedures: bathing him, calling upon his soul, filling his mouth,[2] the smaller clothing ceremony,[3] the great clothing ceremony,[4] laying him in his coffin, and making daily offerings. I followed meekly, obedient, and dazed. Imperial representatives, envoys from the world of high politics, relations, and local dignitaries filed past us offering their condolences and their funeral gifts. Throughout that whirlwind of comings and goings, the summer threw a thick heat haze over the town. Beneath my mourning gown, my hips and buttocks became covered with tiny spots. At night I moaned and turned over in bed, scratching frantically.

The coffin left the house and was taken to the temple of Beloved Happiness, where it stayed for forty-nine days while the monks read sacred texts and prayed for the soul of the deceased. Unfamiliar faces and men with brutish accents invaded the house and occupied the guest rooms. Mother told me that they were my father's nephews, and they had come to escort us to his motherland.

The thoroughbred horses disappeared—apparently sold by the young lords. Soon huge trunks were brought out of the inner quarters, and the governesses, dancing women, servants, and cooks evaporated in turn. One morning, seeing King of Tigers' empty stall, my heart stood

---

[2] The deceased's mouth was filled with grain mixed with pieces of jade or shells depending on his or her social standing.

[3] After displaying the clothes, the deceased was dressed in nineteen costumes.

[4] This took place the day after the smaller clothing ceremony. The number of garments was strictly related to social hierarchy. In this case, fifty costumes would have been used.

still. I ran over to the pavilion where Mother was praying and fell to my knees, calling on Buddha. I rubbed my eyes, which had become infected by so much lamentation and shed every last tear in my body.

Mother remained silent. Then suddenly, for the first time in my life, she held me in her arms and wept with me. The sons had taken the funds and the keys for themselves; the nephews had announced that they would take charge of our assets and be masters of our fate.

IN HIS YOUTH, Father had married a commoner who had given him sons. It was after her death that he obeyed the sovereign's order and married my mother. Even when I was very little, I understood that Father had begat two different worlds. My sisters and I were sunlight and beauty; my brothers, dark, ill-dressed creatures, were the echo of an indelible former life. They had become officials and rarely came home. Father, who had always been so authoritarian toward his subordinates and so severe with us, had given in to his sons' arrogance. He had tried to buy their favor by showering them with gifts. Arguments flared between my parents: Mother would complain about their harsh words and vindictive expressions; Father would defend them, claiming that they were shy and wary of us. Mother pronounced the terrible word "hate." She said they would never forgive her for taking his first wife's place.

At night I would paint Father's face feature by feature: his wide forehead; his pronounced wrinkles; and his square jaw beneath his beautiful, long, white beard. Officials had greeted him with respect, and the common people had prostrated themselves at his feet. One after another they had come before him to plead their case and beg for justice. Father listened to them patiently and gave each of them a reply. He spoke slowly and firmly, intimidating them with his gaze. His physique seemed to occupy a space so fully that it could reach the vaulted ceiling of a pavilion held up by massive pillars. Then I would picture him in his bed clothes, a gray, silk tunic over a white under-robe, held by a mauve sash. He would be reading, leaning his head on one hand that bore an emerald ring carved in the shape of a tiger's head. He would call me over: "Heavenlight, come and read with me." For hours on end he would talk to me about mountains and rivers; he would draw the canals he was having dug to link up the rivers and irrigate the fields. Dawn would come, and Father would leave, taking Glory and Magnificence with him. The world that opened before me now was a dark, narrow, insignificant place.

A new governor had arrived, and we had to vacate the residence for him and go with my brothers to take the coffin to the motherland. We waited for winter before starting out. The caravans of carriages drawn by oxen and horses set off toward that distant land in the north. Men, women, and children dressed in linen tunics with white headbands round their foreheads followed us out of the town of Jing in tears.

I was leaving my town of stone and winged horses. The River Long and the roar of the waves disappeared. I abandoned the tame cormorants and the bobbing junks tossed into the sky. The cavernous temples, the nuns, and the little fishing girls vanished with the wafting incense. Farewell, moon, you who lit the battles of old, you who guided warriors as they rode recklessly through the night. You who know the secrets of my destiny, give me a well-honed weapon, give me your blessing!

TWO

*T*he horizon kept receding further. The road forked and melted into the sun. The roar of the River Han and the seagulls' cries disappeared. The greens, blues, ochres, and mirrored reflections of the paddy-fields vanished. On the far side of the River Huai, the hills smoothed out, and the trees had lost their leaves. Rivers and dry reeds sprang out of the black earth and its metallic glitter. The wind whipped up, squally gusts tormented the fields, and straggly wheat stalks moaned. The horses and oxen lowered their heads to battle against the wind. Little Sister had taken refuge in my carriage; wrapped in furs, we tried in vain to keep warm. All day long I listened to pebbles clattering against the wheels and the howling of the north wind, which deadened my thoughts. My heart was dry; I had no tears left.

One morning, in that ocean of uninterrupted buffeting, I discovered the Yellow River stretching its frozen length away toward the sky. Countless trading caravans had already carved a white track through the ice. Early that afternoon it snowed: The snowflakes of the north, larger than a child's hand, were like millions of birds twirling in the sky. Black and gray became opacity and transparency. The wind dropped. We were dark smudges strung out across this immaculate world as we forged ahead.

Ten days later, just as the fleeting sunlight was about to be eclipsed behind the mountains, hundreds of men and women dressed in white appeared in the snow waving funeral banners. My brothers and cousins dismounted and ran over to meet them.

My heart felt constricted. The thing I so feared was about to happen: I would discover my origins.

A great uncle, head of the Wu clan, took us to the village. My brothers prostrated themselves in the Temple of Ancestors to announce our return. An ageing aunt, mistress of all the women, took us into a house lit by white lanterns. The meal provided for us in mourning was ice cold. Somewhere a dog howled. In the middle of the night, Little Sister came to join me, and we shivered in my bed, which was hard as a sheet of iron.

The next day, in Father's old bedroom, I witnessed the calling of his soul. The coffin and offerings were positioned behind a curtain of gauze. Members of the family tore their clothes and beat their foreheads on the ground, wailing and lamenting. The sorcerer danced until a powerful voice rose up from his throat. He turned to face the north, where the Kingdom of Shades is to be found, and shook one of Father's tunics, calling on him and singing:

O soul, come back!
Why did you leave your body?
Desolate and alone, you now wander the four corners of the Earth!
O soul, go not to the east! For there ten suns have dried out the
seas and set fire to the fields. They will charm you with their
dazzling flames and will burn you to cinders!
O soul, stop before the great swamps of the south! There are
venomous snakes coiled in the mud, and their venom has poisoned
the mists. They will transform themselves into beautiful, naked

women draped with gold necklaces. They will suffocate you with
their supple tongues and drink your blood!
O soul, go not to the west! The desert sands conceal the great Abyss
of the Earth. Storms whip up the stones and bleach skeletons there.
The ground has been roaring and suffering since the creation of
the Universe. Three-eyed vultures and deaf and blind asses wage
war on each other for all eternity.
O soul, do not cross the glaciers of the north. Nine-headed bears
watch over the celestial gates. Snowflakes hide the jade scorpions
lying in wait for wandering souls. Their venom turns the living to
stone and the dead to water!
O soul, come back home! Here your family gives you offerings.
Here there is white rice, brown rice, millet, and sorghum! Here
there is beef soup, turkey stew, and sautéed tortoise meat. Here
there is wine from every region, that earthly nectar and the sweet
headiness it brings! Here is your gentle bed, the gauze curtains, the
silk sheets and downy cushions, and women more fragrant than
orchids!
O soul, do you not long for tender glances, plump lips, and
caressing hands?
O soul, have you forgotten your nights of love making, the
pleasures of the spring?
O soul, return to your body! The celebrations are beginning, and
we are waiting for you to start the ceremonial poem!
O soul, you are here! Forget the calls of ghosts, the world that has
no shadows where the pale moon never sets. You are here, taking
up your cloak again!

The sorcerer collapsed. His assistant took the tunic from between his
limp hands and disappeared behind a curtain.

The soul had returned from the south. After a life of conquest, my
father, who had changed his own destiny by leaving the land of his ancestors, had come back to the house of his birth.

His end had reached his beginning.

Dignitaries, officials, and distant relations hurried to us from the four corners of the region. Once again I prostrated myself behind Mother and my brothers while they received gifts and condolences.

I had no tears left, no voice left. I hid my face behind my sleeves and twisted and squirmed to make myself scream.

Why should Father—a hero as pure as a celestial being, as perfect as a lozenge of jade—have been born into a village where the three hundred members of his clan shared such gloomy houses linked by narrow passageways? Why was his beaming face already melting away behind the coarse features of his relations? I became obsessed with their clumsy gait and their grating accent. These men had his eyes, his ears, his hands, his beard. They offered me fragments of ugliness with which to construct another father.

And there was the dead wife: Her shadow hovered over everything. Without telling Mother, I went to the cemetery to reassure myself that she was really dead. Her tomb was huge, the size of a house, looming up in the middle of a well-tended wood of silver birch. I recognized Father's handwriting carved for all eternity into the impressive stone plinth. He told of the inconsolable sadness of having lost an exemplary wife who had raised their children, tended to their grandparents, and encouraged harmonious relations between members of the clan. I also found two more modest graves for two sons who had been taken by the same epidemic that took their mother. On their plinths Father expressed his regret that he could not leave the Capital and take part in the funeral ceremonies. His responsibility as Minister for Major Works kept him at Court, he said, but every evening his heart escaped to the motherland.

The Wu village was haunted: I could see those dead brothers, two plump, pink little boys playing outside my door. At night I could hear that wife spinning silk. Father had come back, but he was no longer a minister or governor delegate: He did not even know I existed. He spat on the floor, talked loudly, and ate greedily; he loved this illiterate but submissive and thrifty woman; he watched his sons with satisfaction—he had high ambitions for them!

Father's coffin went into the Temple of Ancestors. Once the funeral gifts had been displayed and their donors' names proclaimed, the hearse was raised.

At the head of the cortège, men in white brandished images of the gods to drive away demons. A hundred musicians played trumpets and drums. A hundred Buddhist and Taoist monks recited prayers of appeasement. Hired mourners, with their sparse hair and their blood-splattered faces, ripped their clothes and chanted lamentations. The endless procession wound its way across the plain, between the fields of sprouting wheat. The trees ruffled their green veils, and a scarlet sun rose. The sky leaned in. I had never seen anything more dazzling than the clouds that accompanied Father on his journey to the Shades.

As the fourth son of a modest councilor at the administrative offices in the eastern capital, my father, Wu Shi Yue, had grown up behind brick walls blackened by smoke and punctuated by crudely constructed windows. Very early, the child had displayed a tremendous appetite for knowledge: He delighted in mathematics, geography, and history. The heroes of antiquity and the emperors who founded dynasties became his idols. His cousins made fun of him; they called him "the Madman." At fifteen, he left the village and traveled in the north of China. He found friends who became associates. Against the advice of the clan, he set himself up trading in wood. At the time, Emperor Yang of the Sui dynasty was obsessed with the sumptuous palaces that the Empire was feverishly building. At thirty, Wu Shi Yue had accumulated the region's first great fortune. He was noticed by Li Yuan, the military governor of the province, and became his advisor. In the seventh year of the Great Quarry,[5] the conquest of Korea failed. Emperor Yang carried on with his huge building works with no concern for a people exhausted by military conscription and land taxes. Revolts broke out, and provincial gov-

[5] A.D. 611

ernors proclaimed independence. Wu Shi Yue realized that the Sui dynasty had lost its Celestial Mandate and that the world was waiting for a new master. He offered his personal fortune and his book, *Strategy*, to Li Yuan. He encouraged him to rise up in revolt.

In the thirteenth year of the Great Quarry, Li Yuan marched on the Capital. Wu Shi Yue was in charge of his munitions and supplies. When the victor of that war founded the Tang dynasty and proclaimed himself emperor, he conferred a noble title on Wu Shi Yue and presented him with land, residences, and slaves.

Wu Shi Yue was appointed Minister for Major Works, and he undertook the rebuilding of the ravaged empire. He restored roads, rebuilt bridges, dug canals, and irrigated fields. He developed agriculture, local craft industries, and trade. He contributed to the *Book of Legislation*. When his wife and two of his sons died, he did not have time to go home. Touched by his devotion, the Emperor ordered that he remarry, this time to a girl from the Yang clan who was famed for her virtue and erudition. The wedding was an occasion of great pomp and ceremony: Princess Sunlight of Gui conducted the celebrations. Born a commoner, Wu Shi Yue could see that his career would be safeguarded by an alliance with the most powerful nobility of the Central Plain. He was promised the position of Great Minister; he was to be a great politician who would leave his mark in history. . . . But life had other surprises in store for him.

He had a furious longing for sons from this second union, but three daughters came into the world. In the ninth year of Martial Virtue, when Wu Shi Yue was posted in the Yang province, he heard that there had been a coup in the imperial palace and that the Emperor had abdicated in favor of his son. The new sovereign did not trust generals of the previous emperor: He appointed Wu Shi Yue as Governor Delegate of the Li province and kept him far from Court. Wu Shi Yue was pained by this disgrace. He died of sorrow at the age of fifty-five when he learned of the retired emperor's death.

My father, who had come so close to fulfillment, had failed.

* * *

IN THE VILLAGE, the banquet was in full swing. Every house had its doors and windows flung open as guests drank toasts and devoured feasts. During the period of deep mourning, children of the deceased were forbidden wine, meat, or cooked dishes. With my cold rice soup for every meal, I was growing slender as the funeral coins scattered on the roads. Trying to flee from all the noise and bustle, I wandered through the maze of passages and galleries.

I walked out around a wall-screen, and a garden appeared. The buttercups and pear trees were in blossom. A few rocks formed an island in the middle of a tiny pond. Some men were sitting out on the veranda watching a master of tea boiling water on his stove. I curtseyed to them briefly before scuttling away. A voice called me back:

"Don't be frightened, young lady, come closer."

I turned back and went over to the steps where I curtseyed again.

"Judging by your mourning, you must be a daughter of the Lord of the Ying kingdom," said a man sporting a white beard, dressed in a tunic of dark brocade. "What is your name?"

"Heavenlight."

"Do you know who I am?"

I looked up, and, after looking him over carefully, I replied slowly and clearly:

"You are Governor Delegate of our province of Bing, the Great General Li of the second imperial rank. Your portrait hangs in the pavilion of the Twenty-Four Veterans of the dynasty. The Chinese people venerate you. His Majesty, the sovereign, appointed you as master of our funeral ceremonies. My Lord, I thank you for being here. In heaven, Father is grateful for the honor you do him."

The Great General smiled.

"It is rare to hear a little girl speaking with such assurance. Come up the steps, I would like to offer you a cup of tea."

Beneath the veranda I bowed deeply before sitting amongst the adults.

The Great General spoke to the officials around him: "The Lord of

25

the Ying kingdom was a cultured man who had a nose for business. During the war he excelled as manager of our finances. He spoke little, considered his every word, and worked hard and long. His opinions were always valid. What a shame that he has left us!"

These words felt like a spring of cool water bubbling through my arid heart. I bowed right down to the ground to thank him. The honorable guest asked me about my age, about my mother's grief, my favorite books, and my friends. When he learned that I could ride, he smiled and talked of his Persian steeds, their training, and their exploits.

I had never had a long conversation with an adult, but the Great General spoke simply, without affectation. He listened to me patiently and enthusiastically. His questions were blunt, but his candor gave me confidence; his smile encouraged me; he made me forget that I was a little girl, and I spoke to him on equal terms.

Time flew by, and the general had to leave. In the middle of the garden, he put his hand on my shoulder and said, "Heavenlight, you are an exceptional little girl. I shall take responsibility for your destiny!"

The authority in his voice reminded me of Father's. I was overcome with a most poignant sadness. My tears returned.

MY TENTH YEAR was one long dream pervaded by the image of a catacomb dug into the belly of the mountain. I could not shake off the memory of the death chamber peopled with ceramic statuettes: guards, servants, dancers, horses, camels, houses, and dishes. All around the coffin there were chests and earthenware pots full of clothes, weapons, manuscripts, scrolls of paintings, ornate belt buckles, and an emerald ring carved in the shape of a tiger's head. Suddenly the stone door would close while I was still inside the cave. I struggled to climb back up the slope, but my knees kept giving way, and the icy cold of the underground world was already drawing me in. The smell of damp earth was suffocating. I started to scream: "The mountains are eating me!" But no one heard, no one came to help me.

Great General Li sent me a Persian colt branded with the symbol of his stables. This honor impressed the clan, and Eldest Brother appropriated him. The very next day my horse became his mount.

In the countryside women did not receive an education. To keep the books and tend to the house, they needed only a few figures and as many ideograms to measure the world on the scale of their own minds. All day long three generations of women stayed in their houses spinning, weaving, and embroidering. Mother had never had any contact with that world. She knew nothing of manual skills. She was appalled by their raunchy jokes and embarrassed by their shameless conversations and uninhibited laughter; therefore, she kept away from their gatherings and took refuge in solitude.

The fact that she was different ruffled the other women. They interpreted her silence as contempt. The jibes and insults they hurled over the wall came crashing down in our courtyard: "When you marry a cockerel, you become a hen; when you marry a dog, you become a bitch. When you marry a commoner, you become a commoner. She's no more noble than we are!" "They think they're such princesses. They're just three more mouths to feed and nothing more!" "Parasites!"

Mother remained impassive, fingering her wooden rosary. She had not been taught to defend herself, but she knew how to draw the strength to resist from her Buddhist faith. Our living conditions were deteriorating, and our mourning was becoming a penitence. The clan sold most of our domestic staff. My brothers had cut our allowance back by three-quarters. Meals were distributed from a communal cooking stove, and they often contained rotten vegetables and rice mixed with pebbles. The boiler room ran out of our share of hot water for baths. Sometimes, certain doors were never opened along the passageways, pinning us in. Mother had never complained. Religious fervor made her deaf and blind.

But the clan was pitiless and went to extremes in persecuting us.

At the request of the two brothers, the Council approved their decision to put their mother's remains with my father's. When this news was announced, Mother fainted. If the former wife was to be interred in

27

her master's tomb, Mother would be forbidden to be by his side. Upon her death, she would be repudiated for all eternity. She came to a moment later, without a word, without so much as a sigh. It was the only time I ever saw her falter.

However much I worried about Mother's health, she seemed to grow stronger as our lives deteriorated. Her soul already lived amid the marvels of Buddha's world. Immune to the horror's of daily life, she thought only of her future life. Her body withered, but her face grew radiant. Intrigued and fascinated, I watched this small, fragile woman dominating the turmoil of destiny with a particular kind of strength that goes by the name of serenity.

I was ashamed of my anger. I prayed at the foot of the statue of Amida. I tried to see this world as a shadow-theater filled with illusions, and I sometimes remembered a house of light, color, and vastness. That was on the other side of eternity. At eleven, I was already an old woman. I was sliding through life like a pebble sinking to the bottom of a well. I had decided to accept the village and its walls daubed with grotesque paintings. I had decided to accept the mismatched plates, the smoking candles, the filthy basins, the foul stench of the latrines, and the women who spat on our door. Happiness had died with Father. I had learned to defy sorrow with my eyes open.

PRAYER DID NOTHING to subdue my hate. The desire for revenge was a venomous gall that infiltrated my organs a little more every day.

One morning my anger exploded.

Sheep, the son of a cousin and a sturdy youth, was head of a gang of adolescents who loitered around the village. When they saw Little Sister and me, they would impersonate us and make fun of our good manners. We usually responded to this provocation by looking away. On that particular day, I was holding Little Sister's hand and crossing an alleyway when the boys appeared from behind some trees. They chanted in chorus: "You're just sluts! You're just bastards!"

I felt my pulse pounding at my temples. I stopped and sneered: "My grandfather and my maternal uncle were Great Ministers. My mother is the Emperor's cousin. We are noble, and you, you are commoners, barefoot and worthless, lowlier than dogs!"

"The maternal line counts for nothing," Sheep replied. "Who do you think you are? You're a commoner just like us! Commoner!"

The chorus went on all the louder: "Commoner! Commoner! The toad wants to think he's an ox. He puffs himself up . . . and up . . . and bursts!"

Ever since infancy, my identity had been modeled on Mother's, and she never tired of describing how powerful the Yang clan had been in the days of the old dynasties. Her tales had communicated their pride to me and to be called a commoner by that gang of urchins was one insult I could not tolerate.

I let go of Little Sister's hand and threw myself at Sheep. With one swift blow of my head, I knocked him to the ground. No child from the village had ever dared insult this gang-leader who was known for his strength. Dumbstruck, the gang stepped back and let me roll on the ground with my opponent. Having recovered from the initial daze, he was now punching me. Strangely, this did not hurt; I screamed and struggled, making full use of my nails. Somewhere in the grass, my fingers brushed against a large stone. I picked it up and brought it crashing down on Sheep's head.

Back at home, Mother washed me, dressed my wounds, and did not scold me.

"Venerable Mother," I said as I lay on my bed, "Sheep said that your heritage counts for nothing. Only the father's origins count. Am I a commoner like all my cousins?"

She thought for a moment and replied: "Long ago the Emperor of Peace from the ancient Zhou dynasty had several sons. The lines on his second son's hand featured the august word 'warrior.'[6] When he divided up the Empire, he gave him the domain of Wu, and all his descendants

[6] *Wu* in Chinese characters means "warrior."

bear its name. Now, the kingdom and the palaces have disappeared, and wars have scattered the former inhabitants of the Yellow River region. A new people emigrated into the alluvial plain. Your origins have become a secret that ill-educated men will never know. It is true that in *The Book of Identities* your father's clan, Wu, is classified as a Minor Name. But don't forget that the source of your clan goes back to time immemorial. One of your ancestors is the Emperor of Peace, venerated by sovereigns from all the former dynasties!"

As a punishment, the clan council voted to have me locked up. There was a dilapidated pavilion called Regret in the cemetery. An elderly guard passed food to me through a tiny window, and I lived in darkness with rats, fleas, and cockroaches. During the day I lay with my hands behind my head and drifted in and out of sleep. The silence of the cemetery was more deafening than the roar of a river. When the sun disappeared, the wind would wail mournfully like a woman. Footsteps, snapping twigs, someone breathing; all these sounds hovered round the walls. I closed my eyes and saw colored shapes, dancing flames, white figures and threads of red. When I opened my eyes, I could make out ghosts in the darkness. They wanted to strangle me, to drag me into the eternal shades, but I would chase them out of my room, furiously shaking a broom.

Over the three months after my release from the pavilion, I secretly hoarded rat poison. When I had accumulated a large enough dose, I slipped into the stables.

A few days later the horse that had been a gift from Great General Li Ji died. Eldest Brother blamed it on his groom who fled, fearing a fatal punishment. The men of the clan regretted this death for a long time. They would sigh and say: "He was a magnificent steed."

FIVE NIGHTS SPENT in the Ancestor's cemetery—that was enough to impress all the children in the village. Sheep could not hide his admiration: His gang of urchins became my escort and my servants.

The summer of my twelfth birthday was upon us. To the south of the River Long, the shy retiring hills shrank into a cloak of mist; to the north of the Yellow River, the shameless mountains revealed their forests and their peaks like open books.

I came of age to serve the Goddess of Silk. Every morning, barefoot and without a ladder, I would climb the mulberry trees and pick the tenderest leaves to feed the silk worms. Up in the tops of the trees, I could sense their roots tunneling through the dark earth and see their gnarled arms embracing the sun. Their luxuriant foliage whispered the mysteries of an invisible kingdom. Sometimes I would glimpse the train of a mauve tunic or a green stole. The girls of the village said it was one of the Goddess's servants coming to oversee our work.

Out in the fields the sprouting wheat and maize, the sorghum and sugar cane creeped toward the sky. Soon they surrounded our village. At noon, when the adults were resting with straw hats over their faces, I would run through this ocean of green waves and play war games with the young boys of the clan.

At dusk I would sit by the gate, resting my head on my hands, and watch the clouds bedecking themselves in shimmering colors. The cumulus clouds created faces, mountains, lakes, and drifting boats. Sometimes they would reveal palaces with roofs of crystal, embellished with gold columns and steps of lapis lazuli.

The period of deep mourning came to an end. After the ceremony in which I first wore my hair in a topknot, I was ready to fulfill my destiny as a woman. The clan began having talks with a number of local families, but Father's death had diminished my value, and my brothers were offering only a meager dowry. The few families that showed any interest in this alliance were those of minor landowners.

Mother rejected these unworthy suitors. The Clan Council were impatient to find me a husband and decreed that they would forego her opinion. Mother, who had always been so conciliatory, then lost all her calm. She ordered that we should pack our things and go back to the Capital. The cousins confiscated our belongings and our carriages. I watched this conflict with detachment. At thirteen, I had lost my childish puppy fat; I was fine and slender and wore trousers like a boy. I was not afraid of marriage. Ever since Eldest Sister had left, I had understood that this banishment was every girl's inevitable future. I could marry an untouchable, a dwarf, a madman, an old man . . . and it would be a pleasure to be exiled from that village. I pitied Mother for her blindness: The men of the clan would impose their authority. Sometimes, weary of the ridiculous arguments, I thought it might be simpler to set fire to the grain stores one windy night—the village would perish in the flames, and I would be done with this miserable world.

One morning, an ordinary morning like any other, when I was sharing out the mulberry leaves to the silk worms, a military messenger arrived at the village and gave a letter to the head of the clan. As I swept the courtyard, the elderly uncle unrolled the letter and read it. I was wandering dreamily through the woods, listening to the birdsong, when the head of the clan went to see Mother and showed her the confidential communication. On my return I thought the village seemed strangely quiet; children stood watching for me in doorways; the men were drinking in the principal room; the women were behind curtains, sitting round Mother and smiling at me.

The Great Uncle told me the news: Great General Li Ji, Governor Delegate of our province, had spoken highly of me at the Imperial Court. I was to be called for by a decree from the sovereign to go into service in the Forbidden City.

DISCONCERTED BY THIS unhoped-for honor, the clan decided to move us into a larger, more comfortable house, although they did not actually return our belongings. The women looked at us differently: I could see indignation and envy in their eyes. I lost the freedom to run through the fields and the right to wear trousers. I was confined to my apartments and was subjected to treatments to lighten my skin, which had been tanned by the sun.

Two years after our conversation over a cup of tea, I could only half remember the Great General's face, which I had scarcely seen. But his voice still rang in my ears: It had a magnificent resonance, like some magical scale that allowed my imagination to climb toward a world of inaccessible heights.

The Emperor was no common mortal! As the Son of Heaven, he had the celestial mandate to govern all men. He was protected by the gods, taught by great philosophers, and watched over by benevolent spirits; he was a demigod. His mind was agile as an eagle, his body majestic as a dragon. In the Imperial City, he had the support of ministers and generals, the heroes of our world; in the Inner City, the most beautiful women took turns to fulfill his least desire. To serve the Emperor was to venerate Heaven and Earth, which blessed us with peace and prosperity.

Mother was distraught. She gave me lessons in applying makeup and dressing myself. She crammed my head full of her recipes for cosmetics and medicines. She oversaw my trousseau and tried as best she could to explain the rules of Court to me. Her monologues would sometimes grind to a halt, and she would be unable to hold back her tears and sighs. Going to the kingdom of the divine Emperor would be a one-way journey; I was giving up the outside world forever. The sovereign had no fewer than ten thousand serving women in his gynaeceum. Only very few ever found favor with the Emperor and knew the joys of motherhood. I was too wild, not beautiful enough, and I did not have a powerful father behind me: I had no hope of standing out. I would live and die there, an ephemeral flower living one brief season and never truly blooming.

A delegation of imperial servants dressed in yellow and white tunics arrived. Their leader, a clean-shaven man with a voice like a woman's, inspected the house, explained what form the ceremony would take, gave every detail of the codes of protocol, and ordered pavilions to be built to receive the imperial edict. The summer passed, and the red mulberries turned black behind their foliage. The day of my departure drew near. Mother gave me no peace with her frantic advice and warnings. Little Sister followed me everywhere. I was overwhelmed by a feeling of torpor; my desperate longing to leave the village made me immune to their pain.

An envoy of warriors arrived and presented me with the dowry offered by the Governor Delegate: bolts of brocade, jewelry, books, and fans. When they left, I drifted through the village. I could hear crickets and grasshoppers chirping in cracks of the walls. I felt sorry for those immutable houses: I could not wait to leave.

At dawn one morning, a troop of horsemen appeared on the horizon. All three hundred members of the clan greeted them on bended knee. The Palace envoy stepped down from his carriage, came into the courtyard, and climbed the steps. He unrolled a document and raised his voice: "The second daughter of Wu Shi Yue, descended from a respectable clan, has studied the rites since infancy and has learned to deport herself peacefully and graciously. Her fame has spread through all the gynaecea in the Empire. In keeping with ancient rulings, the Court now honors her with a position in the inner service, with the title of Talented One of the fifth imperial rank. Accept the sovereign's wish, his immeasurable glory and eternal light!"

A cheer of gratitude rang out: "Ten thousand years to the Emperor! Ten thousand years of well-being to the Emperor! Ten thousand and ten million years of well-being to the Emperor!"

My heart leapt with pride. As Talented One of the fifth rank, I immediately overtook my brothers in the imperial hierarchy; they were officials of the seventh rank. The next time we saw each other they would have to prostrate themselves at my feet!

Mother and Little Sister wept. To console them, I pronounced these words that had been tumbling round my heart for days: "My position at the Palace is our one opportunity. Have confidence in my destiny. Do not weep."

Tears are the weapons of the weak and the condolence of the powerful. Little Sister ran behind my carriage. She was no longer a child; she had become a pale, slim adolescent. She waved her arms and was soon nothing but a dark shape in the vast blaze of autumn.

Lulled by the jolting carriage, I too cried. I hated myself for being cold and hard. Little Sister loved me more than I loved her. I was the tree that had stretched its foliage over the entire kingdom of her life. She was a stowaway who had huddled in the safety of my shade. Without me, she would wither and dry up.

ONE MORNING LONG Peace detached itself from the clouds on the horizon. Lit up by the sun, its tall ramparts topped with armed pavilions and surveillance towers looked like a celestial crown laid down on the Central Plain.

A crowd had gathered at the gates. The blues, reds, yellows, and greens of trousers and tunics jostled together, and the wind spread the smell of spices, incense, urine, and fruit. Under the willow trees along the moat, there were horses, oxen, and camels grazing, sneezing lazily, and dozing. There were men in turbans sitting on mats outside their tents. While they waited for a pass to go into the town, they sat eating and haggling amongst themselves. My carriage and its escort traveled past this hubbub of different languages and headed into a long tunnel carved out of walls.

I felt swamped by the sheer noise of the largest city on Earth. The loud cries of the street hawkers mingled with the clatter of horses' hooves, the lowing of oxen, the din from various workshops, and the chiming of bells. From behind the curtain at my window, everything seemed to gleam. The trees vibrated. The air was full of silver clouds. I devoured every sight: the horses' sumptuous bridles, their riders' extravagant hats, the pilgrim monks in their ragged clothes, the trading stalls, and their heaps of wares. There was a succession of enclaves surrounded by high walls. I held tightly to a little purse that had a lock of Mother's hair plaited together with Little Sister's. I found comfort in the thought of all those aunts and cousins who had never left their corner of the countryside. I thought of my mother, who had given up all this; of Little Sister, who would marry a country peasant; of her square courtyard; her beasts of burden; and her fields. I swore to myself that one day I would give them new dignity.

My carriage was already traveling through eternity. I was tiny, alone, and naked. I was moving toward a man, a god, and an empire.

AT THE END of the Avenue of the Scarlet Bird, a crimson wall transformed into a thin line and then into a mountain chain. Having followed the moat around the Imperial City, the military escort came to a halt by a doorway; only carriages could go inside. After walking a short distance, the retinue also came to a halt. Some women held the curtain aside, and I saw a wide pathway paved with golden bricks in the middle of wood. An exquisite fragrance filled my nose. The bustle and noise of the world of men had stopped. I was surrounded by a perfectly unblemished ceremonial silence. I could hear my heart beating. How vulgar that beating sounded now!

A group of servant women greeted me respectfully. They were holding golden basins, silver containers, and towels of woven gold thread, and they asked me to wash my hands and face, then to climb into a litter. I was carried through the forest and then through more walls and gateways. As I made my way deeper and deeper into that sacred land, I began to hear almost imperceptible sounds, the whisper of the leaves, a plucking of stringed instruments, and the tinkle of waterfalls.

We stopped in front of a moon-shaped gate, and I was invited to step down and go into a pavilion. I sat waiting in the middle of a room decorated with frescoes, facing a doorway that looked out over a calm courtyard where a rockery was smothered by an ivy with red berries. Four young girls came toward me along a gallery, taking slow swinging steps and keeping their heads lowered. They came up the steps and into the room with soap, towels, glasses, jugs, and bowls. They washed my hands again and rinsed out my mouth. When they disappeared in a rustle of silk, four more girls appeared to set out a number of low tables and cover them with small dishes.

At home, eating heartily was a great pleasure. Under the gaze of these distinguished servants, I was afraid they might laugh at my manners, so I ate only a few mouthfuls. I was astonished by how refined the imperial dishes were: The vegetables were the texture of meat, the meat tasted like game, and the game looked like flowers.

A bronze bathing tub was brought in; it had a bas-relief design of a huge water lily surrounded by leaves. The bath water was blended with fragrant oil and scented tree bark. Two servants scrubbed me, soaped me, rinsed me, and dried me. Their moves were precise and practiced.

An elderly woman arrived escorted by a legion of young women in men's dress. She wore the tunic of a woman of letters, a man's headdress, and shoes with square toes that curled backwards. She introduced herself and then took my pulse and inspected my hair, my eyes, my tongue, and my breath. In a high, curt voice, she dictated to two scribes the color, smell, and shape of my orifices. She asked me to undress, then measured my hands, arms, shoulders, breasts, hips, thighs, ankles, feet, and toes. "Round, square, triangular, bony . . ." she described. "Red, pink, white. . . ." She asked me to lie down on my back and spread my legs. I obeyed but not without blushing. She made them write down the width and length of my parts, and she penetrated my belly with an ice-cold instrument. "Virgin!" her inspection concluded.

Toward the end of the day, I was visited by a man in a yellow tunic and a lacquered black hat; he was accompanied by many servant women and young men. He had a large belly and a double chin, and, in the powder and rouge of his face, his eyes were just two long slits emphasized by black lines. He greeted me deferentially, complimented me on my appearance, and asked me to follow him. As I walked there were groups of servants going the other way, carrying pink and mauve lanterns. Apart from the rustle of footsteps and clothing, all of them remained absolutely silent.

Gardens and pavilions slipped in and out of my field of vision. Above the gathering darkness, the sky was the color of blood. I thought of Mother, of our dilapidated house. Back there, they would have started the harvest. At this time in the evening, the women would be walking with their children under the cypress trees, the men would be drinking rice alcohol, and great-uncle would be telling ghost stories.

I was frozen by the perfumed air of the Forbidden City.

THREE

*H*eaven and Earth, sun and moon, day and night, man and woman . . . in this world where yin and yang repel and attract each other, the energy of duality is all-powerful. The heart of the Empire, the Absolute Master's estate, did not escape cosmic law. The Outer City, which was dedicated to administration, was the very opposite of the Inner Palace, which was devoted to pleasure. In the former, where there were no women, the Son of Heaven governed as leader of all the officials and generals and fulfilled his duties as high priest by performing rites throughout the year. In the second, the male sex was banished, and only the sovereign, relieved of his sacred duties, drank of the exquisite loveliness of the ten thousand beauties.

In the Outer City, there were soldiers from guards' regiments stationed beneath awnings, each with his brocade tunic under a bronze breastplate, his saber in his leather belt, his bow bound with rattan, and his arrows dipped in crimson stain. The successions of magnificent buildings with tiles of glazed turquoise and green were a solemn, majestic sight. Their imposing proportions represented celestial harmony, their clean lines symbolized earthly fertility. The architecture in the Inner Palace was less conventional. The more gifted master-builders had tried their hand at fantasy and had ventured into exuberance. Martial strength had stepped down; grace and indolence pervaded everything. My eyes, so accustomed to the dimensions of our rustic homes, had to adapt to the excesses here. My nose, which knew the smells of the countryside, could not recognize the subtle fragrances of exotic fruits and rare flowers. There were birds whose cages were like palaces of gold, dispensing their trills with virtuosity. I discovered the heady pleasures of touch: silk, crêpe, satin, brocade, velvet, muslin, gauze, fine porcelain, the coolness of jade dishes, the warmth of lacquered trays, the shimmer of golden goblets, and showers of petals.

There were two long narrow courtyards attached to the Inner City, like two arms protecting a body: The Eastern Palace, the residence of the Imperial Heir and his close government; and on the western side, the Side Quarters reserved for the Court ladies.

The Side Court was a kingdom within the Empire, a painted box inside a golden trunk; it was a labyrinth of tiny rooms separated by walls of adobe clay, bamboo hedges, and narrow passageways. Official pavilions, little gardens, tunnels of wisteria, and countless bedrooms were linked by long covered galleries. Thousands of women came and went with a rustling of sleeves and a murmuring of fans, without ever exposing themselves to the sun or the rain. Imperial hierarchy was scrupulously respected despite the confines of that overpopulated world. The further down someone was on the social scale, the smaller her room, the simpler the décor, and the more modest the furniture. The slave quarter was packed with ramshackle little houses, gloomy rooms, and cold beds; the women there were like insignificant stitches in a vast embroidery.

Nestling under ancient trees, my room was dark; it gleamed with draperies and opened onto a veranda. From my ivory bed I could look through the gauze curtains held up by gold hooks and watch the square of sky marked out by the little courtyard I shared with three other Talented Ones. At dusk, when the sun lingered behind the double ramparts, I could see scattered sparrows spiraling through the inky blueness.

* * *

IN KEEPING WITH my rank, the Court granted me two servants and a governess—a strict, cold woman who managed to give me orders while still entrenched in her inferior position. Ruby and Emerald were twins. They were the daughters of a poor family, and their father had entrusted them to a dealer called Zhang who ran a flourishing trade in the West of the Capital that supplied the Court and dignitaries' families with the prettiest young girls. In the evening, as they uncoiled my hair, they whispered the secrets of the Palace to me. This was how I learned that the imperial servants were not real men: Their parents had cut off their virile parts before selling them to Court. I also discovered that Governess, who was of noble birth, had been the wife of a lord who fought under the standard of the Sui dynasty. After their defeat, the men of her clan had been executed, and she had to become an imperial slave.

In the Palace of Celestial Breath, I followed the training given to new women at Court. The great curtsey, the minor curtsey, greetings of respect, greetings of condescension, greetings from equal to equal, the quick walk, the slow walk . . . there was no spontaneity in the Forbidden City. Natural responses were considered the premise of the people and of Barbarians; all the elegance of our movements derived from the height of restraint. Looking, eating, drinking, sitting down, sleeping, rising, speaking, listening—the most elementary acts in life were meticulously regulated by superstitious and aesthetic codes.

Inner thoughts had to be impregnated with the same rigorous austerity. Moral observance exemplified delicacy of mind; perversion was a crime that could lead to death. One hundred prohibitions were written in fine calligraphy on a ten-panel screen. The study of Inner Law was supplemented by reading *Behaviour of a Lady at Court* by the Empress of Learning and Virtue.

I was improving my skills in music and dance. The directives for clothing taught me to distinguish between the nine official hierarchies—thanks to the variations in colors and the way things were worn.

The moon filled out and wasted away. The trees had already lost their leaves. I lamented my awkwardness, and I envied the more lowly servants who seemed to move around me with such grace and ease. Despite my efforts, my muscles were still taut; I walked too quickly; I could not distribute my weight between my toes and my heels; my inclinations, my prostrations, and my stride lacked reserve—I could not shake off a rough-hewn animal brutality.

The Palace of Celestial Breath grew busier as more new recruits to inner service arrived. These included Talented Xu, whose reputation preceded her: She was the daughter of a learned family and had started talking at just five months. At four she could already comment on Confucius' *Discussions* and recite the poems in the *Anthology*. At eight she started writing and created this verse in the style of songs favored by the ancient kingdom of Chu: "I contemplate the deep, luxurious forest; caressing the branches of the blossoming cinnamon tree, I address the mountain that has lived a thousand years and ask: why this loneliness?"

One winter morning, she finally appeared. Buried in a cape of mauve satin lined with silver fox, her face looked tiny and extraordinarily pale. Her eyes were so long and slanting they reached her temples and were like two timid dashes of calligraphy. She coughed a good deal, and her sickly beauty softened even the surliest of the instructors. From the very first day, she was granted the privilege to withdraw when she deemed that she was tired. According to rumor, she was the one in our group who would be favored by the Emperor. She was a year older than me and had a quiet, learned way about her and all the mysterious charm of a woman who is already promised to someone. She had no difficulty carrying out the Court movements accurately and with a delicate grace. A good many girls buzzed around her, and she soon had a devoted band of admirers as well as a collection of rivals who were quick to criticize her. Not knowing how to approach her, I kept my distance; I feigned indifference.

At night, in my dreams, my former life went on. I walked those strange corridors of time and went back to my childhood. On the banks of the River Long, the wind danced with the huge waves. On my horse, I would fly higher and freer than the seagulls. Waking was brutal. My heart would stop. I was so dazed I would forget who I was and where I was. Then, gradually, the distress would intensify and become harrowing. The chill of the Forbidden City would overrun me.

The pages of life that had already turned could not be opened again.

SINCE THE DEATH of the Empress of Learning and Virtue two years previously, the title of Mistress of the World was still unclaimed. In the Side Court, it was said that Great Chancellor Wu Ji, who was the brother of the noble deceased, had such a tight hold on the government that he would never allow another family to sully her throne. The sovereign had in fact wanted to invest Precious Wife, the daughter of Emperor Yang of the overthrown dynasty and already the mother of two princes, but the ministers of the Outer Court refused to swear loyalty to a descendant of the enemy clan. Then the Emperor's favorite, Yang, was singled out and promoted to Gracious Wife after giving birth to a son. Once again the ministers criticized her because, while in the gynaeceum, she had served the King of Qi who was later killed in a coup. A sullied woman would never be sovereign of China.

But even the most powerful of men could not contain the ambitions of women obsessed with childbearing and fascinated by the dignity of rank. The ten thousand women in the Side Court were ten thousand flowers desperately dreaming of spring. Whether carefully planted out in pots or crudely sown in wasteland, they wilted in the harsh atmosphere of constant waiting, the deprivation of an endless winter. A sniffle, a shiver, a migraine, or a stomachache was enough to cull these souls so worn down with hoping. There were no old women with white hair in the Side Court. Every day the dead were left by the North Gate. Somewhere, far from the ramparts of the Capital, in the cemetery for

Imperial Serving Women, slumbered adolescents who had never seen anything of the world and mature women who, poor creatures, had been too familiar with melancholy.

The pathways in the Side Court wound around like the never-ending threads of a vast spider web. Our pavilions were like dead insects, and the survivors still believed in miracles. Princesses, nobles, and commoners had lost their names and were recognized only by the titles they had been given. I was Talented One Wu, an intruder in the land of gods, a pebble on a tray of fine pearls. I too aspired tentatively to the imperial bed, to be favored by the Son of Heaven.

Rumor had it that the sovereign liked fat women with double chins: I was upset that I was thin. The young girls competed over their jewels, their dresses, and their extravagances. They spent the money given to them by their families on frenzied orders. I had been robbed of my jewels to pay for my cousins' careers. My brothers had sent me nothing. When Mother managed to send me a few small coins, I knew she had secretly sold another of her Buddhist statuettes, the only things of value she still owned. This money made me weep. How could I spend it to buy a pretty hairpin?

Winter came, and the first snow fell on the Side Court. Icicles hanging from the awnings and footprints left in the frost by the birds awakened my dormant energy. Our timetable recommended practicing sport in this season. With my coat thrown off, my sleeves pushed up, and wearing my Tatar boots, I launched myself into the snow. My strength and enthusiasm amazed the Palace intendant instructing us. He suggested I take the archery lessons that were offered to volunteers accompanying the sovereign on his hunting trips.

All the suffering I had endured melted away when I mounted a horse with the brand of the imperial stables. On the archery range, which had been swept of snow, I galloped with the urgency of a blind man hurtling toward a distant thread of light. The wind slapped my face, and the sky whipped up my thoughts. The speed freed me from the torments of frustration, and I felt my pride blossoming once more. Far from the crowd of women, the painted faces, and the affected smiles, I rediscovered the powerful pleasure of being alone.

Before the end of the year, I received my official gowns. In the absence of an Empress, the Precious Wife led the Ladies of the Inner Court and the Ladies of the Outer Court[7] in prostrating themselves before His Majesty to give him their best wishes. Palace etiquette required us to walk with small steps and lowered eyes. Because my rank entitled me to a place far from the throne, during the salutation, I could just see a dark smudge with something resembling a face obscured by a glittering crown.

Back in the Side Court, everyone said that the Emperor wanted to meet his new mistresses and would name a date on which he would receive them. The thought of this put the Pavilion of Celestial Breath into a frenzy of excitement. Soon, one of the Great Intendants told us of the imperial summons. The day before the presentation I could not sleep. Even though I had galloped all afternoon and shot two quivers of a dozen arrows, I felt neither tired nor appeased. A thousand times I went over what I would wear, practiced my walk, and prepared answers in case His Majesty deigned to ask me anything. A thousand times I imagined my joy and pride if I were the chosen one. Mother could forget her poverty and sorrow: No one would dare humiliate her any more. As an imperial favorite and promoted to a superior rank, I would ask for permission for her to visit with Little Sister. When I bore a prince, Mother, as Royal Grandmother, would be given a palace with countless servants. As I shared my pillow with the Son of Heaven, I would remind him that Father had been a Veteran of the dynasty, companion in war to the Noble Emperor Lordly Forebear. I would beg him to grant him a posthumous title as Great Lord of the first rank.

I tried in vain to calm my teeming hopes. The more I laughed at my extravagant dreams, the more desperately I longed to reach this man coveted by his ten thousand serving women. No, I wanted neither priv-

---

[7] These would be imperial princesses and the wives of princes and ministers.

ilege, nor favor, nor glory. I was indifferent to gold, pearls, and sumptuous palaces. I would ask nothing of the sovereign other than to be saved from this fate that condemned me to wither in silence and die, drowning in a swamp of women.

The Son of Heaven was an invincible warrior. Thanks to his dazzling victories, Emperor Lordly Forebear had been able to dethrone Sovereign Yang and inaugurate our Tang dynasty. Throughout the Empire, the people sang of his eventful battles. Recently, during the campaign against the Turks of the East, he had subjugated the barbarian leader with just one war cry. I imagined His Majesty to be powerfully built with a square face and a wide forehead. I pictured him with an intimidating glare, forceful gestures, a loud voice, and a long, well-tended beard. I did not know what I should do once in the imperial bed. We had been told we had to allow him to undress us. Would I have the strength to hold the gaze of a man who had looked Tatars in the eye? What would I feel when he touched my body with the hand that had severed thousands of heads?

I wanted him to be my freedom; I wanted him to be the luminous star throwing its light on my forehead; I wanted him to be that height toward which all my energy would be drawn so that all my ardor and devotion would be beautiful and pure.

THE OFFICERS OF protocol shouted orders in their shrill voices. The Beauties of the fourth rank, the Talented Ones of the fifth rank, and the Treasures of the sixth rank lined up in hierarchical order.

Then silence descended. We stood and waited for the Emperor who was on his way back from the Morning Salutation. Rays of sunlight filtered through the lattice-work of the closed windows and fell on the gleaming black paving stones of the floor, hundreds of wilted flowers.

At the foot of the throne, on a scarlet carpet embroidered with dragons in gold thread, sandalwood burned in three-legged bronze stoves. But the cold was a powerful eagle hovering between the beams and columns, breathing icily over us, scouring our cheeks with its wings of iron. Eyes lowered, hands clasped inside my sleeves, and bent slightly forward, I stood rigidly in the pose of respectful expectation. Time dripped past in the hydraulic clock. My hair was woven together with false hair and wound so tightly around a structure with bronze thread that it tugged at my scalp. My topknot, a cubit and a half high and decorated with five tree-shaped jewels in gold, rubies, sapphires, and other gemstones, symbols of my rank, was weighing me down. The pain crept down my back, my legs, and my arms. I shook from head to toe.

The sounds of a great commotion began, far away at first. Footsteps, coughing, then someone came into the hall. The officer of protocol announced, "The sovereign is preparing to leave the Palace of Audiences!" A wave of panic ran through the group of women who struggled to keep still. Little cries escaped from a few constricted throats. One young girl fainted. Another started to sob. Both were carried out by eunuchs.

Suddenly the musicians struck the bronze bells and sounding stones. The side doors were drawn aside, and two servants dressed in yellow brocade raised the curtains and held them back with gold-plated forked rods. An ice-cold wind filled the hall. After a long time had passed, two valets came in with incense burners and stood to the left and right of the throne. There was another long pause. Two more eunuchs appeared, carrying long-handled, round fans. The imperial servants filed in two by two, then a strident voice cut through the silence: "The Noble Sovereign of the great Tang dynasty!"

My blood froze. I fell to my knees with my forehead on the ground. The accelerated fluttering of my heart mingled with the endless rustling of satin and silk soles rubbing against the carpet, like an impetuous and inexhaustible mountain stream. At the request of the caller, I stood back up but fell to my knees again before making the great curtsey. When I recovered from the dizzying effect of the salutations, I could see through the corners of my eyes that all the candelabras had been lit. There were countless eunuchs around the throne, some carrying the long-handled fans that denoted imperial rank, others holding more everyday objects: towels, boxes of food, glasses, jugs, and bowls.

The General Intendant of the Side Court called forward the ladies of the Court by order of hierarchy and seniority. Waves of heat surged through me. I was covered in sweat. I was afraid my makeup would run, afraid I would not hear my name, afraid I would faint. I was afraid the Emperor would choose a girl ranked before me and that my one chance would vanish before it even arrived.

All of a sudden I heard: "Daughter of Wu Shi Yue, from the district of Wen Shui, in the province of Bing, Talented One Wu."

My head buzzed. I stepped forward, eyes lowered. I made my way slowly toward the throne, and my thighs quaked beneath my dress. At the exact distance required by protocol, facing the imperial dais, I carried out the three great prostrations. At some stage in the proceedings—and I have no idea how because to look at the sovereign constituted a crime punishable by death—I glimpsed a man wrapped in a yellowish brown tunic. He wore a simple headdress of glazed white linen. I managed to make out his features in his puffy, listless face. I was overcome by a feeling of disappointment more icy than the North Wind.

One after another, all the girls were presented to the sovereign who remained silent through the entire ceremony. Each of us was accorded the same amount of time; no one was gratified with a nod, a smile, or a request to come forward and show her face. Once back in the Side Court, I spent the whole rest of the day thinking of that huge, tall hall full of mysterious frescoes. Had the Son of Heaven looked at us at all? I was not sure he had. In any event, up on his throne, how could he have seen the women's faces under their imposing headdresses when they had to keep their heads lowered and their eyes fixed humbly on the ground?

The moon was waning in the sky. Soon it would perish only to be born again. I discovered that Talented One Xu would be received in the imperial bed. A peculiar emotion paralyzed my body like a poison. I scarcely listened to the rumors that claimed the selection had been rigged. As soon as she had arrived at the Palace, Talented One Xu had been under the wing of the Great Chamberlain who came from the same province. This eunuch, who enjoyed the sovereign's complete trust, had engineered for all the names to be erased from the roll-call so that only his candidate was taken to the Palace of Precious Dew.

The new favorite left the Side Court where the living conditions were no longer in keeping with her rank, and she moved into the Middle Court. Something in me had died. I discovered Taoist texts that told of the purification of mind and body, of men who had become immortal, and of union with the celestial breath. I went back to my daily routine of prayers to Buddha, which had stopped when I arrived in the Palace. The world was an illusion, and all desire a source of suffering. How could I have forgotten the teachings of the Great One?

Like the moon, I would be reborn of annihilation.

THE PAVILION OF Celestial Breath closed its doors, and my young companions dispersed, each to her official duties.

The everyday life of a lady at Court was filled with banquets, dancing, and concerts; with the sequence of seasons that required changes of wardrobe; with constant trips between summer palaces and winter residences; with futile events and serious ones; and with light-hearted ceremonies and imposing ones.

The six ministries and twenty-four departments of the imperial gynaeceum had been created during the ancient Zhou dynasty, and each had a share in organizing festivities. There were pavilions that served as offices to the Great Lady Intendants, who directed countless female officials. All of them worked to make our life harmonious and pleasant. In the absence of an Empress, the Precious Wife reigned over our kingdom. She was a weak, gentle character and felt happier entrusting command to her favorite eunuch, General Intendant, in her palace. According to the rules, the four wives of the first rank were responsible for how the women behaved. Not one of these ladies deigned to be soiled by such involvement, and all of them delegated their power.

The duties of a Talented One were to keep records of feasting and days of rest, as well as ensuring that the silk worms were reared satisfactorily. Even though they were paltry tasks, I relied on these occupations to escape boredom. On the very first day, Governess informed me that she would free me from such minor concerns and explained that, from the fifth rank up, it was a woman's duty to be at leisure.

Painted beams, gilded partitions, and fragrant powders entwined us like ivy around trees. This dull, slow life stifled our youth. The freshness and vivacity drained from my companions and me without our knowing when or how. The Court had a liking for fat women, so my companions crammed themselves with food. Their transparent white skin quivered over ample folds of fat. They spent their days perfecting their hair and makeup. Their daily walk through the Northern Gardens was becoming a ritual, and they would spend this time comparing their beauty and exchanging gossip. To escape the loneliness and monotony, some had pet cats and dogs, while others formed friendships and called each other "sister."

There were women everywhere in the Side Court. They trod softly along the galleries, appeared and disappeared behind screens, and let their silhouettes linger on the partitions covered in rice paper. The servants observed a respectful silence, but the mistresses needed to chatter constantly to kill their boredom. A closed door or a secured shutter was tantamount to some inadmissible act, so all the bedrooms had to remain open for impromptu visits. Throughout the day, groups of Court ladies would appear from nowhere, expecting me to offer them tea and to listen to their chattering.

I found refuge in the Inner Institute of Letters where learned eunuchs gave lessons in literature, philosophy, history, geography, astrology, and mathematics to the few students who voluntarily attended their lectures. Books became wings that bore me far away from the Palace. The annals of former dynasties tore me from the immobility of the present. I lived in those vanished kingdoms and I took part in plots, galloped across battlefields, and shared in the rise and fall of heroes.

I visited the library regularly, and I sometimes would run into Talented One Xu, who had already been promoted to the rank of Delicate

Concubine of the second imperial rank. I now had to give her a deep curtsey, and she replied with a condescending nod. Her body had thickened, her expression darkened. Her face had lost its poetic naiveté. When she smiled at me, I could see a vague melancholy on her lips that seemed to express resentment and resignation. I longed to ask her questions but did not dare. A Delicate Concubine would never confide in a Talented One of inferior rank.

Was she not happy on the other side of the wall?

In the Side Court, I may have struggled to be like a perfect lady, but in the exercise quarters, I abandoned all civility. On horseback, with a bow in my hand, I forgot how time passed one slow drip after another, and I became one with my speeding mount and embraced the power of my arrows as they reached their target.

After each training session, I would linger a while at the stables. The eunuch grooms had become my friends: I would recite to them the poems I had read that morning, and they taught me to school foals and told me what was going on in the Palace.

That was how I discovered that, in the days when the sovereign was still only King of Qin, he had set an ambush for his older brothers at the Northern Gate, not far from the stables. The imperial heir and the King of Qi had been killed, and the Emperor Lordly Forebear had been forced to abdicate in his favor. Our sovereign had usurped the throne! Heroes seemed to attach little importance to filial devotion! I was shattered by this revelation.

And in her latest letter Mother told me that Little Sister had succumbed to an epidemic. Poorly tended by the clan, she had died. I lost my appetite; I loathed the dresses, the perfumes, the gardens. The beauty of that Palace was a screen hiding corpses and lies.

I grew thinner while all around me girls reveled in their flesh. I had grown tall and slender, a bundle of muscles on a strong frame.

ONE DAY SHE appeared. Her face was white as snow, like a perfectly circular mirror fashioned by the most adept craftsmen. Her mouth was a crimson cherry, ready to drop from the tree. Her eyes, like the long leaves of the willow, disappeared into the black hair that swept over her temples, and they glittered with a strange light. Seeing her, I forgot my own sorrow, the Side Court, and my sister's decomposing body. I forgot that the world existed, and I understood what eternal friendship meant.

"Are you the girl who loves horses?" her clear, haughty voice woke me from my torpor. "Do you not greet the Gracious Wife?"

I bent my knees and leaned right down to the ground. When I stood back up, she looked me straight in the eye. The other women's eyes were water, ice, fire, and rock; she alone had eyes full of mists and vapors.

"My little cousin, I have heard stories of you," she said, pronouncing each word carefully. Her lips were two petals of red grenadine. "I shall take care of your instruction, my little, wild one."

A mysterious smile appeared in the corners of her mouth, and she left me where I stood: Followed by a dozen servants and ladies-in-waiting, she disappeared into the trees.

That evening I could still see her smooth face; so pure it was almost childlike, her dresses of layered silk and muslin in exquisitely subtle shades. She wore her hair in the shape of a butterfly adorned with the most beautiful jewels I had ever seen. How old was she? I did not know. In the Inner Palace, ladies were careful to hide their age. She was timeless.

We were related through my mother's family. But, in the Side Court, everyone knew that Father had been an ennobled commoner, a wood merchant who had become a dignitary. Was it a mark of respect or out of irony that she had called me cousin? But she too had a dark stain on her past. She had been a concubine to the King of Qi, the third son of the Emperor Lordly Forebear, who was killed at the Northern Gate and stripped of his princely title. Along with the other women in his retinue, she had come into the Side Court as a slave. The new sovereign had taken her to his bed, she had delivered a boy child, and he had offered her the title of wife.

I enjoyed imagining the King of Qi's palace surrounded by his own brother's army: In the gynaeceum eunuchs wailing lamentations, women fleeing to their rooms, and wet nurses hiding the king's sons. Soon the clatter of weapons echoed around the palace, fierce-faced soldiers broke into the inner apartments where no man had dared tread before. They ransacked pavilions, strangled male children, looted treasure, and dragged concubines out by their hair. In all this furious assault, jostled, chained, and wracked with sobs of fear, my cousin was like pear blossom damaged by the rain and sullied in the mud. A feeling of intense suffering and, yet, nameless pleasure swept over me. I could see her face streaming with tears. I could picture her insulted and violated by the soldier's crude and penetrating stares. They thought she was beautiful. They threw her at their master's feet, at the feet of the future sovereign of the empire. He commanded her to expose her white bosom, her belly soft as a turtle dove; he ordered her to dance, writhe, and grovel at his feet. His hands, still warm with blood, caressed her, he sprayed her with his seed. Humiliated and violated, she had to smile, to love, to please.

My body was on fire. I let the full voluptuous pleasure of this poor tortured woman overcome me. Inch by inch, from my toes to the top of my head, my cousin devoured me, made me quiver, glided over my skin. I drank her as a child drinks milk.

THE GRACIOUS WIFE lived on the other side of the wall, in the Middle Court, in one of the palaces surrounded by purple walls with ancient acacias and cypress trees towering over them. She lived in a garden that a modest Talented One was forbidden to enter. For her, virgins picked the delicately colored clouds at dusk to weave with, and palace seamstresses cut out the finest of dresses. Embroiderers with needles of diamonds and threads of sunlight created enchanted images. The divine wife bathed in waters fragranced with extract of moonlight, and she inhaled the breath of the stars. Such a delicate, diaphanous goddess did not eat vulgar, earthly food. The bees offered her their honey, and fruits longed to be chosen to melt on her tongue. When she was thirsty, she moistened her lips on morning dew harvested on lily petals. When she smiled, flowers blanched in jealousy and leaves fell from the trees to kiss the tips of her feet.

She had told me that she would take care of my instruction. Even though she was a distant noble and even though I had no reason to, I believed her. She was the gift that the heavens had sent to console me in suffering. Her misty eyes and indolent voice would soothe the incandescent fires of my tortured life. In her I would find some protection, a screen of silk painted with fabulous landscapes to camouflage death and sorrow. She would teach me to be a woman, and I would offer her my arrogant pride on bended knee!

In fact my longing to see her again supplanted every other agony. Freed from the anguish of mourning, I was now enslaved by a new torment. I did not know this was being in love: Taut as an archer's bow, my soul distended with expectation, my desire tightly coiled, my stomach tensed.

I started to take an interest in my appearance and in what girls wore. In the mornings, I would look at myself in the mirror with her eyes, with her words in my ear. "Do you like me like this?" I would whisper to her in my heart. At night, I lay down with her, in her arms, in the soft waves of her hair.

At the Inner Institute of Letters, I leafed through books trying to find a diagnosis for my illness. The ancient philosophers spoke only of virtue, wisdom, and immortality. I searched through the Annals in vain for similar anecdotes. The official literature in our vast library was filled with dry words, harsh thoughts, and moralizing pronouncements. Our ancestors had built a civilization where affection and tenderness were prohibited. Luckily there were the poets whose words traveled across time and poured limpid delight into my heart. I found my own desperate adoration expressed in their odes to mountain goddesses and water spirits.

When I drew an arrow, I hoped to dazzle her with my strength. I would have liked to give her every horse I schooled. An imperial decree ordered for a female polo team to be formed: I was quick to enlist in the hope that one day she would smile down at me from her imperial tribune. My loneliness was now like a velvet coat in which I wrapped myself so I could better devote my soul to her. I told her about my childhood and asked her a thousand questions. The answers I imagined for her made me feel less alone, not so sad. I needed to see her. My intuition could not be wrong: We would see each other again!

My cousin, the Gracious Wife, continued to be invisible as the air around me. The memory of her was like an old song that I obsessed over but whose notes were gradually melting away. Spring was drawing to an end. The cherry blossom scattered pink and mauve tears on the wind. She had sent me no messenger. Every day the image of her darkened a little more, and her snowy whiteness became a hazy shadow, but I still clung to it to breathe, to live, and to escape from the Side Court and its swarming women.

Days went by, and I turned my entrails into a deep reservoir, collecting this new brand of suffering, drop by drop. My skin was smoother, my hair blacker, my hips more rounded. My breasts swelled beneath my tunic, and people watched me as I walked. More and more women paid court to me, but not one of them thrilled me in the same way, and I coolly rejected their friendship. How could these flitting fireflies touch me when I was promised to her, the motionless star?

A gloomy, gray summer began. The cicadas screeched furiously in the trees. The suffocating heat continued in the night. Tossing and turning on my bed of woven bamboo, I decided to forget her.

The emperor was leaving to spend the summer at his Residence of Nine Merits. All the pavilions started dismantling, packing, and wrapping. Every woman took her own animals, her furniture, her books, and her crockery. I leaned against the balustrade on the terrace and watched my governess scolding the servants. Birds fluttered in their cages, and eunuchs went back and forth to my room bringing out huge trunks. All the commotion seemed so far away.

A young valet in a robe of yellow brocade followed Emerald up the steps. He came over to me and bowed deeply: "The mistress of the Palace of Splendid Dawn, the Gracious Wife Yang, wishes to see you."

My heart leapt: She was coming to me when I had stopped thinking of her. My cousin had asked to meet me the following morning in the Northern Garden, by the Pond of Pearls, to feed the goldfish. I stayed awake all night, unable to believe my happiness. I was terrified by the thought that I might not be beautiful enough, fragrant enough, intelligent enough. At dawn, when I had been dressed and made-up, I listened for the first morning bells announcing that the Side Gate would be open so that I could rush to my appointment.

The mist had not yet lifted in the Northern Garden. The first rays of sunlight infused between the sky and the land, a color wash of dancing pinks, ochres, mauves, and yellows. A pond emerged slowly from the darkness, a mirror of bronze. A long gallery zigzagged over its rippling waters, between the emerald leaves of the lotuses. Seeing my shadow over the water, the fish began to gather. These impatient creatures would have to learn to savor the waiting.

The sun burned off the mists, and a blue sky gradually revealed itself. At my feet, a great meadow of flowers sloped gently down to a new gallery around a raised pavilion. There were a few peonies still opening, the lilac bloomed with furious abandon, and the pomegranate trees were covered in crimson-colored buds. The morning dew quivered on leaves, adding its sparkle to the delight in my heart. The gardening women, dressed in orchid blue and pale pink, were beginning their work. The first concubines to rise came and went through the wood of weeping willows. A group of eunuchs came over to the pond. They scattered grain in the water. The heat was rising. I waved my fan with little effect: My brow was covered in sweat, and my dress was drenched. I stood scouring all four horizons, and my heart quaked at every movement. I thought of going back and changing my clothes, but the fear of missing my appointment nailed me to the spot.

Had she fallen ill? Perhaps, in my euphoria, I had the wrong day. Who had sent that eunuch? Was it a cruel joke?

Ruby woke me from my torpor when she came to tell me that lunch was served. That evening I discovered that the emperor had decided to leave with his favorites in the cool of first light.

THE STARS RIPPLED up above the mountains. Beneath the waves of the Silver River,[8] pavilions, and pagodas, the women and the trees became fish. The summer palace was our aquarium. Despite the cool air and the scent of nocturnal flowers, I could not sleep. In the mountains, there was no archery training and no polo ground. My muscles jittered and maddened me. Ruby and Emerald lay on my doorstep chatting. Their muffled whispering drifted through the gauze curtain and filled the room.

In the Middle Court, the emperor had grown weary of capricious women, and he now cherished only Delicate Concubine Xu. The abandoned wives now waged a communal war against her. The poetess had just lost a boy child in the eighth month: Rumors abounded that she had been poisoned and that the blame lay with one of the jealous favorites. Since our missed appointment, I had had no news of the Gracious Wife. Caught as she was in the torments of intrigue, when would she have time to think of me?

The summer passed. I no longer believed I had anything to wait for. My journey back to Long Peace was one long monotonous swaying of my carriage. I could not wait to see my horse again. The day after our return, a messenger from the Gracious Wife burst into my room: Her Highness was waiting for me to visit; she was free at the end of every afternoon.

Escorted by Ruby and Emerald, I went to her quarters that very day. Surprised by my haste, she received me in her indoor clothes. She offered me tea and asked me about how I had come to be at the palace. I stammered. Her pretty face and her body wrapped in a fragrant cloud made me feel uncomfortable. Beneath her grenadine red tunic, she

---

[8] Known in the West as the "Milky Way."

wore a dress of chrysanthemum yellow muslin through which I could see her shoulders and the tops of her naked breasts. A long shawl of pale green crêpe was wound around her arms and hung limply on the floor. With no wig or framework, she had coiled her hair into a lazy topknot and pierced this black mound with a pin bearing a pearl the size of a quail's egg.

Seeing her so happy and animated, I forgot the purpose of my visit: to warn her of the danger that lay in wait for her. The spiteful rumors accused her of being the poisoner. She had to defend herself! Her misty gaze drifted over me, and this haze of languor was a disguise for her dark eyes probing me.

Suddenly she spoke to me: "My cousin, do you already have an older sister?"

I shook my head to mean no.

"Why not? All the girls in the Side Court have sisters."

I flushed so deeply that I felt my ears burning. How could I tell her that I wanted to remain faithful to her?

"You are not beautiful," she went on. "But there is something un-usual about you that is very striking. The way you look, your body. . . . Has a woman ever offered to take you in hand?"

Then she leaned closer to me and whispered in my ear: "Have you ever been kissed?"

I wanted to be swallowed up by the ground.

"Come, I'll show you my secret garden."

She stood up and I followed her, with my eyes lowered. I heard her flash an impetuous order at my servants: "You may go home. Tell your governess that I shall keep my cousin here to dine. I shall send her back later."

I was ashamed and embarrassed, unable to breathe a word.

After going through a string of rooms and courtyards, she pushed open a crimson door set into a wall painted with the white of pear trees in blossom. The servants stopped and closed the door behind us. There were mauve lanterns lighting a walkway that ran past pomegranate trees laden with fruit on one side and went around a pond covered with lotus flowers on the other.

She took my hand and led me toward a pavilion. My heart beat frantically, and I no longer had any strength in my arms. I sensed that something was about to happen, and it was too late to flee.

The door opened onto a mysterious embracing perfume. I saw a hexagonal room with the dusk filtering through the windowless wooden walls in which craftsmen had carved thousands of apertures in the shape of five-petaled flowers.

"I had this pavilion built so that I could watch the sunset without being dazzled. It's the only time of day when the sky is a faithful reflection of life. Look over there, look at the crimson, the deep red, the violet, the scarlet. Tonight, somewhere in our empire, innocent blood is flowing!"

I opened my eyes wide. In that eruption of red and gold, I could make out her face, a hazy circle of black drawing closer. She took me in her arms. I was amazed when I felt her tongue probing my mouth. She leaned the full weight of her body against me, and I fell down into the cushions with her. Her expert hands untied my belt and peeled off my dress, trousers, and silk slippers.

"Undress me," she said.

I did not know that when sisters slept together they had to be naked, but I obeyed her without hesitating. She removed the golden pin with the pearl, and her long hair tumbled endlessly over her neck. She lay down on this sheet of gleaming hair and drew me on top of her. She put her hand between my thighs. Almost before I felt the agile serpents of her fingers, I gave an involuntary groan.

I started to cry over this undeserved happiness, this little corner of love in my lonely life. My sobbing aroused my cousin. She slid against my body, whispering instructions. I did as she asked. I imitated what she did and watched her face express itself with smiles or frowns. She was trembling and peculiarly tense. Her cheeks grew red and droplets of sweat formed on her brow. The sun slipped off her body. It lingered on the ceiling for a moment, then disappeared through the partitioned wall. She lay in the dark, no longer moving. She was silent for a long time. I was starting to think that she might be dead when she rubbed the flint and lit a candle. Her face was framed by her messy hair, and she looked pale as a ghost.

"I hate night time," she said darkly. "The shades are my enemies. I know that all these women are jealous of my beauty, and they wait until it's dark to cast evil spells over me. Can you hear their voices?"

The garden was quiet; I could hear the rustle of leaves, the earth breathing. But she blocked her ears with her hands to escape the malevolent incantations. In the candlelight the roses of her breasts were so pale that her body seemed almost unreal. Then her face was filled with a grimace of pain, as if a strident sound had just pierced her ear-drums; she shuddered and whipped her hands away. A strange snigger of distress distorted her face, and she started throwing the cushions we had been lying on to the four corners of the room. It was only then that I saw that the floor was made of bronze and mercury—it was a mirror.

"Spread your legs," she said, bringing the candle closer. "Look!"

It was the first time I had seen it, seen that cleft: hairy, convoluted, red—a monstrous lesion.

"Have a good look. It's with that hideous mouth that they sing, they curse, and they spit their venom! Can't you hear their hideous music?"

I tried to put my arms around her. She slapped me and started screaming: "Go away! Go away! You disgust me! You're just a whore, a spy from the Delicate Concubine, a poisoner! Go away!"

"Highness, you're wrong, I mean you no harm. I love you."

I knelt before her with my forehead to the ground. She spat at me like a fury and struck me repeatedly. I hid my face in my hands and wept. Then she collapsed, exhausted; the demon left her, and her lucidity was restored. She crawled over to me and begged me to kiss her. We made love again, but I no longer felt anything. Suddenly she started moaning as if in her death throes, and she drenched me in her moment of ecstasy.

* * *

IN THE SIDE City eyes were constantly spying, ears constantly listening: Soon I was treated to mysterious smiles expressing irony and envy. A feeling of pride mingled with aching sorrow overwhelmed me. What did they know of this wounded, damaged woman's madness? When I kissed the Gracious Wife, I believed I was tasting of some delicacy, but I was just drinking the first draught of a terrible poison. I went over the events of that late afternoon a thousand times, throwing myself into that incandescent pavilion as a fisherman throws his net into the river. As I studied every moment, slowly, minutely, forgotten details emerged. Pleasure, shuddering, uneasiness, disgust—the most contradictory emotions caught at my throat in the day and kept me awake at night.

I was determined not to see her again, not to go back to that abyss that swallowed the sunlight, but this woman who was in thrall to demons could surely read the secrets in my heart. Days passed, and I received no further invitation, and absence—that wily magician—turned my aversion to desire. Daily life came to the fore again, with all its weariness and filth. The women around me were walking wounds. I felt an urgent longing to love, to raise myself to the skies through whatever obsession brought me new hope. The Gracious Wife was a lie, a liberating lie!

The violence erased itself from my memory, and only her astonishing beauty remained to obsess me. What torture it was to feel her gentle breasts on my face and her stomach soft as a newly hatched chick only to wake from this impotent dream! I now missed her cries of ecstasy that had frightened me. At night I smelled the air to try and catch the scent of her hair. One strand at a time, it slid over my breast, but I could not hold it. My life had become more unbearable than before I knew her. Now, I had to stand by my choice even if it would be the death of me!

One afternoon, in the grip of madness, I ran to her palace. She received me with no sign of surprise. We had barely exchanged a few polite words before she dismissed her servants, led me to the Pavilion of Dusk, and pushed me to the floor. She lay on top of me, and once again

I let myself be beaten. Her pleasure became more intense as she inflicted more pain and humiliation on me. I cried. I hated myself. I despised myself for loving such a monster. My tears fuelled her ecstasy. When she had mortified me with insults, when she had stripped me, abused me, and violated me, she sent me back to the women in the Side Court.

I had become her slave. She who understood the strength of silence never called me. My wounds barely had time to heal before I hurried back to her. Sometimes I found her palace empty: She had left; she was serving the imperial bed. My stomach constricted, and my limbs turned to stone. In the emperor's arms, she was a servile slave! I would go back to my world, devastated, dead.

She was not interested in horses, books, or her little boy, the beautiful prince with such sad eyes. She loved jewels, dresses, and tiny little dogs with curly coats. Before making love she was charming, all smiles, gentle. She touched up my makeup, dressed me, made me blush with her shameless jokes. But naked she would gradually go mad, insulting me and trampling over me. It was only when she had unleashed onto me her loathing for all humanity that she reached a form of release, a voluptuous happiness. The Pavilion of Dusk was my torture chamber. She forced strangers on me, girls I did not desire. In that accumulation of mouths and breasts, above the mirror that multiplied the gaping orifices further, she would beat me until I bled. The other women would fondle one another as they watched me. They were naked, with their heads between one another's thighs, their bodies writhing in the blaze of sunlight, shrieking with pleasure; and I felt only loathing.

The seasons changed. I silenced my pain, my body stiffened, my heart was sickened, but still I feigned rapture. There was nothing left to say between us. The tender words had given way to repetitive moans, the fascination had been tarnished by a wearied eroticism. Her gaze was not so misty now; her face was harder. I found her ugly, and she was tiring of my battered body. My visits became less frequent, but I did not know how to bring an end to this liaison. I pitied her: Without me, without my strong muscles that were the lure to her demon, how could she achieve physical gratification? And without that gratification, how could she live?

One evening when I went to her palace, her keepers told me that their mistress was out. When I went back past her door after nightfall, I saw a girl coming out. I hid behind a tree and saw the same servants who used to take me back to the Side Court helping her along, lighting her way with lanterns. I recognized a Forest of Treasure who had arrived at Court a month earlier. She staggered as she walked. Her tears were barely audible, but they reached my ears. While the keepers were distracted, I slipped into the palace and crept into the Pavilion of Dusk.

Through the petal-shaped apertures, I could see there were so many candelabras that the room was lit up as if it were midday. She was lying naked on the cushions, musing happily and eating fruit while the servants massaged her legs. I knocked down the door, pushed aside the terrified girls, and sat astride her. My hands tightened around her neck, and I strangled her with all my might. She struggled. Her face turned purple, and her eyes rolled back in their sockets. The women threw themselves at me in vain, and I abandoned her when I thought she was dead.

That night I dreamt of the sun-bleached skull of a horse. The dark cavities of its eyes, so like a woman's avid orifice, stared at me. I woke screaming. There was blood on my bed: I had just had my first menses.

The Gracious Wife had foreseen this stain in me. She had plucked me in my innocence and betrayed me when I was reduced to corruption. The following day Governess arranged a ceremony to celebrate my reaching fertility. She burned the stained corner of the sheet, then made me drink the ashes blended with warm wine. The women of the Side Court gave me gifts and paid me compliments. My cousin had regained consciousness but was still in bed; she sent me an enamel box containing a pearl necklace and this poem:

Whiteness and purity
May my love bring into bloom
Your scarlet valleys.

I sent back the necklace with a note:

The treasures of the ocean
Must return to the night
Of furious waves.

I stopped seeing her.

THE GRACIOUS WIFE had passed on to me her refined taste in clothes and her experienced eye with women. In that Court so full of extraordinary beauties, I decided to perfect my appearance. My skin was tanned by the sun; my figure was slim with bronzed muscles. I was like a challenge to those pale faces and concealed bodies. My energetic stride sneered at their sickly little footsteps. In contrast to the profusion of jewels, muslins, and embroidered shoes with upturned points, I had my tunics of heavy cloth tailored to fit closely, and my archer's wrists were free of any jewelry. To other women the choice of clothes was a form of ingenious exhibition, a shameless seduction. To me, dresses were like a breastplate that I put on to set off to war against this life.

I was complimented on my elegance, my skin color, my features. I found consolation in a string of casual affairs, girls who, unlike the Gracious Wife, afforded me some pleasure. My memories of the Pavilion of Dusk burned through my entrails. I succeeded in using my charms like a weapon; I learned to play with others' hearts and to master my own desires.

The snow fell, and the days were short and sunless. On the night of the New Year Banquet, I saw my cousin dancing up on a dais between firework displays carried on the heads of two acrobats. Her silhouette swayed and twirled between those sparkling showers, like a bird hovering in its cage decorated with precious stones.

FOUR

One afternoon in the spring, the groom entrusted a Turkish colt to me. The wild animal charged around the outdoor manège, whinnying, jumping, but however furiously he twisted and lurched, I stuck fast in the saddle. When he slowed down, exhausted, I reinforced my every order with a crack of the whip.

I did not realize that this commotion had attracted a good many spectators. When I leapt to the ground, a eunuch ran over and told me that Princess Sun of Jin and the King of Jin wished to give me their compliments.

On the far side of the enclosure, I found a girl in boy's clothing, and the young king, who wore a tunic of willow-green brocade embroidered with golden lions over a second tunic in daffodil yellow. The princess's eyes shone, and she could scarcely conceal her admiration. The king flushed as he accepted my greeting. He had beautiful elongated eyes and was shy as a little girl.

The princess, a happy fluttering creature, chattered constantly. She asked me the secret of my courage, then she wanted to know everything about me: my name, age, and position. The king listened. When he heard that I was from Bing, he emerged from his silence and told me that the sovereign had appointed him the great governor of that glorious province.

"When my noble grandfather, Emperor Lordly Forebear, was a mere military governor, he encouraged his children to practice the martial arts," he confided solemnly. "And so, when he rose up against the Sui's corrupt Court, my honorable sovereign father, my uncles, and my aunt, Princess Sun of Ping, brandished their swords and rode at the head of their armies. As the descendant of those intrepid warriors, I am preparing to conquer the world. When I am older, I shall subjugate the Barbarians of the dark kingdoms, and I shall impose China's supremacy over the entire world!"

The young king's ambitions were in contrast to his slight frame and the fact that his forehead was still covered by a youthful fringe. But I looked into his face—the face of a dreamer—with envy. I too would have preferred to die on a battlefield than to wither slowly in the Side Court.

"May we call you Heavenlight?" asked the Princess. "Father calls me Little Bull and my brother Little Phoenix."

She turned to the king and asked: "Heavenlight could use those secret names? Would you agree?"

"I give you my permission, Talented One. But do not tell anyone."

The gynaeceum had produced fourteen sons and twenty daughters for the Emperor. Two of the boys had died very young. In keeping with Court custom—ever wary of pretenders to the throne—the remaining princes were required to leave the Inner Palace as soon as they received the royal seal, and they went to live in their official residences in the noble district of Long Peace. But Little Phoenix and Little Bull were the children of the Empress of Learning and Virtue. Her untimely death had robbed them of the only protection they had in the Forbidden City. United in their grief, they had become inseparable. The emperor had taken pity on them and had made a special decree allowing the young king to prolong his stay in the Inner Court.

I did not know what had led the other to me, and I could not explain how this friendship began, but it would become a pact of life and death. The princess was nine, the prince eleven, and I was fourteen. They were fascinated by my strength and saw me as an idol, a protector. I sympathized with their bereavement, which reminded me of my own. I missed Little Sister. I would give my time and my patience to this princess to appease the sorrow.

I shared a love of horses and archery with Little Phoenix. Together we plotted the routes of his future expeditions across geographical maps. Through him I lived my dream of being a man, of being strong and free. In time, this weakling who strove to look so aloof and proud admitted to me how alone and afraid he felt. His elder brothers had left the Forbidden City. The eldest, who was his full brother, was ensconced in his Eastern Palace playing the part of an authoritarian Supreme Son. He would not tolerate being outshone by his younger brothers. The favorites in the gynaeceum tried their best to distance Little Phoenix from the sovereign, who was so busy with affairs of state that months could go by without his speaking to the boy. Little Phoenix was shy and self-effacing. He had to settle for living in an imaginary world where he now included me in his great conquests overseas.

Puberty is a fleeting moment of beauty. When Little Phoenix was fourteen, he lifted his fringe from his forehead and tied his hair in a top-knot. After his coming of age ceremony, the ministers pointed out to the sovereign that it was no longer suitable to keep this man in his gynaeceum. Little Phoenix left us and went to live in his royal residence. A few months later, he arrived at the Outer Court in the robes of an imperial official and began taking his part in political life. The Great High Princess[9] of Shared Peace arranged his betrothal to one of her granddaughters, a young lady of high birth from the Wang clan in the province of Bing, whose grandfather had been a Great Minister in the

---

[9] The Great High Princess is the title given to the paternal aunt of the Emperor.

Wei dynasty of the west and whose uncle had recently married a County Princess.[10]

After her beloved brother left, Little Bull was a broken creature. My young princess was wasting away, and I was tormented by her cruel question: "Why does human life have to mean constant separation?" The day the king was married, Little Bull shut herself in her room and spoke to no one. She weakened under the weight of her melancholy. As the winter began, she succumbed to a violent fever; three days later, she escaped to the heavens.

I saw the king again when her body was ceremonially placed in her coffin. He had grown: Beneath the white linen tunic, it was now a man who wept in sorrow. He appeared at the far end of a path even though I was trying to avoid him. His voice now had the deep resonance of an adult's.

"I killed her," he said, stamping his feet in anguish. "I killed her!"

We were both guilty; we had both been loved. I forgot propriety and cried with him in the whistling wind.

The snow of my eighteenth year fell around us and covered the ground.

BEYOND THE NORTHERN Gate, the Imperial Park—the vastest domain under the heavens[11]—stretched out to the west, its forests teeming with game and its rivers rich in fish. In the autumn, when the sun-scorched leaves turned to ochre, the ground reverberated to the sound of horns and drums, making dogs bark and tamed leopards roar. Horsemen bearing banners and standards appeared like the furious clouds of a rainstorm. The banners would part, and the emperor would appear beneath his yellow satin parasol, astride his favorite mount, drawing back his bow adorned with gold carvings. When he galloped like this, his solid body seemed to lose its weightiness and become lighter. The Master of the

[10] The County Princess is the title given to the daughter of imperial princes and princesses.
[11] The Imperial Park had a perimeter of 60km.

World was supple and agile; he was once again the invincible hero who had subjugated the Empire by force of arms.

Banquets were held on the banks of the river. Whole boars and stags were spit-roasted, and bets were taken on the Turkish generals as they wrestled, stripped to the waist and oiled with animal fat. Kings and ministers took part in Tatar-style dancing, and the Emperor deigned to beat out the rhythm on a tambourine.

On that particular day, drunk and in high spirits, His Majesty called for the horse called Winged Lion, which had been a gift from the King of the West. Generals and captains came forward in turn, each hoping to drink from the cup promised by the sovereign to whoever could master this huge beast with the golden mane. Drums rolled, and the enraged Winged Lion snorted and bucked, arching his back and launching himself into a full gallop only to stop dead in his tracks, throwing his rider to the ground.

Cries of amazement and disappointment filled the air. Inflamed by this cruel game, the Emperor ordered for his sleeves to be rolled up and prepared to take up the challenge. The Great Ministers threw themselves to their knees:

"His Majesty must take care of his divine self."

"It is not acceptable for the sovereign to put his life in danger."

"The sages would condemn such foolhardiness."

"Majesty, do not forget your responsibilities to the State!"

Unsure how to proceed, the Emperor tapped his foot on the ground and looked around him.

"Well, is there no one who can master this horse?"

Hearing these words, I stepped forward and prostrated myself on the ground.

"Your servant requests permission to try her luck!"

For the first time, the sovereign turned his eye on me. Amazed and amused, he asked: "My generals were unable to control this beast. Young girl, are you not afraid to die beneath my mount's flailing hooves?"

I replied more calmly than I would have believed possible: "Majesty, creatures of violence must be mastered with violence. I shall make so bold as to ask for three tools: a whip, a hammer, and a dagger. First, I shall give him a lesson with the whip. If he disobeys me, I shall blow him on the head with the hammer. If he still rebels, I shall slit his throat."

The Emperor roared with laughter. He praised my attitude and told the Supreme Son that it was an excellent metaphor for the strategy he applied to the Tatar people. The very next day he summoned me to serve in his inner palace. Dressed in man's robes, with my tablet and ink pot attached to my belt and my calligraphy brush through my topknot, I joined the ranks of the secretaries.

THE PALACE OF Precious Dew was displaying its beds of irises and orchids. With its ceilings as high as the vault of the heavens, its curtains of pearls, its screens inscribed with calligraphy, and its succession of sinuous galleries, it was a labyrinth of intrigue. Its countless doors opened onto a little corner of sky, a sloping roof, a window in the shape of a crescent moon, a rockery smothered in the twisted limbs of a wisteria or an emerald pond around which white cranes flitted. Each of these ingenious touches meant that every guest felt that the Son of Heaven favored him alone.

From my position behind screens of gauze and sliding doors, I could watch the endless streams of jealous concubines and princes hoping to find recognition. Taoist monks and doctors argued over the pile of immortality. When ministers and generals appeared and disappeared at the entrance to secret passageways, I knew that, somewhere in the Empire, rebel heads would roll.

The poetess Xu was having difficulty standing up to the combined forces of her rivals. Following her miscarriage, the Delicate Concubine had withdrawn from the Emperor's entourage and now led a sad and solitary life. The Gracious Wife was still struggling valiantly to maintain the sovereign's favor. I was now half a head taller than the woman who had introduced me to the delights and horrors of love. Her eyes had lost their languid mistiness, and her leaden face exhaled an air of repeated debauchery. Her sugary words were sibilant nonsense. I could not believe that I had been enslaved to this monster.

But I had learned to play games the way women do. So as not to have her as an enemy, I flattered her with well-placed lies. My promises kept her desires at bay, and I no longer abandoned myself to her. First love is a crossing to another world.

I sometimes met Little Phoenix, who came to offer his greetings. He would manage to shake off the following of eunuchs and slip away with me behind a column or a tree. He would give me secret presents bought at peasant fairs: a wooden comb, a terracotta doll, a little horse made of sugar. These very ordinary trinkets were priceless in our Inner City. In exchange for his presents, he insisted that I listen to him describe his inextricable affairs with his young mistresses and I give him my advice. I watched my king growing up with a heavy heart. He was no longer the fevered adolescent who dreamed of magnificent battles against the Barbarians. His adult life was a succession of female conquests in which any feeling of glory disappeared the day after the victory. Still dissatisfied in his search for an ideal woman, he abandoned himself wholeheartedly to pointless suffering and transient happiness.

He too was a prisoner of the forced inactivity of the imperial court; was there a better drug for him to find than love?

One afternoon Little Phoenix appeared at the entrance to the manège where I was schooling a horse. He called for his usual mount and galloped over to me.

Still far away, he called: "Did you know that the King of Qi, the son of Wife Yin, has led a revolt against Sovereign Father? He's killed the Governor Delegate of his province-kingdom and proclaimed himself Emperor. Sovereign Father is furious. His ministers have approved an immediate repression. The armies of nine counties are marching toward the rebel cities!"

When he was closer to me, I could see tears on his cheeks.

"This morning at the Emperor's audience, my elder brother, Supreme Son, and my second brother, the King of Wei, each accused the other of being allied to the insurgent. I thought they were going to fight before the sovereign. Heavenlight, my brothers are going mad!"

The Supreme Son and the King of Wei, who was second in line to the throne, were both born of the Empress of Learning and Virtue, and their rivalry in the Imperial City went back to their childhood. As the Emperor grew older, he was losing patience with the eldest, who preferred debauchery to study, and his affection was turning to the younger son who seemed more serious and intelligent. Seeing his title threatened, the heir became even more bullish and vindictive. As he drew close to his goal, the King of Wei became increasingly nervous and vapid. Their hatred for each other spread throughout the Court, and partisan clans had formed. Both camps slandered each other before the sovereign who, distressed by the conflict, could not reach a decision. The heir wanted his younger brother dead to secure his position; the King of Wei cursed his elder brother who held a place he did not deserve. Each of them secretly resented the sovereign for defending his adversary, and each of them was quite capable of seizing the throne by launching a coup. Princes turning to fratricide and usurping thrones was the curse of our dynasty!

Little Phoenix interrupted my thoughts: "After the audience, the heir's carriage held mine up as we turned a corner. He demanded that I speak ill of his enemy in front of Father. Later, I received a visit from the King of Wei in my palace. 'Neutrality is a sign of weakness punishable by death,' he told me. What should I do? How can I take either part? They are both guilty of sowing the seeds of unrest in the Palace. One of them is colluding with the rebels and has betrayed us. Heavenlight, I don't want to be involved with any plotting and scheming! I'm afraid!"

I tried to reassure him: "Your uncle the Great Chancellor Wu Ji, the brother of the honorable late Empress, has the sovereign's ear. In the past, he took his Majesty's part when he confronted his brothers; today he best understands the tragedy of the situation. The sovereign is too closely involved to act, but I know that he has instructed Lord Wu Ji to conduct a secret enquiry. Soon we shall know the truth. Your brothers are trying to frighten you. They are the ones who are dying of fear! Don't trouble yourself; no one will have time to do you harm."

The atmosphere at the Palace of Precious Dew darkened. The Emperor was sullen and silent; he refused his favorite entry to his palace and condemned his servants to beatings for the least oversight. At night he would call for a slave, a little sweeping girl he had discovered one day, and this provoked acute indignation amongst the Court ladies.

The rebel province was overcome by the imperial army's attack. The King of Qi was brought to the Capital in chains. A decree from the sovereign stripped him of his position, his title, and his nobility. Now deposed, reduced to the state of commoner and imprisoned, he received the order to commit suicide.

The enquiry conducted by Wu Ji revealed a conspiracy against the sovereign led by the heir and supported by members of the imperial family and high dignitaries. In prison the Supreme Son confessed his crimes. He lost his title and the right to wear the insignia of nobility. His eldest son was stripped of the mandate of Imperial Grandson. Both were exiled. Their chief accomplices were the King of Han, who was the sovereign's brother; the prince consort Dou He, whose father had been one of the twenty-four veterans who founded the dynasty; the son of the High Princess of Vastness Zhao Jie; the Minister for Human Affairs; and Ho Jiun Ji, the great victor of the Gaochang War. All of them were imprisoned and had to wait until the autumn[12] for their capital punishment. Except for the imperial princesses, the female members of their families became slaves in the Side Court. Their male descendants were granted the Emperor's clemency; he did not want to see any more heads severed. They were whipped and banished to the south of the Mountain of the Extreme.

[12] In the days of the Tang dynasty, executions were carried out once a year in mid-autumn.

Little Phoenix would come to me in the middle of the manège and confide his distress in me. He was deeply affected by this series of condemnations and seemed more helpless than ever. One day he broke down in tears.

"There are arrests at the audience every day. The guards rip the head-dresses and ivory tablets from conspirators, then drag them from their places amongst the officials. My heart beats so fast I fear I will pass out. Heavenlight, all these men have sworn loyalty to the sovereign—how can they break their word? My uncles and aunts grew up with Father; why are they trying to assassinate him now? If it had only been Elder Brother who rebelled, I might understand. But why these crowds of traitors, these hordes of conspirators? People have always said that Father is a good and fair ruler and that he is one of the best sovereigns the Empire has had. Why would his inferiors want to overthrow him?"

"Highness, from the snatches of conversation I have overheard between the sovereign and his confidants, I have learned that most men are hungry for power and wealth, that the smallest promise of obtaining them can make men change their minds. Ambitious men like that confuse their own interests with the future of the Empire and cannot distinguish between a good sovereign and a bad emperor."

My explanation was not enough to calm Little Phoenix. He went further: "I have also heard that half these people are condemned without proof. They are guilty simply of being the friends of the conspirators. Why has Father become so cruel!"

"Highness, promise me you will not say those words before anyone else. You must silence these thoughts in front of your brothers. Your compassion might be denounced. You in turn would be suspected of being allied to the conspirators."

"Oh, Heavenlight, I regret Empress Mother's death more than ever. She would know how to soften Father's harshness and how to heal my uncle's murderous madness!"

"Highness, wipe your tears, you who dream of being a conqueror, do not be conquered by pity. The sovereign must defend his crown for he has built a powerful empire and made the people happy. Tomorrow, free of these troubles, he will strive again for the prosperity of the dynasty. Compared to this substantial task that benefits millions of individuals, the hundred or so men who are to be decapitated count for nothing!"

Little Phoenix sighed: "Now that my brother the King of Wei has removed his opponent, the title of heir automatically falls to him. He's a suspicious man, a grudge-bearer. His accession will be the beginning of the end. He will kill all his brothers to keep his crown."

"The Emperor has not yet announced the name of his successor. This delay proves that he is hesitating, that he has another possibility in mind."

"What could this other possibility be? The King of Wu, the son of Precious Wife?"

"You, Highness!" I cried indignantly. "Your uncle Wu Ji, the head of the Great Ministers who faithfully keeps alive the memory of the Empress of Learning and Virtue, would never let the child of an imperial concubine accede to the throne. Your heart is pure and your generosity vast. You would be a good and fair sovereign; you would bring prosperity and peace to the Empire."

Terrified, he shook his head. "There is such madness in your ideas! The King of Wu has been reciting poems since he was four years old. He is the child prodigy, Father's favorite. I'm just an ordinary prince. I have no desire to reign. My brothers are fascinated by power, but it disgusts me. I would prefer the perilous campaigns of an army commander, far from the plotting at Court. I shall go and talk to my uncle who knows Sovereign Father's intentions. I will concede my place to the King of Wu."

"From his mother's side, the King of Wu bears the blood of Emperor Yang of the overthrown dynasty. He will never be sovereign of ours. If you speak now to Wu Ji, head of the Great Ministers, he will think that you are actually maneuvering to be given the title. It is too soon to guess the future and too late to act. Let life decide this for you!"

A few days later Little Phoenix's destiny played itself out in the most extraordinary way. The dismissed prince wrote to his father from prison: ". . . Your servant had already been distinguished with the position of heir, what more could I ask for? Slandered and persecuted by the King of Wei, I sought advice from my counselors to find peace. It was these men and their intrigue that drove me to criminal means. . . . If Your Majesty now appoints the King of Wei as successor, you would be fulfilling the wishes of an underhanded man who will have achieved all he was scheming for. . . ."

After reading this, the Emperor realized that nominating the King of Wei would encourage all the princes to covet the title of heir, and the Empire would not know another moment's peace. The Great Minister Wu Ji then suggested the King of Jin to the sovereign. He was the ninth imperial son, but the third to be born of the late Empress. Little Phoenix, until then forgotten, became the perfect candidate, and the Court, bowing before Wu Ji's power, upheld him unanimously.

The King of Wei was stripped of his dignity and exiled to the county of Dong Lai. Little Phoenix was proclaimed heir: He rejected the responsibility but, as refusal was all part of the ritual of imperial nomination, no one realized that his intention was very real. When he wanted to offer his title to the King of Wu, the ministers praised his modesty. In the confusion, Little Phoenix received the seal of Supreme Son.

The sovereign had the following pronouncement inscribed in the *Imperial Records*: "When the heir strays from his duty and when the king plots to have him removed, both fall from grace."

WHEN THE NEW heir took up residence in the Eastern Palace, one of his concubines brought a son into the world. At sixteen, Little Phoenix was blessed with every earthly happiness.

I congratulated him, and he replied with a melancholy smile.

"I wanted neither the child nor the title. Both events caught me unawares. When I look at myself in the mirror in the morning, I cannot understand why I already have descendants. In Court, after the audience, dignitaries, and minister gather around me, some ask for my opinion; others give me their advice. Before, great ministers could walk past me as if I were transparent. Now they give me deep bows and invite me to their banquets. Even Sovereign Father has changed. Only yesterday he was distant and treated me like a little boy. Now he showers me with his warmth and attention, as he did with the King of Wei before his downfall. Heavenlight, I don't recognize myself. I feel I have slipped into a stranger's body."

"Little Phoenix, the world has not changed. You have grown up. You are no longer a child lost in dreams. You have become a man, a man of destiny! The sovereign has offered you the seal of the future. With your hands and your thoughts, you will rule the world—you will change it. You will be able to wipe away the lies, to right the wrongs, and spread goodness and compassion!"

"Heavenlight, your words are reassuring and encouraging. But when I am far from you, I lose my confidence again. All this responsibility is beyond me. I am not educated enough; I know nothing about politics. The fact that there are three councils, six ministries, and twenty-four departments gives me a migraine. Amongst all the uncles and brothers and the aunts and sisters who are rushing to offer their loyalty, I cannot tell who is a friend and who is an enemy. I don't think I am intelligent enough to recognize the traitors and liars who are twice, three times, even four times my age. I'm frightened of people. I will never be ready to reign."

"Confidence has a long apprenticeship," I consoled him. "Like physical strength, it is accrued with experience and exercise. You have modesty and lucidity, two qualities that are essential to becoming a good sovereign. Fear nothing, Highness; the Emperor is keeping watch over your education. The Great General Li Ji is your tutor; he is an honest and devoted warrior. You shall be a great sovereign if you do not retreat in the face of difficulty."

"All this means little to me. I would be the happiest of men if I could have you by my side," he said, looking deep into my eyes.

"Highness," I replied in amazement, "I am already by your side!"

"Heavenlight, are you so very blind?" he asked and ran away.

I was filled with a sweet sadness mingled with anger. I remembered the first time we had met: The boy had been smaller than me. Now he was taller than me and wore the beginnings of a mustache. Was I so very blind? Little Phoenix had become a man. He was no longer a little boy seeking the wisdom and consolation of a sister; the feelings he now nurtured for me were a man's. He saw me as a woman!

The heir found a thousand excuses to visit the Palace of Precious Dew. He tried to catch my eye, but I avoided him and lowered my eyes. As a Talented One of the fifth rank, my body and soul belonged to the sovereign even though he had never honored me. Little Phoenix was expecting an incestuous affection from me that I could not grant him. How had he dared confuse me with those poor women he had seduced and promptly abandoned? How could he allow himself to consider me as an object of amusement and distraction? I wanted us to be connected by an undying friendship, and he was offering me a transient love that would fade with time.

He managed to follow me to the private washroom. He stood blocking the doorway and spoke: "Why are you hiding yourself? Why don't you want to speak to me? If I have behaved tactlessly, please forgive me!"

I avoided his eyes and said: "Before, your Highness was a child, now he has become and man and is heir to the Empire. The Ancients say that a man and a woman should keep a respectful distance. I no longer wish to speak freely with your Highness. Let me go."

"Talented One, you are so formal with me now! Why are you so cold and unkind? And I think of you every day. Here, look, I've been to the market to buy the quince jelly you like so much. Don't you know that since Little Bull's death you are the person dearest to me? Heavenlight, be kind, give me a smile. Tell me you're not angry."

Hearing him speaking like that, I thought I might have misinterpreted his intentions. I regretted being susceptible and ate the delicacy he had put in my hand.

Nothing would ever be the same again.

My conversations with Little Phoenix had lost all their spontaneity. Now that he was Supreme Son, he was careful about his clothes and makeup. His tunics were sumptuous garments gleaming with pearls and precious stones. His face, with its light dusting of powder, looked even more pure and delicate. The perfume he wore made my heart beat faster, and I often forgot what I wanted to say to him. Somewhere deep inside I felt a new kind of happiness. For the first time in that Forbidden City, someone was showing an interest in my life and my death. Little Phoenix said that, without me, he would never overcome his fears and his weakness; he did not know that, without him, I would be just one more unhappy soul among the ten thousand women growing a little older every day in the Inner Palace.

In the Eighteenth year of Pure Contemplation, the kingdom of Korea invaded the kingdom of Sinra on the peninsular.[13] When the King of Sinra called for his help, the Emperor decided to set off on a campaign against our hereditary enemies, the Koreans. On the fourteenth day of the tenth moon, the ceremonial regiments, the imperial guards, the government, and the gynaeceum escorted the sovereign to the eastern capital, Luoyang, where an army of one hundred thousand warriors was to gather.

As the horses galloped on, I looked through the curtains of my carriage and could see troops maneuvering in a cloud of dust on the horizon. That night, the imperial bivouacs stretched out over the entire plain that was turned into an ocean of light by the countless camp fires.

One night, when I was taking out my topknot before the mirror, someone raised the curtain to my tent without asking to be announced. I recognized the heir, wrapped in a thick fur coat. Seeing him, Ruby and Emerald prostrated themselves and withdrew. I understood too late that they were accomplices to this reckless act. The heir was already

---

[13] The Korea of today was once occupied by three kingdoms: Korea, Sinra, and Paiktchei. The Korean kingdom was inhabited by the Tatar Mongols and the Tobhas, who had already defeated the armies of Emperor Yang of the Sui dynasty.

sprawling on a cushion behind me. He was agitated and told me how he had stepped over drunken servants and slipped through the guards.

I begged him to leave. But he protested: "As I've been unable to flee my retinue during the daytime since we left the Capital, it is now half a moon since we have seen each other. Tonight, I decided to take a risk because I have come to tell you something important."

I could see him in the mirror, still trying to catch my eye. I stood up, put on my coat, and made for the door. He caught the hem of my tunic.

"We are alone. My people are watching the door. No one knows I am here. Listen to me first, then I shall leave."

"Well then, please, may your Highness move further away from me and sit down."

Little Phoenix went and sat obediently in a corner. I sat facing him at the far side of the room. He looked at his hands on his knees and said nothing. I watched a candle spilling its tears, and I too was silent. Suddenly he looked up.

"Heavenlight, I am to have a second child."

I was about to congratulate him when he said: "Those women don't count. There is only one person who fills my days and nights," he said, and then lowered his voice before adding, "she is not like all the women at Court: the bland, formal, calculating women. She is spontaneous as a horse, pure as a river, free as the air. I venerate her, and I fear her. I suffer when I think I cannot be one with her."

He broke off. His eyes were like two dancing flames in the half darkness. Outside the North Wind blew, and one of the watchmen struck the gong. It was late. Then he suddenly started stammering: "I want to teach you what true pleasure is. I know that you would like the abandon, the excesses. I'll be gentle with you, you'll see. And you would slowly become a woman. You would be the most beautiful woman in the Empire!"

Tears came to my eyes, but my voice was hard: "Go, Highness. What your Highness is doing is improper."

He stared at me for a moment, then stood up and slipped away.

* * *

LUOYANG, THE EASTERN capital. Along the avenues icicles hung from every roof, and the trees were covered with buds of frost. The River Luo was frozen, a long, winding sigh reaching up to the weary sky. In the Forbidden City, only the winter plum trees braved the cold with their subtle fragrance. I stayed in the pavilions with my hands inside my sleeves and my feet up against bronze heaters, and I learned news of the outside world from the eunuchs. It seemed that regiments had come from the four corners of the Empire and had set up camp beside the town. Their garrisons had turned the countryside into an ocean of banners and horses. Accompanied by the heir, the Emperor would climb to the highest point of the Southern Gate and take command of the soldiers' training sessions.

At the beginning of January, the peripatetic monk Xuan Zang returned, and this delayed our armies' departure. After covering tens of thousands of lis[14] and living for seventeen years traveling the western kingdoms, he came back to the eastern capital laden with sacred manuscripts gathered in the land of Buddha. The Emperor received him during his audience, covered him with gifts, and appointed him master monk at the Temple of Immense Felicity. The Precious Wife invited Xuan Zang to the Inner Court, and he stepped up onto a stage of lotus flowers where he gave a speech about the Buddha of the Future, Maitreya, who had promised to be reincarnated on Earth to guide millions of believers toward eternal peace.

But the Emperor and his generals were more interested in the victories of this world. The sovereign was already armed with his golden breastplate threaded with red laces and was leaving Luoyang by the Southern Gate. Three thousand musicians played the tune of the *Glorious Departure*. Lances, axes, and tridents gleamed; horses and carts whipped up dust that swirled for days without settling.

In the sovereign's absence, the heir took over regency from his East-

---

[14] One li is equal to a half kilometer.

ern Palace, and entry to our gynaeceum was forbidden to men. News of the war reached us through screens and partitions. Our squadrons had wound their way up the coast and reached Korea. The city of Peisha fell, and eight thousand Koreans were taken prisoner. The troops of my benefactor, Great General Li Ji, crossed the River Liao and laid siege to a port. The army commanded by the sovereign had met with more grim resistance. The Koreans were brutal warriors and adept archers, and they defended their territories with all the energy of despair.

Neither the war cries nor the smell of blood breached the high walls of the Forbidden City. Spring came back to Luoyang. Court ladies set out in little groups to enjoy picnics by the banks of the river. Peach trees scattered their petals, and carefree peonies rustled in the wind. In the master's absence, the jealousies and intrigues had stopped, but the favorites began to tire of this peaceful, untroubled existence. I missed Little Phoenix. This separation meant he was with me with every breath I took. Women no longer satisfied my soul's desire, and their constant, insistent attentions only made me more obsessed with my absent brother.

In the ninth moon, the chrysanthemums in the Palace of Luoyang vied with one another in beauty and insolence. In the north of the Empire, a precocious winter had already set in. Snow fell thick and deep. The cold wore down our soldiers who were still in summer dress; the Emperor was forced to lift the siege, and the army retreated toward the central lands. The arduous crossing through swamplands exhausted the men and their horses. Accompanied by a light cavalry, the heir rode out to meet the sovereign, only to find an ailing man and a defeated conqueror.

The Court returned to Long Peace in the third moon of the following year. Spring had returned, but the Emperor was still bedridden. Every two days, the heir received the morning salutation in his Eastern Palace. The rest of the time he fulfilled his filial duties by his father's bedside. In the Palace of Precious Dew, we were almost never apart. Being together again was not as joyful as I had imagined. When I was far from him, I hugged the image of him to me. When he was close, I despaired that I would never cross the invisible barrier that separated an heir from a Talented One. I struggled with a thousand contradictory feelings and preferred to say nothing and suffer in silence.

One night the wind changed for the worst, and the sovereign became paralyzed down one side of his body. He grew even more irritable and suspicious. From where he lay in the depths of his palace, he imagined plots brewing in the Outer Court where, he claimed, his prolonged absence was kindling usurpers' ambitions. He asked Wu Ji to conduct investigations, and the persecutions began again. Soon, a great many imperial officers and state officials were condemned to be beheaded.

Fearing that the Supreme Son might be intriguing against him in his Eastern Palace, the Emperor ordered Little Phoenix to move to the Palace of Precious Dew and to sleep close to his own bedroom. To give some comfort to the prince who was now far from his own concubines, he sent him the most beautiful virgins from his gynaeceum every night. In the evening, before the doors were closed, I watched in despair as these women were conducted into Little Phoenix's pavilion surrounded by lanterns and torches. I would go back to the Side Court along dark pathways. The trees rustled and tears rolled down my cheeks for no reason.

ONE AFTERNOON, WHEN I was waiting in the sovereign's bed chamber for him to wake, Little Phoenix appeared and dragged me forcibly behind a screen. He put his arms around me. Unlike women's arms that were supple and soft, his were strong and muscled. He held me against his chest, a hard flat surface like carved stone, so that I could hear the rapid beating of his heart. He lay his head on my shoulder and his cheek against mine. His tender young beard tickled my skin, and I heard him whisper: "It's you that I want. It's you I make love to every evening."

Little Phoenix deflowered me during the course of a journey to a summer palace. Despite our precautions, our liaison could not escape the watchful eyes of those who spied behind curtains, nor the ears that lingered behind doors. But the Emperor now never left his bed, and the heir regent was all-powerful. Instead of denouncing me, the eunuchs and servant women flattered me as a way of pleasing the future sovereign. I never knew whether the Emperor got wind of the rumors. It seems likely that this lady's man, who had once taken wives from his own father and brothers, was quite indifferent to an attachment between a son of his and an anonymous Talented One. The imperial Court was a world of constraints and contradictions: It was easy to die for a mistake, and it was easy to break a taboo.

While the Emperor still had plans to invade Korea, his life was slipping away. His belly swelled up like a mountain and made him howl in pain. But this intrepid warrior defied his suffering and dictated an entire book, *The Art of Being Sovereign*, to his heir. As I stood beside the door awaiting orders, I could hear his dark, determined voice reverberating. Memories of war and political tactics were intertwined with moral and philosophical reflections. The sentences punctuated by groans of pain; the heroic silences and the eerie sighs made me falter with admiration and sorrow.

In the Side Court, people whispered secretly that the astrologers had foreseen a change of reign in this twenty-third year of Pure Contemplation. The favorites removed their jewelry and ripped the pearls from their tunics. They gave their treasure to eunuchs who were financing services in the four corners of the Empire to pray for a miraculous recovery.

There was much talk of the future. But was there any future for the concubines of a dead sovereign? The mothers of kings may have been able to join their children posted in the province-kingdoms, but ordinary women had to choose between living in the funerary palace of the August Deceased, becoming nuns in monasteries, or dying alone in the Side Court.

The heir swore that he would offer me another life. He talked to me of a sumptuous palace and an elevated rank. I did not believe his naïve promises. When the sovereign finally floundered along the river of this life, his treasures, clothes, horses, and the laughter of his women, all these beauties, would have to sink with him into the shades and into oblivion. Would Little Phoenix have the strength to save me while a whole world drowned?

Not believing his end was near, the Emperor continued to travel. He escaped the heat of summer in the mountains of Zhong Nan and the frosts of winter beside hot springs. The imperial caravans swayed, lulling weary bodies and awakening the senses. At night, the heir would disguise himself as a eunuch and slip into my tent. He caressed me softly and sweetly. But only very rarely did I let myself succumb to pleasure. Terrified by a fear I could not name, I wept in silence and feigned happiness. After he left, I would lie awake for hours with my eyes wide open. I denounced myself for feeling something. I was afraid of conceiving a child. I was horrified by the thought that I secretly longed for the sovereign's death. I dreamed of that deliverance even though I knew I would always be a slave to the Forbidden City. I hated myself for using my body as a bargaining tool: I was copulating with the heir to ensure my own future. But could I have any legitimacy in that future thanks to an act of incest? When Little Phoenix held me tightly in his arms, I resented his selfish desire that made him deaf to my distress. As soon as he was far from me, I forgave him for being my downfall and loved him with all my strength. He was my only hope.

The news spread through all of China: The Emperor was in his final agonies. The people were terrified, and inflation began spiraling because of ill-considered buying and because merchants started stockpiling cereals, salt, and bolts of brocade. Our spies in the west and the north spotted movements of the Tatar cavalry regiments. The Empire was waiting for a seismic event, our enemies their hour of victory. Amid all this agitation, I watched my own metamorphosis with displeasure. My breasts were growing, my cheeks had become chubbier, my mouth fuller. My body was ignoring my own unhappiness: I had become beautiful just when beauty would no longer be of any use.

On the twenty-sixth day of the fifth moon in the twenty-third year of Pure Contemplation, in his summer Palace in the Zhong Nan Mountains, the Emperor of the Yellow People with Black Hair completed his earthly mandate and rose up to the heavens to sit amongst the powerful gods. The sun hid behind the clouds; Earth was plunged into darkness. For twenty-seven days, the Imperial City groaned with tears and prayers, and the various ceremonies—calling the Emperor's soul, bathing him, the clothing ceremonies, laying him in his coffin, and the official closing of the coffin—were carried out with unprecedented pomp and splendor.

On the first day of the sixth moon, in his Eastern Palace, the twenty-two-year-old heir succeeded the late Emperor by putting on the imperial tunic painted with the twelve sacred symbols and by wearing the crown with twenty-four tiers of jade pearls. The music for the celebrations sailed over the red walls and hovered along the deserted galleries of the Inner Court. Bronze bells and sounding stones intoned the knell of his wives and concubines. Stifled tears and pious prayers escaped from every gloomy little room where the scarlet wall hangings had been covered over with white fabric.

I stayed at the bedside of the Delicate Concubine Xu, trying to persuade her not to let herself die. Beneath her linen sheet, she weighed little more than a feather. She spat blood and was wracked by violent coughing. She reached out for me with her frozen, bony hand. We talked endlessly about our first few years in the Side Court, the Institute of Letters, and the late sovereign. I begged her to receive a doctor. She smiled and gave me no reply. I could see in her eyes her determination to follow the master into the next world.

She died a few days later, and her death buried once and for all the intrigues between the Precious Wife, the Gracious Wife, and all the imperial favorites. Rivalries and alliances, loathing and attraction had been dissolved. Their existence had been a pointless tragedy, just as the talent of one prodigious poetess had been.

Every woman in the Forbidden City—beautiful or ugly, intelligent or foolish, refined or vulgar—was fragrant dust. The whirlwind of history would carry them away, making no distinctions.

THE SOVEREIGN HEIR gave the late sovereign the posthumous title of Emperor Eternal Ancestor. The man who had ruled the vastest empire under the skies had lost his final battle. Heroes are damned. No mortal conquers Death.

In tears, the imperial concubines packed their bags. After the sovereign's burial, they had to hand over their palaces to the new Emperor's mistresses. The Precious Wife and the Gracious Wife followed their king-sons and exiled themselves in distant provinces. Other favorites resolved to take their vows. Oppressed by sadness and uncertainty, I tried in vain to contact Little Phoenix. He was now the all-powerful Emperor of China. From now on his friendship was a favor over which all men and women would fight. I had written to him, but he had sent no reply. His first wife would soon be recognized as Empress; his mistresses would leave the Eastern Palace and come to live in the Middle Court with their own intrigues. I would have no place in that horde of younger, more beautiful women. Why should I stay at the Side Court and wait for an unlikely summons from a man who would be surrounded by ten thousand beauties?

One night, in my dreams, I saw the peripatetic monk Xuan Zang sitting in the middle of a lotus flower. His eyes stood out from his weather-beaten face with the incandescent brilliance of the sun. When I woke, I understood that Buddha had spoken to me through this image. I had been an apprentice nun at just seven; I was afraid neither of discipline nor of abstinence. A visionary monk had revealed my spiritual vocation to Mother: I should go back to the monastery.

On a date decided by the astrologers, the Emperor raised a great parade and left the Forbidden City. More than one hundred thousand people followed him and made their way to the Mountain of Nine

Horses, where the imperial tomb had just been completed. One thousand soldiers drew the imperial hearse, and behind it Little Phoenix and his wives, the ministers and princes, and the princesses and concubines of the August deceased formed a river of white tunics.

One night I was woken by a bustle of activity outside my tent. Two people lifted the curtain and put two lanterns on the ground. A third person came in but was not announced. I rose quickly and prostrated myself before the Emperor.

"Heavenlight," he said. "I am so sorry I have been silent. My uncle Wu Ji is making my life impossible! With the funeral arrangements, electing a new government, and drawing up peace treaties with Turkish tribes, I don't have one quiet moment."

My throat felt constricted.

"I've missed you," he went on. "In my most difficult moments, I have often thought that if you had been by my side, you would have advised and comforted me. Heavenlight, I have come to tell you that I have not forgotten you. I beg you to be patient. Another month or two apart, and we shall be together all the time."

Tears filled my eyes.

"Too late, Majesty. After the funeral, I have to go to a monastery."

The smile vanished from his face. He was so taken aback he could not speak.

"Majesty, you signed the authorization. I received Your Majesty's decree and his gift three days ago."

"Do you think I read everything I sign? How could I know your name was among the list of concubines who were leaving? Why are you behaving like this? I wanted to be with you until the skies fall in, and you abandon me already!"

Prostrated on the ground before him, I wept.

"Majesty, your servant belonged to the previous Emperor. My inclusion in Your Majesty's household would have caused such a scandal that Your Majesty's reputation would have been blighted: It would not be long before people found out that our liaison began when the previous Emperor was still alive; Your Majesty would be accused of abusing his father's trust. Your Majesty has just taken command of the Empire. Those who harbor dreams of usurping the throne would use slander such as this to weaken you. If Your Majesty is determined to lead his empire to prosperity, then he must forget me!"

"Heavenlight, why did you give yourself to me? Why did you let me believe that we might stay together forever? What does this crown matter! I never wanted to be Emperor. If you become a nun, I shall abdicate, shave my head, and become a monk in the neighboring monastery."

He clasped me tightly in his arms.

"Heavenlight, I beg you, don't abandon me. I am the Emperor. I do as I please. I shall execute all those who are against us. I command you to obey your master, your sovereign: Stay, Heavenlight, stay by my side!"

Little Phoenix's words wrung my breast with pain.

"Let me leave, Majesty," I cried. "Leaving this secular life is a kind of death that erases all the impurities of the previous life. There I shall observe the twenty-seven months of mourning. Day and night I shall pray for the soul of the late sovereign. After that time, Your Majesty may call me back to the Palace. Coming out of the temple is a rebirth, and no one would be able to contest my legitimacy. Majesty, it is our only hope!"

The Emperor wept. But he knew that once I had made up my mind, nothing could sway me. He sighed and lay down beside me. With my head on his chest, I listened to his heart beating. I could carry that music to the ends of the earth!

I did not close my eyes all night. My own determination tortured me. Time fled by in the darkness; soon it would be dawn, and this night would be a mere memory. In this world of constant change, who could promise me a happy reunion after my ordeal?

* * *

I HANDED OUT my jewels, dresses, shawls, and furs. I offered my trinkets and furniture to the eunuchs. I burned all the love letters, the melancholy calligraphy, and the handkerchiefs still perfumed with the tears of women who had been my lovers.

In the Monastery of Rebirth, I cut my hair—a great black river streamed to the ground. My head was shaved, I was stripped of my clothes down to the last silk undergarment, and I was wrapped in a tunic of black cotton. In the bath I scrubbed myself furiously to erase every trace of my past life, the heady smell of sandalwood, musk, and irises. I renounced everything, abandoned everything. I was prepared to suffer annihilation to be reborn.

As soon as we arrived, the Great Nun lectured the novices: "Children, my women are answerable to a father and his changing fortunes. As adults, they attach themselves to a fickle husband. Sometimes abandoned, sometimes adulated, wracked with jealousy and sick with suspicion, women die of sorrow; they slip away in childbirth and are struck down by illness. Man is woman's enemy! Fathers barter and haggle to marry us off. Husbands lie and exploit us. Children betray us and kill us! Noblewomen, townswomen, peasant women—all of them are like beasts of burden pulling the cart of a pointless existence. Never think that living out that sort of existence will set you free for your future life. Without prayer, without Buddha's help, the lives to come will be an eternal repetition. I am often asked how a woman can obtain her freedom. I reply that a woman's freedom begins when she understands the word 'independence'—refusing the softness of silk, the delights of fine food, the bands of passion and the enslavement of motherhood—renouncing pleasures, longings, and illusions! Forget your breasts that nourish only sorrow, forget your bellies that conceive only crime, reject the soft caresses that are the source of all pain. Breaking with the home, with men, and with pleasure is the first step toward deliverance!"

I learned later that this Great Nun had been a favorite of Emperor

Yang of the overthrown dynasty, and the nuns in the monastery had all served emperors. To erase all memories of Court and to repent of its sins of vanity, the community applied the strictest laws. The imperial annuities that arrived every month meant we could survive in misery. We were forbidden visits by relations or to write letters. We were forbidden to speak to one another or to meet—except during prayer times. There was a constant succession of lectures and confessionals. The senior bonzes, elderly withered creatures themselves, toiled to extract the youth from our bodies as if it were gangrene.

The wind howled a mournful funeral song. High walls as white as shrouds surrounded the temples with their curved roofs. There were scrubby clumps of grass along the path where we let the sheep and goats graze. There were no mirrors, no sheets of gold. There was no face powder, no perfume, no laughter. There were no birds in cages, no red carp in bowls, no soft silken carpets, golden floor tiles, marble basins, or pillars of fragrant wood. There was no red, or pink, violet, or yellow. Wan was the color of nuns, black the soot from the tapers, gray the cotton dresses, blue the sky, and green the forest that hemmed us in.

My bed was a plank of wood. No more meat or wine, no more drunken happiness, no more poetry improvised by moonlight, no more musical instruments being played, no more picnics beside the river, no more cranes flying upward, black silhouettes against the velvet skies. Every night without these pleasures chafed me. Their gloomy silence incited me to tortuous meditation.

The first winter was harsh. I was cold. Ruby and Emerald, who had followed me and become nuns, had chapped hands from washing my clothes in freezing water. I stole the lamp oil to rub into their wounds. Morning prayer was held when it was still dark. We recited the sutra, a muted droning, despite the bouts of coughing. In the palace, we had been served five meals a day; in the monastery, the nuns were allowed to take meals only in the morning and at midday. I was possessed by my hunger all afternoon. I missed the horses and, without books, I could no longer escape.

I was called Perfect Clarity. My face as it had been in my previous life faded in my memory. Without mirrors, the other nuns became my reflection: bushy eyebrows, dry skin, walking skeletons.

During the second winter, an epidemic swept through the monastery, and I came down with a violent fever. For days on end, I saw the monastery as a funereal city peopled with ghosts. I called for Little Phoenix. I begged him to take me away from the kingdom of the dead. Hugging a beautiful concubine in his arms, he would say: "Heavenlight, you left me. You wanted to be exiled. You cannot blame me if I forget you."

When I came back to my senses, the bells were ringing and funeral orations filled my ears. Since the monastery forbade the use of medicines and healed the sick with prayer, the scourge had taken the lives of some twenty bonzes. Would I be the next to be inscribed on the list of the dead? Down to the depths of my entrails, I could feel Mother's pain now that she no longer had news of me. If I were to die, would this pious woman who had known every misfortune be able to confront her suffering simply by fingering her rosary beads?

Buddha blessed me with a miracle. I survived that winter by drinking tea. When I finally recovered, it was already springtime. The sun that dazzled me then was no longer the sun of yesterday, and I was no longer the same person. Something in me had been burned out. I no longer felt any desire. I was no longer hungry, and I no longer hoped for anything. The sutras seemed intelligible to me now. I started studying Sanskrit and prepared to undertake a great imaginary pilgrimage to discover the origins of Buddhism.

A huge ceremony of offerings was addressed to the late emperor's spirit, bringing an end to the period of mourning. Ruby and Emerald started waiting by the gates, looking out for messengers from the Palace. Days passed, months drifted by, their impatience wore thin, their hopes dwindled. Little Phoenix, Master of the World, had forgotten me. I was no longer sad, but Ruby and Emerald wept in secret, and my only regret was that I had led them into this tomb in which they were buried alive.

I had just turned twenty-eight, the age when a woman should break with her illusions of a better life.

FIVE

*R*uby ran to me so quickly that she tripped. She leapt back to her feet and cried: "The messenger from Court has just left! The Emperor wishes to come to the monastery to burn incense, make offerings to the late sovereign's spirit, and distribute gifts to the former imperial concubines. Mistress, he has not forgotten you!"

The community was gripped with fevered activity. Rumor and whispering echoed behind every wall. The nuns, who had once been so gifted in the art of intrigue, had guessed that the Son of Heaven was coming to see a woman. Irritated and honored in equal measures, the Council of Great Nuns had no choice but to restore the temples and dormitories and to erect a pavilion intended as his August Resting Place. Fences sprang up around the building sites to shield us from the workmen's eyes, but the symphony of hammering put an end to silence and meditation. I felt responsible, guilty, for this all-consuming confusion, but I was more disturbed at the thought of seeing a face that had so faded in my memory.

A delegation of eunuchs came to inspect the premises and to establish the laws of protocol. Then, at dawn on the twentieth day of the first moon, the imperial regiments circled the forest, and we knelt before the gates of the monastery. A long time passed before we saw golden panels with ornate calligraphy appearing on the horizon. The wind dropped, and the birds fell silent. Eunuchs and imperial guards marched past us in a two by two procession that went on for many hours, then the Emperor eventually stepped over the Threshold of Purity.

After three years of separation, Little Phoenix was unrecognizable. He wore a beard that gave him an air of authority, and he walked with quiet purpose. While he received the prostration of the nuns, he sat like a statue on his tall seat, a sacred icon, an inaccessible god. After the celebration, the gifts were distributed: One after the other the nuns approached the sovereign, and he gave each of them a tunic and a sandalwood rosary. Their gray dresses, shaven heads, and unpowdered faces filed past in ceremonial silence. Little Phoenix did not recognize me. Heavenlight had died inside Perfect Clarity's body!

The Emperor withdrew to eat a vegetarian meal, and I ran to my cell to weep. Someone knocked at my door. A senior nun informed me of an imperial summons: His Majesty wished to speak of religious piety with me.

Several eunuchs took me to a pavilion and closed the door behind me. Little Phoenix was sitting in the middle of the room. He looked astonished at the sight of me, and all at once I could measure the suffering I had endured. My legs gave way, and I sank to my knees. He rushed over to me and supported me in his arms.

"Heavenlight, I've missed you!"

His voice was deeper. His hands that gripped me were those of a stranger. When he drew me to him, I stiffened and stepped back.

"Are you not happy to see me again?" he asked, surprised. "Are you angry? You know full well that everything I do has become a major event requiring protocol and preparations and the deployment of thousands of servants. It has taken me a long time to find a pretext to foil the Empress and my uncle Wu Ji who oppose my every decision."

He tried to stroke my face, but I lowered my head. He led me over to the imperial bed, which was already prepared for him to sleep. Prostrating myself on the ground, I broke down and wept.

"What is it, Heavenlight? Do you no longer love me?"

I was speechless with despair.

"Heavenlight, these three years have been like a long, dark nightmare to me!"

The Emperor turned me over onto my back. I struggled in silence. His hands tore my dress feverishly. Muttering incoherent supplications, he crushed me beneath his weight. His hands were more experienced, his caresses more brutal. In the past, overcome with emotion, he would climax quickly, but now he knew how to prolong his pleasure. After three years of abstinence, the moment of penetration was painful to me. My tears fell, and Little Phoenix became more and more aroused. Eventually he collapsed with a long sigh.

While we ate together, he was happy and relaxed, giving me news of my horses. He told me about the building work he had undertaken and described the artists and poets he had discovered. The winter sun came through the casements and danced on the tables between the dishes. I recognized the flush on Little Phoenix's cheeks when he had climaxed. A vanished world slowly reappeared and wrapped me in its indecipherable melancholy.

A eunuch scratched at the door and warned the sovereign that it was time for him to change. The happiness fell from his face; he frowned and fell silent. We had not yet talked of my future. Was he going to leave and disappear from my life forever?

The eunuchs became more insistent. Wearily, he drained the last cup of tea.

"Heavenlight, do you know that I have been very unhappy? Last year my sister the High Princess Sun of Gao plotted against me with her husband, the son of Fang Xuan Ling, a minister who was a close confidant of the previous Emperor. They managed to enlist support from my aunts, the Great High Princess Sun of Dan and the Great High Princess of Ba Ling, and my uncle the King of Jing. My own family wanted to overthrow me to put my brother the King of Wu on the throne. I had to let my uncle Wu Ji arrange their trial and sign the papers sentencing them to death. Up on my imperial throne, I am like a man sitting alone at the top of a mountain, surrounded by vultures ravenous for power. Heavenlight, I am already tired of reigning. Every morning I strive to be worthy of Sovereign Father, but the ministers take my orders lightly and obey only my uncle Wu Ji. In the evenings, in the Inner Palace, I find it hard to sleep. I am possessed by the obsessions that have tormented every Emperor before me. Lying in the dark, I listen for the drip, drip of poison, the sly footsteps of an assassin, and the rumblings of revolt.

He broke off to wipe away his tears. Standing before this unveiled divinity, I let my torments subside. I held out my arms to him, and he wept on my shoulder. Then I helped him change and repowder his face. As he stood before the mirror, he explained: "For you to return to the Palace, the Empress must draw up a decree and affix her seal to it. She is a jealous, unpredictable woman, and she supports her uncle whom I appointed Great Minister in a rush of generosity. He now dares to disagree with me over everything. Tired of resisting him, I have often given in to his absurd demands. But this time I am determined to see the fight through to the end. That is why I have left my seed in your belly. It is proof of our love. The heir who is born of your belly will give me the courage to defy the impossible."

Looking in the mirror, I thought I could see a malicious smile on his face. Little Phoenix had just caught me in a trap. If I were with child, I could no longer stay at the monastery and would have to go back to the Palace. After he left, I collapsed at Buddha's feet. Let him show me the way!

Barely five days later a miracle happened: The Empress called me back to Court, appointing me as one of her ladies-in-waiting. A carriage escorted by eunuchs and soldiers came to collect me from the monastery. I left the nuns, their thin bodies, and their silent loathing of men without regret. Buddha had spoken. My fate lay elsewhere.

* * *

FASHION HAD CHANGED in the Side Court. Women wore their hair in elaborate topknots, shaped like birds with outstretched wings, dragons coiled on themselves, and galloping horses. They pinned fresh flowers and long strings of pearls into them. On their red-powdered cheeks, they stuck bees in yellow silk. They wore long, pleated skirts just under the rib cage to exaggerate their nearly bare breasts and expose their shoulders, which were veiled under wide-sleeved muslin tunics.

I was cradled within the eternal landscape of the Middle Court. The palaces, lakes, and gardens were all still the same color, in the same light, breathing to the same rhythm. Their immutable music played itself out to the very end of the sacred world. But the servants' faces had become overrun by wrinkles; the dead would be absent forever; the survivors had been subject to promotion or deposition. Some areas were now full of life, others had been condemned to dust.

Courtesy required that I introduce myself to the Mistress of the Palace as soon as I arrive and thank her for signing the decree for my return. Not to awaken her jealousy, I had chosen a tunic in saffron-colored brocade and leggings in crimson satin, and I wrapped a mauve turban around my head to hide my shaved scalp.

I thought she would send me away contemptuously, but she received me eagerly. In the days when I had served the previous emperor, I had seen her from a distance, and she must not even have known I existed. She sat, frozen in a majestic pose, on a platform before a screen painted with powdered gold and bearing the calligraphy of a great master. Her hands lay in her lap, and she had a pink peony pinned into a topknot two cubits high. Her features were pure and regular, finely chiseled by her distinguished birth in which the noblest bloodlines in the Empire had been combined. She must have been twenty years old, but she looked fifteen. Her face was expressionless. Only her huge eyes, examining me from head to toe, betrayed her inner turmoil. To her left, at the foot of the steps, there was a woman who was nearly forty. From the resemblance between them, I guessed that this must be the Lady Mother.

I prostrated myself at the Empress's feet before bowing deeply to her mother. I expressed my profound gratitude, and the sovereign asked me a few questions about my living quarters, then fell silent. She had the voice of a little girl. I sensed that she was shy and reserved—in noble women, silence was a sign of elegance. I was preparing to ask her permission to withdraw when the Lady Mother spoke out in her haughty voice: "Talented One, when the sovereign returned from his pilgrimage to the Monastery of Rebirth, the Empress learned of the sin that had been committed. Given that her heart knows no jealousy and that, as an exemplary wife, she considers her master's happiness as her own, she suggested that he should recall you to the palace to quell the scandal that would have damaged his august reputation. We here are well aware that you served the previous emperor. To obtain your return, the mistress had to disobey ancestral codes, and this offense attracted reprimands from the Outer Court. I hope that you now recognize the error of your ways and that this boundless generosity will be repaid with your grateful devotion."

I struck my forehead against the ground several times, repeating the words: "Majesty, your servant shall never forget your goodness."

The Lady Mother eyed me with a hostile sneer and went on: "Talented One, you are already familiar with the laws of the Inner Court, and I shall not enumerate them for you. The Empress rewards worthiness and punishes crime. She may occasionally choose to offer lapsed women a second chance, but she expects absolute obedience in exchange for this clemency. To ensure that you do not commit a further error that would cost you your life, Her Majesty has instructed me to warn you against a particularly perverse and dangerous person: Lady Xiao. She was born into a lowly, fallen family. As a child she knew poverty and trailed through the streets of the eastern capital. Our family took her in out of pity, and I appointed her as a maid to Her Majesty during her childhood. We lavished her with care, and this creature—so full of bad manners learned in the depths of Luoyang—metamorphosed in a few short years. When Her Majesty was married to the sovereign, she took Lady Xiao with her to Long Peace. Unbeknown to her mistress, Lady Xiao seduced the prince and plotted to ensure that she was raised to the rank of Resplendent Wife. This distinction only fuelled her excessive ambition and her insatiable greed. Under her evil spell, the Emperor is forgetting his duties and losing his mind. The Empress called you back to the Palace because she is counting on you to exorcise the sovereign and to help him return to the path he must tread."

The Lady Mother's words clarified the ambivalent nature of the hasty ruling made on my behalf. Jealous of the favors enjoyed by the Resplendent Wife, the Empress wanted to use me to deflect the sovereign's passion. On my return to the lodgings in the Side Court, I came across a woman whose beauty was stupefying. The Resplendent Wife Xiao feigned surprise and introduced herself to me. She was sheathed in a dress of crêpe and a muslin tunic, and above her right breast she flaunted a beauty spot in the form of an avaricious wasp.

I curtsied deeply before her.

She returned my greeting and said in an eager, affable voice: "It is indeed you, the Talented One of two reigns! I have heard that you are twenty-eight, but you look ten years younger. Is it true that the nuns have magic recipes to preserve eternal youth? It seems that your friends, the monks, know the secrets of ecstasy and are more virile than ordinary men. Come and talk to me of all this when your Empress gives you the time. I invite you to take lunch on my boat. The poor girl must have spoken to you of me, anyway. I expect that, once again, she ground her teeth and shed many tears! So much the better if her morbid jealousy drives her insane! She is barren, and she resents every belly capable of bearing a child. No one is stopping her from conceiving, but her own perfidious nature has dried her out!"

She came closer to me and hissed in my ear: "I know that the Empress had you brought back to the Palace to steal the sovereign from me. You should know that she has already pushed a number of unfortunate girls into his arms. Alas for her, at the moment, it is I who command

His Majesty's heart in this Inner Palace. Every woman who has tried to dispute his favors with me has met an unpleasant end. Some died, struck down by the lightning wrath of the heavens; others were sent away to the Cold Palace. Do you know that frozen place where women fester in dank dungeons and in their own excrement? It makes me laugh to think of the beauties who have ended up in those dung heaps. Only the other month, the Emperor authorized me to expedite some shrew who wanted to poison me. Do you know what became of her? I had her arms and legs cut off and threw her into a vat of wine. She died blind drunk!" Then, with a peel of laughter, she walked away.

IN THE CLOSED world of the gynaeceum, despite the gardens and parkland extending beyond the horizon, despite the insurmountable walls separating pavilions and palaces, the tangled web of our fate was inescapable. Why did these women love each other to the point of madness? Why did they loathe one another so vehemently, and why did sworn enemies feel such horror and fascination for one another? Why should furious hate become obsession, then intoxication and the very reason to live?

Because love and hate were the two heads of the demon.

The Empress had been married at fourteen, and now, at twenty-two, her stomach was still flat, while in the other palace, a succession of concubines and slaves brought imperial children into the world. Infertility is a major crime committed toward the ancestors, and any man whose wife is sterile is free to repudiate her. Many former Empresses had lost their title on these grounds, and the Empress Wang was well aware of the danger that threatened her.

Like the noble women who grew up in the closed world of the gynaeceum's apartments, she valued the comfort and refinement of an artificial existence. She was afraid of life's urges and enthusiasms, bored by copulation; from the very day she was married, she had received the Emperor's advances by playing dead. But, to conceive a son, she would suffer anything, even rape. At first light every day, she prepared herself feverishly to appear beautiful. Her Lady Mother forced her to drink medicinal infusions for fertility and to have warm fluids injected between her thighs. As the sun began to fall still, there would be no sign of the Emperor. She would sit in the middle of her day room, with her hands on her knees, a black silhouette against the vermilion silk carpets covering the ground, and her heart would curse him. She swore to herself that she would no longer live in such humiliation once she had delivered a son. Night stole through the palace, and servants lit candles and lanterns. Her face lit up at the tiniest rustling sound; she would get up and run to the door. The women she sent out as spies came back one after the other: His Majesty had finished dining! He had ordered his litter to be prepared. His Majesty was about to leave his palace! He was heading for the apartments of the Resplendent Wife!

The Empress would collapse, and her shrill cries would echo round the room: "Snuff out the lights! Snuff out the lights!" She would shrug off every hand offering to help her and would spend the night on the spot where she had fallen. With day break the servants would come and open the shutters. The hope and disappointment began again with the sun as it circled endlessly across the sky.

Her rival, the Resplendent Wife, had had her belly filled three times, and her son had been given the crown of Yong, the kingdom-province that boasted the capital Long Peace and one that was usually reserved for the eldest son of the Mistress of the Palace. Every time the Empress heard her accursed name, she faltered and dissolved into tears: She wanted to drive this whore out of the Forbidden City. She accused her of practicing black magic to make her sterile; she was a demon incarnate in a woman's body who wanted to steal her throne and destroy the Empire!

At twenty-three the Resplendent Wife's heart was ravaged. The more the emperor cherished her, the more she feared. At the height of her beauty, aging obsessed her and she trembled to be abandoned one day. In government, ministers despised her very existence, and in the gynaeceum the women leagued against her. Her desperate loneliness, her violent sensuality, and her fierce struggle to survive had a strange hold over the Emperor, who was weary of bland, characterless women. With the Empress he had to observe rituals and ensure he spoke in imperial vernacular. Sleeping with the Mistress of the World was a sacred duty, an attempt at procreation, an anxiety that chilled his entrails. In his favorite's palace, he could dispense with the solemn poses and courteous conventions. His pleasure had only one aim: to be satisfied.

Despite his renewed promises to the Resplendent Wife, the Emperor could not remain faithful. He succumbed to all temptations, and his every adventure was devastating to her. On those evenings when he disappeared into other pavilions, she could see herself reduced once more to the starving orphan wandering barefoot through the streets of Luoyang. The thought of losing her savior, her boat in the ocean of misery, drove her demented with worry.

Younger and more beautiful ladies constantly challenged her. With the passing of every moon, when the blood flowed between her legs, she had to resign herself to the nights of silence, alone with her own stain.

She always had to think, calculate, lie, and smile when she wanted only to weep. Her adversaries were as cunning and determined as she was. She confronted her rivals more and more often, but her strength was flagging. The Empress and her Lady Mother had declared war: They were waiting for the sovereign to grow weary of her and throw her into the Cold Palace. She sought relief in drugs, but found the mornings all the more painful. One morning she decided that the title of Empress would be the remedy to so much suffering that she should now fight to give her son the title of heir. She enlisted her slanderous tongue and her fevered imagination: Night after night, she succeeded in inciting the sovereign's disgust for his sacred wife.

The duel between the two rivals spread terror throughout the Inner City. The two camps in this battle had concentrated the energies of all these women on the brink of madness. Poisoned wine, toxic clothes, and fans dusted with fatal powders were frequently found in their palaces. Servants died mysteriously instead of their mistresses, but the investigations never went any further than the eunuch valets. Some servants were punished for their betrayal: They were beaten to death, put into a sack, and thrown into the imperial river that flowed beyond the thick walls and into the outside world. The Emperor became fearful: Unable to untangle the web of crimes and to impose his authority, pursued by fits of weeping and threats of suicide, he wanted to escape but did not know which way to turn.

Once again he relied on me to give him counsel, to support his will, and to provide a haven of peace.

I HAD LOST some of my naiveté and gained strength. These women with their pointless scheming could not contain me, and I watched the volatile world of the gynaeceum with a detached eye. The Forbidden City had buried my youth, and in the monastery, I had died and come back to life. Friends, enemies, and mistresses had all disappeared. I was a ghost from a lost world, still going from one season to the next and still living for one man alone.

But this time it was not a provincial adolescent terrified by the sensuality and corruption of the Inner Palace: Women would bow to my strategy and my experience. From the very first day, I succeeded in securing the loyalty of servants who had grown weary of the despotic Empress and the vindictive favorite. My instructions were respected and carried out; the Court Ladies wanted to escape the conflict between the two mistresses, and, in me, they found the peace and wisdom they sought. At first they were disconcerted by my disdain for tunics that revealed too much flesh, then they decided that modesty was more sensuous. The Court started to imitate my warrior-nun style. The young girls tried in vain to squeeze their ample waists into the wide belts of sculpted leather in an attempt to make themselves attractive. They had neither my slender figure, nor my muscles, nor my fine waist. They did not know that my habit was my armor.

I was ashamed of our sex and disgusted by its aggressiveness. I attended to the daily management of the Palace as a way of forgetting all the misery it harbored. The Middle Court appreciated my abilities, and the Empress entrusted me with more and more responsibility. Little Phoenix tried to find me the whole time and constantly sought my advice.

At night, despite his supplications, I refused to join him in his palace. He then alighted on the idea of summoning me to his offices to dictate letters. He had the entrance to the pavilion closed and welcomed me in the entrance to the secret passage. He would smile at me as he tore off his tunic, untied his silk trousers, and bared his vigorous body. My heart would beat wildly. I would let him kiss me and draw me down to the carpet. Our muscles rubbed against each other; our sweat mingled. When Little Phoenix penetrated me, I was surprised that I did not feel pain, but I recognized the pleasures of this act. Soon a feeling of warmth would roll around within my belly and spread throughout my body. I kept my eyes open and saw Little Phoenix's face blending with the frescoes on the ceiling. I saw the gods dancing on clouds and pouring millions of petals on us. I saw myself raised up from among the hordes of chained women who were still struggling. Then, at last, I was borne away from this life, from its short-lived seasons and its murderous weakness.

After making love, Little Phoenix would rest his head on my knees and whisper all his problems to me. When he had acceded to the throne, he had had no experience and had left important matters to his uncle Wu Ji. Since then the Great Chancellor had taken a liking to ruling the Empire and paid little attention to his opinions; Little Phoenix was inexplicably afraid of his all-powerful uncle, and he lamented that he had betrayed his Emperor Father's wishes and become a puppet sovereign. I encouraged him to impose his authority gradually on the government. To avoid the balance of power falling once again into the hands of an ambitious lord, I offered to read political reports for him and to help him prepare for his audiences.

Having served the Eternal Ancestor as a secretary for many years, I still remembered his words. When Little Phoenix spread out the various ministers' requests before my eyes, the words they used held no mystery for me, and I had no difficulty finding answers. Soon Little Phoenix reported back that, unaware of the authorship of these suggestions, the Council of Great Ministers had praised them, and Wu Ji had bowed before his resolutions for the first time. The Outer Court's reaction boosted my confidence, and I returned to work in Little Phoenix's offices every day. After his moment of jubilant ecstasy, the sovereign would succumb to sleep while I read State reports and wrote up my commentaries. With every sentence, the teachings dictated by the Eternal Ancestor on his deathbed came back to me. By dictating his book *The Art of Being Sovereign* to Little Phoenix, he had linked me to his future reign.

At twenty-nine years old, I saw a ray of light for the first time: My life was beginning to have some meaning. Fifteen years earlier, when Little Phoenix had still been King of Jin, he had come over to me when he saw me mastering a horse. For him, I would master an empire.

ONE MORNING, PREY to nausea and dizziness, I stayed curled in the depths of my bed and could not rise. From the other side of the curtain, the imperial doctor took my pulse and congratulated me. I was carrying within me an imperial descendant! This news struck me dumb. Little Phoenix was overcome with joy: He sent me jewels, bolts of silk, and dishes that were served at his table. His delight only increased my confusion. I had decided not to attempt to rival the Empress Wang and the Resplendent Wife Xiao. I did not want to quarrel over a man's favors with any woman in the gynaeceum. I had sworn to myself that I would be free of women's servitude, but this imperial embryo made me its slave. This was no ordinary child stirring in my belly: I could be carrying a king, a pretender to the throne.

My breasts swelled; my skin became clearer; my waist tripled in size. I had to abandon my leather belt and tie a long ribbon around my hips. The doctors forbade me to ride; I lost my sprightly stride and now took only small steps. When I saw the Emperor pressing his ear to the great mountain of fat that was my stomach, I found it hard to hide my bitterness. Never again would I be his mother or his older sister. When the child was born, I would become a concubine, dependent on his capricious desires.

I had been slender, slight, and strong. I was becoming heavy, nervous, and vulnerable. I was afraid of tripping; I would wake in the night dreaming of the assassins sent by the Empress and the Resplendent Wife. Fearing I might be poisoned like the Delicate Concubine Xu, who had lost her child at the end of the eighth month, I ate only dishes prepared by Ruby and Emerald on a stove set up in my room.

The hatred between the Empress and the Resplendent Wife was reaching its height. Having ruthlessly put pressure on the sovereign, the favorite wrenched a promise from him that he would designate her son as heir. But in the Outer Court, the Great Ministers were unanimous in opposing this pernicious nomination that would inevitably bring about the deposition of Empress Wang. They suggested to the Empress that she should adopt Prince Loyalty, who had been borne of a slave girl, then force the Master of the World to recognize him as the Supreme Son.

The turmoil churning in the Forbidden City afforded me unhoped-for peace. I made sure I was forgotten. Ruby and Emerald hid me in one of those countless modest pavilions in the heart of the Side Court. The midwife hung a wide ribbon from the top of the bed and told me to pull on it with all my might in moments of extreme pain. In my dark burrow with its shutters and windows closed, I lost all notion of time. The contractions became increasingly violent. My sweat mingled with my tears. Between my shrieks, I could hear the women weeping, and one voice saying my hips were too narrow. No, I don't want to die! I am stronger than suffering. I push, I tear, I dig into the depths of my entrails to bring this life out into the light!

The loud cries of a newborn baby bring me around.

"Mistress, greatest congratulations! It is a prince!"

When Mother brought me into this world, did she know that she would have a king among her descendants? Emerald showed me the swaddled bundle of life. Through his veins the divine blood of the Son of Heaven flowed. It was a miracle that my mind had trouble grasping.

His name would be Splendor. Splendor like the legendary first name of Lao-tzu, the founder of Taoism, the glorious ancestor of the Tang dynasties.

WHEN THE DAYS tainted with blood had passed, Little Phoenix ran to my pavilion. As he came toward me, I realized that childbirth was a huge upheaval from which every woman emerges transformed. I could tell from his eyes that I was radiant. I heard my voice ring out, it was more human, more soothing. I was more alert, my senses more acute; I could read my sovereign's thoughts as if they were in an open book. I could make his heart quiver and dictate my wishes to him with a smile.

The Emperor presented me with the Palace of Wandering Clouds. By his decree, I was granted the seal of Courteous Concubine of the second rank, the highest remaining position in the gynaeceum. Little Phoenix also immediately offered my son the kingdom of Dai, thereby having me venerated by the entire world as the mother of a king.

Splendor's birth was my own rebirth. Every ray of light, every last caterpillar on a tiny leaf, every twinkle of sunlight on the lake, and every startled flight of a bird made me tremble with joy. A gray curtain had been raised, a world of delights had been proven possible in the Forbidden City.

My dearest wish was finally realized: An imperial regiment galloped to the province of Bing, Mother stepped into a carriage that I had hastened to her, and she left the village of Wu amid great pomp and ceremony. She received from the sovereign's hand a vast residence staffed by countless servants in the noble quarter of Long Peace. Elder sister, who had been widowed four years previously, joined Mother in the capital. Both were given permission to enter the gynaeceum. Our tears set free all the sorrow of our separation; a wound was wiped from my heart. My glory and fortune were now theirs. Thanks to me, they would now know happiness.

The Emperor deserted the Empress's bedchamber. The Emperor neglected the Resplendent Wife. The Emperor spent all his nights at the Palace of Wandering Clouds where my family had become his. I ignored the Empress Wang who screamed that it was scandalous and her Lady Mother who accused me of betraying my mistress's goodness. I no longer forbade myself happiness nor tried to hide my maternal pride.

Since her son had been removed from succession to the throne, the Resplendent Wife had shut herself away in her palace and drugged herself. When, on my insistence, the Emperor determined to force his way in, he no longer recognized the favorite who was reduced to little more than a skeleton. She wept as she enumerated her aching disappointments and heaped insults on me. She wagged an accusing finger, bony as a chicken's leg. A torrent of confused words and bestial groans streamed from her scrawny frame. She threw herself at the sovereign and begged him to love her.

Little Phoenix came back to the Wandering Clouds in tears. He blamed himself for destroying this woman who had once been so beautiful. I comforted him and gave him a cheering piece of news: His seed had impregnated my belly a second time.

My name was on everyone's lips in high society in Long Peace. Dignitaries who were only now discovering my existence could not understand this miracle: The Empress was in disgrace, and all the glory of the Resplendent Wife was a thing of the past. In two years, I had banished both women from the Emperor's heart.

My origins and my past were a source of gossip. Born of an ennobled commoner, a Talented One in the previous Emperor's court, a nun in the Monastery of Rebirth, my life had been an adventure worthy of popular legend. As they approached thirty, Court ladies—however beautiful—became almost worthless, but I had the love of a sovereign three years my junior! Vipered tongues claimed that I had magical sexual powers and boundless ambition. The Empress and the Resplendent Wife were determined to depict me as a she-devil. They took turns slandering me before the sovereign. While one accused me of pouring poison in her glass, the other claimed that I had taken a monk as a lover, and he had fathered Splendor. Then, when they saw that the Emperor did not believe a single word, these mortal enemies became inseparable friends. The Empress praised the Resplendent Wife's gentleness, and she in turn recognized her former mistress's generosity.

Confronted with these violent attacks, I had to organize my defense. At five months pregnant, I was forbidden all sexual relations. For fear that Little Phoenix would go back to frequenting other pavilions where he might give credence to the spiteful gossip, I offered him Elder Sister's body.

The rumors and defamation did not reach the sovereign while he was blinded and deafened by a new carnal passion. Purity took over for me in the imperial bedchamber and fought valiantly for our mutual happiness. Knowing that she was beside Little Phoenix meant I could concentrate on the forthcoming birth. My narrow hips might kill me yet. If I were to die, I would be delivered from the abuses of the Forbidden City. If I were to live, I would be reborn stronger than ever!

A princess opened her eyes to the world one spring morning. I gave my daughter the most beautiful cradle in the world and the fattest wet-nurses. Her cries made me smile and weep in turn. She would be happy and fragile like her father and ardent and stubborn like her mother. She would be impetuous as the Eternal Ancestor and gentle and good as Mother. I would make her an erudite poetess, a peerless horsewoman. She would experience every happiness that is forbidden to women and the freedoms I had never known!

The Court ladies filed through my palace to present their compliments. Entire halls were filled with gifts from dignitaries. I received the Empress and the Resplendent Wife, who decided to make the trip to see me together, hand in hand. Even though Ruby and Emerald whispered to me that their good wishes were not heartfelt, I thanked them warmly. I would find a way of being reconciled with them.

The Emperor accepted my suggestion and granted a special audience to General Li Ji, who had recommended me to the Court sixteen years previously. The warrior had been promoted and was now an eminent member of the Council of Great Ministers. His face had not changed, and his silvery beard was still magnificent. From his embarrassed expression, I could see that there was nothing about me that resembled the little girl devastated by mourning for her beloved father. I had become a woman who could exercise both charm and authority over him. Sixteen years after our first meeting, the conversation had changed, but time had not broken our bond. He had been put to the side by Wu Ji, who had been contemptuous of his commoner's origins, and he was now prepared to offer me his loyalty and to defend the sovereign's authority.

My belly was growing smaller, and my agility was returning. Childbirth had been a trial, an initiation from which my strength had emerged all the greater. The Emperor put his trust in me blindly. The chief eunuchs, the Great Intendants of the six inner ministries, and the directors of the twenty-four departments took orders only from me. I was no longer an anonymous woman among ten thousand beauties, but the true mistress of the Inner Palace.

At that time I was maneuvering to regain the supreme power that had been confiscated by the ministers. I worked day and night urgently sorting through case files so as to pre-empt Wu Ji's decisions sent out by his chancellery. As I toiled, I forgot the rancorous feelings that were never far away.

One afternoon when Little Phoenix and I were riding through the Imperial Park, Ruby, Emerald, and a group of eunuchs appeared at the end of the track. They threw themselves to their knees and beat their chests, wailing lamentations.

"Your slaves deserve a thousand deaths!" they cried. "The imperial infant has just departed this life!"

My head spun, and my voice was strangled: "Only this morning she was laughing with me."

Ruby struck her forehead on the ground so forcefully that she split her scalp. The blood flowed down over her face, and she wept as she explained: "Majesty, Highness, early this afternoon the Empress came to see the infant. She took her in her arms and played with her. Looking into the cradle a little later, the nurse noticed that the baby had turned blue. She had stopped breathing!"

I faltered, my ears were buzzing, and somewhere I thought I heard Little Phoenix sobbing: "The Empress has dared to poison my daughter!"

The cortège returned to the Inner City. I let myself be led, stiff, mute, dead. I do not know how I was able to dismount and climb onto a litter. Trees, pavilions, walls, countless faces . . . all these things appeared before me and only deepened my pain. My governesses, servants, and valets were all kneeling at the gates of my palace. Our two litters were borne across a garden seething with people, a place already like the most dismal of cemeteries. Emerald brought the tiny babe to the Emperor, and he bathed her with his tears. I refused to touch her ice-cold body.

For seven days, I stayed huddled in my room with the shutters closed, and I did not open my eyes. For seven days I could not keep food down; everything seemed to taste of fish. I would hear a baby crying, and panic would surge through me. I would call Ruby: "Why does the Princess keep crying? We must change her wet nurse!"

Emerald and Ruby concluded from this strange behavior that I had been put under a spell. They suggested secretly calling for an exorcist, but Mother rejected this practice that was forbidden in the Palace and had a statue of Buddha installed in my room. The monotonous droning of her prayers filled my heart that had been so dried by grief. Deprived of food, my body became lighter and lighter, and one day it flew away. I slipped into a moonless, starless night. I struggled in vain to find a glimmer of light, then I realized that I had become deaf and dumb. I was dead! Dead? No, I must live and have my revenge. I was not yet defeated! It was then that two faces appeared in the darkness: Father and the Eternal Ancestor. Their features became confused and formed one dazzling moon that started to speak: "The Resplendent Wife and the Empress have been exposed. They summoned sorcerers to the gynaeceum and wanted to see you dead. I have had the objects of their curses burned and those two madwomen imprisoned. Now your sickness will expire; you can sleep in peace."

I opened my eyes. Little Phoenix was lying beside me on my bed, resting his head on his arm, and watching me lovingly. I turned my head: Mother had disappeared, but in the center of my room, lit up by hundreds of candles, was a gleaming golden statue of Buddha.

He drew me into his arms and asked me if I would like to have some soup. I remembered then that my daughter was dead. My tears fell for the first time since her death.

A servant brought a tray. Little Phoenix wiped my tears with a handkerchief, then he picked up the bowl and fed me with a spoon.

"Heavenlight, when I met you, you were no taller than I, and you were galloping on a magnificent horse. When you came over to greet me on that day, it felt to me as if every part of you was entering into my body, and I told myself: 'I would like to marry a woman like her.'"

He paused for a long time and sighed: "Then I became a man. Women revealed their mystery to me. I became the prey of my desires, explored passion and sensuality, the sweet tragedy of love. Young girls fought one another off to please me, but, in exchange, I had to satisfy their sexual demands and sentimental wants. I would have liked to experience the thrill and the agony, but I knew only scheming, self-interested embraces: One wanted a relation to be nominated for government, another demanded a golden necklace, a third wanted a bigger palace and to wear new dresses. So I opened the treasury wide; I squandered it. I learned to lie in order to console, to promise in order to escape. I alternated between compliments and lecturing because I am weak and a coward. The feigned tenderness, the jealousies, the treats, and the tears sickened me, but I was so very afraid of being alone!

"When you returned from the monastery, you were so changed: You had become more intense, more determined. By your side, I felt free, at my ease, delivered. I was so happy to be able to count on your strength once again! And yet, even in those moments of happiness, I still did not know that it was love. You were merely a breath of reason in all the madness, a dependency that did me some good, a habit that made my life a little easier. . . .

"When I came to see you yesterday, your face was ashen. Your hair was wrapped around you like a black shroud. Thinking you were dead, I screamed in despair. It was then that I realized that you alone exist, that we two alone exist in this world, and that the rest is just shadows, ideas, and absurd dreams. A wave of heat surged through me. Borne by this extraordinary force, I knew that I would readily die for you. All the anxieties and the nameless torments that have haunted me since my childhood suddenly disappeared. Heavenlight, now I know what it is to love!

"Heavenlight, I want to prove to you that I love you, I want to protect you from the slander, the poisons, and the black magic. I want to offer you the honor you deserve. The world shall prostrate itself at the feet of the woman who has brought me grace. The Empress will be dismissed. You shall take her place. Together we shall reign over Earth for a thousand years, for ten thousand years, until the skies fall in."

Tears sprang to my eyes. Did I deserve such distinction? The sovereign had chosen me among the thousands of women in his gynaeceum. He was offering me the supreme title, proof of absolute love. What could I give him in return? I was already his slave; I had already given him my body and my soul. He was the only man I had known. Like a dog devoted to his master, like a newborn babe clinging to the breast that feeds it, had I loved him wholly and sincerely? Little Phoenix was my destiny, and I was his Heavenlight. He freed me from the prison of those women condemned to a slow death, I delivered him from his frigid existence in the Forbidden City. We were two children joined together by pity and a feeling of revolt.

Did an emperor and his concubine have the right to know the pleasures of love, so carefree, so light, and so insolent?

* * *

ANOTHER PREGNANCY WAS a sign sent from the gods to consolidate my legitimacy. Removing an empress regarded as the Mistress of the World proved a delicate affair of state and required an agreement from the dignitaries of the Council of Great Ministers. A confrontation with these powerful lords would be a bitter and dangerous one, but I was determined to break through this final barrier so that I could embrace my freedom and join Little Phoenix on top of the world.

On my advice, the sovereign first dismissed Empress Wang's uncle who had the title of Great Minister.

My name, Wu, was an insignificant one, and my commoner's background a handicap in that Forbidden City where men and women placed much weight on how noble their blood was. I decided to proclaim my father's glory to increase my prestige. It was, therefore, decided that the Emperor should hold a ceremony commemorating the dynasty's veterans while traveling in the province of Bing. Among the thirteen now-dead individuals who received homage from the sovereign, Father was promoted to the posthumous title of Great Governor of Bing of the first imperial rank.

The Empress of China had to be a perfect Mistress of the Palace and a model of virtue for all Chinese women. I wrote a book called *Inner Warnings* in which I denounced the luxury and idleness of Court ladies and praised hard work and thriftiness.

The birth of a second prince gave me an opportunity to rise up in the imperial hierarchy. As the four seals for wives of the first rank had already been allocated, I suggested we create a fifth one called the Luminous Wife. When the sovereign mentioned the plan during an audience, Wu Ji, who was already very worried by my ascension, said it was scandalous. His supporters backed him up, saying that ancestral institutions could not be modified and any changes would debase the Inner Court and undermine the Empire. I learned of their indignation and advised Little Phoenix to save our efforts for other things and give up on this idea. Wu Ji would be the instigator: I would go straight from a Courteous Concubine to an Empress.

In the sixth year of Eternal Magnificence, tension grew at Court. The sovereign's determination to remove Empress Wang in my favor was common knowledge among Court officials. With the exception of Great General Li Ji, every member of the Council of Great Ministers remained united behind Wu Ji, who was frustrated that his nephew no longer followed his recommendations. Trying to find grounds for reconciliation, I urged Little Phoenix to visit his uncle, and we deigned to present ourselves at his door with ten carriages filled with bolts of brocade and golden tableware. During the banquet, the sovereign promised honorary distinctions to Wu Ji's three sons and tentatively broached the contentious subject. Without looking up at me once, the Great Chancellor cut short all my illusions. Disobeying a father's wishes is a sin, he told us sternly. It is impossible to repudiate an Empress chosen by a deceased sovereign.

Little Phoenix was not a gifted speaker. As Wu Ji had made him emperor, he was unwilling to raise his voice or disobey his charismatic uncle. On our return to the gynaeceum, he shed tears of despair in my arms, ready to accept fate. The humiliation I had just endured seared my very soul. Suddenly, I perceived the truth that lay beneath Wu Ji's words: As a chancellor designated by the previous sovereign, he was defending the barren Empress to ensure the power of his regency. For his partisans and himself, dismissing the Empress would not simply be a breach of the Eternal Ancestor's wishes, but it would also disrupt the Empire's ancient orders and culminate in Little Phoenix taking political command.

Wu Ji's cold calculation could not kill the flame of love. To win the duel, I buried my feelings and deployed my most manipulative strategies. His weapon would be turned against him. I would be icier and more merciless than him.

The Court had been suffering the rule of the sectarian old man for too long. This Chancellor, trusted by the previous emperor and the sovereign heir, had been the author of frequent bloody purges. It was not long before I identified his implacable enemies and promised them the opportunity for revenge. I rallied the talented officials, mostly commoners who had been neglected by the imperial uncle, leader of the aristocratic clique. I gave them the hope of rising in the court's hierarchy, when the concubine of modest origins would become the Mistress of the World.

A low ranked official called Li Yi Fu was the first to dare to break the silence Wu Ji had imposed on the Court: He publicly called for the Empress to be removed from office because she was barren. After the audience, the Emperor and I received him in the Inner Palace. His courage was rewarded with a flagon of rare pearls. He was soon raised to the position of Vice-Chancellor. From then on more officials resolved to follow his example every day, and they made sure the government was aware of their exasperation. When I could see that opinion was swinging in my favor, I encouraged Little Phoenix to make his determination clear to the Council of Great Ministers.

On that particular day, after the morning salutation, the sovereign called the Council into his offices in the Inner Palace. I hid behind a gauze screen and heard Little Phoenix stammering the words I had dictated to him: "The greatest crime a wife can commit is to fail to procreate. The Empress has no descendants; the Courteous Concubine has two sons. I would like to name her as Empress. What do you think of this?"

Chu Sui Liang, one of Wu Ji's faithful followers, spoke up loudly: "The Empress is descended from an illustrious clan. During the last reign, she served the previous Emperor without committing the least misdemeanor. Before leaving this world, His Majesty took your servant's hand and told him: 'I entrust to you my son and my daughter-in-law.' That voice still rings in my ears to this day. The Empress is still young. She might one day bear a child. The crime of which you accuse her is unfounded. Your servant does not dare obey you and betray the wishes of the Eternal Ancestor."

Irritated, the sovereign raised his voice: "The Empress has committed crimes too shameful to mention. The Chinese people cannot venerate a woman who has failed in her moral duties and sunk into perversion. The

Courteous Concubine is dazzling in her virtue; she would be a perfect model for the women of China."

"There is absolutely no proof to support the accusations leveled at the Empress," Chu Sui Liang replied. "Some doctors feel that the imperial child suffocated as a result of gases released by the coal in her overheated bedchamber. Others say that someone might have poisoned the princess to attribute the murder to the sovereign lady who was unlucky enough to be near her. As for the crime of practicing black magic, I am very much afraid that there is some plot against her and that the sovereign lady may fall into the trap a second time. Ambitious women have unfathomable hearts. If Your Majesty is determined to designate a new sovereign lady, I beg you to choose one among the Empire's noble families. Why this lady Wu? The Courteous Concubine served the previous Emperor; everyone knows that, and Your Majesty cannot deny it. When you have reigned for ten thousand years, what will people say of this incest? Your Majesty follows the path of light. Why would you cover yourself with mire? The decline of the Empire will begin the day the Courteous Concubine ascends to the throne. By resisting your wishes, your servant surely deserves ten thousand tortures, but I would willingly choose death to not fail in the duty entrusted to me by the previous Emperor!"

If Chun Sui Liang was to be believed, I had killed my own daughter to achieve the rank of Empress. I could remain silent no longer; I burst out: "Have this hideous creature destroyed, this vile animal who dares to suggest such slander before the sovereign!"

Wu Ji's icy voice replied: "Sui Liang received a decree from the previous Emperor: 'All his sins shall be forgiven.' No one can touch him."

Chu Sui Liang suddenly launched himself at the platform on which Little Phoenix was sitting and cracked his head against one of the steps. His head split open, and the blood ran down his face.

"Majesty," he proclaimed, "if you do not listen to me, your servant would rather die!"

"Get out!" the Emperor exploded angrily. "Throw this insolent creature out of my palace! Get out, all of you, out, leave me alone."

119

But the Great Ministers had decided to see their fight through to the end. That very evening, Han Yuan had this letter sent to the sovereign: "Your servant has heard that if the king appoints his queen, then they are to represent Heaven and Earth. Their complementary virtues, like the sun and the moon, are to light up the four oceans; but if the sun and the moon are darkened, darkness reigns over the world. Like husband, like wife—even the common people can find their own kind. Can the Son of Heaven act against his nature? An Empress is the mother of ten thousand kingdoms; she is a conductor of good and evil. That is why the Emperor Yellow was assisted by Mo Mu, whose face was ugly, and the King of Yin lost his way because of the very beautiful Lady Da Ji. As for the great Zhou dynasty, it was destroyed by mistress Bao Si, a bewitchingly beautiful woman. I hope Your Majesty will choose in such a way that he is not a laughing stock for all eternity."

Lai Ji wrote, "Your servant has read that the Emperor appointed his empress to honor the temples of the Ancestors, to watch over the earth and the heavens, to represent the forces of this earth, and to act as a model for the imperial princesses. That is why she was chosen from an illustrious family. She must be peaceful, virtuous, submissive, and unselfish; she must earn the respect of the four seas and satisfy the wishes of the gods. That is why the Emperor of Letters founded the Zhou dynasty, but the commoner Bao Si ruined it with her smile; the Emperor of Piety of the Han dynasty married a slave girl, the slender dancer Summer Swallow; he had no further descendants, and his empire collapsed. Look at the tragedies of these two dynasties and think about our own!"

Wu Ji was clearly behind all this slander. He and his companions were already stained with the blood of their political enemies; how could they scorn my name, I who had neither poisoned nor made curses, nor organized assassinations? They knew my face; they could see I was no devastating beauty. Could they then not see that something other than physical pleasure tied me to Little Phoenix and that we were determined to be together for eternity? How dare they announce that they had spied some evil force in me because I was of lowly origins! By calling me a conspirator capable of destroying an entire dynasty, these men were betraying their fear: With my help, the sovereign would wrest the power that they had held for too long. I, a concubine imprisoned in the Imperial City, had enough will to confront every one of these men!

The caricature the ministers painted of me hurt, but the insults only strengthened my resolve. I adopted the fierce determination they attributed to me, stripped Chu Sui Liang of his duties for treason, and drove him out of the Capital. Great General Li Ji secured the army's support for me. Wu Ji was powerless as he watched his enemies taking orders from the Emperor and the officials who were commoners climbing to the rank of minister. In the depths of the gynaeceum, I received permission from Little Phoenix to correspond with our supporters in the Outer Court. And so, under my instructions, Great General Li Ji announced that the government should not concern itself with the sovereign's private affairs. Xu Jing Zong, the Minister of Rites, exclaimed, "When a peasant becomes rich after a good harvest, he feels the temptation to take a more beautiful wife. When a prince ascends to the imperial throne, should he not choose a wife of higher quality? The Son of Heaven is master of the four seas; why does he not have the right to appoint his empress? This is no one's business. Let us not weary ourselves!"

A petition was put before the Great Secretariat and transmitted to the Emperor: One hundred officials wanted the Empress to be revoked. The Council of Great Ministers was forced to accept this imperial decree immediately: "The Empress Wang and the Resplendent Wife Xiao, having committed murder, are stripped of their positions and deposed to become commoners. Their mothers and brothers shall be exiled to the south of the Extreme Mountain."

Six days later, in keeping with ritual, the Court called for a new mistress. The Emperor published the edict that I had written myself: "Lady Wu is descended from an ancient and glorious lineage. She has been chosen by the Inner Court, which values her intelligence and virtue.

Her presence has swiftly filled the garden of orchids with light. She has spread her goodness and sweetness to the women of the gynaeceum. In the past, I fulfilled my filial duties to the Emperor Father, who granted me the privilege of never leaving his side. Seeing that I tended him so well that I forgot to sleep and without ever being disturbed by the beauties all around me, the Emperor decided to reward my attentions by offering me Lady Wu, like the concubine Zheng Jiun whom the Emperor of Annunciation of the Han dynasty gave to his heir long ago. In keeping with the wishes of the previous sovereign, I have decided to appoint her Empress."

On the first day of the eleventh moon in that sixth year of Eternal Magnificence, I was dressed in a full tunic of dark indigo painted with pheasants, those venerated symbols of power and fertility, and I wore my leather belt with the gold clasp hung with jade ornaments. The Great General was appointed as the Imperial Envoy, and I received from his hand the Empress's seal and golden blade. So for this event to be a celebration of victory, I would not settle for holding the festivities in the intimacy of the gynaeceum, as prescribed by Imperial Protocol. At my instigation, the Emperor summoned kings and princes, ministers and generals, governors and foreign ambassadors, and a gathering of ten thousand subjects before the gates of the Inner Palace.

Twelve trees of gold set with pearls and diamonds, twelve carved flowers, and two phoenixes with their wings outstretched were pinned to my topknot that was two cubits high and crafted over many hours by the imperial hairdressers. My head weighed down on my shoulders like a palace, a mountain, a star. As I climbed the steps to the top of the Gate of Serene Loyalty, I saw the immaculate blue of the sky draw nearer. The music played by three thousand musicians and the cheers from dignitaries who had come from the four corners of the Empire faded as I rose up. Suddenly I stepped into the silence of vastness. Up there, there was not a breath of wind; eternity spread its wings like a giant bird. An intense heat and a proud, dazzling light emanated from the sun. Beside Little Phoenix, I could see the earth unfolding like a painting: the fields, rivers, mountains, and the millions of Chinese souls prostrating themselves at my feet and begging for my protection.

I was thirty years old, and my second life was beginning. I had no more fears or worries. A new path appeared for me at the top of the Gate of Serene Loyalty, inviting me to reach heights not known to any man. With Little Phoenix, I would build the greatest dynasty of all time; I would beget the most beautiful civilization.

On that day I knew that I would face other difficulties, that loneliness would be my faithful companion, that this new life would be a succession of deaths and rebirths, and that intense joy would be born from the depths of suffering and despair. I, the ordinary restless child, the plain adolescent, the commoner who had been a nun twice, would prove to be a Daughter of Heaven.

WITH THE NEW Year, a new cosmic cycle began. May the nightmares of the past be erased forever! May the Empire know peace and prosperity! Convinced that words had magical benedictory powers, I advised Little Phoenix to inaugurate an era named Dazzling Prosperity.

Plants germinated in the depths of the soil. Rivers wakened to the call of spring. Trees covered themselves in green veils. At the ministers' insistence, Loyalty was discharged from the position of heir, and Splendor was named Supreme Son. I freed the prisoners in the Cold Palace and shut up the former Empress and the Resplendent Wife there, having stripped them of their titles.

I was right to be wary of my husband's capricious heart. My people intercepted a poem that the Resplendent Wife had written to him, using her own blood as ink and a piece of her dress as paper.

I questioned the sovereign: "I've heard that you have been to see those two commoners in their cell. Their tears and their lies moved you, and you have promised them your mercy. Have you forgotten their dark plots that disturbed the peace of your Palace? Do you want me to abandon the imperial seal and give myself up to them once more? Your pity is a dangerous thing: It puts the Empire in danger!"

Little Phoenix had never seen me angry, and he was quite dumb-struck like a child seeing his mother's rage for the first time.

I had always despised fits of jealousy but—by raising my voice, by playing the wounded wife and the cruel stepmother—I realized that this device that millions of women had been using since the dawn of time was more effective than a considered conversation. Paralyzed by my angry screams and my blazing eyes, he tried to justify the weakness he had demonstrated by saying that he had been put under a spell by the two women. I pretended to believe him: "Both those commoners are familiar with black magic; it is hardly surprising if they cast evil spells on you from the depths of their dungeon. I can see only one way of exorcising you. According to the laws of the Inner Court, any criminal who tries to put spells on the sovereign instead of repenting is condemned to one hundred lashings with a wooden plank."

I immediately wrote out the order for this to be carried out and affixed my seal as Mistress of the Palace. Little Phoenix was silent and ashamed, letting me act as I saw fit and lacking the courage to intervene. To be sure that the punishment would be severely enforced, I sent Ruby and Emerald to watch the procedure. It was not long before they reported that Wang, the dethroned sovereign, had prostrated herself three times in the direction of the Middle Court and wished the Emperor a long life and the Empress much happiness before being reduced to a seething mass of meat. The demoted Resplendent Wife had sworn that in her next life, she would be reincarnated as a cat and I as a rat, and she would drink my blood and tear me into a thousand pieces. Her voice soon stuck in her throat as the black lacquered planks tore off her skin and broke her bones. Her blood, flesh, and excrement mingled together, and she had her last breath after twenty strokes.

I had the bodies thrown into the leopards' den. I forbade the two criminals' families to bear the names Wang and Xiao. From then on they would be called Python and Stray Cat.

I slept fitfully in the Forbidden City: My rivals appeared to me in my dreams with their hair torn out and their flesh bloodied. I was haunted by the thought that their supporters would want revenge. But I decided to preempt any reprisals. To demonstrate my generosity, I requested promotions for Han Yuan and Lai Ji who had dared to write to the sovereign, and I praised their sense of responsibility and the courage they had shown in being so candid. Ashamed and frightened, they refused the titles the Emperor offered them and left Court.

Chu Sui Liang and Liu Shi, the uncle of the deposed Empress, received orders to go into exile at the ends of Earth. But Wu Ji was still chancellor. The old man, furious in his isolation, publicly contested my every decision. I had to wait for years to orchestrate his downfall. Wu Ji was indicted in the fourth year of Dazzling Prosperity. In a letter of accusation that covered a full three scrolls of paper, the imperial magistrates demonstrated that the Great Chancellor had been the instigator of my daughter's death: Through Liu Shi, he had supplied the then sovereign lady with a phial of aconite.

Little Phoenix wept when he heard these shocking revelations. Then he was gripped by anger, and he exiled him from the Capital. On his journey, the former chancellor received orders to kill himself: He hanged himself from the rafters of an inn. The death of Wu Ji—the previous Empress's brother, and the sovereign's uncle, who had been a chancellor for two reigns—announced a new era. This man who had been feared and venerated as a demi-god had proved to be fragile as a clay statue. His demise would serve as an example to anyone who might dare wish me harm.

Even though they had retired, Han Yuan and Lai Ji did not escape capital punishment. Chu Sui Liang was already dead, but the deposed Empress's uncle was called back from exile and decapitated at Long Peace. The Court confiscated the assets and lands that these noble clans had accumulated through a succession of dynasties: I distributed this fabulous fortune to the commoners who were now ministers and who would be devoted to my cause.

In his tomb, Father received the posthumous title of Master of the Kingdom of Zhou. His funeral stone was now in the temple of the Emperor Eternal Ancestor, and the Court made daily offerings to him. An imperial decree raised Mother to the rank of Lady of the Kingdom of Dai, and Elder Sister to Lady of the Kingdom of Han.

In this world beneath the Heavens, no one could fail to know the glory of the Wu family. My brothers and cousins hastened to Court to offer me their obsequious congratulations. The men of the clan had aged. They groveled before the sovereign and prostrated themselves at my feet in the hopes that I would promise them elevated positions. In the annals of other dynasties, there were many empresses who had granted the men of their own clan command of the armies and key posts in government. Once in Court, these relations from the outside helped to defend the sovereign's authority against ambitious princes and powerful ministers. My brothers and cousins had neither the political vision nor the necessary education to take on any administrative responsibility. I could not forget the misery they had inflicted on us. They were shameless, thankless creatures; they would never set an example as men of State. Little Phoenix was prepared to welcome them to Court for the sake of my prestige and his imperial dignity: It was hardly fitting for close relations of an empress to remain simple administrators. But I was reluctant to include these worthless individuals in the government simply because they were lucky enough to be born my brothers and cousins. If men like that were granted promotions without earning them, without any effort, would they swear unfailing loyalty to me, would they prove perfectly obedient? After weighing up the arguments for and against, I decided to raise the men of my clan to a symbolic rank within the hierarchy, and I accorded them modest responsibilities that would mean they could take part in the morning salutation.

A few months later, during the Feast of the Moon, Mother gathered all the members of the family in her palace and asked them, "Do you still remember our lives yesterday? And what do you think of the abundance and honor we enjoy today?"

Cousin Wei Liang, who was disappointed not to have been given a more significant promotion, replied: "We are descended from the most highly skilled warriors in the dynasty, and we have climbed through the administrative ranks by our own efforts. Having no claim to the highest ranks in the hierarchy, we are forced to accept these new positions to please the Empress. This special favor weighs on our conscience. Good Lady, there is truly no glory in this!"

When Mother told me of this conversation, their lack of gratitude now and their oppression in the past inflamed me. I immediately wrote the Emperor a long letter, my hand working furiously across each page, denouncing the privileges of these relations from outside the Court and citing frequent historical examples when unworthy men had been heaped with honors and had usurped supreme power. To cut the evil back to the very root, I suggested my relations be sent away from Court to far off provinces. The ministers greeted my request with enthusiasm. My determination had dissipated their fears that my family would become embroiled in politics. The men of my clan had barely taken up their positions before they were driven out of Court like criminals.

Shortly thereafter, I received letters from them begging for my clemency, and I replied to their supplications by writing the book *A Warning to Relations from Outside*.

My brothers died in their postings. Their bodies were taken to the Cemetery of Ancestors. And so I buried the shadow over my glory forever.

six

The same scene kept coming back to me in my dreams: Elder Sister emerging from her room wrapped in crimson silk, her face carefully made up, and every eyebrow plucked, resplendent as a goddess. I was about to take her hand when a surging crowd of strangers knocked me aside. My anguished cries were drowned out by deafening music. She was carried away by the jubilant crowd and disappeared forever.

When she was fourteen, Purity had married into the He Lan clan. Her husband was a gangly, sickly boy of fifteen who soon began a career in local government. As the years passed, he made little progress in the imperial hierarchy, but he became very well read, could hold a conversation about the Great Classics, and was an able painter on silk paper. Like most young aristocrats, he did not go home when he left work. The young lords of the town would take turns organizing banquets in the Houses of Flowers and would invite the most famous courtesans to join them at the table. Clandestine loves flourished as they teased each other. A young poetess introduced a young lord to the astonishing pleasures of the flesh, but she refused to become his concubine and slave in his gynaeceum. In his efforts to persuade her, he visited her pavilion with tenacious regularity and squandered his fortune. Precious stones could buy her smile but not her faithfulness. Other men had found their way into the courtesan's rooms: A poor but educated man offering her a roll of silk could hope to be given a cup of tea; rich merchants with gold might be granted a perfumed kiss. When, at the age of twenty-five, she was found hanging from a beam, the whole town was devastated, but no one knew which thwarted love had made her kill herself. Without her, life had lost its spice: Elder Sister's husband succumbed to the incurable illness of his grief. He died six months later.

At twenty-five, Elder Sister was a widow and a mother of two. She had put away her colored gowns and wrapped herself in dark tunics. She no longer left her apartments where she divided her days between reading and prayer. Believing her life was over, she hoped to find happiness for her future life through Buddhism.

I still remembered the image of her as a beautiful adolescent whose coquettish pouting seduced every person she met. When Purity had appeared at the gates of the palace, I saw a woman from the provincial aristocracy who was chillingly severe. She was covered in layers of tunics of heavy purple-blue-black satin and looked like a crow bearing evil omens. I made her take off her sinister clothes and dress in silks and muslins. I looked at her closely while she changed. What an extraordinary surprise to find she no longer had the straight legs, thin arms, and flat stomach of the sister I used to glimpse at in her bath! Her monastic clothes had been hiding a fertile bosom and generous hips: an ivory sculpture!

The servants had then announced the sovereign's arrival, and Elder Sister had wanted to escape, but I held her back. She had insisted on putting her gloomy clothes back on and had prostrated herself on the ground, trembling shyly. Little Phoenix looked closely at her, and his expert eye saw beyond her immediate appearance. The novelty of a widow appealed to the sovereign, overwhelmed by the polished sweetness of the Court ladies. I encouraged him to seduce her. Through him

I hoped to slip inside of a woman who had been close to me and very distant. The union between Little Phoenix and Purity took place in a pavilion I had prepared. That night my soul was in turmoil, accompanying my husband as he explored a sacred kingdom.

At thirty-one, when most women are in decline, Elder Sister had rediscovered her youth. Her silk gowns and crepe muslin tunics had revealed a proud and happy bosom. Her face had thrown off its gloomy veil and adopted a thousand languid expressions, displaying her sensual delight. She who had never been loved had now discovered the fervent caresses of an emperor. Her chastity had been breached, and she had allowed herself to be borne away on a wave of pleasure.

I had watched my sister blossoming with the pride of a craftsman contemplating his masterpiece. I had offered her part of my palace, a pavilion surrounded by blazing azaleas and camellias, with orange blossom and jasmine wafting their subtle fragrances around it. The Emperor had stopped pursuing the beauties to spend alternate nights in our beds.

That summer the Zhong Nan mountain was covered with pale, pastel colors and heady moisture. The cicadas moaned in the trees. The silken breeze gently stroked our shoulders. Our three-way agreement was an invitation toward the highest pinnacle of desire. One evening, when the musicians were singing age-old melodies outside the door, Little Phoenix affected drunkenness and tumbled Elder Sister and myself down onto his bed sewn with leaves of jade.

I hardly had time to think, my fingers glided over her delicate skin, and my lips pressed up against my sister's. I felt as if I were holding myself in my arms and kissing my own burning lips. I moved carefully, afraid of hurting her, but Little Phoenix guided me in my discovery of her body, as if climbing a magnificent mountain. Her breasts were the peaks wreathed in eternal mists. Her stomach, a deep lake reflecting the blue of the sky. Snatches of our childhood came back to me. I saw Purity pulling a wooden duck behind her. I remembered Little Sister, a restless child who craved affection. Mother's youthful figure loomed up from the past with her high topknot, her collar left open, her noble bearing, and her dazzlingly white breasts. I did not know what Elder Sister was thinking: She kept her eyes obstinately closed. Her awkward gestures implied that she had never made love with a woman. Was she shocked by my experience? Little Phoenix had penetrated me when my sister's naked body rolled on top of mine. I gripped hold of Purity's shoulders, for I wanted to take her with me on my celestial journey. Suddenly, two streams of tears spilled from the corners of her eyes.

Elder Sister was ashamed. Elder Sister was an ordinary, sensible woman, who kept her feet firmly on the ground.

Purity had fallen in love with my god-like husband. She would be punished for this impossible passion.

WHEN I LEFT the village of Wu, I had wanted to console my mother and to give myself courage when I said: "My position at the Palace is our one opportunity. Have confidence in my destiny. Do not weep."

Sixteen years of separation—a split second or a whole eternity. When I arranged for Mother to be brought to the Forbidden City, I had been proud of fulfilling my promise. I had wanted to dazzle her with the riches and the glory waiting for her here, but my blood had frozen in my veins at the sight of this stooped old woman leaning on her cane. I had forgotten that Mother had borne me when she was forty-six and that she could grow old. She prostrated herself at my feet. In keeping with Court etiquette, I returned her greeting with a slight nod of my head. A searing pain carved through me: The happiness I claimed to be offering her was laughable.

Ever since childhood, Mother had demonstrated a tendency toward philosophy and a contempt for manual labor. She had abandoned the women's duties prescribed by the ancestors to devote herself to a spiritual quest. When a team of workmen had restored her apartments in her family home, they had found a piece of paper hidden in a cleft in a beam. On it she had written the maxim for her existence: "Never to do evil and to spread generosity of heart to the four corners of the country." Her father, the famous Great Minister Yang Da, had exclaimed, "My daughter is the future of our family!"

Until I took up my position at the palace, I had always venerated Mother as an idol: Her erudition was quite equal to a man's. Her words were inspired; she had a serene strength that had protected me from the vices of the men in the clan. When she came to present herself at Court, I saw that sixteen years of misery had gradually worn her down; she had become passive, pessimistic, and conciliatory. Her words of wisdom that had rung comfortingly in my ears were reduced to the weary moans of a frightened old woman.

Mother had passed her fervor on to me. I had stolen her valiance. She had dreamed of seeing me married happily to a minor official and was terrified to see me fighting for the position of Empress.

"Once the moon is full," she warned me, "it begins to wane; the higher we climb, the harder we fall. A man should learn to be satisfied with what he already has!"

Her pronouncements had irritated me, and I replied: "You have misunderstood me, good lady. Empress Wang has tarnished her title. Under her rule, the Inner Palace has sunk into chaos, and the sovereign's life is in danger. I am determined to make His Majesty happy and peaceful. This is not a question of personal ambition."

Later she had defended my rivals: "No one should kill a woman who can no longer do any harm. Buddha would have granted both criminals the chance to repent! Majesty, I beg you, shut them away in a monastery—give them an opportunity to pray for their future existence."

"Buddha grants his unlimited compassion to the living because he is invincible," I replied. "I am a mere mortal. Here in the Forbidden City, every life hangs by a thread. Even if I feel pity in my heart, my reason forbids it. Good lady, what you are asking is impossible."

Later Mother learned of the sovereign's liaison with Elder Sister. In veiled terms she criticized me for corrupting Purity's virtue.

"The primary virtue in life," I told her, "is order. Thanks to Purity, I have secured the imperial seed exclusively. Now there are no births anywhere outside my palace, and there is only one uncontested Mistress in the Inner City. That is how I have succeeded in imposing virtue that has been neglected for so long. The concubines have stopped their jealous posturing, the eunuchs no longer dare dally in intrigues. I have banished frivolity and introduced a mood of restraint. The Court ladies have followed my example by removing their jewels and wearing simple gowns and leggings. They have started studying the Great Classics and practicing sport. I have had the names of their titles changed: They are no longer called Precious Wife, Gracious Wife, or Delicious Concubine—all names that reduced them to sexual objects. They have become Supervisor of Piety, Overseer of Morality, and Servant of Wisdom. With the money that I have saved on our clothes, I have financed the construction of Buddhist temples so that messages from the Great One can spread to the four corners of Earth. Good lady, the sovereign's kindness has seen an unloved widow blossom. The happiness of millions of people has resulted from her corruption. Purity is more virtuous than any religion!"

Mother was outraged, and she started to pray day and night to secure Buddha's forgiveness for our incestuous affections. Purity was indifferent to her torment. I heaped honors and gifts on Mother and started treating her like a little girl. At the time, my sister and I could not imagine the fears of a woman who had seen a dynasty fall, a fortune dissolve, and fate overturned.

To us the inconstancies of this ephemeral world were still a source of poetic melancholy and negligible suffering.

I had enjoyed Little Phoenix's favor for ten years, a miraculously long time for carnal passion to survive. Even though I had added to his sensual delight by offering him the young virgins I called to my bed, I knew that he would eventually tire of these repeated orgies and that one day he would succumb to a new infatuation. At thirty, Little Phoenix had become slow and listless. I felt responsible for this apathy that betrayed the boredom in his soul. While I was looking for a trustworthy young woman capable of reawakening his sexual energy, I learned that the sovereign's heart had been inflamed once more and that his conquest had already been consummated. Her name was Harmony. She was Purity's daughter.

Even when she was just twelve years old, word of her beauty had spread through both capitals. Key families and Court dignitaries had sent their most persuasive emissaries to my sister. Mother had opposed a very early marriage; at eighty, she could not bear to be separated from her granddaughter. The matrimonial negotiations broke up and then began again several times. None of them was ever very serious.

Harmony had been raised by her grandmother. The one reaching the twilight of her years idolized the one flowering with the dawn. The spoiled child had become a rebellious adolescent; the charms of puberty had probably awakened the sovereign's attentions. It was also possible that this precocious niece had always nurtured a fascination for an inaccessible uncle. With her wide, curving brow; her fine, willful mouth, and her proud, haughty bearing; she was like me . . . alas, even down to her taste for incest.

I closed my eyes to this clandestine love. But the day Purity learned of this betrayal, she flew into a rage. One morning, a group of eunuchs burst into my palace. An argument had broken out between the Lady of the Kingdom of Han and her young rival. "The noble lady slapped her daughter," I was told. "She called for a strong rope with which to strangle her!"

I ran to my sister's pavilion. The governess's cries announcing my arrival immediately calmed both women. Purity was lying prostrate, and Harmony was kneeling stiff and motionless beside her. Her face was rigid as an iron mask and showed no trace of tears. She was staring darkly at the ground and greeted me with one sharp gesture.

"What does this mean?" I asked them. "You have fought in the Inner Palace and for that you both deserve twenty strokes of the plank! For two women of my clan to argue like common shrews is an insult to my favor and my patience! Take Harmony away, shut her up, and have her copy out *The Book of the Virtuous Women* ten times!"

Once Harmony and her retinue had moved away, I spoke to my sister: "How could you get so angry that you forgot the dignity required by your rank? Before making such a scene, think of the mocking smiles of all the ladies and the laughter of all the high-ranking women in the Outer Court. Everyone envies the power our household enjoys. Why give them an opportunity to gossip about us? Have you thought of Mother? She is eighty-three. How would she cope with the sorrow if she saw you strangle her favorite granddaughter! Your extreme nobility demands that you be a model for every woman in the Empire. Is this any way to behave?"

Crippled with shame, she walked on her knees, pressed her forehead to the ground, and asked my forgiveness. I ordered the servants to serve us tea. A eunuch master of ceremonies appeared. He pounded the tea in the canister, brought the spring water to a boil, rinsed the cups, and let the green powder infuse before adding a pinch of salt.

Purity confided her distress to me: "Majesty, I have projected so many hopes and ambitions onto Harmony! All these dreams are now dashed forever. The gods have just robbed me of both the sovereign and my daughter. Who would dare to wed a young woman deflowered by the Son of Heaven? Why did I not marry her sooner? Is this a divine punishment for failing to observe abstinence as a widow?"

Tears streamed down her cheeks, but she went on: "Majesty, I beg you, as my daughter's body is sullied, send her to a monastery, exile her far from the capital. As a nun, she will learn to pray for her future life, and Buddha will forgive her for her impurity."

As I gave her no reply, she insisted: "Children come into the world to ensure the continuation of the lineage. They grow up to fulfill their filial duties toward their parents. Why does this she-devil want to rob me of the dearest thing I have in the world? Why did I give birth to my own rival in love? Majesty, I offer you her life. Please apply the laws of the clan to her: the death sentence for those who dishonor us!"

I repressed my pity and announced icily: "Good lady, you are jealous. Is that a sentiment worthy of your rank? Did you think the Emperor belonged to you alone, that his favor would last forever?"

Purity's face twisted with pain.

"Majesty, have you forgotten the suffering you endured when the two commoners were alive? Have you never wanted to have the Emperor to yourself for one day, for one month, for life? I have not allowed any other woman touch him but you. For all these years, I have fought for him to be ours alone, and now my own daughter challenges me. When I close my eyes, I can see the longing in their eyes; I hear the Son of Heaven whispering tender words; I imagine his expression when he is holding her in his arms. I am an old woman of thirty-seven, while, at fifteen, Harmony is at the height of her beauty. How can I compete with her? Such treachery! Such ingratitude! Such scandal! One of us must die!"

I tried to reason with her: "Good lady, you make me laugh. You who read the Sacred Writings so fervently, you who have been reciting the sutra beside our venerable Mother since childhood, have you still not grasped that the law of impermanence applies to all things? That a man's heart is far more vulnerable than a pearl of glass and is pervaded by inconstancy? Our sovereign has never loved one particular woman. He is permanently in pursuit of love, excitement, and his own delight. Neither you nor I can confront the whims of his heart; it would be as pointless and pretentious as trying to stop the sun from shining or the moon from waning. We can choose only resignation."

"I would rather die."

I hardened my tone still further: "Good lady, you have been raised to the first imperial rank. You are treated in a way worthy of a princess by blood. You owe all that to His Majesty. We are both on a downward spiral: We will never again be as fresh as we once were; we will not be able to keep a man for long when he thirsts for new beauty. Be grateful that his favor is staying in the family, that it is not some scheming outsider who would fight me for the title of Empress. Never forget how my deposed rivals Wang and Xiao ended their days. We too could fall like them."

Purity opened her eyes wide with horror, then threw her hands over her face. She let out a rasping sob.

"I see now!" she cried. "A few years ago you pushed me into the sovereign's arms so that I could keep him in your bed. Now you think I am old and tired, so you looked for a young girl who could act as bait for you and you chose Harmony! You can think only of holding on to your power!"

"Good lady, you have gone mad," I said, leaping to my feet. "For all these years, I have never thought of my own happiness! I have struggled and upheld our family's dignity, and I have worked for the prosperity of the Empire. Everything I have endured has been turned into the beautiful silks you wear and the sumptuous palace in which you live. There is not one thread, not one grain, not one crumb of your gilded existence that you do not owe to my hard work. Now you can meditate on that—I am leaving."

Elder Sister threw herself at me and blocked my path with her body. She tore open her dress, and her breasts sprang out.

"Look, Majesty, I'm not yet ugly. I have no lines on my face or my breasts. I rub my groin with powders of pearl every day; it is still soft enough to accommodate the divine member. Majesty, give me back your Little Phoenix. I swear I shall satisfy his every desire. I will be grateful to you even into the next life!"

Elder Sister's sobs rang out, echoing back to us through the deserted halls so that they sounded like the howls of some desperate animal. I sighed and left her to her pain.

When the Emperor came home from his hunting trip at twilight, he ran to my room.

"Heavenlight," he said, watching my face closely, "I have heard that the Lady of the Kingdom of Han was angry and that you have had Harmony locked up. Why?"

I was saddened by Elder Sister's selfishness and heartbroken at my husband's frivolity, and I resented Harmony for upsetting the equilibrium that I had established in the Inner Palace.

My silence frightened the sovereign. He took my hands.

"For all these years," he said, "I have had only you in my heart. The other women are just so much dust, butterflies for a day. You, though, are a tree that has taken root in my flesh."

His tender words did nothing to move me. My husband used sweet caressing words like these to manipulate women's hearts.

"The Lady of the Kingdom of Han is becoming unbalanced," he admitted. "She spies on me and makes scenes. She cries all night and makes my life dark and sinister. If she were not your sister, I would have withdrawn her title and sent her to the Cold Palace."

"The Lady of the Kingdom of Han has served His Majesty with devotion," I said with a note of irony. "Have you forgotten the days of happiness so quickly?"

"I no longer desire her. I am tired of her fits of jealousy. I don't want to make love with a bundle of tears. Do you understand that?"

"Is that a good reason to show an interest in Harmony? Now that you have done the rounds of the women in my clan, have you thought of what lies in store for them in their future?"

The Emperor flushed scarlet.

"I never think about that sort of thing," he stammered, "because you are there to help me resolve all my problems. I have even entrusted my government and my empire to you. She's very like you, the girl. So wild . . . so ardent! My sweet Heavenlight, life is short, and Harmony is my one last desire. Let me have her, and in return you shall have more honor than any empress has ever had!"

"Your Majesty has been suffering from violent migraines for some time," I said in a gentler voice. "Your treatment requires a period of abstinence. Is this the time to be abandoning yourself to excesses?"

"My impatience to hold Harmony in my arms does me more harm than anything else. Please arrange this for me, please."

"Your Majesty has already fathered seven princes, enough to ensure the continuity of his dynasty. Like all the women in the gynaeceum, Harmony must undergo treatment to stop her bearing children."

The Emperor drew me into his arms.

"Do as you please. You are the Mistress of the Palace!"

Harmony had refused her meal in the pavilion where she was locked up. When my serving women opened the door and lit the candles, she turned to look at me; she looked disheveled but showed no hint of remorse. It was as if she had lost all the heedless joy of childhood in one night. Her drawn features and her dark expression were those of a woman consumed by hatred.

With her forehead on the ground, she said, "Majesty, send me to a monastery or to the Cold Palace, condemn me to death, I would have no regrets. My body already belongs to the Son of Heaven. I am happy to offer him my life."

Harmony's impetuousness reminded me of my own. I had experienced this same voluptuous suffering, this heroic sadness, but I had lost my innocence: I no longer believed in that ridiculous word—love.

I ordered the young girl to look up. I looked her right in the eye and said: "I shall spare your life because you are the daughter of the Lady of the Kingdom of Han, my beloved sister, and because the Lady of the Kingdom of Dai, my venerable mother, would die of grief if you left this sullied Earth before she did. You are fifteen. The path of life before you is long. Today I am giving you a choice: Either I arrange to find you a good marriage and you shall have a husband and children, or I shall offer you a palace in the Inner Court. But you should know that, like your mother's, your liaison with His Majesty will never be official. You will remain the Empress's niece. Your body will never be touched by mortal men again; you will never have children."

Harmony prostrated herself three times. "Who am I to make such a decision?" she said darkly. "My fate depends on the sovereign's wishes. If he prefers my mother, I should kill myself straight away."

Instead of expressing her gratitude, she was defying my authority.

And yet I felt no anger. I had become a spectator to all their insanities in the name of love.

ELDER SISTER BEGAN to wither.

On a ruling from the sovereign, Harmony received the title of Lady of the Kingdom of Wei and was raised to the first imperial rank. This august favor granted her a magnificence that no other princess could hope to rival. A lake was dug in the grounds of her residence to the south of the Imperial City. The excavated earth was used to create hills topped with pavilions several floors high overlooking the Capital. It was in the center of this body of clear water, in the endless meadows of lotuses and water lilies, that the favorite received the Emperor and his retinue. Their boats glided through the mist with musicians at the prow playing the latest melodies and dancing girls on the bridge twirling their long sleeves. Acrobats spun in the air at the top of the masts and created shapes together with extraordinary virtuosity.

The Lady of the Kingdom of Wei also owned several pavilions within the walls of the Forbidden City. She came and went between the two palaces on a Persian horse branded with the imperial iron. Dressed as a man, preceded by eunuchs and a detachment of guards, and followed by young girls dressed as pages, she would gallop through the avenues of Long Peace raising clouds of dust.

Mother and daughter no longer spoke to each other. They were rivals in love and murderously jealous of each other. When Purity received a piece of jewelry, Harmony would demand one twice as valuable. When His Majesty, consumed with nostalgia, furtively visited the mother for a cup of tea, the daughter would immediately be informed by her spies and would send word that she was dying of some strange illness. Horrified, the Emperor would leap up, and Purity would throw herself at his feet and soak the bottom of his tunic with her bitter tears. The sovereign would have to tear himself from her embraces with a broken heart and an aching soul.

The mother aged as the daughter blossomed. The august visits to Purity's palace became less frequent and then stopped. The sovereign no longer summoned Elder Sister to his banquets for fear that the two women might argue. The favorite's arrogance irritated me, but I held my anger in check. The fragile harmony within the gynaeceum depended on the calm and generosity of its Empress, and I pretended to know nothing of the turbulence amongst its capricious younger members.

Elder Sister followed me everywhere with her weeping. She was deaf to my reasoning and went around in circles of her own despair. I eventually tired of her miserable monologues; there were affairs of State calling for my attention: Famine and epidemics were ravaging the south. I turned away from my sister's unhappiness in love and devoted myself to my people's suffering.

In our Inner Palace, which was the size of an entire town, it was easy to melt into the labyrinth of passageways and to disappear in the tangle of gardens. Elder Sister was still alive, but she was already a ghost. My people informed me that her terrible sorrow had made her lose weight. She now refused to leave her palace for fear that people would make fun of her thin, wasted frame. The turmoil in the Court settled. Harmony was growing more charming; her laughter brightened our ageing pavilions. The household became accustomed to Elder Sister's absence. They forgot her.

One evening when I summoned Elder Sister to my room to gossip with her, I was informed that she had not been living in the Forbidden City for three months. She had gone back to her property. I sent eunuchs to give her dishes served at my table, and they came back to tell me that the Lady of the Kingdom of Han was confined to bed. She was taking a drug that made her forget her heartbreak; she was living a half life, barely awake. I sent her a letter talking to her of life's simple pleasures, of my affection for her, and of the future. I begged her to get up and come back to my side. I promised I would find men who would cherish her without the sovereign knowing. She replied only once to my countless letters. Her words quavered across paper white as a shroud: "Loving just once is enough for me."

In the first year of the age of Dazzling Prosperity, on the first day of the seventh moon, I was informed that Elder Sister was dying. I rushed the imperial doctors to her bedside, and, at nightfall, their messengers knocked at the doors to my palace: The previous evening the Lady of the Kingdom of Han had taken a mortal poison. She had just exhaled her last breath.

An icy chill swept over me. I remembered the pale, ravishing child reading by candlelight. I remembered the scene when, dressed like a goddess, she had set off for a distant land to wed her destiny. My life was a tree that had spread too wide and robbed my sisters of light. They had both been like fragile flowers uprooted by a storm and laid at the foot of my altar.

THE EMPEROR WEPT over Purity's death and called for an imperial funeral. He raised Mother to the position of Lady of the Kingdom of Rong and granted her the ultimate privilege of coming into the Palace on a litter. I adopted Purity's son and named him as heir to my late father. To the detriment of my brothers' children, when Intelligence was twenty years old, he inherited the title and the revenue of the Great Lord of the Kingdom of Zhou, he became the principal officiating priest in the worship of the Wu ancestors, and he took on his duties at Court.

The generous offerings and elaborate ceremonies devoted to the deceased did nothing to heal my sorrow. I could not shake off a feeling of guilt. To cut short this pointless grief, I gave orders to close the residences that had belonged to the Lady of the Kingdom of Han.

But her death had thrown the shadow of doubt over my life. Instead of accepting the changing of the seasons, the loss of her happiness and the decline in her beauty, Purity had rebelled against the laws of nature. The demon she had fought had been nothing other than an obsessive desire to make time stand still. Mutilating herself and destroying herself were her ways of refusing inevitable failure. There was a nobility and veracity in that desperate gesture that constantly troubled me.

I felt I was growing old, floating. Everything pitted an Empress nearing forty against a young favorite: The beauty treatments and the beneficial effects of medicine that were a constraint and a necessity to the first were a distraction and a waste to the second. Specialists had started to treat my failing kidneys, my slackening intestines, and my back damaged by the weight of my headdresses. The eunuch masseurs ran their vigorous hands over my face to smooth my wrinkles; they rubbed my breasts, pulled my stomach, and twisted my buttocks to firm up the muscles. All these manipulations convinced me that this body, which had brought four children into the world, would soon be a wasteland.

In the sixth moon of the second year of the Breath of the Dragon, I brought a chubby pink boy into the world. His laughter and tears gave me new confidence. I called him Miracle. Let him drive the demons from my life and fill my horizons with his golden beams of light!

The blissful happiness of this event devastated Harmony. Now over twenty, the very noble Lady of the Kingdom of Wei could not escape the torments that ambush women at particular points in their lives: All the pride of youth was also a fear of decrepitude. To keep the sovereign's favor for any length of time, she felt she must have a child.

She summoned Mother with her tears and sent her to me as an emissary. I offered a cushion to the Lady of the Kingdom of Rong who had hardly made herself comfortable before she started describing the agonies of imposed sterility and begging for my clemency.

Determined not to give in, I told her: "Only concubines, wives, officiators, servant girls, and ladies in finery—in fact all the women inscribed on the register of the gynaeceum—may conceive for His Majesty. The Lady of the Kingdom of Wei is a relation from the outside. She has palaces outside the crimson walls of the Forbidden City. Her freedom means she could conceive a child by a man in the ordinary world. If, by mistake, the Emperor recognized the infant as his own, it would be a terrible blow to the imperial lineage."

"Majesty," Mother began, trying to move me with her words, "I have survived every hardship in life thanks to my children. Without you I would have let myself die of grief when my husband died. The most appalling suffering in life is to be alone in old age. I do not want Harmony to end her days alone. My granddaughter is prepared to give up her freedom and to accept all the constraints of the Inner Court. Give her a title as an imperial concubine; she could have a child quite legitimately . . ."

"Good lady," I interrupted her sharply, "in every era of dynastic history, imperial children have been used as weapons by ambitious favorites. The births of princes have brought more disruption than happiness. That is why the sovereign and I have decided to control women's fertility to serve him. It is their duty to entertain the Son of Heaven and mine to be responsible for procreation. This ruling is a guarantee of peace within the Palace and of stability in the Empire. At present I have brought four sons into the world: The continuation of the dynasty is guaranteed; the sovereign is satisfied of that. He does not need any more children. Harmony will be lucky not to risk her life in childbirth. She will live longer, and her beauty will be more easily sustained. She should understand my concern and be grateful for it!"

"Majesty," Mother said, falling to her knees and sobbing, "I shall soon die, and I want Harmony's future to be secured while I am still alive. She is your niece. She owes you her upbringing and her destiny. She will always be your servant, indebted to you. Majesty, she will never betray you. Please let her know the joys of motherhood!"

I held my anger in check and lifted her to her feet as I said playfully: "Madam, are you encouraging incest now? Do you no longer fear the wrath of the gods? If Harmony is so determined about this idea, then she must leave the Capital, secretly marry someone, and have children!"

In that year the Emperor handed over all his political affairs to me.

His signature on the decrees that I wrote was now a mere formality. The fate of an entire people weighed on my shoulders, and I was submerged in affairs of state. In the frenzy of work, I mourned Elder Sister. I went to bed late at night and rose early in the morning, and I was no longer concerned about the sovereign who had stopped visiting my bedchamber.

My silence and indifference only increased Harmony's resentment. She secretly accused me of having killed her mother with poison and claimed that she in turn was in danger. When I was informed of her strange complaints, I summoned her and reprimanded her fiercely. The favorite kept her head lowered, but there was a provocative irony in her prostration. News of my anger spread, and the next day the sovereign brought me a precious gift: The preface to *The Orchid's Pavilion* written by the master calligrapher Wang Xi Zhi. My heart leapt with joy, but I was still wary and with good cause: He went on to express his wish to confer a vacant title of concubine on Harmony.

"Majesty," I told him, "your servant has never forgotten that she was once a Talented One in your august father's court, and she is still infinitely grateful to Your Majesty who defied custom by making her Empress. But would it be sensible for Your Majesty to turn his back on conventions twice in the same reign by receiving the niece of this Empress—whose legitimacy is still contested—into the Gyneaceum ten years later? Imagine the consternation of the Outer Court and the rest of the world! Future historians will not be able to distinguish between love and flippancy or sincerity and perversion. Their frivolous comments would cast a shadow over Your Majesty's glorious reputation! Would Your Majesty deign to give me an answer: Is there a difference between an imperial wife and the favor the Lady of the Kingdom of Wei enjoys? Your Majesty's generosity is boundless, and this favorite has not been neglected in any way. Why make a change for the worse when Your Majesty treads the path of righteousness?"

My celestial husband lost heart, and I spoke in a softer voice: "My mother, the honorable Lady of the Kingdom of Rong, has spoiled Harmony. This young woman belongs to a new generation that knows nothing of duty and sacrifice. Her boredom is the sickness that comes with a life of luxury and leisure. I shall put her to work! Would she like to conduct the Inner Institute of Letters?"

THE EUNUCHS' CRIES shattered the calm of my palace. My intendant, still breathless from running frantically, threw himself at my feet: "His Majesty the Emperor has secretly called Great Secretary Shang Guan Yi to his offices. He has asked him to draw up an edict to have Your Majesty dismissed!"

I threw down the brush I was using to make notes on ministerial letters. I did not even wait for my litter to arrive but picked up the hem of my dress and strode out. I was crushed under a weight of conflicting emotions. I admired the poet Shang Guan Yi's literary talent and his moral rectitude and had asked the sovereign to confer the seal of Great Secretary on him. Instead of showing gratitude, he was now plotting my downfall. His betrayal did not hurt me, but it cast doubt on my intuition about character. How could I have been mistaken? After Wu Ji's death, when Loyalty was deposed as heir, I had eliminated all their close supporters, but, not wanting to see too much blood spilt, I had limited the scope of the persecutions. Was it the survivors of these events who were scheming for their revenge now? My role as advisor to the sovereign had shocked the dignitaries bristling with ancestral prejudices who relegated women to the ranks of animals and children. They had become increasingly anxious and dissatisfied as my authority grew. They saw my part in political life as nothing better than meddling. Was it they who were plotting to distance me from power? Harmony was the third possible threat within the Inner City. I realized that my own niece had become a dangerous rival. Without her slanderous words that had instilled doubts in my husband's heart, would he have taken this step?

As I drew aside the door to his offices, I saw the color drain from the Emperor's face. A scroll of paper was spread out on a low table before him; the ink was still wet. He tried in vain to cover it with the sleeves of his tunic. Behind him the Great Secretary Shang Guan Yi had backed away as I came in, and he had melted into the shadows.

I fell to my knees.

"Twenty five years of agreement and happiness, four imperial princes—the fruits of a union that I believed would last forever—is all this already coming to an end? Majesty, have you forgotten our daughter's death, have you forgotten Future's difficult birth, all the turmoil we have confronted? If I were sterile, I would be resigned to the dishonor of dismissal and the pain of abandonment without speaking out to defend myself. But the heir to the throne and the imperial princes will demand an explanation. What should I tell them? Ever since Your Majesty conferred the position of Empress on me, not one day, not one night has passed when I have not thought of my responsibilities and my duty: to incarnate celestial goodness, to help Your Majesty, to keep harmony in the Forbidden City, and to be a model to all Chinese women. If I have committed unforgivable errors, if I have failed in my commitments, if I have neglected my virtue as a woman, please tell me of these things before repudiating me!"

Unsure how to react, the Emperor stammered: "I have been told that you brought a Taoist into the palace and that you asked him to use evil magic. I have been told that you wanted to dispose of me and become regent. You know that the use of witchcraft is punishable by death."

"I knew Your Majesty," I interrupted him, "when he still bore the title of King of Jin. Ever since then my fate has been tied up with his. I have followed Your Majesty as you have risen. Now I am like a wave carried by the power of the ocean. Without his support, without his generosity, I would be the froth on the beach that evaporates at dawn. I cannot help but wish Your Majesty ten thousand years of life. Have you already forgotten? When you were first struck with a migraine, you ordered me to find monks who might exorcise the demons haunting the Inner Palaces. The leader of the Taoist monks on the Mountain of the Celestial Terrace recommended Master Gou. To trick the evil spirits that manifest themselves a thousand different ways, he disguised himself as a eunuch and proceeded to pursue them with utmost discretion. I said nothing of this to not frighten Your Majesty. You could speak to him yourself and to the leader of the Taoist monks and to the eunuch who is Great Intendant of the Inner Court. The malicious rumors you have heard are trying to destroy the harmony between us, which is the envy of many, but lies can never stand up to the clarity of the truth. Majesty, please verify what your servant has told you before accusing her unjustly: Call for an enquiry! The facts and the witnesses will persuade you of my innocence."

"It is true," said the Emperor, scratching his head, "that the hatred and ambition people have attributed to you are unlikely from you. I do now remember that order . . ."

My anger and my indignation finally exploded: "Am I a usurper? Am I a plotter and an assassin? While empresses from previous dynasties tried to submit governments to the authority of their relations from outside the Palace, I exiled my own brothers to distant provinces to show the entire world my selflessness. What more could I ask for in this life when my husband is the Emperor, my son is the heir, and I carry twenty-four trees in blossom on my headdress? Granted, I read the political reports that Your Majesty entrusts to me, and I occasionally give the Court advice, but my position as Empress and my duties as Mother of the People grant me those responsibilities. How could I silence my opinions when Your Majesty has always encouraged me to express them? For ten whole years, I have been working constantly for the prosperity of the dynasty. How can my commitment to the greatness of the Empire be confused with ambition or my devotion to Your Majesty be distorted into crimes of a usurper?"

I moved toward him on my knees.

"Majesty, show me what you have written."

The Emperor flushed with shame. He picked up the imperial decree and tore it to pieces.

"It was not I; it was Shang Guan Yi who wrote it. Do not hold this against me."

"Shang Guan Yi," I said, turning toward him, "when His Majesty raised you to the position of Great Secretary, it was so that you could act as his best adviser. Instead of showing gratitude and serving the cause of the Empire, you have manipulated his trust and sown discord through the Palace! Do you acknowledge your crimes?"

Silent and quaking with fear, the traitor struck his forehead on the ground.

Once back at my palace, I sent a letter to the Great Chancellor Xu Jing Zong, ordering him to lead an investigation into Shang Guan Yi and the eunuch Wang Fu Sheng who had slandered my name. In three days he untangled the threads of a dark plot: Ten years earlier Shang Guan Yi had been an advisor in the Eastern Palace of the heir Loyalty where the eunuch Wang Fu Sheng was in charge of running the palace affairs. When Loyalty lost his title and was banished from the Capital, the two vassals had sworn to ensure their master's return. By pretending to be upright and loyal to the sovereign, they had earned his trust and duped the vigilance of the government.

On the morning of the thirteenth day of the twelfth moon, eunuch messengers ran constantly to and fro through the corridors of the Forbidden City bringing me news of the audience.

After the prostrations, the Great Chancellor's resounding voice boomed: "Majesty, ever since her accession, the Empress's virtue has illuminated the entire land of China. The fragrance of her reputation has been carried on the wind and spread to the furthest limits of the deserts and the very extremities of the oceans. Not one day has passed in which the Yellow People in this vast world under the heavens have not rejoiced in this favor granted them by the gods. Defaming the Mistress of the Empire and plotting against the Mother of the Supreme Son is to commit a crime against the sovereign who appointed her. Behind these traitors whose faces have been revealed today lurks the shadow of the commoner Loyalty, who was banished from Court for addressing disrespectful words to Your Majesty. Instead of meditating on filial piety, the banished commoner has disguised himself as a woman and trained in witchcraft; he intends to raise an army against the Court, clinging to the feverish hope that he will one day be Master of the World. He is behind this plot that stands to serve his ambitions! Here are his servants' confessions and the intercepted letters between Shang Guan Yi and his former master."

A good many ministers stepped forward from their positions and took turns to speak. Some praised me, and others denounced the conspiracy. The sovereign ordered the arrest of the guilty parties. The soldiers of the guard took up their arms and seized Shang Guan Yi, who protested his innocence in vain. They tore off his cap that had distinguished him as a scholar, his ivory tablet, and his dignitary's belt. With his hair awry and his tunic torn, he was dragged from the audience hall.

It was not long before judgment was passed: Three ministers of justice unanimously called for the death sentence against the principle conspirators. The imperial decree fell, and Shang Guan Yi and Wang Fu Sheng were executed along with their entire families. In the house where he was living under close surveillance, Loyalty received orders to commit suicide. In Court, Liu Xiang Dao lost his title of Great Minister for having been a close friend to Shang Guan Yi. I exiled every politician about whom there was the least whiff of suspicion.

The sovereign was affected by the betrayal of those he had believed to be loyal. When he had ordered Shang Guan Yi to write the edict for my deposition, he had been acting out of anger. Now how appalled he was to realize that a marital quarrel had served the purposes of a huge conspiracy! When I had refused to grant Harmony a title as concubine, enraged, the Emperor had realized that my authority overshadowed his own.

After our reconciliation, I was more careful about how I behaved and expressed myself. I was annoyed with myself for neglecting a man's pride and a sovereign's sensibilities. The incident dulled Little Phoenix's appetite for politics. He was tormented by arthritis and headaches; incapacitated by these difficulties, he could no longer concentrate on debates. On the grounds that peace and prosperity reigned over the Empire, he abolished the morning salutations held at dawn every day, and the officials now gathered only every other day. Soon, weary of asking questions and holding discussions in his audiences, he suggested having a gauze screen behind his throne and putting my seat there.

People had known for some time that the sovereign made no decisions without consulting me and that eunuch messengers went backward and forward between the Outer City and the gynaeceum during audiences. This shuttling lost a great deal of time for the government and delayed emergencies. Never in the history of the dynasties had an empress reigned behind a curtain while her husband was alive, but, since Shang Guan Yi's execution, the dignitaries had been afraid of angering me. The plan received approval from the majority; I stepped outside the City of Women for the first time and attended the audience with my husband.

The first year of the Era of the Crowned Sky was marked by the consecration of Tai Mountain. The splendor of this event erased the shadow cast over Court by the traitors' executions. Great Remission was granted to the world, and several banished officials saw their exclusion from the Capital reversed. My cousins in their distant postings immediately asked for permission to come and congratulate me. Half way through the seventh moon, both men, who had waited patiently for their turn in the imperial lodgings, were able to prostrate themselves at my feet. In keeping with custom, they offered me specialties from the regions in which they were posted.

I deigned to invite them to a family feast with Mother, Harmony, and Intelligence in the Inner palace. The awnings were raised round the hall, letting darkness glide over our gowns. The wind rustled through the chrysanthemums and breathed its bitter perfume over us. Dancing girls waved their sleeves of orange and mauve brocade. Their melancholy voices sang of the wild geese leaving for far-off lands.

The eunuchs carried in lychee wine brought by my cousins. The elder of the two brothers stood up, poured the wine into my goblet, and offered it to me. I ordered Harmony to test the temperature because, according to legend, this wine was drunk very cold. The Lady of the Kingdom of Wei stood up and emptied the glass.

"Delicious."

Her voice strangled in her throat. She was gripped by a violent convulsion, and she rolled to the ground, groaning terribly. Then she suddenly stopped moving. Eunuchs and servants ran in. I screamed murder and had my cousins seized. Mother fainted. Intelligence turned over his sister's stiffened body: Black blood was flowing from the five orifices of her face. She was dead.

The following day the moon was full. The banquet celebrating the middle of autumn was cancelled. The Emperor dined alone with me. He drowned his heartbreak in drunken tears and promised to condemn to death the two men who had failed in their attempt to poison me.

The moon in all her immaculate purity hung in the sky, laughing at this world of dust. She congratulated me for my carefully considered maneuvers and invited me to share in her eternal solitude.

AT THE AGE of ninety-one, Mother abandoned our sullied earth. The thought of her parting had tormented me for so long that once it had become a reality, it distressed me less. During her lifetime, she had never completely understood me. Now that she was dead, she had joined the divinities that brightened my nights with their gentle shining. Her funeral arrangements provided an opportunity for an extraordinary display of wealth and esteem. The sovereign abstained from appearing at the morning audience three times, and the Court and government followed their master's example by observing the deep mourning usually reserved for empresses. The Chinese people dressed in linen and hemp to weep her august passing. Monasteries at the four corners of Earth rang their bells and prayed for her celestial journey. The glorious apotheosis that Mother enjoyed after her death was proof of my power. On the day of her burial, the funeral cortege processing out of the town stretched for more than one hundred lis. After the Emperor's parade and the parade of kings and princesses, came the ministers, foreign princes, dignitaries, and crowds of common people. Over and above all this pomp and splendor, I wanted the woman who had brought me into the world to be paid special homage. The imperial regiments played their horns, blew their war bugles, and beat their battle drums. Like the Princess of the Sun of Ping, an exceptional woman who had fought to found the dynasty, Mother was to leave our world with the military honors granted only to men.

Until her dying day, Mother had cherished and protected Intelligence. It was only after she was buried that I authorized judges to investigate this nephew I could no longer tolerate. His mother and his sister had been imperial favorites, and he himself bore the flamboyant title of Lord of the Kingdom of Zhou: Having power thrust upon him so easily had gone to his head. He was beautiful and captivating, which had given him a reputation as a womanizer. Instead of thinking of his career, he had concentrated on his countless amorous adventures. With a group of affluent young peers, he had squandered his inheritance in the pursuit of unknown pleasures. He had even gone so far as to seduce the girl betrothed to the Supreme Son while she was making an offering in a temple. For fear of being seen, they would meet in secret in an inn beside the serpentine river on the edge of a wood of apricot trees. Their love was discovered by chance; my husband was furious and banished the betrothed girl's family. While he was in prison, Intelligence screamed that I had poisoned his sister and had had him arrested for fear of his vengeance. The jailors silenced his absurd pronouncements with a sound beating.

Winter had come. My disgraced nephew lost his title and his fortune and was banished from the Capital. I sent a faithful guardsman to give him some warm clothes in his camp on the Mountain of the Extreme. When the lieutenant returned, he presented me with a silk belt on a silver tray. He informed me that, overcome with shame and remorse, Intelligence had asked to be hanged from a tree.

I no longer had any relations from the outside in Court, and this absence weakened my position. My family had been built and dismantled to suit me. I had given every one of them wealth and position, but Elder Sister's renunciation had been the first betrayal, which had invited others. Instead of following my rise, they had chosen to fall. My childhood was dead; there were no longer any faces around me to remind me of the distant landscape of innocence. Father and Mother had slipped away, and my sisters had followed them. I had to carry on, accompanied by my regrets.

I called my nephews from my father's clan back from banishment to fill this void. I conferred the title of Father's heir and head of the clan on Piety, the eldest. One family had been destroyed, and a new one would be built. With my brothers' and cousins' sons back in favor, I set up the village of Wu in Court. The younger generation understood that I had power over their success or their demise. They would show fear and adulation for me. I would help them weave a labyrinth of power that would allow me to govern with nothing to fear.

A great emptiness had been carved out in my soul; I watched all the effervescence of the world with a derisive smile. I still had the warmth of life within me, though, and enthusiasm for the future. There was still the Tang dynasty and its vast provinces. The millions of souls in the Empire had become a huge family in which I was the embodiment of an energetic and authoritarian mother. I was over forty, and I held in my hand an invisible sword that sliced through every illusion. The sharpness of the blade gave me its icy and dazzling strength. I no longer believed in the compassion of men; I believed in that of the gods. I had averted my eyes from my suffering and fixed them on the stars.

SEVI

The Emperor Lordly Forebear had brandished his sword and conquered the Chinese lands with arms. When the Emperor Eternal Ancestor had risen to the throne, he had healed the wounds of a ravaged country. Thirty years after it was founded, our Tang dynasty had all the fragile grandeur of a convalescing empire. In our hands it would see unprecedented prosperity or fall back into poverty. It would be a unified power or would splinter into kingdoms.

Our august predecessor had been chiefly preoccupied with agrarian developments, and, like him, we continued to lower land taxes. Weaving factories proliferated along the banks of both great rivers. To encourage households all over China, I set an example by rearing silk worms in the imperial parks. While the sovereign personally took part in more and more ritual ceremonies for the cultivation of the land, I conducted the meticulous celebrations for harvesting mulberry leaves so that the Goddess of Weavers would give us her blessing.

Caravans came from the west in search of porcelain and silk, breathing new life into our civilization. Our women, tired of being swaddled in several layers of dresses with long sleeves, now chose tunics with nar-

157

wide trousers, and leather boots that freed their feet from
...aints of rigid shoes with curled toes. The dizzying height of
...aditional headdresses required hours of work, and they were so
...vy that they impaired our movements. The desert women wore their
hair simply dressed, crowned with light felt hats; by imitating them, we
could walk or run as fast as men.

The craze for exotic spices and foreign foods kept expanding. Furniture from western kingdoms streamed into China, piled on camels'
backs. High-level chairs and tables and raised beds allowed us to stretch
our legs and brought beneficial comforts to our everyday lives. Our ancestral arts favored restraint, purity, and metaphysical abstraction, but
this quest for a spiritual essence denied the warmth of the senses and
the whims of the heart. The music from the oasis conquered us with its
powerful impulsive rhythms and immodest palpitations. The twirling
dances from those parts—so different from the Chinese dances that included restricted and graceful slowness and ritual gestures—showed us
all the beauty of spontaneity and reconciled for us the sensuous pleasures that our sages had neglected for so long.

Imperial patrols guaranteed the safety of the Silk Road through the
Gobi desert. Inside the Great Wall, new inns had been built to make
the journey easier for travelers. In Long Peace I opened academies to
provide a forum for foreign scholars and Chinese tutors to pass on their
knowledge, train interpreters, and compile dictionaries in every language.

Officials complained about the growing number of temples dedicated to unknown idols, but I ignored these pointless concerns. Buddha
was a god who had been revealed to the West, and the spread of the
Buddhist faith had never eclipsed the glory of the deities we had venerated since the dawn of time. Every religion was a blade that allowed its
faithful to carve up the lie that is life. I encouraged my people to choose
the tool that suited them best.

In my eyes, a country's enthusiasm for other customs was the mark
of a great civilization that could absorb every difference. This new

wealth and the abundance of our own ancient heritage had transformed China into a stellar empire that shone beyond its own borders. Distant kingdoms dreamed of Long Peace as a city destined to be happy and prosperous. Our history, which had been related through the dynasties by Court chroniclers, was a generous source from which men could draw ideas and reflections. Our criteria for elegance became the universal points of reference for good taste. Western kings and far-eastern princes sent their scholars to our Court to study politics, justice, administration, military organization, medicine, literature, the arts, and architecture. Numerous foreign capitals took their inspiration from the example set by Long Peace, and their imperial palaces were smaller copies of ours. Chinese was the most widespread language in the world, and it became the official language of diplomacy with which every kingdom could communicate. The morals and ethics of Confucius were adopted by many countries and served as a code of behavior and an official doctrine.

Inside the Great Wall, I encouraged trade between the towns of the Yellow River and the River Long. I constantly created new routes to stimulate exchanges between different regions. Nevertheless, the rivers remained my own preferred means of transport. Forty years later, I still could not forget the huge sailing boats laden with mountains of goods. Every year I opened a new canal to provide irrigation for the fields and a link between the rivers.

Long Peace, the greatest trading town under heaven, prospered. Luoyang, Yangzhou, and Jinzhou became commercial crossroads where commoner clans accrued new fortunes. Since the dawn of time, merchants had occupied the lowest rung on the social ladder. Previous Courts had treated them as thieves, but I recognized their active participation in the country's prosperity: Their greed spurred on an increase in expertise and furthered productivity among farmers and craftsmen; their speculations guaranteed closer links between the north and the south and the towns and the country. Their dynamic outlook contrasted with the weighty aristocracy with their Great Names and their autocratic way of life that was now hampering the Empire's development.

These old families were major landowners and had reached their peak during the Wei and Jin dynasties. Within their fortified farms, which were like completely independent kingdoms, they intermarried and defied central authority by refusing any interference from the outside world. When our Tang dynasty was founded and the Emperor Lordly Forebear distributed noble titles to his comrades in arms, this gesture was frowned on. When the Emperor Eternal Ancestor published his *Book of Clans* in which he put the imperial family before the Great Names, he too was jeered at. As the daughter of an ennobled merchant, I would never forget how the old aristocracy had treated me with contempt. More than any previous sovereign, I wanted to dismantle an outdated world and its obsolete hierarchy.

An imperial decree forbade a dozen of the key families from arranging marriages with one another. Two ministers who had been born commoners were given the responsibility of establishing a new social order. They wrote the *Book of Names*, which was accepted as an authority so that the new titles given out by the sovereign came before the old nobility.

Ever since ancient times, the Court had recruited its highest officials from the Empire's aristocratic clans, and their duties had been handed down from father to son. Politics was a matter of inheritance, something that was constantly redistributed among the privileged. Matrimonial alliances reinforced the influence of ambitious households that held sway over sovereigns. Emperor Yang of the previous dynasty had invented a system of recruitment by public competition that allowed scholars to earn state responsibilities and the title of mandarin. But until now this method of selection had been restricted to the appointment of minor officials whose careers would always be limited because of their origins.

Now our empire was evolving: Demographic growth and increasing wealth in the towns meant we needed an efficient administrative system and well-supported imperial authority. Finely dressed noblemen who could quote the Classics and hold metaphysical conversations were living in a world far removed from reality. How could they give judicious advice to a sovereign who would never set foot outside the Forbidden City?

My reform received Little Phoenix's approval; he had a taste for overturning customs. A decree was published ordering the ministers and provincial governors to recommend capable men to the Court, regardless to their origins. Soon the sovereign followed my advice and encouraged widespread competition for the mandarinate by honoring the final exam with his sacred presence.

Sitting behind the throne, surrounded by curtains of mauve gauze, I watched the scholars in contention for the title. They knelt before their writing desks where the paper, quills, and ink had been prepared for them by eunuchs; some shook with fear, and others struggled to keep their calm. I remembered my own anguish and feverish excitement when I was presented to the Eternal Ancestor for the first time. Unlike the previous sovereign who had not known how to choose among his ten thousand beauties, I vowed to myself never to ignore any man who might some day become a pillar of the Empire.

The Court finally opened its doors wide. A son of a Great Name would consider his nomination to be rightfully his whereas an ennobled Minor Name would show gratitude to his benefactor. The number of commoner-born ministers increased as the sovereign's authority grew. Life was no longer fated. Education offered those of lowly birth an opportunity to rise. Now, through competition, thousands could aspire to a better lot.

THE STARS HAD foretold glory.

For four consecutive years, the sun, rain, and snow lavished Chinese soil with their generosity. From the heart of the imperial city to the four horizons, the old society perished, and a new world was born. Fields impregnated with the sweat of toiling peasants undulated voluptuously beneath the sky. Silks and brocades slithered off the looms, each a loving whisper from its weaver. Outlying lands became populated, and smoke from kitchen fires spiraled up into the sky in every direction. Every five lis another cockerel crowed, and another flock of sheep bleated. New barns were raised in the provinces to store the exceptional harvests; bolts of silk accumulated in the imperial storehouses. The price of rice fell to five sapeks per bushel.

Emperor Yang of the overthrown dynasty had had ostentatious tastes: His court and his dignitaries, following his example, had been carried away in a whirlwind of spending on pointless pleasures. Art and poetry in his time had predicted decline: Poets, calligraphers, and painters had been prisoners of a world full of refined form but devoid of content. Their affected sentiments and vapid pomposity betrayed their impotence. Under my husband's reign, our Tang dynasty shook off this decadent style. A person's energy was now more important than their aesthetic learning, and appearances reflected inner depths and breadth of spirit. By wearing dresses that were worn and darned, I imposed a more sober fashion on the Court, and by using calligraphy stripped of any superfluous frills, I communicated my preference for the essential to Court officials. I myself read the papers written by the candidates in imperial competitions, and I selected those whose writing impressed me. The mannerist poets disappeared from Court: Their superficial moaning was replaced by powerful verses with simple rhythms full of vibrant emotion.

Our empire was an earthly oasis, a grain-store for the heavens, and it became the envy of the many nomadic tribes whose constant travels were dictated by pasture and water sources. Since the dawn of time, the Chinese people had been living with this fear: stampeding archers appearing out of the desert and closing in on our villages, throwing our harvests and our women onto their horses' backs, and leaving our fields devastated and our houses burned to the ground.

Unlike the Emperor Eternal Ancestor who had tried to keep us safe by conquering them and occupying their unworkable land from the steppes of Mongolia to the Gobi desert, I forced my husband to give these wild regions their autonomy and to appoint the local dignitaries as governors. The previous emperor had secured the obedience of these unstable regions with brutal bloodshed, but I bought it with the gold that my people gave willingly to avoid war. In a few years, the revolts had dwindled, but I knew that this period of calm was deceptive. The nomadic peoples had a predatory streak and a longing for freedom that no violence or gentleness would ever quell. My only fear was that they might unite against us. Thanks to the loose tongues of Chinese arms traders, I succeeded in maintaining the discord between the different tribes and in kindling hatred between their leaders. I prolonged the peace by alternating military repression and secret agreements.

When an empire embarks on a cycle of growth, it instills spirit and courage in its warriors. In the fifth year of Dazzling Prosperity, our vessels were called to the kingdom of Sinra, which was in danger once again; they vanquished the Paiktchei invaders and captured their royal family. Our generals offered the latter to Long Peace as victory trophies, and they prostrated themselves at the sovereign's feet and begged for his clemency. Against the advice of our ministers, who wanted them to be executed, I took the initiative of recognizing the prince and heir as governor and sent him home with supplies to feed his people who were starving in the aftermath of war.

Now isolated, the kingdom of Korea lived its final hour of arrogance. My husband still hoped to have revenge for his father's defeat. Exalted by their successive victories and carried by a sense of their own invincibility, our soldiers broke the defenses of a ferocious army, laid siege to the capital Ping yang, and forced the Korean court to recognize the suzerainty of our empire.

Emperor Yang of the previous dynasty had raised an army of a million soldiers against Korea three times, and three times his expeditions had failed. His dogged determination had exhausted the people and had cost him the crown. Emperor Eternal Ancestor, the conqueror blessed by the gods, had in turn failed to subjugate this little kingdom. He had come home sickened by his failure, and the regret had killed him. Our victory erased the dark pages of the past and drew out the thorn deep in the flesh of our history. The people saw our military successes as a celebration of their power, while my husband—who had suffered for being the son of a great sovereign—saw it as proof of his own power and virility. He who had never wanted to govern, he who loathed politics, was beginning to believe what I told him every day: His reign was still more glorious than his father's.

Euphoria spread through the country and reached its apotheosis when dragons appeared in the southern provinces. The honorable sages of Antiquity said that these kings of the River and the Ocean only manifested themselves when peace and happiness reigned on Earth. The erudite scholars of the government's astrology department interpreted this extraordinary phenomenon as a sign of approval from Heaven addressed to its Son. Our ministers felt they were living in the most enlightened Court of all time, and this filled them with pride and audacity. Several of them begged the sovereign to undertake a pilgrimage to Tai Mountain to make an oblation to Heaven and Earth.

According to the *Book of Rites*, this ancient celebration was carried out by emperors who had accomplished some extraordinary earthly feat. The Annals recorded that—after the Yellow Emperor and the mythical sovereigns—only two emperors had dared take the steep path up Tai Mountain and aspired to saluting the skies: the First Emperor, who had unified China, and the Martial Emperor of the Han dynasty, who had conquered the Barbarians and extended our territories as far as the setting sun.

During his reign, the Emperor Eternal Ancestor had intended to make this sacred pilgrimage, but the fragile state of his convalescing empire had forced him to abandon the plan. I begged my husband to carry out this unfulfilled wish. The ancients said that Tai was the sovereign of all mountains, that at its summit a door opened into the celestial world. I dreamed of grasping the mysterious power of mountains: As they reared up impetuously, the earth joined the sky.

My enthusiasm could not sweep aside Little Phoenix's scruples; like every son crushed by the weight of a daunting inheritance, he was wracked with despondency and doubt when he had to surpass himself. He said that his crown had fallen to him by accident, and, as a simple mortal and a humble servant of the Empire, he wondered: Was he invested with the Celestial Will, was he worthy of being the one and only initiated person on Earth, was he the sublime sacrifice that the people made to the gods, and was he the Savior of the World? Up there in the mists and the eternal wind, would he not be dizzied by his own ascension and his solitude?

My eyes filled with tears.

"Yes, Majesty, you are this providential son. You have been chosen by the gods to incarnate goodness and generosity; you are the sovereign who will drive out poverty and suffering on Earth!"

The Emperor wept too. He was haunted by a painful childhood deprived of a mother's love and a distressing adolescence shattered by scheming and fratricide. He could not free himself from the demons coiled within his heart and chose to huddle in the shadows of the Forbidden City.

Two years later, the Palace servants found the footprint of a griffon[15] on the imperial steps to the Pavilion of Perfection. The Ancient Books described this sacred animal's appearance on Earth as a harbinger of victory and peace. I saw this extraordinary event as a divine sign: I had to bear my husband up to the highest point in life, to the pinnacle of humanity.

The news sent a thrill of excitement through Court officials. I secretly encouraged learned courtiers to send petitions to the sovereign calling for him to climb Tai Mountain. Soon provincial governors, district administrators, chiefs of southern tribes, and western kings joined in unison to make the same request. The sovereign could not decline the invitation of the heavens or his people's request. He was persuaded.

---

[15] The legendary animal of ancient China has a stag's antlers, the head and body of a lion covered in scales, and the wings and talons of an eagle.

* * *

IN THE THIRD month of the fourth year of the Virtue of the Griffon, the Emperor transferred his Court to the eastern capital and arranged to set out with foreign kings and tribal chiefs from the world over. My august husband conducted an extraordinary deliberation during which ministers and scholars used the annals and the books of doctrine to establish the protocol for the ceremonies. They chose sacred melodies and dances and agreed on the list of participants and officiators. I planned the construction of the imperial route and the erection of altars; I renewed the armies' ceremonial uniforms and took measures to prevent skirmishes along our borders and avoid a possible coup in the capital during the Emperor's absence.

The ritual for the petition began in the tenth month. During a solemn audience the Supreme Son, the kings and great lords, followed by the Great Ministers, magistrates, advisers, Governor Delegates and foreign princes, all presented their official requests to the sovereign, asking him to make the ascent of the sacred mountain. After refusing three times to demonstrate his humility, my husband announced to the world that he had decided to undertake the pilgrimage. I immediately sent my congratulations to the sovereign, along with a letter in which I disputed the ancestral law that banned all women from the ritual ceremonies. I demanded the right to be the second officiator for the Sacrifice to the Earth.

"According to the rules of the Rites, two ministers will assist the sovereign during the Libation to the Earth. Man is the incarnation of the celestial breath and woman represents earthly powers. Eternity is the product of the transmutation born of the union between Heaven and Earth. How can it be that women should be excluded from the sacrifice which pays homage to her original element? During the ceremony, the shades of every empress will be invoked in prayers for fertility. Is it conceivable that the spirits of these august deceased should appear before strangers, all of them men? Without their honorable presence, the ritual would be incomplete, and no blessing would be granted. It is true that, in China's history, no woman has ever been admitted to the supreme Service of the Empire. Should we persist with a shortcoming of the Ancients to the detriment of the future?"

When my letter was read in public during the morning audience, it shocked the Court. I saw amazement and consternation on our ministers' faces, but the sovereign found my arguments irrefutable: He expressed his approval, and the debate was closed. I would be the first woman to discover the mysteries of these celebrations.

On the twenty-eighth day of the tenth month, there was a chill northern wind, and the coral-colored sun hung in a crystal clear sky. Luoyang was deserted: The main avenue was covered in wet sand, and it gleamed like a golden sword laid down by the gods.

Men in yellow brocade marched slowly from the Southern Gate of the Forbidden City. They held signs with the words "Make way, keep clear" written on them in powdered gold, and they shouted to announce the beginning of the imperial procession.

There was a succession of parades for different dignitaries: first the Administrator from the district of Ten Thousand Years, the Governor of Long Peace, the Great Lord Overseer, and the Minister for Armies; then the Great Generals of the Golden Scepter of the Right and the Left. Both wore purple brocade, black breastplates with red lacing, and gold-plated helmets; they were mounted on horses with plaited manes and tails. They each carried a quiver of twenty-two arrows on their backs, and sabers hung from their leather belts in sheaths inlaid with precious stones. Behind them came an escort of four horsemen holding the lance adorned with yak hair as a symbol of victory.

Two lieutenants of the Golden Scepter headed up a square formation of forty-eight soldiers with scarves wound around their topknots, bronze breastplates, crimson trousers, quivers on their backs, and sabers on their belts. They were accompanied by twenty-four armored foot soldiers.

A group of standard bearers held their banners aloft in the wind, displaying the Crimson Bird, the god of the south.

Then came the procession of six carriages with roadmen marching before them. Each carriage was drawn by four horses and carried fourteen coachmen. The first measured the distance; the second established the direction; the third was decorated with white cranes; the fourth bore the flag of the phoenix; the fifth transported the Great Seer and dispelled evil; the sixth was driven by a soldier of the Golden Scepter armed with a crossbow and was covered in wild animal skins.

Then came two lieutenants of the Golden Scepter and their twelve mounted lancers and archers.

Next came the troop of imperial musicians: twelve drums, twelve golden kettledrums, 120 large drums, and 120 long horns. Small drums, a choir, pipes, and Tatar flutes were lined up in groups of twelve, while 112 flautists with larger flutes marched ahead of the two drums setting the rhythm. Then came the bamboo flutes, pipes, mouth organs, more Tatar flutes, and mouth organs made of peach wood. Then there were another twelve drums, twelve golden kettledrums, 112 small tambourines, and 112 bugles. Twelve more drums decorated with feathers headed up a square formation comprising a choir, pipes, and Tatar flutes. All of them began to play the solemn melody of the *Emperor's Departure*.

Then came the parades of banners. The two Palace Overseers rode ahead of the Great Librarian and the Great Annalist. The sovereign carriages of Geomancy and of Measures were escorted by roadmen and followed by twelve drums and twelve gold drums.

Then came the procession of long-handled serrated sabers and behind them two rows of twenty-four imperial horses.

The flag of the Green Dragon, the god of the east, and of the White Tiger, the god of the west, swished apart to reveal two lieutenants leading two square formations of twenty-five cavalrymen, twenty of them lancers, four crossbow carriers, and one archer.

Following this was the procession of ministers and councilors from the Great Chancellery, the Great Secretariat, the Office of Supreme Affairs, and the Office of Overseers, all riding two by two.

Two generals headed up twelve divisions, totaling 1,536 men, arranged according to the color of their uniforms.

Two lieutenant-generals from the Imperial Guard commanding sixty soldiers from a division of reinforcements, two lieutenant-generals from the Cavalry in charge of fifty-six horsemen, and four lieutenants leading 102 foot soldiers made an impressive sight.

Then came the parade of the Jade route: the Jade carriage towed by thirty-two coachmen dressed in emerald green was accompanied by five more carriages, the General of One Thousand Bulls, and the two great generals of the Guard of the Left and the Right bearing imperial sabers; behind them were two imperial horses and two Gate Keepers holding long-handled sabers.

Then there were two soldiers bearing two banners of the Imperial Gate, escorted by four men on foot, all wearing tunics in imperial yellow. There were twenty-four sergeants from the regiments that guarded the Gates trotting between six rows of soldiers from the cavalry and reinforcements, and twelve rows from the regiments that guarded the Left and the Right.

Then followed long-handled fans made of feathers from venerated pheasants, borne by horsemen. Then the imperial litter with its eight bearers. Next there were four small fans, twelve fans of precious feathers, and two parasols covered in flowers. Four men marched ahead of the imperial vehicle which, having been designed for just such elaborate large-scale journeys, dripped with gold and precious stones and looked like a legendary reptile. It was made up of a sequence of platforms covered with giant palanquins and connected with hooks so that the whole train was articulated and flexible. It proudly displayed its two hundred coachmen in their black scarves, yellow tunics, mauve trousers, and purple belts and its countless horses harnessed in the most beautiful jewels in the Empire. As they reached the wide road covered in wet sand at the gates of the city, the reins were released: Every shaft and axle began to creak, and the train set off across the universe with a roar of thunder.

It was followed by the Palace eunuchs carrying the sovereign's personal belongings and twenty-four horses from the imperial stables; by a procession of lance-bearers, feather fans, painted silk fans, and yellow parasols; and by a musical rearguard of hundreds of instruments.

The pavilion of the Black Warrior was first in the march-past of crimson banners, lances decorated with yak hair, and sticks topped with peacock feathers.

Then there was another yellow banner escorted by two Palace Overseers and their four assistants. The Rectangular carriage, with its two hundred coachmen, traveled ahead of the Small carriage with sixty coachmen, followed by imperial scribes and red, emerald green, yellow, white, and black banners carried by the eight soldiers from the Regiments of War of the Left and the Right.

After the procession of the Regiments of Vehemence came the parade of the Path of Gold, the Path of Ivory, the Path of Leather and the Path of Wood.

Followed by a procession in the following order four carriages celebrating agriculture; twelve magnificent vehicles drawn by oxen; the carriage of the Guard of the Seal; the carriage of the Golden Scepter; and the carriage of the Leopard's Tail, a symbol of Majestic Fear;

the two hundred guardsmen of Vehemence in breastplates, carrying shields and bearing weapons of war in their right hands;

the forty-eight guards horses;

the twenty-four standards of sacred animals with their armed escort;

the procession of the Black Warrior, the god of the north, divided into armored troops in five colors;

the Empress's parade with her horsemen, footmen, officers, musicians, eunuchs, and ladies-in-waiting (their numbers all predetermined by the Rites);

in strict hierarchical order, the processions of imperial concubines, each scrupulously respecting the prescribed number of long-handled fans, the color of her clothes, and the ornamentation of her carriages;

the parade of the Supreme Son with his regiments and troops of musicians, followed by his wife's parade;

the processions of kings and those of their wives;

the processions of the county kings and those of their wives;

then the processions of princesses;

the processions of imperial Great Lords and those of their wives;

the processions of ministers and the processions of the Barbarian kings, tribal chiefs, and foreign ambassadors;

at the back came the animals from the imperial Park: tigers, leopards, elephants, rhinoceroses, stags, ostriches, and birds in aviaries, and the builders, cooks, wet nurses, scribes, tailors, silversmiths, cupbearers, doctors, pharmacists, grooms and horses, slaves, and beasts of burden.

For half a moon, more than one hundred thousand people came out of the town of Luoyang and set off on the imperial journey that traced one perfect straight line across the wintry plain. During the day the processions moved forward in a powerful river of brightly colored waves. At night the bivouacs and camp fires transformed the land into a starry sky. Never in the Annals of the dynasties had such a display of magnificence been recorded: An entire nation was migrating to the east, toward the ocean.

So we could join the sun!

HOW COULD ANYONE forget Tai Mountain with its snowy peaks challenging the skies? How can I describe its immaculate grandeur that reduced the imperial procession to a narrow black thread? Long after we left, the sights and sounds would still come back to me in the depths of the night: the mysterious ceremonies, the huge altars shaped like discs and squares, and the sacred dancers with their painted sleeves twirling between the smoke and mist. In my dreams I heard the mountain's hoarse breath mingling with the chiming of sounding stones and bronze bells. I pictured the camp fires outside tents covered in sheets of gold, the flames flickering in antique basins, and the torches erected along the Sacred Path, an endless string of vertical lights. The sovereign's request for prosperity had been engraved onto a golden blade, and at the top of the mountain, he sealed it behind a rock. There in the howling of the wind and the falling snow, I abandoned a part of my soul. Tai Mountain already belonged to the past, but its magic lived on. I had found something more precious than the celebrations: the loneliness of a former life, a fragment of shattered reminiscences, and a quest for a true origin.

Our pilgrimage turned into a roaming progression across the northeast of the Empire. When we reached Confucius's homeland, the Emperor paid homage to the Sage. As the Court headed north to the birthplace of Lao-tzu, it made offerings to this founder of Taoist thought who was an ancestor of the imperial household. Our return journey was overrun by a radiant spring and its blossoming trees. In the Palace of the Joined Jade Disc, Little Phoenix and I wrote a commemorative hymn together. It was engraved onto a stela that would be erected at the top of Tai Mountain, among the celestial clouds. How long would that stone monument glittering with powdered gold withstand the cruel weather? After a thousand springs and autumns, after the snow had covered Earth ten thousand times, it would crumble into dust. The imperial route would be eroded away, the turmoil of one hundred thousand men marching jubilantly would dissipate. From Luoyang to Long Peace, the magnificence of the present was already being swallowed up in the vastness of the skies.

This sanctification had marked the high point of a cycle that would, inevitably, fall into decline. The ascent of Tai Mountain had given me strength, but it had left my husband somehow damaged. Like a warrior who has won his victory or a poet who has written his most inspired odes, he decided to renounce speech and actions for silence and contemplation.

Since my niece's death, my husband no longer had a favorite. When he honored my bedchamber, it was to find an older sister's consolation in my arms. As he aged, his distress took the form of fits of mysticism. His health was failing: As well as the frequent migraines, he suffered from arthritis and chronic dysentery. He spent more and more time confined to bed, and his absence became the norm for the outer court.

During the audience, he resigned himself to playing a symbolic role in the morning salutation and let me lead political debates from behind the gauze screen.

He dedicated himself to his passion for medicine, he built up a huge pharmacy in his palace and would go to sleep surrounded by the smell of bitter herbs. He actively oversaw the compiling of an encyclopaedia of medications and even went so far as to receive herbalists and sorcerers to discuss the beneficial effects of plants. His fascination for alchemy and immortality pills was long-held, and he became fervent in these obsessions. He had altars and magic furnaces built. Like the First Emperor and the Martial Emperor of the Han dynasty, he dreamed of transmuting the body into pure spirit. The red cinnabar that he took failed to cure his illnesses, but it changed his personality. He was sometimes sleepy and sometimes feverish, sometimes full of dreams and sometimes despondent; his days of dejection were punctuated by periods of hyperactivity.

He now slept with adolescents, both boys and girls. According to Taoist medicine, their virginal bodies could rebalance his vital fluids and restore his vigor. In his search for cures, he dragged the Court on journeys with him. New cities were built. Up in the mountains, our palaces snaked between the clouds. As he listened to monkeys howling, tigers roaring, and birds chattering, his earthly sufferings were washed away. He was dazzled by tall waterfalls tumbling from rocky peaks and by rainbows hovering over ancient trees. He bathed in hot springs and explored deep caves and underground rivers, already tasting the indolent existence of the gods.

The years were flying by. Our bodies aged, and our souls trembled. I watched, powerless, as my husband drifted in the opposite direction from myself. He became slow while I remained alert; he became fragile while I remained robust. He was frequently indisposed, and I had never even experienced a migraine. His voice was weak and breathless, mine loud and full of energy. The heir, Splendor, was only sixteen years old when he was designated as regent, so I had to take responsibility for all affairs of State. I would rise when it was still dark, come summer or winter, to receive the salutation of officials that was set at daybreak by the ancestral calendar. As my husband weakened, my authority increased further. Ten years earlier, the Palace intrigues and the complexity of imperial decisions had irked me and I had sometimes felt oppressed by the impotence of power. Now, the government that I had appointed was proving its competence and obedience, and I had acquired all the assurance of a woman on the threshold of maturity. The art of commanding became a martial drill, a religious sacrifice. I was both involved and detached as I manipulated the opinions, vanities, and ever-changing truths of men.

I floated above this sullied world like a drop of oil in water.

The sovereign's mania for traveling upset the smooth running of the Court, which sought discipline and routine. The work undertaken to satisfy his whims required hundreds of thousands of laborers. Mountains were razed to the ground, and entire forests fed the furnaces used to fire imperial bricks. Precious woods, alabasters, granites, and exotic plants arrived down the rivers and were then transported on carts drawn by oxen and horses. Having imposed restrictions on the people for the sake of the economy, I was annoyed to see my husband setting such a poor example with his profligacy. As he lost interest in politics, he became increasingly fanatical about war: He went from one province to another, visiting garrisons, reveling in their grandiose military displays. The subtle balances I had maintained within the Empire were upset by his impulsive decisions and his obsession for interpreting any kind of attack as a personal affront to his pride—which he now confused with the dignity of China itself.

The deep discord between us triggered a violent argument: Irritated by the severity of my comments to him, the Emperor shook with rage from head to toe and accused me of crossing him with the sole intention of making him unhappy. When I saw the tears on his cheeks and the pain he was enduring from an excruciating headache, I regretted giving full vent to my feelings. How could I forbid an ailing man from proving his power with military deployments? How could I deprive an already weary soul of his futile but precious earthly pleasures? How could I stand in the way of a weakening man tasting the last joys of this life?

At forty two I had brought a daughter into the world; she was called Moon and was given the title of Princess of Eternal Peace. After the birth of the daughter I had so longed for, we had brought an end to our sexual relationship. The sovereign still occasionally showed some enthusiasm for me, but I knew that his doctors had forbidden him from spilling his vital sap, and I myself no longer had any right to desire. The tormented love that I had felt for the only man in my life disappeared, and long-held resentments resurfaced. A bitterness mingled with disappointment secretly overran my heart. I was sad to see him turn his back on a vast empire and a glorious heritage for the sake of his own well-being. I had hoped that, as time passed, he would become a great sovereign, but he had proved to be full of fears and laziness. There were still days when I was moved by his helpless charm and his affable kindness, but there were others when his capricious moods and his selfish longings infuriated me. I disguised my growing weariness with him by lavishing him with affection and attention: I tended to his aches and pains, found new distractions for him, and made sure that I could devote time, patience, and maternal love to him.

I was drowning in the waves of daily life. The caravans and imperial parades snaked through the four seasons between Heaven and Earth. Clothed in green, red, yellow, then white, the trees were resplendent and then withered; flowers exploded and then fell silent. Day after day, night after night, the role of Empress became a full-time occupation, and the discipline I had imposed on my existence wrapped itself around me. I myself had made the chains that bound me, and I headed toward death with open eyes and a dry heart.

An unusually hard drought followed by a famine ravaged the Central Plain. Overwhelmed by the suffering and sorrow of the people, I decided to take on the anger of the gods myself: Considering myself unworthy of my position, I offered my abdication.

*   *   *

MY HUSBAND REJECTED my request, and the Outer Court, in a state of panic, signed a petition begging me to remain on the throne. In the first year of the age of the Supreme Element[16], Little Phoenix took the title of Celestial Emperor offered by the Court, and during the course of the ceremony, he conferred on me the golden blade and seal of the Celestial Empress. The fine gauze behind the throne that screened my seat was removed, and in palaces where receptions were held, two thrones now stood side by side. Up in the heavens, the stars foretold a luminous future for me, and yet, I could see only shadows.

My husband and his ministers had capitulated. My power was no longer contested. I returned to work giving audiences and scrutinizing political reports, as a weaver returns to her loom. I no longer needed to fight to secure my position. For the first time in my life, I tasted the bitterness of boredom. But it was in one of these moments of darkness that Heaven heard my prayer: It sent me a sign, a gift, a sparkle, and my life was suddenly set alight.

The precocious literary talents of a little servant girl had met with high praise in a report written by the eunuch professors at the Institute of Letters in the Inner Court. I was intrigued by her family name: I discovered that she was the granddaughter of Shang Guan Yi, the poet chancellor who had plotted my dismissal. After the execution of male members of her clan, she had followed her mother in becoming an imperial slave. I had her poems sent to me. Her calligraphy revealed a firm but supple wrist, and her verses had the direct elegance of simple cadences. If I had not been informed, I would never have guessed that these words had been written by a fourteen-year-old girl.

The child was summoned to my palace. Her fringe concealed the tattoos borne by the condemned, and she replied to my questions with considerable aplomb. Her blend of shyness and an indefinable assurance gave her charm. Listening to her, I remembered the Gracious Wife and her soft voice. My stomach lurched: This child reminded me of

---

[16] A.D. 674

that devastating passion. Her huge eyes seduced me. Her smile was defiant. I could hear her unspoken question: "Would you dare to love me?"

That very evening, trembling in every limb, Gentleness offered me her virginity, and I initiated her in the realms of pleasure. I had just turned fifty. I had had her father, her grandfather, and all her brothers executed. I was the jailor and torturer whose tyranny she worshipped. She was the pale flower I would transform into a resplendent peony.

Sensual delight colored my world. Love is insolent. Disguised as a page, Gentleness followed me day and night from my palace to the audience hall. When I sat, she remained standing; when I held secret meetings with ministers, she kept watch at the door; when I flew into a rage, her expression of silent amazement appeased me. When I ordered her to rest, she would retire to her room and write. Her poetry soothed me with its chaste descriptions of festivities and journeys. As I held her in my arms, I wondered when she would betray me and avenge her clan's extermination. Hers was a perfume of innocence and poison. Shy caresses preceded her violent release, shaken by an unknown pain. She would scream, and she would cry.

Her sleeping face held the dangers that made me feel young and strong.

TIME DIES, AND time is born again, but men's lives are a one-way journey. Imperial birthdays were excuses for sumptuous festivities. Fireworks and banquets were laid on for the people in every town—our imperial generosity being matched by our subjects' dissolute celebrations for a transient pleasure. From one year to the next, our ages accumulated and weighed us down. From one year to the next, these birthdays changed and saw me mourning our long-buried youth. The sovereign's inevitable deterioration gave real meaning to a vague concept: Death was lying in wait for us.

But it was the Supreme Son who succumbed to coughing and breathlessness. Splendor left us forever. The passing of his beloved heir affected the Celestial Emperor so profoundly that it provoked chest pains. United with my husband in grief and anguish, I forgot my resentments. Little Phoenix clung to me more than ever, as the shipwrecked cling to a piece of flotsam. And the fear of losing him paralyzed me more than ever. The memory of Father's death, which had been such a brutal loss, came back to haunt me. I could clearly remember the utter dejection of those childhood days. Would I have the strength to survive another such onslaught? Little Phoenix and I had been living as prisoners of the Forbidden City for forty years now. His very presence was the air I breathed; he was the balancing pole to my tightrope-walking soul. How would I cope with the emptiness and loneliness when he joined the gods and embraced freedom?

Medicine, prayer, and magic services secretly arranged in monasteries sustained the Emperor but did not cure him. There were more and more bad omens. I had just announced a pilgrimage to Mount Song for another blessing from Heaven, but a Tibetan attack forced me to abandon the expedition. During the Eternal Ancestor's reign, the Court had planned to build a Temple of Clarity dedicated to the sacred religions, as a symbol of union between imperial power and the will of Heaven. The idea had matured, and now the architects' plans were ready, but an incident ruffled the serenity of the proceedings and delayed this building project that had been wanted for so long. Wisdom, my second son, tried to usurp the throne. He was stripped of his title as heir and driven from the Capital.

There was a succession of terrible natural catastrophes. After a winter that yielded no snow, cereal production dropped in the north and the region near Luoyang declared penury. Later a very wet summer saw the Yellow River burst its banks, and the floods were followed by an epidemic that killed tens of thousands of horses and cows. The following year, clouds of locusts descended on the fields, and an earthquake rocked both capitals. The Ancients said that when the natural elements were unsettled in this way, great misfortune would befall the Empire. They even specified that if, amid all this fury, the Earth began to tremble, Heaven was announcing the death of an eminent man.

Exploiting the difficulties our empire was suffering, the Turks rose up against us. Negotiations with them failed, and I had to send imperial troops to put down the rebellion with bloodshed. I may have maintained the country's stability by force of arms, but in the Inner Palace, I was completely disarmed by just one man's illnesses.

In the residential city of the Celestial Oblation, my husband's body doubled in size, and violent spells of dizziness and headaches pinned him to his bed. He lay behind the curtains moaning while a crowd of doctors thronged round him. The Supreme Son and the Great Ministers knelt beside him. It was their duty to approve prescriptions and to taste each remedy. I dismissed all these people whose agitated bustling was only weakening my husband. I set up my own bed and my writing table in his palace of rest. With one hand I countersigned political decisions, and with the other, I held the sovereign's limp, clammy hand. He was soothed by my presence; drinking in my strength, he seemed to improve and asked for food.

I spoon-fed him some soup; thirty years earlier, he had been the one who did this for me. I remembered his distraught face full of love, his tentative voice asking me to be his empress. Tears clouded my eyes: if only I could die and he could be resuscitated!

But the gods remained deaf to my pleas. Once again Little Phoenix would betray my hopes. One evening when he had been bled from his head, his pains disappeared, his eyes regained their sight, and he smiled at me.

"Sovereign Father appeared to me in a dream," he murmured. "He invited me to follow him, and I started to float through a sea of clouds. Father led me through the fog and raised his arm to point to the horizon. The mists dispersed to reveal a golden palace surrounded by light, and flying round it were phoenixes with wings in nine colors. I realized that this was the celestial residence of Sovereign Father, Empress Mother, and my beloved sister, Little Bull. Music began to play, an extraordinary tinkling sound. A procession of immortals came from far away to greet me. And I decided to come back to Earth to tell you that I'm leaving!"

Tears streamed over my face.

"Empress," the sovereign continued, "my time has been accounted for. What a shame the heir is not ready to reign—this one concern means I cannot leave in peace."

"Your Majesty tortures himself in vain," I cried. "He will soon be well again. Next year he will undertake the pilgrimage to Mount Song, and Heaven will bless him and grant him the secret of immortality."

"I'm so tired of living in pain. The apparition of Sovereign Father has calmed my fears. Death is nothing. It is abandoning a rotting, worthless body; it is a soul ascending. The peak of the sacred mountain, which is the highest most point to the living, will be nothing but a blade of grass when I am in the heavens. Be happy—I am to be delivered!"

I was silenced by Little Phoenix's words. It was too late to hold back a man who had laid eyes on the marvels of the afterlife. In his eyes all the riches and delights of this world were now mere filth and dust.

"Majesty," I said despairingly, "allow me to follow you; I want to continue serving you."

"Heavenlight, I have been a very ordinary sovereign. My only good quality has been that I have succeeded in surrounding myself with people more able than me. I have never liked being on the throne or giving commands. But I was able to make a great empress of you. If I had to enumerate the achievements of my time on Earth, I would say that you were my masterpiece. Before we are temporarily parted—because, later, you will come to join me—I wanted to thank you for your patience, for the sacrifices you have made, for risking your own life to give me heirs. Forgive me if I caused you suffering."

I was overwhelmed by the thoughts milling in my mind. I was about to reply when the sovereign interrupted me, his voice reduced to a feeble hiss: "Heavenlight, your hour has not yet come. You must stay here to watch over the dynasty. The heir is too young; when I die, he will not know how to run an empire weakened by natural disasters and uprisings. I have faith in your experience. You will know how to master the situation and restore order and stability to the world. Heavenlight, look after yourself; I am trusting you with my people and my empire."

His eyes closed, and I cried: "Little Phoenix, don't abandon me!"

I thought I saw a mischievous smile on his face as he whispered almost inaudibly: "I've always wanted to die before you, did you know that?"

THE COURT HASTILY left the Palace of Celestial Oblations. The Celestial Emperor lay on his bed in a carriage drawn by two hundred coachmen. The imperial road to the eastern capital would be the route he took toward his death. To reach the world of clouds and eternal ease, my husband endured his final torment. I stayed beside him, grimly fascinated by the terrifying process of dematerialization that would render him immortal: his skin had to be burned of its filth until only purity and incandescence were left. The soul that had been called up by the gods had to break free from the flesh that housed it to fly up to the heavens.

At Luoyang, border troubles forced me to leave the dying sovereign's side to hold audiences alongside the heir regent. For the first time I was inattentive, distracted, listening out for messengers coming to bring me news of his death. Human affairs seemed so futile to me now that I had seen the splendors of another world through my husband's agony. When the meeting was over, I hurried back to the Inner Palace and went back to my prayers at Little Phoenix's bedside. It was now he, a dying man, who gave me strength and warmth and illuminated my entire existence.

On the third night of the twelfth moon in the second year of Eternal Purity, the astrologers were burning tortoise scales, and they announced the word "severing." The following morning the Celestial Emperor woke and found that his pains had disappeared. He spoke clearly, and he himself wanted to announce the Great Remission and the Changing of the Era to the name the Magnificent Path. Doctors and eunuchs managed to lift him from his bed and to wrap him in fur-lined tunics. A litter carried him through the narrow passageways of the Forbidden City and took him to the pavilion at the top of the Gate of Celestial Law.

On the far side of the moat, beyond the square formations of cavalry and foot soldiers, were the common people who had come from the four corners of the city. They prostrated themselves before him. Morning snow had covered the roofs of the eastern capital; temples, bell-towers, and pagodas looked alike in the flurrying greyness, and princely pavilions could hardly be distinguished from merchant's houses and more humble dwellings.

For a moment the Celestial Emperor's gaze lingered on the horizon to the west and focused through the fog and falling snow on Long Peace, his native town. Drums, bells, and gongs began to sound. The sovereign could not read his decree because the jubilant people were already crying "Long live the Emperor!"

That afternoon he summoned ministers; the Supreme Son; the King of Yu, Sun; and Moon, the Princess of Eternal Peace to his bedside. He dictated his will: ". . . seven days will be sufficient for the funeral ceremonies; the heir will ascend to the throne in the presence of the coffin; the tomb and the funeral city will be built in sober style; the government will consult the Celestial Empress on important military and political matters."

Early in the evening, my husband woke feeling very short of breath. He asked for an anaesthetizing drug, and, before sinking back into sleep, he called me over to his bed and took my hand.

Night fell, but I dared not move. As I held his hand in mine, I was his last link with the world of the living. There in the flickering candlelight, with his hollow cheeks, sunken eyes, and dry lips, he already looked like a pallid corpse. A cold current suddenly ran through the palm of my hand, and I heard muted music, a tinkling of crystal, silver bells and jade flutes.

Little Phoenix's face relaxed. Smoothed of their suffering, his motionless features had all the elegance of sculpted marble and the beauty of an enigmatic mask. His half-open eyes continued to watch the gods as they gathered invisibly around him. His lips were drawn out to the corners of his mouth, already in an expression of rapture.

I waited for the divine music to fade before rising to my feet. Eunuchs opened the doors of the palace wide. In the lantern light, I saw no hint of white snow in the square courtyard, so full was it of princes and ministers prostrating themselves on the ground. Town criers chorused the words I murmured: "The Emperor of China has risen up to Heaven. The greatest empire in the world has been orphaned."

The people dressed themselves in the white of mourning. Music, laughter, and banquets vanished from every household. For seven days the Court carried out the simplified version of the twenty-seven ceremonies for putting the body in its coffin. For seven days the city of Luoyang rang to the sound of lamentations, esoteric prayers, and Buddhist recitations. For seven days incense dispersed from ritual basins and columns of gray smoke haunted the sky.

In his will my celestial husband had not specified where his tomb should be built. But as he stood at the top of the Gate of Celestial Law, his gaze had led me to understand that he wanted to return to his birthplace. Against the advice of ministers who wanted to bury him close to Luoyang, I rushed a delegation to Long Peace: Ministers of Human Affairs, engineers from the Department of Major Works, and experts in geomancy from the Funerals Department.

This commission sent messengers back to me with sketches and descriptions of the sites they had inspected. On my very first reading, I was drawn to Liang Mountain to the northeast of Long Peace, a site whose astral position corresponded to the number one and to the element of the heavens. It backed onto a chain of lush green hills and, on its eastern side, looked out over the Mountain of Nine Horses where the Eternal Ancestor was buried, while on its western side it quenched its thirst in the River Wu, a limpid source that barred the route to any demons from the Shades. The plain around the River Wei came and prostrated itself before the mountain's southerly face that was defended by two hills, the towers of celestial archers.

A second delegation went to join the first, and they confirmed the prognosis: The mists that rose up from the vegetation on Liang Mountain were the breath of the dragon. It dominated this earthly world and drew on the energies of the sky. It would be a glorious site for a tomb and a guarantee for the Empire's eternal prosperity. I summoned the Great Astrologer Li Chun Feng to my palace and asked him to proceed with the verification. As I would join my husband later, once I was dead, the time and place of our births were converted into numbers and added to those of our children and our ancestors, then divided between the Five Elements, and combined with the twenty-four astral houses and the twelve terrestrial branches. The mathematical calculations lasted three days and three nights, and the results proved to be in agreement with the ideal suggested by the geomancy experts.

The work started as soon the thaw began. Every evening my soul flew westward to a subterranean palace that was growing in the belly of Liang Mountain. The dark, dank galleries grew longer, making their way slowly and painfully to the center of the Earth. The imperial chamber was positioned in the unfathomable depths of life, in the heart of a labyrinth of corridors set with trap doors, arrows and poisons to steer looters toward the false tombs. Frescoes were drawn: Gold, silver, ochre, violet, faces, bodies, and gowns appeared along the whitewashed corridors. I ordered a fresco representing the imperial parade with its thousands and thousands of men and horses. Along the way to the celestial kingdom, even my sister and my niece found their places behind my retinue.

Ramparts were built around the mountain-tomb. A scale model of Long Peace was built district by district with, right in the centre, a sacred citadel dedicated to religion and offerings. The sovereign's personal bed clothes were transported to a palace identical to the one he had occupied in his lifetime, recreated at the top of the mountain. All along the Divine Way, the central axis of the funeral town, I positioned statues of lions, winged horses, and ministers accompanied by our sixty-one vassal kings.

I disobeyed the ancestral tradition of erecting a commemorative stela for a sovereign, and I built a granite monument on which craftsmen engraved an epitaph of eight thousand characters, a long poem in which I spoke of my celestial husband's life and glorious reign.

On the fifteenth day of the fifth month, the imperial procession set off for the west, led by my son, Future. All along the way, dignitaries, merchants, craftsmen, and peasants set up altars. There was an endless succession of paper houses decorated with gold leaf. White flags, ribbons of hemp, and funeral money fluttered in the wind and blotted out the sky.

The horses had no plumes, and princesses went without their jewels. The musicians played funeral airs as they walked. My husband's hearse, covered in a white sheet and drawn by one thousand soldiers in mourning, moved away in a cloud of dust.

I ordered the annalists to compose the *Book of Events*, depicting his reign, transcribing his audiences and conversations, narrating his hunting expeditions, and describing how he harangued his warriors. For posterity, they drew up the portrait of a great sovereign.

I closed the residential palaces—the Palace of Ten thousand Sources, the Palace of the Fragrant Cinnamon Tree, and the Palace of Celestial Offerings—they were only so many wonders, so many painful memories, and worthless luxuries.

Who had Little Phoenix been? Eternity would not have been long enough for me to find an answer. He was the motionless core of a vast world, staying still while life spun slowly round him. When I thought I had grasped the flame within him, seen into it, possessed it, it was already far away, glimmering, extinguished.

EIGHT

Future ascended to the throne and inaugurated a new reign. He awarded the august deceased the posthumous title of Lordly Ancestor, appointed his first wife's eldest son as Supreme Son and took up residence in the Inner Court. To make space for him, I had to send Little Phoenix's concubines to monasteries, scores of middle-aged women prostrating themselves on the steps of my palace before leaving in tears.

The bustle of these upheavals broke the silence that had enveloped the Forbidden City since its master's death. The austerity of mourning gave way before these women who were eager to display their youth and beauty. The First Lady, who was now Empress, made her stamp as an arrogant mistress. She attempted to prove that my time had passed, and it was her turn to shine. She was impatient to play the same role I had had alongside the previous emperor.

I pretended not to hear Emerald and Ruby criticizing the intrusion: "The Empress is competing with the imperial concubines for the most sumptuous gowns." I turned a deaf ear to reports that the Empress had driven out my old female officials and recruited girls in their prime. I became furious when I discovered that she was fond of women and had made overtures to Gentleness. Her game of love disguised a plot. By seducing my secretary, she attempted to discover my secrets.

My anger was compounded by my despair at my son's mediocre abilities in the Outer Court. Through my husband's death, I had been elevated to the position of Supreme Empress, and, as Mother Regent, I now had it in my power to issue decrees. My presence during audiences guaranteed some continuity in political orientation and ensured that the make-up of the government remained stable. The two thrones had now been reversed throughout the Forbidden City: I now occupied the seat of honor. The very first day after the period of mourning ended, the Emperor tried to demonstrate his independence. In the Council meeting, he reeled off a series of grandiose ideas that made the Great Ministers blench in horror. We had to send troops to the western border and exterminate the nomadic tribes to preempt their attacks; the rebellious state of Korea must be made to bow before the Empire—three hundred thousand troops should be sent there! The palaces of Luoyang were too confined—the Forbidden City needed expanding, and two polo grounds should be built!

I sat on my throne, silenced by my shame. The Great Ministers openly refuted these impetuous suggestions. After the floods, the earthquake, and the epidemic, the north was reduced to terrible poverty. In some regions, people had resorted to cannibalism. Military expeditions should only be carried out by professional troops. Any major works had to be delayed, not to say cancelled. Piqued by these harsh words, the Emperor turned to me: "These men are deliberately contradicting me. Supreme Majesty, you don't need me here to govern; I'm leaving!"

My third son had had a very difficult birth. For ten whole days, I had battled with the pain, refusing the doctors' advice that I should sacrifice him. It was only thanks to the prayers of the peripatetik monk Xuan Zhang, who had brought us the Great Sutras from India, that this seventh prince of the imperial household had come into the world. Just one year after he was born, Future had received the crown of the Kingdom of Zhou and the seal of the Great Governor of the province of Luo, which included the eastern capital. At twenty, he had become King of Ying and Great Governor of the province of Yong that surrounded the town of Long Peace. For many years, he had attracted attention on the polo ground wearing his floppy hat at a jaunty angle, with his sleeves rolled up and shrieking at the top of his lungs, or at imperial banquets where he would dance gracefully to the tune of *The Snows of Early Spring*. He was a fervent enthusiast of cock fighting and organized tournaments with his brothers, provoking my celestial husband's anger because the latter saw a perverse hint of fratricide in this cruel sport. After Splendor's premature death and Wisdom's dismissal three year's before the Emperor's death, the title of Supreme Son had fallen on this boy who had grown up in the shadow of his two elder brothers. Men reveal their true qualities once they have risen or fallen. Emperor Yang of the previous dynasty, for example, had been a humble and thrifty heir, but had proved to be a despotic and extravagant sovereign. Future had once been a naïve, enthusiastic child, but now that he had been crowned, he was revealing his appalling nature as a pretentious and impulsive man.

My husband had entrusted his people and his empire to me. The Yellow Land devastated by four years of famine was like a vast arid field that needed sowing with new hope. Instead of helping me rebuild it, my son could think only of exploiting the privileges of being Emperor. The young Empress had an ill-fated influence over him; it was she who was encouraging him to set himself free.

A few days later I was informed that the Great Secretary Pei Yan wished to have a secret meeting with me. I sent Gentleness to find him, and he took an underground passageway to reach my calligraphy pavilion. When he saw me, he prostrated himself completely, from head to toe. I was curious to know why he used this salutation that demonstrated total submission, and I ordered him to speak without delay. That very morning, he said, the sovereign's private officials had come for him to take him to the Palace. Future had dictated two decrees to

189

him. In the first, the son of his wet-nurse was granted a noble position in the fifth imperial rank, and in the second, the Sovereign Lady's father was appointed Chancellor and made a member of the Council of Great Ministers. All imperial orders had to be approved and published by the Imperial Secretariat, and Pei Yan had tried to dissuade the sovereign, explaining that such unreasonable promotions would encourage the political ambition of the Empress's family. Future had been so irritated that he had thrown his ink well at the old man, shouting: "I am the Emperor! I do as I please! I shall not only name the Empress's father Chancellor, but I shall also offer him my empire! No one will be able to stop me!"

"Supreme Majesty," Pei Yan wailed, "the Empress Wei Xuan Zhen's noble father was military attaché in the province of Pu. When his venerable daughter was elevated to the position of Heir's Wife three years ago, he was promoted to governor of the district of Yu. He has not yet completed his term of office. As he is a man of no particular merit, his extraordinary elevation through the imperial hierarchy would awaken suspicions among officials. Your Supreme Majesty once wrote *A Warning to Relations from Outside* in which she denounced abuses of power by the families of empresses. Could she now bear to see Lord Wei admitted to the Council of Great Ministers and allow the Empress's clan to take command of Court? The word of a Chinese Emperor is irreversible. For him to announce before his minister and servants that he will give his Empire to Lord Wei amounts to a solemn undertaking that must be respected. Supreme Majesty, dark clouds have come to eclipse the sun. Earth is shaking with fear. Birds are circling over the Forbidden City, afraid to settle. The Tang dynasty is in danger!"

I remained silent. Pei Yan inched closer to me on his knees and prostrated himself.

"Supreme Majesty, the rightful Emperor wants to give this throne conquered by his ancestors to an outsider. This betrayal is not mere negligence; it is a crime that must be punished! The previous sovereign often used to say that all human beings are equals in the face of justice. May your Supreme Majesty apply the law!"

"Lord Pei, please give me one night in which to think."

That evening I ate little. After a long period of prayer, I felt cleansed of all the mire of this earthly world. I took Gentleness with me and climbed to the top of the tower at the observatory. Up there the air was piercingly pure. The moon threw her icy beams over the astronomer's spheres. In the last three years, the celestial area representing the throne had become darker and darker. That evening I saw through a light veil of clouds that the stars were almost extinguished.

On the sixth day of the second month in the era of the Sacred Heir, I invited court officials to undertake the morning salutation in the Palace of the Crimson Zenith, which was usually reserved for the annual Great Veneration. When Future sat on his throne, I took the seat to his right. He immediately sent a eunuch to ask my serving women why I had called him there and whether we were expecting a visit from a foreign king.

The jangling of weapons reverberated around the hall as men climbed the steps to the palace. The Great Secretary Pei Yan and the vice-secretary; the Great General of the cavalry of the Left, overseer of the imperial Forest of Plumes Guard of the Left; and the Great General of the leading army, overseer of the imperial Forest of Plumes Guard of the Right; came into the audience hall in battle dress.

Pei Yan took a scroll from his sleeve and read out loud the decree I had dictated to him in secret the previous evening: "My son, the Emperor Sacred Heir, the fourth Emperor of the Tang dynasty, has turned his back on the teachings of the previous sovereign by neglecting his sacred duty and by dishonoring his ancestors. His actions have tarnished the reputation of imperial authority. Exercising the power passed on to me by the Emperor Lordly Ancestor, I shall therefore withdraw his crown. He shall be disinherited of all his noble allowances and positions and will bear the simple title of King of Lu Ling."

Pei Yan stowed the scroll in his sleeve and climbed onto the stage. He pulled the sovereign from his throne.

"Mother!" my son cried in astonishment. "What mistake have I made?"

Instead of questioning the legitimacy of my actions, Future was behaving like a child found in the wrong.

"You offered the Empire to Wei Xuan Zhen," I said icily. "That was your mistake!"

"It was said in jest, mother."

"An emperor does not speak in jest before his subjects."

"Venerable Mother, forgive me! I shall not do it again!"

The man who had reigned for two months over the world's greatest empire broke down and wept. Princes and Great Ministers remained prostrate at the foot of the stage in the hall. My eyes swept over them looking for my fourth son, Miracle. He crouched with his forehead to the ground, shaking from head to toe.

THE KING OF Yu was called to my palace. When I informed him of the date of his coronation, he stammered: "Venerable Mother, Empress Supreme, our dynasty was founded fifty years ago by the Emperor Lordly Forebear. Since then, the Emperor Eternal Ancestor and my Sovereign Father allowed peace and virtue to triumph over the world. Such a past poses a challenge for their successor. As the youngest in the family, I have never wished for the crown. I have not prepared myself to reign. The honor and power you want to bestow on me are too heavy to bear, and your son has neither the knowledge nor the strength necessary to take them on. To disappoint you would be a crime that your son dares not commit. I would rather remain King of Yu. I beg you, Supreme Mother, choose another candidate!"

Of my four sons, Miracle was the most like my husband. At twenty he still had a pale face and a naïve expression, and his voice reminded me of Little Phoenix's as a young man when he too refused to be emperor. A man who does not like power will suffer from its cruelty. He would be unable to raise his hand in punishment or to untangle the web woven by good and evil. He would be unable to subdue the relations and dignitaries who pose a constant threat to the throne.

"You are my last son," I sighed. "You shall receive the sacred seal of the dynasty. I have no other choice. You must accept your duty."

Miracle's beautiful face was bathed in tears.

"Supreme Mother, my second brother, Wisdom, has been banished for three years. The months of loneliness, the harsh terrain of the south and the weeping of the wind have taught him the error of his past ways. His heart is full of pain and regret. I am sure that if you call him back to the Capital, you will see he has changed completely. He will prostrate himself at your feet and ask your forgiveness. Supreme Mother, I beg your clemency, forgive him the mistakes of youth! He would be a sovereign worthy of your respect."

Hearing Wisdom's name infuriated me.

"Have you received letters from this banished commoner?" I asked, scowling. "Any exchange of information with those excluded from Court is a crime of betrayal punishable with imprisonment and exile. As King of Yu, you should not allow yourself to flout the law."

But Miracle insisted, "Supreme Mother, Wisdom is ready to—"

"Wisdom," I interrupted him, "committed an unforgivable crime in trying to usurp the throne. Even if my heart felt pity for him in his exile, I could not call him back to Court. Such an action would prove a destructive influence for posterity. It would serve as encouragement for every prince to rebel against his sovereign father. As for your brother, Future, I do acknowledge that his rash words did not correspond with his true intentions, but I am obliged to apply the ancestral ruling because to tolerate such negligence would debase the power granted to an emperor. Without respect and without fear, reigning would become child's play, and the dynasty would be overthrown. It is pointless discussing this further: You shall be Emperor of China."

A few days later, I watched with satisfaction as Miracle officially acceded to the throne. Chants and incense, praises from officials, cheers from soldiers, and feasting offered to the people helped to erase the dark days. The new sovereign's wife, Lady Liu, became Empress, and their eldest son took the title of Supreme Son. I inaugurated a new era called the Awakening of Culture. Future and his wife were exiled to the south of the River Long where they would have to meditate on the vanities of this world as they contemplated the inhospitable terrain. Members of the deposed empress's clan were deported to the province of Qin and would perish in poverty.

The new sovereign refused to reign and gave a decree that paid homage to the role I had played beside the late emperor, recognized his own lack of political experience, and announced his decision to entrust the Empire to me. He had his throne removed from the Palace of Audiences and left me to receive the morning salutations alone. He shut himself away in his palace with his discreet retinue and court and appeared by my side only for major occasions.

One evening, my people informed me that the commoner, Wisdom, was secretly planning to escape from his guarded residence. Letters addressed to his uncles and cousins in posts in kingdom-provinces had been intercepted. In them, this unworthy son claimed that my regency was a usurpation and called on all princes by birth to rebel.

I was wracked with sorrow and fury, but I had no time to waste on pointless lamentations. That very night, I called for Qiu Shen Ji, the Great General of the Cavalry of the Left, overseer of the imperial Forest of Plumes Guard, and sent him hastily to the mountainous province of Ba with an army of one thousand cavalrymen. Their mission was to dissuade Wisdom from launching into such foolish behavior again.

My second son had been born in the fifth year of the era of Eternal Shining, in the month of December, during the pilgrimage to the tomb of the Emperor Eternal Ancestor, in an eerily white landscape where naked trees pierced the fog with their slender branches. I carried this embryo in my belly as if issuing a challenge to the Outer Court that refused to grant me a title. Wisdom came into the world as the first snows fell. His life would be one of cold elegance and anxious agitation.

From his earliest years during childhood, it had pained him to be the younger brother of the Supreme Son. There were two years between the boys, and Wisdom had been appointed as his brother's official companion. They were taught by the same masters, read the same books, played the same sports, and were even the same height, and yet the inequalities between them could be seen everywhere: the number of valets, the different salutations, the choice of meals, the colors of their clothes associated with their rank, and the attention paid to them by the Sovereign Father. Wisdom was the King of Yong and would always be his brother's servant.

When he was eight years old, Wisdom left the Forbidden City and moved into his royal palace. He was taught by officials I had chosen and grew up in the outside world, slipping into adulthood behind my back. At fifteen he climbed up the Vermilion Steps and started attending the morning salutation. During ritual ceremonies and imperial banquets, he made sure he was the most elegantly dressed courtier. As well as the ceremonial tunics prescribed by his rank, he always added details that secretly transgressed restrictions and highlighted the fact that he was different. He was made-up by the most skilled, graceful hands; enveloped in the most subtle fragrances; and surrounded by beautiful adolescents with cherry-red lips: His magnificence eclipsed the Supreme Son.

My eldest son, the lamented Splendor, had not worn his name well. He had suffered from shortness of breath even as a child, and had looked on the world with the tenderness and indulgence of a young man struggling under the weight of his own death. Wisdom was eloquent; Splendor spoke only softly. The younger had pink cheeks, the elder a pale face dotted with sickly red patches. The prince liked rare jewels, precious fabrics, wine, and good cheer; the heir to the throne was happy with sober tunics, vegetables, and tea.

One winter's day when Splendor was having difficulty breathing, he begged me to listen to him: "My health is failing, and I am growing weaker. Despite my wishes, I will not be able to perform my duties to the full. Now, the Imperial Father's successor should be a vigorous man: Wisdom is strong and gifted—he will one day make an excellent sovereign. Please do not take my birthright into consideration! I would be happy to surrender my title as Supreme Son to him."

Since the very highest dynasty, there have been countless brothers in the imperial family who have fought for the position of Supreme Son. It was a rare thing for an eldest son to offer his future to someone he deemed worthier than himself. Moved by this selfless act, I took his hand in mine. It was the first time I had touched one of my sons, and this unaccustomed contact made me shudder with happiness and sorrow. Splendor lifted himself up and rested his head on my knees; I held him tightly in my arms.

"It is you that your Sovereign Father and I wish to see on the throne," I told him, stroking his hair. "It is you who have the virtues necessary to be sovereign. You must regain your health!"

Tears trickled over my child's cheeks: "Thank you, Venerable Mother, thank you."

At the time, unbeknown to be me, Wisdom had spies planted in his brother's entourage. It was only later that I learned that this conversation had sown the seed of furious resentment in a jealous brother's heart.

I did not have the time to make a great emperor of Splendor; I did not have the time to teach him the truth about cruelty and compassion, tolerance and punishment; I did not have the time to tell him how to turn cowards into brave men, to make the lazy hardworking, and to make traitors loyal. Splendor died suddenly. Once again Buddha was showing me that everything is illusion.

My beloved son was buried on the Mountain of Eternal Peace near Luoyang. He was given the posthumous title of Emperor of Piety; this was the first time since the ancient dynasties that a king had been raised to the absolute rank after his death. The frescoes along the long subterranean corridor depicted the sumptuous delights of the afterlife. At the entrance I commissioned paintings of scenes showing feasting, hunting, and games with horses whinnying and dogs barking. The very chariots could be heard rumbling, the banners cracking in the wind, and the horns sounding to announce the Emperor's arrival. On the star-studded vaulted ceiling of the funeral chamber, the sun gazed across at the moon, and the most beautiful wives strolled through a garden of blooming peonies. I hoped that Splendor, who had renounced the light and the changeability of this world, would still be living amid happiness and beauty thousands of years later.

Wisdom succeeded his brother in the title of Supreme Son and became actively involved with politics. In his Eastern Palace, he received intellectuals who acted as his scribes, and he started compiling books. My husband's health was failing at the time, and I was informed that officials were secretly gathering in the heir's household and criticizing my interference in affairs of State. It was not long before Wisdom gave his father a new version of *The History of the Later Han Dynasty* in which he rebuked regent empress mothers and referred to them as usurpers. I responded by writing two books intended for him: *Advice to the Supreme Son* and *The Anthology of Sons Famous for Their Filial Devotion*.

Wisdom cherished a particular adolescent whom he had had castrated. In the evenings, behind the closed doors of his palace, he organized feasts where he ran naked through the gardens with his guards and this emasculated favorite. When the noises from these orgies reached my husband over the walls of the Eastern Palace, he was furious and decided to punish the adolescent responsible for corrupting the king. The beautiful boy was snatched on a street corner and beaten by hired thugs, and he made some unexpected revelations: His master had had the Taoist Ming Chong Yan assassinated for refusing to poison me, and he was now planning a coup.

The Eastern Palace was searched, and the stables were found to be housing hundreds of weapons and breastplates, ready to equip a light cavalry. The coup was stopped just in time, and Wisdom was stripped of his title and banished from the Capital.

I discovered from his entourage that he knew I was not his true mother: Twenty years earlier, on the great pilgrimage, Elder Sister had delivered an illegitimate boy conceived with my husband. The very next day I had brought a stillborn child into the world. Ruby and Emerald were responsible for informing the sovereign and for swapping the infants. Claiming that she felt unwell, Mother left with the prince's chill body wrapped in her coat and buried him in a monastery.

My son lay beneath a stela with no inscription. Wisdom, who was destined to be abandoned, could have taken his place on the throne. But the truth that we learn is more murderous than lies. Convinced that he was unloved, obsessed by imaginary hatred, he mistook my strict expectations and my severity for the deliberate oppression and gratuitous nastiness of a stepmother. In our eternal China, nothing comes closer to absolute power than the position of heir, and there is nothing more perilous than life spent so close to the flame. Some, like Wisdom, tried to force fate: The door was open, but it led only to downfall.

The Great General sent me a dispatch: Wisdom had hanged himself in his room. I had his body interred immediately, beneath a meager mound with no ornamentation, in an underground chamber with a few everyday objects. To appease evil minds who would have seen this as an assassination dressed up as suicide, I summoned the dignitaries to a lamentation ceremony. I wept tears of regret in public and granted a pardon to this rebellious son, restoring his crown as the King of Yong, the title he had borne as a youth.

My efforts to be joined to my children by a simple bond of happiness had proved fruitless. From the moment they were born, the distance between princes and an empress had only grown wider. I never breastfed my babies and had to disguise my jealousy as I watched them clutching avidly at other women's breasts. As a young mother, I had been powerless to change the ancestral rules. My children were raised and instructed by high-ranking officials; they were taught to be afraid of me and to venerate me as a divinity. They grew up without learning so much as one poem from me. Whatever the circumstances, my thoughts and words for them took the form of orders transcribed onto silk by secretaries that they received on bended knee. At fifteen they were married and learned of physical pleasure. Their courts lay outside the Imperial City, and they opened their doors to ministers' sons, guards, and their own ambitious cousins starting out on their careers. Their servants led them to believe that they were great men. Splendor decided to bide his time, and Wisdom wanted to make his mark. Miracle chose silence and Future rebellion.

At sixty, when women my age enjoyed the warmth of a happy home and played with their grandchildren, I felt more alone than ever. Little Phoenix had made his way to the heavens, and I to the abyss. Two of my sons now lay underground, and one was banished. Fearing that Wisdom's supporters would get hold of his heirs and use their names to raise a rebel army, I had my grandsons repatriated into the Eastern Capital and shut away in a wing of the Forbidden City. Future's family had gone with him into exile. Along the mountainous roads, his wife had brought a little girl into the world prematurely. With no midwife, Future himself had pulled her from her mother's belly and hauled off his own tunic to swaddle her.

Gentleness stayed by my side, a young woman now, speechlessly contemplating my sorrow.

A FEW LETTERS sent by Wisdom had escaped the vigilance of the guards and had been propagated over the world. Seven months after his suicide, an insurrection erupted. Li Jing Yei, the grandson and heir of the Great General Li Ji, who had recommended me to the Forbidden City fifty years earlier, led a rebel army. He had been driven out of the Capital for corruption, and he and his supporters hoped to come back to Court as liberators. They succeeded by occupying the strategic town of Yang and gave command to a man who looked like Wisdom and claimed that the king was not dead, that they were acting on his orders. In the span of ten days, they gathered an army of one hundred thousand volunteers, a rabble of hooligans and bandits lured by the promise of incredible booty.

That morning I received the officials' salutation in Luoyang. The pillars in the Palace of Virtuous Authority were like black dragons reaching up for the dark skies. Fires blazed along the rows, lighting the ministers' anxious frightened faces. After the prostration and the prayer for long life, Pei Yan handed me the declaration that the rioters had distributed through districts that were now in their control.

Gentleness spread the scroll out on my table. The first verse seemed to jump off the page at me like a jet of venom: "The aforementioned regent Lady Wu is the issue of vile origins. In her youth she was summoned by the Emperor Eternal Ancestor, then she seduced Sovereign Father, debauched the Inner Palace, and bewitched the Supreme Son. She supplanted the Empress with her slander; her treacherous smile drove our master into an incestuous trap. Her heart is slyer than a lizard's and crueler than a she-wolf's. She is possessed by demons; she tortures loyal servants. She killed her sisters and assassinated her brothers. She hastened the sovereign's death and poisoned her mother. Now that she has committed these murders, she no longer hides her usurpatory ambitions. She has imprisoned the heirs to the throne and entrusted affairs of State to members of her family. She is a cannibal, eating her way through the imperial lineage; she is evil, putting the dynasty in peril. Her crimes have provoked the wrath of men and of the gods. Her very existence sullies the purity of Heaven and Earth. . . ."

In the second half of the manifesto, its author sang the praises of the rebel leader Li Jing Yei: ". . . Jing Yei, a former servant to the Imperial Court, the son of noble and glorious lords, has been denied power because he denounced corruption. Since then his indignation has grown more furious than a rainstorm, and he has sworn that he will free the throne from these vampires. Summoned by the disappointment of this world beneath the heavens and mandated by the Will of the People, he has raised the flag of revolt to cleanse away the scum of humanity. As far as the Land of One Hundred Tribes to the south and the limits of the Mountains of Rivers in the north, iron horsemen jostle to be first in line, wheels of jade rumble constantly onwards, everyone is marching on the enemy. Our grain stores are full of red sorghum from the four seas; our yellow banners advance inexorably as impetuous waves in a storm. The whinnying of our horses silences the North Wind itself, the gleaming blades of our swords outshine the celestial constellations. Our troops have only to whisper for entire hills and valleys to collapse; when our troops utter war cries, the clouds and the wind change color. With this strength, what enemy can resist us? With this strength, what city could withstand us?"

The third part was the height of pathos: ". . . The earth poured onto His Majesty's tomb is not yet dry, and already his orphans no longer have a right to exist. . . . If you still cling to the warmth of your home, you will be lost in the labyrinth of fate! If you do not grasp the providential hour, you will flounder in the hour of downfall! Answer me now—this very moment: Who shall be sovereign of the Empire, who shall own the Black Lands, who shall be master of the Yellow People!"

I closed the scroll and looked up. I asked who had wielded this quill. Someone in the audience hall replied that it was the scholar Luo Bin Wang.

"Surely he has a reputation for having been a precociously gifted poet, already famous by the time he was seven? What a shame that his flamboyant style and powerful gift should have been used to serve these intriguers. For a poet to become an instrument of politics, for the genius of an artist to debase itself and surrender itself to be used for dishonest propaganda—what a pity! How is it that I did not hear of him sooner? The fault lies with the Great Ministers who have neglected such talent. Mistakes like this must not be made again!"

My calm reaction astonished the ministers and reassured the generals. The Meeting could go ahead in an atmosphere of confidence. Suddenly, in among the vociferous opinions that needed quashing immediately, Great Secretary Pei Yan made his voice heard: "Supreme Majesty, your servant feels it would not be sensible to raise an imperial army!"

Surprised by his attitude, I asked him why.

"His Majesty the Emperor Heir has already reached adulthood, but Your Supreme Majesty is still governing in his place. This irregular situation means that the rebels are right to call for the reign of a prince by blood. If your Supreme Majesty hands over the reins and gives power to the sovereign, all this agitation will no longer be legitimate and could be calmed with no crossing of swords."

I was more stunned by Pei Yan's words than by the rioters' shattering manifesto. Thirty years earlier, this Great Secretary had been nothing more than an impoverished scholar from commoner stock. I myself had noticed him during the last stage of the imperial competition, and, on my orders, he had been received at the Splendid Institute of Letters, the school of higher administrative studies established by the sovereign Eternal Ancestor to train future ministers. As a reclusive Mandarin, he knew neither how to build up a network of contacts nor how to espouse a political leaning. His career had taken off only when I perceived his qualities as a hardworking and incorruptible official. In fifteen years, under my protection, he had climbed up the imperial hierarchy and had become head of government. Now, when I most needed his support, his conciliatory attitude was worse than a betrayal. Instead of condemning the rebels, he was acting as their mouthpiece by publicly accusing me of monopolizing power for too long.

Outside the day was dawning. A continuous stream of light flooded the audience hall, and the sun opened its arms to me. I disguised my anger and smiled.

"Lord Pei, I helped the previous sovereign for almost twenty years without making a single mistake. Heaven and Earth demonstrated their satisfaction during the Great Sanctification, and the Chinese people have recognized the value of my advice by giving me the title of Celestial Empress. My regency is now the only guarantee of imperial stability after all the troubles that have afflicted the land of China. That is why the previous sovereign and the sovereign heir both confided the dynasty to me. It would not be difficult to hand power to my son, but this small gesture would be an unconditional surrender on my part. In the eyes of the people, it would be as if I recognized these unfounded accusations and encouraged every lawless creature to disrespect our authority. Even though I have for some time fostered the desire to withdraw gently from the affairs of this world, it will not be possible in the immediate future. The imperial order has been flouted. The prestige of ancestral sovereigns has been called into question. In such a situation, no prince by blood thrust into the forefront of the political scene would be respected by his vassals. He would simply be manipulated. Lord Pei Yan, you who once demonstrated such extraordinary perceptiveness, why are you now so blind?"

BACK IN THE gynaeceum, it took me a long time to recover from Pei Yan's insolence, and I was weighed down by a dark feeling of foreboding. I gave orders for the guard around Future's residence in exile to be reinforced, then I sent spies to listen to Miracle's conversations with officials.

The overseeing magistrate Cui Cha asked for a secret audience.

"On his death bed," he whispered, "the previous emperor asked Pei Yan to watch over the government. This bequeathed power must have nurtured some unspeakable ambition in him. That is why, instead of defending your Supreme Majesty, he is now asking you to abandon your regency. Everyone knows that the sovereign heir has no political experience and that he would not be a firm ruler. Calling the sovereign back to the throne would be to entrust power to Pei Yan. Your Supreme Majesty should be wary of this."

This comment complied with my own investigations. I delayed sending an imperial army out against the rioters and increased the number of guards protecting the Inner City. Within a few days, secret enquiries into Pei Yan's activities revealed that one of the principal organizers of the revolt was his nephew. Apart from this relationship, there was nothing to prove the Great Secretary's guilt.

I had made my decision, even if there were still doubts that should have worked in Pei Yan's favor. It no longer mattered to me whether he was guilty or innocent. The riot led by Li Jing Yei, grandson of the Great General who was a veteran of the dynasty, had sown the seeds of unease in the Outer Court. Men who had obeyed me blindly were beginning to doubt my legitimacy. Pei Yan's position served only to reinforce this destructive tendency. Pei Yan had been made Great Secretary on my husband's wishes, and with my support, he had dethroned my son Future. His power had become a danger that I had to suppress quickly.

One wintry morning during the salutation, I ordered Pei Yan's arrest. The generals of the Forest of Plumes Guard led their troops into the Palace. Taken by surprise, a number of ministers pleaded his innocence, but the Great Secretary submitted without protest or tears as he was stripped of his cap of lacquered black linen, his ivory tablet, and his leather belt sewn with jade discs.

During that same ceremony, I sent orders for Great General Li Ji's grave to be destroyed because he had begat an insurgent grandson. "Let the name Li, presented to him by the Emperor Eternal Ancestor[17], be withdrawn. Scatter his bones over the countryside!" By persecuting this dead minister who had been so close to me, I was warning any living person who might dare betray me. That day the imperial divisions received orders to set out. Three hundred thousand armored soldiers hastened to the occupied cities. Soon news of victories was sent back to me. The so-called rebel army was nothing but a horde of beggars who fled when they saw our banners. A revolt had broken out within their own ranks. Forty days after their dramatic declaration, the insurgent soldiers were asking to surrender by offering me the severed heads of Xu Jing Yei[18] and his followers. I had them paraded on pikes through

[17] In imperial China, Emperors often presented close dignitaries with their family name, a gesture intended as a sign of supreme favor. Before being called Li Ji, the Great General had had the name Xu Ji.

[18] Li Jing Yei, before the family name Li awarded by the Emperor Eternal Ancestor was withdrawn.

the centre of Luoyang where they soon streamed with spittle from my people.

My imperial officers executed every last survivor of the rebel chiefs. When Cheng Wu Ting, Great General of the regiment of Eagles of the Right, was denounced to me for having secret meetings with the rioters, I asked for no further proof, and, despite his reputation as the conqueror of the Turks and the Koreans, I sent the Great General of the regiment of Eagles of the Left to behead him in his barracks.

After Pei Yan was arrested and his quarters had been searched, the examining magistrate informed me that the Great Secretary had lived in a state of destitution. His furniture was rudimentary and his rooms quite without ornamentation. In his six-year term of office as a Great Minister, he had managed to save up a few bags of rice and a dozen rolls of silk, gifts given to him by my late husband and myself.

I was moved by the man's honesty. In prison he would not admit to the crime of which he was accused and never proclaimed his innocence. In mid-autumn he was decapitated in the middle of a public crossroads. Before dying he allegedly asked for forgiveness from his banished brothers: "When I was in power, I never let you benefit from my position; now, because of me, you have been exiled to the ends of Earth. I am so sorry!"

I chose to ignore whether he deserved to die. His condemnation had been a deciding factor in the fight against the insurgents. I secretly ordered for his head and body to be collected and given a decent burial in the countryside near Luoyang. Occasionally, on the anniversary of his death, I would send a few offerings and prayers to his grave.

Within the Forbidden City, my voice echoed solemnly around the Palace of Virtuous Authority: "Gentlemen, I have never disappointed Heaven, you know that well! I served the previous sovereign for more than twenty years, and the Empire's affairs have caused me much concern! I have watched over the stability and happiness of this world. I have offered wealth and nobility to all of you. Since the previous sovereign abandoned you and entrusted me with command, I have never troubled with my own health; my every thought has been for the happiness of the people. These rebels were ministers, generals, and Court officials. Where, then, is loyalty, and where is honor? Shame on you! I am not afraid of treacherous, rebellious men. I ask of you: Who among you would be more powerful, more sour-tempered, and more stubborn than hereditary minister Pei Yan? Who would be more violent, more reckless, and more inflamed than Xu Jing Yei descended from one of the dynasty's Veterans? Who would be more experienced, more adroit, and more tactical than Cheng Wu Ting who never suffered military defeat? Those three men were believed to be indomitable! When they tried to betray me, I cut off their heads. If you consider yourself better than them, then you must revolt straight away. If not, work together and save all your energies for helping me in affairs of State. Prove yourselves worthy of posterity!"

IN THE FIRST month of the first year in the era of the Residence of Sunlight, I begat a new world. The imperial banners of ancient times disappeared from the city's ramparts, and my golden standards edged with mauve now flapped in the wind. At Court I distributed new colors to the dignitary's clothes: mauve to scholars and generals above the third rank, crimson to the fourth rank, and vermilion to the fifth rank. The sixth rank had to make do with dark emerald green, while the seventh rank wore light green. The eighth and ninth ranks, at the very bottom of the grading system, were given consolation for their humility; I attributed the color of blossoming springtime to them. In government, I did away with the age-old names given to ministers of state. Inspired by the venerable Zhou dynasty from which our Wu clan descended, I wanted politics to be a celebration of life from now on. I published an edict renaming the Great Chancellery the Terrace of Divine Birds; the Great Secretariat became the Pavilion of the Phoenix; and the Ministry of Supreme Affairs became the Lodge of Prosperous Letters. The six ministers responsible for the administration of the Inner City, human affairs, religious rites, armaments, punishments, and major works became Officers of the Heavens, the Earth, Spring, Summer, Autumn, and Winter, respectively.

When stars move across the sky, they transcribe a mathematical perfection. When flowers open, they reveal a universe of harmonious architecture. The seasons unfold in keeping with the order of creation—Germinating, flourishing, ripening, wilting, because where there is death, there is also harvesting. The pinnacle of poetry is silence; a painter's crowning achievement is the white of a virgin sheet of paper; sages meditate with a vacant mind; the illumination of Buddha is the extinction of the world. A sovereign's ultimate power is the abstinence of his authority. The sovereign's will is motionless, highly concentrated, serving as a vehicle for Nature's intelligence in maintaining the balance between light and darkness of the shades. The sovereign's command is calm, steady and determined, transcending the universal evolution of perpetual motion. The sovereign's hand is infinitely powerful and infinitely gentle, applying the invisible laws that fertilize the fields, shift the stars, and call forth migrating birds.

Four months after the era of the Residence of Sunlight was inaugurated, I was ready to pass to the higher phase of my policies.

The era of Lowered Arms and Joined Hands announced my resolve to govern the world without recourse to violence but in a posture of prayer. Before me I would have the gods who had stepped down from the heavens, leading us to happiness, and behind me, a whole country prostrate on the ground. From now on, there would be no arms raised, brandishing the lance of repression. There would be no fruitless struggle and pointless agitation. The demons had been driven out; I would dominate the turmoil of this world with immutable strength.

NİNE

My periods had stopped.

The moon waxed and waned in vain. The crimson tide had run dry.

In this lowly world, women are the ocean's pearls, their brilliance derived from the stain of their flesh. The blood had been the thread linking me to an underground world where a grim labyrinth twisted around a perpetual furnace. It had been the source of all my energy.

As Supreme Empress I had to conceal my failing, but the changes in my mood did not escape my old servant Emerald. One evening she forced me to accept a visit from a woman doctor, an austere creature who wore a man's hat. After a brief examination the doctor prostrated herself and congratulated me: My divine body had returned to its original state. The serenity accorded me by my resting senses would allow me to achieve immortality at last. I did not like the term "resting," and I interrupted her croaking pronouncements with a desultory wave. None of these women who officiated in the palace had known the violence of a phallus or the seismic upheavals of childbirth; virginity had made diaphanous creatures of them. A tree emptied of its sap loses its leaves and dries out. Stripped of my womanly barbarity, it was as if I were dead. The gods were imposing a virtuous widowhood on me, and I accepted their censure. The pleasures of the flesh no longer interested me. Carnal gratification would be the sacrifice I made to the heavens.

My duties running the Empire came to the fore again. Once again I was the weaver before her loom, unraveling inextricable threads. During the day, surrounded by ministers and generals, I forgot my age, my weariness, and the absence of a man to listen to me and support me. In the evening, sitting before my mirror in the Inner Court, I watched as my women dismantled my topknot, my pride, and my deceptive youth. Servants smoothed little squares of dampened silk over my face, and the white powders and red makeup melted away. I had to contemplate my bare skin and the wrinkles that had begun to knit their mesh in the corners of my eyes and lips. There in the candlelight, the mirror invited me to step into the abyss. I pictured Little Phoenix young and beautiful, his eyes brimming with desire. Then an aloof young woman appeared behind him, laughing, teasing him, and then drawing him up onto her horse. Shoulder to shoulder, hip to hip, they disappeared into the dark night of my memory.

Without Little Phoenix, his migraines, and his turbulent emotions, the Inner Court felt empty. In that huge garden that seemed to have been deserted by human beings, every tree whispered, every piece of furniture spoke, every window exhaled a perfume that reawakened snatches of the past. I slept alone and was tormented by insomnia. I would wake Gentleness and order her to walk before me, carrying a lantern. As I arrived in each successive pavilion, the women who kept watch at night prostrated themselves and held open the doors. The rooms I dared not venture into by day were fully lit. Here a zither he had caressed; over there, in front of the aquarium, I could still hear his childlike laugh; here, beneath this window, we once argued; over there, his calligraphy brushes and inkpots—his books still lying open. Sometimes Little Phoenix seemed to walk so close to me, whispering words of love; sometimes I would lose him behind a painted balustrade, as I turned along one of the galleries. He always eventually disappeared into the bushes, into infinity. Sometimes I would even ask for the door to the stables to be opened. When they saw me, his horses would stamp and snort with joy. I would put my arms around his favorite mount, Song of Snow, who would stare at me with sad, steady eyes. I would bury my head in that fine mane and weep.

The shadows had taken Little Phoenix, my father, my mother, my sisters, my niece, and my rivals. For the time being, I had learned to forget my body, which was "resting." I grew accustomed to the lofty height of the throne on which I now sat alone. Alone, I manipulated the pawns on the vast chessboard of an empire orphaned by its master. I was nothing more than a mind, a mind contemplating the world below with chilled compassion.

POLITICAL AFFAIRS KEPT me breathing. I extended the time I dedicated to my work on into the evening to avoid my palace, my prison, my tomb.

The transition in reigns was an opportunity for plots to be revealed, for hidden ambitions to betray themselves. These little problems that needed resolving distracted me and occupied my solitude.

One night, a strange dream disturbed me. Someone was scratching at the door to my pavilion. As there seemed to be no servant on duty, I went to open the door myself. It was dark outside, and there was a little boy standing on the steps. A man! Who had let him into the gynaeceum where all males were forbidden? The child held up both his hands, holding a tiny box. "Could you give me some salt? Please?" Behind me, the room was deserted. In front of me, beyond the threshold, the dark rooftops of the Imperial City spread out to infinity. The wind blew, and I was gripped by an uncontrollable fear. Was he a professional killer, a hired assassin? And yet I could not find the resolve to close the door on him. Perhaps he needed my help? How could I refuse him a few grains of salt? I shook with fear, but in that agonizing moment of hesitation, I decided, in spite of myself, to let him in. As the stranger stepped over the threshold, my fear suddenly dissolved, and I woke feeling amazed and happy.

I confided this dream to the Princess of Gold, the youngest daughter of Emperor Lordly Ancestor, and my friend for thirty years. The princess thought for a while and then smiled at me mischievously: "Does your Supreme Majesty not think that salt gives food its taste? When there is no salt, life is bland and flavorless!"

I could not help myself sighing. In my dream, it had not in fact been a little boy asking for salt, but I, Supreme Empress, begging for the savor of life! The previous sovereign had given me back my freedom. Whatever I wished was now granted. In all of China, I had no other master but myself; I had become my own jailor, and I was my own prisoner.

My distress did not go unnoticed by the princess. She went on: "For a year now, Your Supreme Majesty has worked day and night. She receives me little, but I know she is hiding her sorrow from me, and only keeps going because she has a will of iron. Has she considered that every human body is a fragile organism and that, by accumulating too much melancholy, by neglecting the need for relaxation, it will eventually be exhausted and may suddenly succumb to some fatal illness? It seems that Your Majesty's body has entered into the age of rest. I can, therefore, offer a remedy that will disperse your sadness and fortify your health!"

Intrigued, I asked her what it was.

"Supreme Majesty," she said, blinking slowly, "the yin element must be mixed with the yang element, and the combined force of these two primordial energies creates the seasons, makes the flowers bloom, raises up the wind, and brings forth the rain. Even though Your Supreme Majesty's soul is as virile as a warrior's, your body remains that of a woman. Since our Celestial Sovereign was called to the heavens, the dark exhalations of yin have accumulated in your organs. The weight of them darkens your mood, causes gloominess, diminishes your strength, and beckons old age! Majesty, your servant has in her possession a remedy full of the power of the sun, the remedy you so need. It will recapture forever the freshness of your features, the suppleness in your limbs, and the elation in your spirit!"

Her charlatanism made me smile: the Princess of Gold—a great bulky woman who was impossible to age—was a constant whirlwind of celebrations and pleasure. Born into a jade cradle, raised in the closed universe of the Imperial Court, she maintained a constant battle against the extinction of desire that threatens all such high-born creatures. Strangely, I who loved sobriety, exactitude, and profundity, had become fond of her guileless eagerness, her desperate frivolity, and her debauched escapades that overflowed with joy and tears.

"Come then, princess, do not toy with my impatience, make out the prescription!"

She waved her painted silk fan and breathed these words: "It is late now. I shall go home and find the formula. May Your Majesty reserve the night of the next full moon for me, I shall return with my medication!"

WHEN THE NIGHT of the full moon came, I dined with the Princess of Gold. She became a little drunk and told me stories that would have caused any respectable woman to blush: princesses and their passing fancies for officers of the guard, princes and their attachments to their pages. She laughed as she related all these fatal encounters, all these terrible separations that had torn apart those silken hearts.

It was only after dinner—when, weary of listening to her and of laughing idiotically, I decided to go to bed—that she followed me into my bedroom, helped me to undress, and insisted once more on the excellence of her remedy. I ordered her to show me these magic pills. She smiled mysteriously and asked that the servants withdrew. Then she blew out the candles, and she too slipped away, taking Gentleness by the hand.

I waited on my bed, with my head lying along my arm. In accordance with my instructions, the blinds were left raised every night of the full moon. Outside, the celestial mirror projected the motionless shadows of the bamboos and the millennial cypress trees onto my windows. A long time passed before anyone came in. I called for Emerald and Ruby, but neither of them answered. Suddenly I heard the rustle of a dress, and the door was drawn aside. A tall, unfamiliar silhouette appeared. I thought she must be one of the princess's attendants, and she did in fact raise the bed curtain and give me a cup of sweetened infusion. Then she whispered very quietly that she was to massage me to stimulate the effects of the medicine.

I lay full length on my front. Two strong hands applied slow pressure to the acupuncture points at the nape of my neck. They slid into my hair and rubbed my head, wearied from the constant wigs and golden hair pins. Then they moved down over my shoulders and settled on my spine. The fingers were supple and charged with pleasing energies; wherever they applied pressure, my muscles were eased, and a life-giving warmth spread through my body. I was overcome by a hazy sleepiness and a sense of exaltation. I suspected that the masseuse was herself part of the magic remedy the princess had given me: She was not like any of those I already had. Her palms were wide and vigorous, and they relaxed me while at the same time reawakening ardors that had been extinguished since my husband's death.

Further down, after she had anointed my thighs with fragrant oil, the stranger's manipulations became more equivocal. Her hands glided over my buttocks, sometimes sliding delicately off course. The silent language of her fingers made my blood seethe within me. I encouraged her by spreading my legs slightly. Her middle fingers plunged into the core of me and grew bolder. My prolonged abstinence had made me all the more sensitive, and her caresses provoked quivers that rippled through me. The stranger was an expert. She overcame my nervous agitation and steered me to the first pleasurable climax with great precision. Slowly, she turned me onto my back and took my face in her hands. As she rubbed my cheeks, my eyes, my forehead, and my earlobes, she made me blaze with desire. I rose up abruptly and clasped her in my arms. She fell onto me, and I tore her tunic. Her skin smelled of honey and orchids. Her chest was flat and muscled like a man's, her stomach firm, and I felt an erect phallus.

A man!

A man in my bed, in the bed of the Supreme Empress, widow of the Sovereign Lordly Ancestor!

I leapt up, but he held me in his arms, against his burning member.

"Yes, Supreme Majesty, do not be afraid. I am a man. My name is Little Treasure. I am your remedy. Tomorrow, you will have me beheaded or quartered by chariots. But tonight, let yourself go, allow me to love you."

I cannot give a reason for my capitulation; it is impossible. I, Empress, sworn to virtue. I, a woman preoccupied with matters of State. I, a warrior who had never removed her armor, I, who considered men to be dust and who conversed with the stars. On that night I betrayed Little Phoenix, for whom my heart still mourned. I allowed myself that one weakness by revealing myself, without shame or regret, to a stranger.

My couplings with the Emperor of China had been a conscientious duty. By the time I was thirty, I had become obsessed with perfection and hygiene. I had had my genitals massaged for fear that they would lose their firm outline. I had abstained from spicy food and had drunk infusions to perfume my breath and my sweat. My body had been anointed with oil of peony and rubbed with cedar bark before being delivered, plucked and powdered, to my husband.

When Little Treasure parted my legs, my genitals were neither combed nor perfumed. I had the same nudity, the same lack of artifice as an ordinary woman. It was nearly twenty years since I had felt a phallus in my belly. The stranger tore me in two. For the first time I let myself neglect the man's gratification to concentrate on my own pleasure. Little Treasure moved his hips with masterful skill. He listened to my shivers and conducted the music of my sighs. Where had he learned the art of copulation? It mattered little; the following day I would send him to his death.

215

Suddenly my body began to boil. A scream was torn from my lungs. With great assurance and little effort, the stranger had just delivered me an orgasm, a firework of ten thousand dazzling sparks.

I SPENT A feverish night.

One moment I dreamed that I had tied him up in a sack and thrown him into the river in the grounds; the next I saw him lying poisoned. I was suddenly afraid that I would not wake in time to receive the morning salutation. Then I wondered how I would look my servants in the eye and whether I should have all their eyes gouged out and their tongues cut off.

I woke with a start. In the half light, the stranger was sleeping naked on the crumpled sheets. His bronze skin gleamed. Filled by this giant frame, the bed looked narrow as a cradle. He was very young with a hint of a moustache on his lips. Quite suddenly he opened his eyes and smiled at me.

I had never seen such a happy smile. I was so surprised by it that I forgot my dark thoughts and let him draw me to him. He made love to me again. This time I realized that, in the distant past, Little Phoenix had never granted me such intense pleasure. Unlike my husband, who thought only of his own gratification, the young man guided my body and steered it till it folded on itself, stretched out, and executed contortions. I became his zither, and he made my every string hum, discovering resonances I had not known until then. Dawn was growing lighter. I realized that my muscles were almost intact, that my firm breasts were those of an adolescent. My belly that had brought forth six children had kept its vigorous round outline. Little Treasure's dark eyes betrayed his furious passion and reflected this flattering truth: I was still beautiful and desirable.

GENTLENESS SCRATCHED AT the door and announced that I was late for the morning salutation.

"The Supreme Empress is unwell," I replied. "She will not go to the audience. Tell the officials to withdraw and return to their ministries. Tell the Great Ministers to prepare written reports. There will be no meeting today."

Little Phoenix had often announced this decree while in the grips of a short-lived passion for a young favorite. I remembered finding it irritating, but now how I regretted battering him with my moralizing! For the first time I could appreciate that, beyond the interests of the Empire and my duties as sovereign, I had an obligation to the impetuous demands of my body!

I let my serving women in at midday. They arranged my hair in silence, eyes lowered. I sent Little Treasure to Ruby, who washed him in a side pavilion. He came back wearing a eunuch's tunic. I made sure he shared my morning meal with me. He devoured it, and his appetite and vulgar manners fascinated me. As he ate, he answered my questions, often simply smiling at me instead of speaking.

As the third son of well-to-do peasants, Little Treasure had been educated by the master scribe in his village. At fourteen he slipped away from home for the first time and tried his luck in the imperial competitions held in the regional academy. In the space of three years, he failed three times, but, as he loitered in the streets, he glimpsed a better world. At eighteen he fled an arranged marriage to a cousin from his village and made his way to Luoyang.

He came to the eastern city that I had just named Sacred Capital and wandered aimlessly with no money or relations to call on. He did have a few contacts, beggars from the same district as himself, who found him precarious work as a porter, a mason, or a swindler. He learned to lie, steal, and defend himself; he shivered under the bridges and was kicked by passers by as he gazed enviously at horses with precious stones in their harnesses and carriages draped in gleaming gold cloth. He was eventually taken on by a Taoist who secretly concocted aphrodisiacs and was entrusted with bamboo boxes carrying precious pills with mysterious ingredients. He walked through the streets improvising cheerful tunes expounding their miraculous effects. In the poorest quarters, he would sell a pill for one *sou*, claiming it would cure every kind of sexual ill. In the noble districts, he became friends with footmen and lackeys, swapping these so-called contraceptives for things stolen from their masters. These medicines proved curiously effective, and Little Treasure became famous. Wherever he went there was always someone calling to him cheerfully, warm bread waiting for him, cups of tea offered on the pavement, and children running behind him joining in the chorus of his songs. One day a guard who worked for the Princess of Gold asked him whether he knew a good masseur, and Little Treasure recommended himself. He went into the princely palace by the back door and had not set foot in the outside world since.

The princess liked to bring on a dozen or so beautiful young men in the Side Court of her palace. They were bathed, fed, and perfumed, living like parrots in a cage. Eunuchs taught them how to massage their aging mistress, and on Her Highness's orders, servants offered them their bodies to improve their performance. At night they were summoned in rotation. Occasionally some of them performed services outside the palace—gifts the princess gave to her friends. On her very first night with Little Treasure, she had recognized such exceptional sensuality in him that she set him up in his own pavilion and insisted that he followed a strict diet to purify his skin, hair, intestines, and blood. Apart from the experienced women whom the princess sent to him to widen his knowledge, Little Treasure never laid eyes on anyone. He was dying of hunger and boredom. Then, one evening, someone had called him from his rooms and entrusted him with the sacred mission for which he had been intended.

"Why are you telling me all this?" I asked him, amazed that a stranger should reveal his shameful past without embarrassment or artifice.

"Because when I opened my eyes this morning, I saw the gleam of a sword in your eyes. You will have me executed; I know you will. I left my village five years ago, and I have done nothing but invent lies ever since. I have not had a single friend I could tell the truth about my life. I will die later today. When I'm dead, I will no longer be ashamed of where I came from or my past! Thank you, Majesty, for listening to me."

"It's true, you may well die. Any man who enters the Inner City without my decree is punished with death. But your life has touched me, and I would, therefore, like to give you a chance. You will be castrated, and you will become my eunuch. To ensure that you keep silence about the favor granted to you last night, you will be given a poison that will strike you dumb, but you will be given a position on a par with the fifth imperial rank, and I will allow you to hold my horse's bridle when I ride out."

Little Treasure gave a derisory snort: "Supreme Majesty, fortune and rank mean nothing to me if I lose this little tool between my legs, this gift from my ancestors. It is thanks to him that I live and breathe. If he is taken from me, I would waste away. I would rather die straight away!"

I had never heard such vulgar language, and I marveled at it.

"How old are you, my child? Are you not afraid of death?"

"Supreme Majesty, I was born in the deepest darkest corner of the countryside. My life brought me to this palace, and I have loved the most beautiful and noble woman on this earth. I shall never have another night like that. My twenty-fourth year can be my last—I would die with no regrets!"

I liked his reckless attitude. I would not decide on Little Treasure's fate before the moon was next full. I kept him hidden in my palace like a domesticated animal. Day after day I would come back from the Great Meetings still weighed down with concerns, and I grew accustomed to his enthusiastic greetings and his jubilant chirping that made me forget my busy day. As he gesticulated enthusiastically and told me about what he had done, he revealed a Sacred Capital that I had not known existed: sordid suburbs peopled by lepers and freed slaves converged on plots of wasteland where acrobats, magicians, and monkey-tamers performed. Waterborne gambling clubs and brothels glided along the rivers Luo and Yi. In mid-autumn every year, crowds gathered around the crossroads where executions were carried out. The saber whistled through the air, the head flew off, leaving the body motionless while a stream of crimson blood jetted out of it.

Little Treasure's voice became more serious when he spoke of his homeland. Then scenes would unfold before my eyes with low houses made of beaten earth, and little boys running through the fields naked. I could smell the sheep and the fragrance of apple blossom. I could hear the bustle of a river and the birdsong at dusk. I forgot my serving women, those cold pale dolls, and my ministers with their fabricated elegance and false virtue. The village of Wu loomed in my memory with its mulberry trees and fields of wheat. I pictured a sturdy, little girl with bronzed skin jumping, singing, and climbing. I felt the sun burning my forehead once again and inhaled the happy smell of wet straw mixed with pig dung.

At the age of sixty, I learned that a man could give me more different kinds of pleasure than a woman. Little Treasure had revealed the wealth of all the senses to me. His inevitable death and my desire to hold him in my arms one last time made my ecstasy all the more intense. My face changed imperceptibly: Roses bloomed in my cheeks once more, the hard edge had gone from my eyes. My ruby-red lips glowed without makeup. Sitting on the throne for the morning salutation, I displayed my metamorphosis unashamedly. My voice had new energy, and my responses came more swiftly. I would sometimes smile for no reason during a political debate, and my embarrassed ministers would lower their eyes and prostrate themselves.

One afternoon, during a concert when Little Treasure was sitting behind me, I noticed that he was secretly stroking Gentleness's hand. My breast seethed with anger. As a prisoner in the gynaeceum, he could seduce all the youngest, prettiest, and sweetest serving women behind my back. These women who had been cut off from the outside world all dreamed of knowing the pleasure only a man could offer. Who could resist this incorrigible charmer with his tireless member? I was overcome by morbid jealousy. I had never been so determined to have exclusive rights to a body, a skin, a beating heart. Little Treasure was my little dog, my toy. I, the Supreme Empress, was his owner, his goddess, the depository of his life or death. I knocked over the table and dismissed the musicians with one violent gesture. Alerted by my anger, the young man swore he was faithful to me, and Gentleness prostrated herself at my feet, bathing the hem of my gown with her tears. Ruby pleaded her innocence, and I gave full vent to my anger: "You are all accomplices in this crime! Call the doctors! Have every orifice examined! Throw Gentleness into the Cold Palace for one hundred strokes of the stick!"

The Palace guards tied Gentleness up and pulled her out by her hair. With the young girl's terrified screams still echoing, Little Treasure dragged me forcibly into my bedroom and began massaging me to relax me. He slipped his clothes off in a flash and held me in his arms.

"Supreme Majesty, let me kiss you before I die."

"I shall have you grilled on a fire; I shall have you flayed by a thousand knives; I shall have you cut in half."

"Supreme Majesty, don't scream. Your threats don't frighten me. There is nothing that can hold me back when I desire a woman. At the moment, it is you that I want."

As I lay beneath him, I was wracked by violent spasms and crushed by huge burning waves. It suddenly seemed as if it was my husband holding me by the hips. Men's freedom is their unfaithfulness: the Son of Heaven or the son of a peasant, they could both reduce me to the mediocre torments of a woman.

THE PRINCESS OF Gold informed me that the Outer Court had heard of Gentleness's disgrace and had learned that there was a man in the gynaeceum.

"Supreme Majesty," she said, "if you cannot bring yourself to eliminate him, give him back to me, and I shall make him disappear."

"Princess, this matter is of no concern to you."

My old governess Emerald had the courage to whisper in my ear: "Supreme Majesty, you cannot keep a man in your rooms for ever. Even if your servant watches night and day over the virtue of the Court ladies, I shall stumble across the inevitable one morning. Lord Little Treasure is twenty-four—he is a bull, and you are shutting him away in a birdcage. Let him go, I beg you."

"My poor Emerald, if he leaves, he will talk about me to the whole world! I must kill him. But I cannot . . ."

One of the eunuch officers who oversaw palace protocol wrote to me: "Some time ago the Emperor Eternal Ancestor appreciated the talents of a pipa-player from the Western Kingdom, but it was only once he had been castrated that the sovereign gave him permission to go into the gynaeceum and to teach the Court ladies his divine art. If Little Treasure's knowledge can be of use to Your Supreme Majesty, your servant asks that he undergoes the procedure of castration before having access to the Inner Court. If not you shall be covered with opprobrium."

In the end, my daughter Moon, the Princess of Eternal Peace, released me from my predicament: "Supreme Majesty, Little Treasure is an indispensable remedy to maintain your health and the balance of your energies, and those are qualities that warrant reward. Your child has found a solution that will satisfy both protocol and your own requirements. The Emperor of Clarity of the Eastern Han dynasty erected the Temple of the White Horse to the west of Luoyang some time ago. It was the first Buddhist temple to be built on Chinese soil. Alas, having survived countless dynasties and frequent wars, its fires no longer attract any pilgrims and the temple has fallen into ruins. Why does Your Majesty not present her servant with this sacred place? With his shaven head and his rosary in his hands, a master monk would be allowed to circulate freely in the Inner Palace and no one would be able to reproach Your Majesty for wanting to listen to the wise words of this Buddhist."

My daughter disappeared, and I received Gentleness whom I had freed from the Cold Palace. The girl had been spared the one hundred strokes on my orders, but she had suffered the harsh treatment meted out to all imperial prisoners. In only a few days, she had become thin as a reed.

"I can make you powerful or take your life, do you know that?"

She prostrated herself at my feet in tears, and I sighed: "I know that, here in the Inner Court, Court Ladies, officials, and overseers are only too eager to obey you, and outside these walls, princesses shower you with compliments, and ministers and magistrates bend over backwards to please you. Your mother has been raised from the position of seamstress in the Side Court to the ranks of nobility once more. She has taken up residence in a palace, and I myself have given her precious stones and countless servants. You already have everything a woman could dream of! If you want to take a lover, choose one from among the princes and kings. Leave Little Treasure to me. He is mine."

In my bed chamber that evening I dismissed my serving women and ordered Little Treasure to kneel. My mind was made up: If he did not love me and wanted to leave, he would be killed at the gates of the Forbidden City. If he loved me and decided to become a monk, I would give him honor and glory.

I eyed him sternly.

"You will not be executed or mutilated. I shall give you your freedom."

A little shiver ran through him.

"Will I still be able to see Your Supreme Majesty?" he whispered.

As I gave no reply, he looked up. His beautiful face was bathed in tears: I had not realized that this hard-hearted man could falter too.

"Supreme Majesty, I beg you. Keep me. Don't abandon me! Think of your servant as a dog who asks only for a little food and to stay by your side."

I contained my emotions as I told him, "I cannot keep a man in the Inner Palace."

"Then have me castrated! What does that matter to me now! Never mind if I can no longer give you pleasure and if I become like all the other eunuchs with their flaccid flesh and cloying eyes. I only hope my heart will stay intact and will still love you."

"I would not let you leave as you arrived," I said, trying to test him. "Once outside the Palace, you would be rich. The money I give you would be enough to buy the most beautiful concubines, to start a large family, set up a business, and become a respectable man. Why do you want to remain a slave when you could be a master with women and land? If you wanted you could own merchant ships that could transport you up and down the Empire with their scarlet sails billowing in the wind."

The young man only wept more desperately: "Supreme Majesty, forgive me for hiding the truth from you. I did not leave my village because of an arranged marriage. The great epidemic in the first year of the Era of Eternal Purity killed my parents, my grandparents, and my brothers and sisters. I fled after burying all their bodies in the fields. After that I roamed around Luoyang with death hovering over me. In five aimless years I was beaten, robbed, and raped; I was spat at, kicked, and insulted. You are the first and only woman who took me in her arms as anything more than a tool. No woman in the world, not even my mother, looked at me with the tenderness that you do. Supreme Majesty, forgive me. Keep me in your gynaeceum or have me killed! Don't abandon me!"

Little Treasure's words tore me apart. His distress awakened my own. I sighed and drew him into my arms: "Then you must listen to me and do as I ask. You, the son of a peasant, the vagrant, the aphrodisiac-seller, you shall be respected by the world. If you obey me I shall make you, a man off the streets of Luoyang, into a glorious Lord in the Imperial Court."

LITTLE TREASURE'S SUFFERING was that of my people, and I felt ashamed for living in artificial abundance within a fortified city. This Court bathing in its happiness was a miraculous island in an ocean of misery. When I resolved to change Little Treasure's fate, the fate of one child picked up by the wayside of life, it was not merely to reward his devotion: He was my window to this world of despair. The Mandarin Competitions had allowed thousands of scholarly individuals to enjoy a better life, but diplomas could in turn become barriers, and opening doors could transform into exclusion. Peasant children, orphans, and abandoned youngsters still had no right to fulfill their talents. Little Treasure was one of these battered, frustrated creatures, and I was offering him a chance.

On my orders, the young man shaved his head and became a monk. As a member of the bonze community, he broke with his past and became unimpeachable. He surrendered the name Feng and the common first name Little Treasure, and I gave him the Buddhist title of Scribe of Loyalty. I asked my daughter's husband, Xue Shao, to recognize him as a distant uncle, and from then on, he bore the name of the famous aristocratic Xue clan.

The impostor proved to be a genius: Scribe of Loyalty had that raw intelligence that has never been damaged by academic study. His time as a vagrant had sharpened his intuition, which was more effective than any bureaucratic reflections. His audacity and imagination made his tongue more agile than the wooden-mouthed administrators. His many experiences in his past life had metamorphosed into peculiar knowledge. Although he knew nothing of design, he restored the monastery of the White Horse with great aplomb. After leafing through some sutras and memorizing a few formulaic prayers, he stepped up onto the stage and preached with thundering conviction. All of Luoyang gathered round to hear sermons by the imperial lover. They found a magnificent temple filled with white lotus flowers and columns of incense escaping from huge basins to darken the sky. Through this intoxicating fog, monks could be heard chanting a steady, dull drone. Suddenly Celestial Kings loomed up taller than mountains, and a long line of bodhisattvas opened out, beaming with light. The faithful would eventually find Scribe of Loyalty in the very depths of the hall, sitting with his hands joined in prayer in the middle of a golden lotus glittering with millions of diamonds. With his wide forehead, lowered eyes, and bulbous earlobes, he was almost a celestial apparition. He himself started rumors that quickly spread throughout the city; soon the Capital was venerating him as the reincarnation of a famous Indian monk who had the gift of healing and magical powers.

A man's glory lies in his clothes. When my guards removed the lacquered linen cap, ivory tablet, and jade-studded leather belt from a disgraced minister, the statesman with his unruly hair and wild eyes lost all his imposing presence, already reduced to a convict or a slave. Wrapped in his purple tunic, astride an imperial charger, preceded by palace eunuchs and followed by his acolytes, Little Treasure, the aphrodisiac-seller, had no trouble establishing himself as the most elegant aristocrat in the Imperial City.

The more prudish ministers in the Outer Court eyed the scandalous Scribe of Loyalty scornfully and sent me letters of protest, reminding me of stories I already knew: Sovereigns besotted by their favorites neglected their duties; their passions had been the ruination of dynasties. Others, always alert and at the ready, fought for opportunities to win favor with this new figure of power. Generals prostrated themselves before the monk, addressing him as Master. My nephews—arrogant, impetuous princes—held his bridle for him as he mounted his horse. I watched these scenes from my lofty position on my throne with a sly smile.

Scribe of Loyalty was a lie that had become a truth.

Scribe of Loyalty was the merciless mirror I held up to this absurd world.

IN THE SECOND year of the Era of Lowered Arms and Joined Hands, I put my second invention into operation: At the entrance to the Forbidden City, I installed a giant bronze urn embossed with inscriptions worked in pure gold by my goldsmiths. The urn was divided into four compartments and was to be used to receive letters from the people.

An imperial decree was posted up in the four corners of the Empire: "Any individual who has no official State duties may now address Her

Supreme Majesty freely by placing their written statements in the Urn of Truth. The eastern side of the urn is reserved for recommending competent officials and for comments on sound imperial decisions. The southern side is intended for censure of social and political events. The western side is for denouncing crimes and offences. The northern side will be used for astrological predictions and reports of premonitory dreams concerning the fate of the Empire."

This first edict was followed by a second: "During their travels to the Sacred Capital, those bearing messages intended for the Supreme Empress will be given a daily payment and will be provided with bed and board by the regional authorities. Any imperial administrator committing the crime of questioning his guests, intercepting their letters, or impeding their journey to the Capital will be punished by death."

It was not long before a third decree was sent out: "Any man, regardless of his origins, bearing useful advice or having suffered an injustice, shall be received by Her Supreme Majesty in person."

My announcements put the Empire into turmoil. Convoys organized by provincial governments formed long uninterrupted streams of people along the country's roads. The people queued up outside the Forbidden City to reach the Urn of Truth. Imperial bailiffs collected the letters at dusk and brought them to me at night. Banquets and concerts were temporarily suspended in my palace. I chose the best pupils from the women at the Inner Institute of Letters as my readers. Ornate chandeliers were extinguished, and only candles on short candlesticks were kept alight. The young women did not wear topknots or official court tunics and sat with their bare feet in silk slippers. They were virgins in flesh and in their judgments, and they were shocked by the vulgar turns of phrase. From time to time, Gentleness would lay down the work and call for wine and fruit. She would sit behind me and massage my tired temples. Somewhere in the depths of the room, a girl would play the zither, and another would accompany her with the clear notes of a bamboo flute. When they fell silent, the only sounds were the rustle of paper and the whisper of silk sleeves. Scribe of Loyalty would arrive late in the night, and, when he appeared, the young girls would flee in every direction like flocks of birds disappearing into the darkness.

A palace in the Outer City was prepared to receive the people. At certain times throughout the afternoon, I would sit on my throne surrounded by gauze curtains, watching all of China file past.

> A peasant came to complain about the taxes on his land.
> A butcher denounced a dignitary who had taken his wife.
> A fisherman suggested that a canal should be built in his region.
> An impoverished scholar in love with a courtesan begged me to free his beloved.
> A madman talked about the end of the world.
> A woman from my region came to thank me for encouraging widows to remarry.
> Another brought me a basket of eggs.

Countless hundreds of them were terrified by the majestic palaces and the imposing military parades around me. Intoxicated by their fears and their veneration, they could not utter a word and carried on striking their foreheads on the ground until they were led away by eunuchs.

I delighted in hearing all the regional accents; I was touched by people's modest dreams and humble longings; and I suffered for those in despair—the starving, the old, and the orphans.

Learned, self-taught men without diplomas were given official positions. Strong and supple young men joined the army. Criminals saw their punishments reduced. To every creature who called on my help, I tried to grant clemency, justice, and happiness.

I was consumed by the vastness of China. The silhouettes on the far side of the curtain became confusing and overran me like a fever. All these people—thin, fat, tall, short, deformed, and ill—grasping the hem of my gowns pressed against my retina and invaded my dreams to ask for my goodness once again. The more I gave, the bigger the crowd of supplicants grew. All these miseries that were being revealed to me were just tiny portions of an infinite suffering.

I was proud, and I was disappointed; I was happy, and I felt guilty. Through these hundreds of lives, I was trying to find an answer to all the sorrows and pains of this world, but the solution melted away like water on sand. The root of these evils was still impenetrable.

During one of these sessions, the Council of Great Ministers brought me a petition in which my imperial officials begged me to suspend the public audiences in the interests of my own health.

"Supreme Majesty," said the Great Chancellor, prostrating himself, "no other sovereign has deigned to receive the people. And yet the Scholarly King of Zhou, the Emperor Lordly Forebear of the Han dynasty, the Scholarly Emperor of the Wei dynasty, and the Emperor Eternal Ancestor were all able to fulfill their celestial duties successfully and gloriously. A good sovereign knows the suffering and the joy of the people, but also knows how to delegate concerns to servants. That is why the ancient Zhou dynasty created the position of inspector and disguised these men as beggars before sending them out to every province. Her Supreme Majesty's health is the Chinese people's most precious resource. If she were exhausted, the entire world would be deprived of every joy. She must save her strength and her energy for the most important decisions."

"When I introduced the Urn of Truth," I replied, "and opened the Forbidden City to the people, this act was not intended to mock previous emperors, but to warn future sovereigns. Shut away in his palace and surrounded by courtiers dressed in brocade, the Master of the Empire knows nothing of hunger, poverty, and the trials of life. If he is the motionless center of the hub, then let the world come to him! The public audiences over the last few months have shown me the truth: As I treat each successive case, my power seems to diminish. Every act of kindness is a drop of water added to a constantly moving river. By granting my favors to some, I have withheld them from others who dared ask me for nothing. I must not take the place of the gods by handing out the fates of men. A sovereign's power is an illusion and a promise. Only Buddha's compassion can turn suffering into perpetual joy. I now accept your request, and I shall suspend the public audiences. But the Urn of Truth will continue to receive the complaints of the people. Politics can heal, but it cannot cure. Only a spiritual force can overcome ailing flesh and aching souls. He who is in the light forgets hunger and thirst. Let us pray that our empire will know religious bliss and be lifted up to the heavens."

TEN

I, the wandering child, I, the shaven-headed nun, I, the concubine who preferred the power of separation to the weakness of attachment, I, the Empress who was both in and out of life here and elsewhere—I noticed with stupefaction that a miracle had come to pass: I had laid down roots at the city of Luoyang.

Since my husband had joined the heavens, I had never returned to Long Peace. The seething metropolis of a million inhabitants had swept aside all the illusions of a provincial Talented One. I did not miss its markets and rows of little shops, its avenues of jostling horses and pedestrians. That town had forged me and perverted me. Away from it, I could at last forgive its feverish debauchery, its easy wealth; I no longer criticized its gleeful dissipation, its titillating exuberance. I had freed myself once and for all from a Forbidden City built by the emperors of Tang, haunted by the ghosts of murdered princes and poisoned concubines. Long Peace, which had robbed me of my youth, would be punished by my absence.

Specialists in genealogy had proved that my clan, the Wus, were descended from the lineage of the King of Peace from the ancient Zhou dynasty. Twelve hundred years previously, this Great Ancestor had moved his capital from Long Peace to Luoyang, lying on its fertile plain and surrounded by steep mountains on three sides. The wide, peaceful River Luo flowed through the city where it was joined by many other rivers. Geomancy experts had seen happy prosperity in the configuration of the surrounding countryside, and strategists, liked its central location, protected it from Tatar invasions. Emperor Yang of the overthrown dynasty had raised millions of peasants to dig the Great Canal[19], setting off from the Eastern Gate and linking the five rivers of China.

In Long Peace there were sweat and dust and the heavy ruts left by carts. In Luoyang there were green canals, red sails, and the grinding of oars. Luoyang did not move, and the world came to it on the waves. Boats laden with grain, precious woods, bolts of silk, packages of tea, and jars of wine set off from the provinces and unloaded their wares before the imperial palace.

Luoyang had welcomed me as a triumphant empress. The city had been destroyed by war and had surrendered itself, naked, to my imagination. I had exercised my thoughts over every restored quayside, every new stretch of canal. I had redesigned the ramparts of its rectangular fortifications. I had reinstated its ten avenues bisected by ten wide boulevards and its 130 separate districts. I had planted the double row of scarlet grenadine trees and pink peach trees in the middle of the boulevards and constructed stone bridges shaped like rainbows and wooden bridges that opened to allow boats to pass with their sails filled with the wind. I had restored and enlarged the Forbidden City and the Imperial Park. I had built the three imperial temples to the east of the Palace to house the spirits of the Emperor Lordly Forebear, the Emperor Eternal Ancestor, and the Emperor Lordly Ancestor, called there from Long Peace. I had erected the Temple of Adoration where my

[19] Built between A.D. 605 and 611 and covering 2,700 km.

forebears now received offerings on a par with those given to the three sovereigns of the dynasty.

Long Peace was banished. In Luoyang the wind blew over crimson peonies. From the top of the Pagoda of Contemplation, I could see the River Luo glittering in the middle of the Imperial Park. The Palaces of Spring and Autumn appeared in the depths of the forest where pavilions of cherry blossoms and terraces of orchid melted into the shadow. Galleries wound their way along the banks of rivers and became bridges launching out toward little islands, discs of emerald in the water. To the south, the low-lying city spread its panorama. Sailing ships glided across the sky. It was no longer clear where boats were setting out and where birds were flying off; tiled roofs and thatched roofs were smudges of turquoise and yellow between the canals. In the gap between blue and green on the horizon, a thread of black hovered. I could just make out the sacred valley through which the River Yi flowed. Devout Buddhists had dug thousands of caves along the cliffs on its right bank and had erected their idols in them over the centuries. My childhood wish had been granted there: A mountain had been sculpted and transformed into Buddha Vairocana of the Great Sun, accompanied by his bodhisattva servants. I had lent the giant statue my oval face, the thoughtful curve of my brow, my long slanting eyes, and my full-pouting lips, now immortalized in a distant smile.

Further away, there were forests and rivers, endless fields, and busy little towns. The golden and purple banners I had designed blew in the wind throughout the land of China. Men were dead. I was mistress of this eternal world.

LITTLE PHOENIX, HIS sickly cheeks and wan smile, was gradually erased by images of the Emperor Lordly Ancestor. Astride his horse, with his bow in his hand, he was a haughty and invincible warrior. On his throne, with his hands on his knees, wearing his ochre-yellow tunic and his cap of lacquered linen, he was dazzling in his majesty. At the top of Tai Mountain, wearing the crown with twenty-four tiers of jade pearls and the scarlet and black cloak embroidered with symbols of sovereignty, holding up the goblet of libations in his hands, he was the great priest of this earthly world.

Little Phoenix, the feverish adolescent and unfaithful husband. Little Phoenix, who had been my brother and my lover, had now become an effigy, a transparent glory, a sparkling light. His soul had wandered through the palace before joining the Emperor Eternal Ancestor in the heavens. They were both now a source of vague heat and icy inspiration to me, open to my contemplation but unattainable, on high.

They were both near to me and very far away; they had become stars.

My bed had been a desert for twenty years, and I had stumbled on Little Treasure as if onto an oasis. I forgot the damp embrace and herbal smell of medicinal infusions. I now savored his cool skin, firm muscles, and proud virility unashamedly. Love, which makes the weak weaker, had strengthened my powerful soul. I wanted to show the government that ecstasy by night robbed me of none of my lucidity by day.

New reforms were instigated: The best legal minds were summoned to examine the laws and compile new codes. In the past, the Mandarin Competitions had been organized to suit the government's needs. I now wanted them to take place once a year and the final session to be held in my presence. I broadened the scope of the trials and decreed that it was no longer compulsory to submit a dissertation on the Great Classics. I included poetry—that music of the gods and window to our souls—as the most infallible test of talent.

A decree went out expressing my determination not to miss a single hint of genius: "The Empire's prosperity is a duty for every one of us. Every individual—whether an official or of no distinction, nobleman or commoner, Chinese or foreign, gifted in the field of culture, economics, defense, education, justice, or major works—should present themselves to the recruiting officers without a letter of recommendation."

I poached more time from recreational activities and wrote *The Ethics of a Servant of the State* and *A New Warning to Imperial Officials*, in which

I made reflections on loyalty and competence. I published an essay on agriculture and had the largest astronomical sphere beneath the sky erected at the Northern Gate to the Palace. I diligently replied to the people's requests thrown into the Urn of Truth. With one hand I managed the administration of the provinces, while with the other, I continued to weave a web of intrigue to weaken the Barbarian tribes in the west.

My reawakening to life stimulated the rebirth of the Empire. The years of famine and epidemics were forgotten. Grain stores were filled once more; there was abundant meat, game and fish in the markets. The generosity of Heaven and Earth inspired me to brave the heights before which my husband, the Sovereign Lordly Ancestor, had faltered. Above and beyond secular power, was the reign of the gods. Above and beyond the seal of Supreme Empress, was the scepter of a high priestess, the incarnation of Divine Justice.

In the fourth year of the Era of Lowered Arms and Joined Hands, I detailed a holy man, the master monk Scribe of Loyalty, to knock down the reception palace at the entrance to the Forbidden City and to build the Temple of Clarity on its ruins. This site would provide a home for the sacred sanctuary. This project had been abandoned in my husband's time, but it would be my masterpiece. The construction of this temple would make all petty human squabbles meaningless. An entire empire, an entire people would be called up by a divine force and would burn with the desire to reach heaven. Exalted souls disdain suffering. Poverty—my enemy and my rival—would soon be reduced to ashes and dust.

IT WAS NOT long before the gods expressed their satisfaction through a number of extraordinary phenomena. Since I began governing the Empire as Supreme Empress, the Officer of Rites in the Palace had already recorded some thirty promising apparitions, atmospheric events, and astral configurations that indicated celestial approval.

These good omens culminated one morning in a fisherman on the River Luo bringing up a stone with cracks on its surface that formed an inscription. During the morning audience, ministers and soothsayers deciphered the oracle and translated these characters: "DIVINE MOTHER ON THIS EARTH, THROUGH HER, THE EMPEROR'S REIGN SHALL BE PROSPEROUS AND EVERLASTING." For the first time since the world sprang forth from chaos, the gods were identifying a woman as the human sovereign! The news spread throughout the Empire, and letters of congratulation fell around me like snowflakes: "Your Majesty has pursued the former sovereign's unfinished work. Her endeavor and her humility have touched the gods. That is why this divine writing has been sent to the world for the third time since civilization began. . . . As a representative of the female element in us, Your Majesty is invested with male strength. The union of these two opposites has produced the great harmony now enjoyed by our ten thousand kingdoms. That is why Heaven has appointed her Mistress of all people."

My past—with its downfalls and resurrections, its opportunities and difficulties—had already convinced me that I bore the mark of a very singular fate on my forehead. I had known suffering and had brushed with death. Every time that I was pushed to the very limits of despair, abandoned by men and gods, I managed to find the strength to triumph within myself, in my own body. That was the stamp, the voice, the music of providence. The oracle had just revealed the hidden truth behind all these trials: The gods were appointing me as their representative on Earth, having forged me with the consuming power of flames and the sudden chill of water.

Why Heavenlight? Why the little girl who loved horses? Why this strange ascension by such a devious route? Even the dead had served me as stepping stones to reach the heights. Why had it taken the deaths of my first master, Emperor Eternal Ancestor; my husband, the Sovereign Lordly Ancestor, my sons Splendor and Wisdom, and my sisters, Purity and Clarity, to reveal me, to accomplish what I was to be? Why did I know how to draw strength from the infirmities of birth? Why had my status as a woman and a commoner, my failings, been turned into triumphs? All the questions that had always tormented me disappeared. The gods had given me their answer at last.

I left it to the Court to award me the pompous and ambiguous title of Divine Mother Sacred Emperor that interwove masculinity and femininity. I left it to my nephews to engrave the three imperial seals with the simple name Sacred Emperor. All this feverish activity that demonstrated the delight of some of my courtiers and subjects provoked only anger in others.

One morning, the audience hall was shaken by a dispatch: In their respective provinces, the King of Yue and the King of the County of Lang Xie—Little Phoenix's brother and nephew—were rising up and calling on the world to overthrow the "usurper." I smiled at this grotesque spectacle: a dead husband's family openly seeking to punish a widow for not knowing "a woman's place." There was nothing to fear. The gods who had chosen me would defend me. I replied to their war cries and their furious indignation, which wanted to restore male supremacy, by sending them my faithful armies. Yet again there was a miracle: Only twenty days later the insurrection was quashed and the rebels' heads hung before the Southern Gate of the Forbidden City. Their supporters within the Court were pursued by the magistrates of Autumnal Duties and the inspectors from the Lodge of Purification. Other plots came to light: kings and princesses received orders to hang themselves in their palaces. During one of the enquiries, I was informed that the Prince Consort Xue Xiao, Lieutenant General of the Guards, and his brothers had also sworn allegiance to the insurgents. My daughter, Moon, wept by my bedside and begged my clemency. Despite her anguish, I decided to make an example of my son-in-law and to demonstrate my merciless repression. I spared him the shame of a public execution and had him starved to death in prison.

An illegitimate authority that knows no respect crumbles at the first signs of uprising. A revolt that dies down in a few days is a disturbance that did not have the people's approval. The silence in my empire was a tacit recognition of my legitimacy. I had indeed worked tirelessly for the Tang dynasty for nearly thirty years, and everyone recognized that I was the source of its prosperity. Why should I go on reigning behind an incompetent son and reducing him to a puppet emperor? I had already changed banners, renamed ministers, and made Luoyang my capital. I had squashed revolutions and subdued the Tatars. I had allowed poetry and the arts to flourish and had seen justice triumph. The people were well fed. The world had me to thank for its beauty. Why let the hazy title of Divine Mother Sacred Emperor and the shadowy suggestion of usurpation hover over me? Why should I not formally and enthusiastically take up the mandate offered to me by Heaven?

On the fifteenth day of the twelfth month in the fourth year of the Era of Lowered Arms and Joined Hands, two months after the insurrection led by the royal princes, I broke the ancestral law that forbade women to officiate in the rites of celebration. In the name of the Sacred Emperor, I raised the great imperial parade that had once served my husband. Followed by my son, the Emperor, and his heir, by officials and governor delegates, Barbarian kings, foreign ambassadors, and an entire people in a state of feverish, exalted excitement, I traveled to the banks of the River Luo. There I stepped up onto the altar to the strains of ten thousand musicians playing the fourteen verses of *Rejoicing and Veneration*, which I had composed. At the top of this great monument, there were a thousand wild birds, a thousand game birds, a thousand sheep and goats, a thousand bulls and cows, a thousand jars of grain, a thousand jugs of wine, and countless rare creatures sent as gifts by vassal kingdoms; these made up my offering to the goddess of the River Luo who had sent me the divine message.

The very next day Scribe of Loyalty announced that the Temple of Clarity had been completed. The Morning Salutation became an audience granted to the Barbarian ministers and kings.

The sacred building was made up of three circular sections, one on top of the other; it was built on a square platform and looked liked a pagoda on a massive scale. Inside, two hundred and forty millennial trees had been used to support a network of horizontal beams that acted as a base for the pillars on the floor above. Beams and rafters painted with powdered gold were interwoven in an increasingly complicated pattern to reach the vaulted ceiling covered in frescoes depicting the marvels of the gods. Its substantial system of curving roofs covered in varnished blue-green tiles unfurled into the sky. The top of the roof looked down on the entire world from a height never before achieved: 280 cubits, which was twice as high as the tallest imperial palace. Upon it, nine seething golden dragons—gods of the seas and symbols of masculine strength—held up a scarlet phoenix, king of birds and the emblem of the Empress Mother of Heaven. The creature's wings were set with gemstones that caught the sun's rays and twinkled dazzlingly up to the clouds.

The sanctuary consecrated to Heaven, to the Kings of the Five Directions, and to the spirits of emperor ancestors, was forbidden to profane eyes; I therefore revealed only the front area intended for imperial receptions. There were twenty-four windows on the third floor representing the twenty-four winds of the four seasons, and twelve on the second floor representing the twelve earthly cycles. The beams of light from these converged on a stage consisting of a disc of celestial turquoise laid on a square of earthly yellow. I climbed the steps and sat on the throne, a simple seat low on the ground, draped with a mat of woven, white satin. But the rays of sunlight playing around me were so bright they might have been hideous dragons, fearless warriors, or an entire celestial army begat by the breath of the gods. The ministers and kings were terrified, and they threw themselves to their knees and prostrated themselves, crying: "The Sacred Emperor is truly a divinity!"

Brimming with pride, I announced, "In his lifetime, the previous emperor wanted to raise the Temple of Clarity. On the day of the sanctification on Tai Mountain, that wish received Heaven's blessing. But the propitious time was a long time coming. Today peace reigns throughout the world, and the people live in plenty. The gods have given me their permission. I have dared to resurrect ancient religion and to turn myth into reality. The Temple of Clarity is a sanctuary intended for Supreme Celebration, a solemn place that shall be venerated by the people. It has been built according to the laws of nature to represent Heaven and Earth, and it drives away demons and absorbs impurities. That is why I shall call it the Sacred Temple of the Ten Thousand Elements. May every man, beast, plant, and mineral on our Earth be protected by it!"

The cheers were still echoing when the year came to an end. Snow fell tender on Luoyang. On New Year's Day, with my ministers' approval, I overstepped ancestral law again.

After the purification, I put on the ink-red emperor's tunics and men's-style shoes. On my man's topknot, I wore my husband's crown decorated with twenty-four tiers of jade pearls. With the jade scepter in my hand and hugging the hopes of an entire people to my breast, I stepped into the heart of the Temple of the Ten Thousand Elements and communed with Heaven and the spirits of the ancestors. After the ceremony, I stood high up by the Gate of Celestial Law to announce the Great Remission of sins and to inaugurate the Era of Eternal Prosperity. Two days later, I gathered my officials in the temple and sat on the sacred throne. In the name of Heaven, I instructed them in the nine virtues. A few days after that, I ordered that the temple be opened to the public and invited my people to visit it. From the top of the Pagoda of Contemplation, I observed with pride a continuous stream of pilgrims form outside the Forbidden City. The previous emperors had all failed. But I, a woman, had been capable of raising the highest temple in history. The rebel princes were right: I was the usurper of men's dreams.

SCRIBE OF LOYALTY threw himself at my feet: The master monk, Clarity of Law, had just translated the sutra of the Great Cloud in which certain passages justified my position as the master of the earthly world.

"While he was preaching," Scribe of Loyalty took the scroll from his sleeve and read, "Buddha addressed a celestial daughter named Purity of Heavenlight and said: 'In a former life you once heard the sutra of Great Nirvana. Because of this providential incident, you have taken the form of a celestial being. Now, having heard my teachings, you shall abandon this ethereal body and assume the mortal flesh of a woman. You shall reign over the earth and shall be the bodhisattva who redeems the lowly world.' "

"Sacred Majesty," my lover cried, "ever since I was called to your service, I have wondered who you were. You are proud yet humble, tormented yet naïve. You are deep as the night, limpid as a mirror, ardent as the sun, and icy as the moon. You restore traditions and reinvent codes. You are in the present and navigate through the past while already projecting yourself into the future. You are a woman and a man, one and several, movement and immobility. The better I know you, the more I am amazed by the infinity that lies within you. This sutra of the Great Cloud that has come from India has just revealed your origins: You are that celestial daughter! You are the Savior of the World; you are the bodhisattva of the Future!"

Seeing that I gave no reply, he drew closer on his knees.

"Majesty, do you not remember the distant past when you lived in the kingdom of the skies?"

Images flitted past: I saw myself as a little girl on a big white horse. I was galloping by the banks of the River Long, trying in vain to take off toward the sky in the speed of my mount. With my hands under my chin, I watched the clouds lit up by the setting sun, and then—amid the shadows and flashes of color—I could see palaces with pillars of gold, terraces of mist, and ponds of sapphire. How I longed to be one of those celestial beings clothed in light! I saw myself as a young concubine imprisoned in the gynaeceum with its ten thousand beauties fighting for the favors of just one man. I remembered how ardently I wanted to tear myself away from the earthly world, its pitiful hatred and mediocre frustrations. I saw myself as Empress of China, my topknot crowned with the twenty-four gem-studded golden trees, climbing the steps to the Gate of Serene Loyalty. The officials were cheering, and the sky opened out its expanses of blue above my sovereign head, a pathway to climb toward a world hidden from men and women. I understood my passion for horses, those earthly clouds, and my love of mountains, those staircases toward the gates of Heaven. I understood why I was drawn to heights, why I had the strength to recover when I fell into the abyss, and why I so loved undertaking major constructions: temples, statues, columns, plinths, all reaching toward the zenith. My compassion and my indifference to human misery could now be explained. Throughout this existence, I had been trying to turn my back on Earth to reach Heaven, my homeland, my birthplace.

Scribe of Loyalty withdrew and had the newly translated sutra disclosed. My nephews used the opportunity to instigate my deification. They were impatient to be the imperial household and change my husband's relations into outsiders. The monasteries of the Great Cloud built in the four corners of the Empire rang their bonze bells, whipping up fervor among the people. As a celestial daughter and bodhisattva who would be Savior of the World, I was hope and happiness and the promise of a better life. From that moment on, the people prayed for my well-being before statues of Buddha Maitreya of the Future who bore my enigmatic smile. They begged me to lead them back to the path of deliverance toward the Heaven of Pure Rejoicing. With this faith, I was ready to defy the ancestors, the deceased, and the living—to become the first woman emperor of all time.

The Tang dynasty, founded by conquerors and sullied by blood and warfare, would be turned like the page of a book. Every form of renewal is a purification. I did away with the calendar of the ancient Xia dynasty and applied the Zhou calendar, used by my glorious ancestors, in which the new year begins in the eleventh moon. I undertook to change the way things were written by publishing a series of new characters including my name, Heavenlight, now represented as the Sun and the Moon carried by the Heavens. My eldest nephew, Piety, had recently been named Great Chancellor of the Left, and while he busied himself trying to alter the course of history, I very quietly suggested my decision to the government: My sacred mission would be accomplished only if I inaugurated a new dynasty based on peace, compassion, and divine justice.

On the morning of the third day of the ninth moon-phase, shouting broke out by the Gate to the Forbidden City and interrupted the morning salutation. The overseeing magistrate, Fu Yu Yi, stepped forward and presented me with a petition signed by the 900 men and women kneeling before the southern entrance. I had the scroll opened; it was covered with signatures, some beautiful, some hideous, others simple thumbprints: "The sky does not have two suns; the earth does not recognize two kings. Your Sacred Majesty must obey the will of the gods who entrust the sovereignty of the Empire to her. Heaven is commanding her to inaugurate a new dynasty, and to gratify her son, her successor, with her name—Wu. So that henceforth her lineage may prosper and illuminate the four seas for eternity."

Without waiting for a reaction from the high-ranking officials, I dictated my reply: "I, who obey the wishes of the previous emperor; I who am devoted to serving Heaven and who long for peace in the world and joy in the hearts of every people; I am determined to take on my duties without claiming any glory."

A ripple rang through the audience hall. Several ministers stepped forward from the ranks, trying to make me accept the celestial invitation and reasons of State. Their numbers were far from the majority. I rejected their request but rewarded Fu Yu Yi, who had understood my intention. I immediately appointed him councilor to the Chancellery.

The following day I learned that the 900 inhabitants of Luoyang had still not moved. They had been joined by monks and Taoists, traders and beggars, children and the elderly. Twelve thousand people were now kneeling before the Forbidden City, determined to rise to their feet only once I agreed to satisfy the petition. Accompanied by my ministers, I climbed to the highest level of the Pagoda of Contemplation and saw a carpet of prostrate figures before the Forbidden City. My heart faltered with emotion. This change of dynasty would see no bloodshed or violence. For the first time in our history, the people were choosing their sovereign. Let their wishes be heard!

Still, I hardened my tone to voice my refusal: "The sun shines, but it wears no crown. The gods govern this earth, but our offerings are paltry in the face of their goodness. Buddha's power lies in his boundless and universal compassion. He asks only for prayer. The sovereign who transcends divine goodness, and the blessings of our forebears must be the most humble servant of the Empire, an officiator in religious rituals constrained to moral purity. The sovereign should have no belongings or glory. My power was passed on to me by the previous emperor; my vocation was revealed by Heaven. I deserve no special title."

Two days later there were sixty thousand people outside the Southern Gate; they had come from the four corners of the Empire calling for my eternal reign. During the morning salutation, the officials, officers, princes, and barbarian kings also presented me with a petition. The Great Eunuch Overseer took it upon himself to give me a letter sent by the entire population of the gynaeceum. I also received a letter from my daughter, the Princess of Eternal Peace, expressing the wish of all the women dignitaries to see me found a new dynasty. Finally, my son Miracle, whose silent existence had been a mute form of opposition, announced to the world that he had abdicated. He publicly asked for my permission to abandon his paternal name, Li, and to bear my name, Wu.

Voices strangled with emotion cried out in every direction to try and persuade me: "At dawn this morning, a phoenix flew over the Southern Gate, followed by hundreds of different birds. Then thousands of scarlet sparrows came from east of the horizon, escorted by golden orioles. When the sun rose, clouds tinged with happiness spread over the sky for a long time before dispersing. The whole capital witnessed this marvel, and your servants heard your people proclaiming: 'The presence of these celestial beings heralds a sacred revolution! Scarlet sparrows symbolize fire, golden orioles represent the earth. Now, according to the law of the five elements, fire begets the earth. That is why the golden orioles escorting the scarlet sparrows announce a celestial oracle: The son shall follow the mother, shall bear the maternal name!'

"In the *Book of Mutation*, the Ancients observed: 'When a great man receives the mandate of Heaven, he can overturn the former order, and his actions are called Revolution.' Your servants have learned that when a great man obeys the will of Heaven, he becomes invincible; when he obeys the will of the people, his lineage will prosper. Today Heaven has appointed Your Majesty master, and the people have asked for Your Majesty as a mother. The law of Heaven is destiny; the intentions of the people are fate. Your Majesty is disobeying Heaven and showing contempt for the people, but she is choosing virtue and modesty: These actions run counter to the course of history and to the Law of Distribution. Your servants will no longer be able to venerate you! Your Majesty's refusal is a betrayal of Heaven and a blow to the people: How can you govern now?"

After uttering the refusal three times, in keeping with the ancient code, I bowed before the Will of Heaven. The imperial soothsayers and Great Ministers chose the ninth day of the ninth moon, the day of the Double Sun, to celebrate my enthronement.

On that morning, I wore over my white tunic the indigo-colored imperial cloak embroidered with twelve rows of sacred drawings and painted with dragons riding astride clouds. With the crown of twenty-four tiers of jade pearls on my head and the emerald scepter in my hand, I climbed the steps to the Gate of Celestial Law amid the ringing of bronze bells and the chiming of sounding stones. I was preceded by a cortège of servants from the Inner Court and followed by princes and Great Ministers. I announced to the world the beginning of my dynasty, the Zhou dynasty. Its peace and prosperity would be inaugurated by the Era of the Celestial Mandate. Cheers from officials and shouts of joy from the people rang out. Heaven descended and wrapped me in its crystalline blue. All the power of the House of Tang was expiring, and a woman who had become Emperor was founding her own dynasty without scorching Chinese soil with war. This marvel confirmed once more that I truly was the envoy of the gods.

The whole world knew that my terrestrial legitimacy could be traced right back to the ancient Zhou dynasty whose kings were my ancestors. I took every opportunity to proclaim that I was descended from them by using their crimson banners—the color of fire, the element they venerated. The Sacred Hearth of the Empire was transferred from Long Peace to Luoyang, which was promoted to Imperial Capital. I went back through the family tree, and seven generations of ancestors were given the posthumous title of emperor. Seven temples were built to the east of the Forbidden City, and here their spirits could receive offerings and adorations. My son Miracle became the Imperial Descendent and enjoyed the privileges accorded to the Supreme Son. Piety, Spirit, and Tranquility, the eldest three of my nephews, became kings, and their cousins were raised to the rank of county kings. Having been a wood merchant, a fighting warrior, and then a dignitary kept far from the Court, Father could rise up at last, thanks to his daughter's accession. In her lifetime, Mother would have been terrified to have given birth to an emperor, a god. As it was, they were both silenced by their pride.

They were exhumed and reburied with the posthumous titles of Emperor and Empress of Pious Clarity.

I stopped asking myself: Who am I? And where do I come from?

The Court had just offered me the title of August Sovereign Divinity. I was the Beginning, the Source of Sources. I was the identity, the root that would become a tree in the centuries to come.

ELEVEN

The world forgot Confucius's maxim: "It is as scandalous for a woman to meddle with politics as for a hen to crow like a cockerel." Men forgot their indignation at seeing a widow emerge from the gynaeceum and command an empire, and all the rumors about my sexual exploits faded. The cheers of the people still reverberated through the Forbidden City; it was these heartfelt cries of a humble people— rather than any crown or imperial cloak—which restored the confidence of a sovereign dented by betrayal and revolts among her officials. I had become an inescapable truth, and now, as I sat on my throne facing my ministers and generals, I no longer saw them all as potential traitors.

I no longer needed the blood-thirsty judges—who I myself had appointed after Xu Jing Yei's uprising three years earlier—to quash further conspiracies. I began to understand that some of them had earned promotion by exposing imaginary plots. It was time to reestablish justice in the special judgment court I had built within the Forbidden City, behind the Gate of Magnificent Landscape. I decided to eliminate those prosecutors and magistrates who were acting on their own initiative like the princes of independent kingdoms. A secret investigation revealed that they brought charges with no more proof than a simple denunciation; and, from the moment of their arrest, all of the accused were subjected to torture during interrogations. The tortures were given names such as "the phoenix spreading its wings," "the braced donkey," "the immortal offering divine fruit" and "the Daughter of Jade climbing the ladder." To ensure that no culprit was spared, these trials condemned innocent men. On the pretext of quashing rebellions, the judges had created a parallel power that was beyond my control.

Their spies were proliferating throughout the Empire, even within the walls of my palace. To strike quickly and efficiently, I chose one judge who was familiar with the network's every secret, strength, and weakness. Lai Jun Chen, famed for his cruelty, was the Lodge of Purification's prosecutor. A former criminal, he had been sentenced to death by beheading. When I had opened my court four years before and given audience to humble commoners, he had obliged his jailor to accompany him to the capital, where he had dared to plead his innocence before me. I had pardoned his crimes and appointed him as prosecutor to hunt down his fellow creatures. The man who owed me his life received his orders without comment. One by one, he exterminated his colleagues, patiently and methodically. I learned that, to obtain a confession from Zhou Xing—a judge reputed to be a sinister torturer—Lai Jun Chen invited him to dine with him, and during the course of the meal, he asked his advice on how to interrogate especially resistant conspirators. Zhou Xing replied, "Put them in an earthenware jar over a pile of logs, set light to it, and let them cook dry. Even the dumb speak then." It was then that the prosecutor drew the arrest warrant from his sleeve and announced, "At the entrance to this room, there is an earthenware jar set up on a blazing fire. Her Majesty suspects you of stirring up a plot against her. I beg permission to interrogate you on this matter."

Lai Jun Chen triumphed over his own kind.

Decapitated: Qiu Shen Ji, Great General of the Golden Scepter of the Left, who crushed rebellious armies in their blood.

Decapitated: Magistrate Suo Yuan Li, a Turk scholar with the eyes of a lynx, an eagle nose, and a Barbarian heart.

Exiled: Zhou Xing, the ill jurist who drew his strength from his fevered interrogations. He was eventually assassinated.

Decapitated: Fu Yu Yi, the councilor for the chancellery who instigated the people's petition calling for my enthronement.

Decapitated: Justice of the Peace Wang Hong Yi.

Decapitated: Judge Ho Si Zhi, the illiterate peasant who thrived on his intuitions and his ferocious cruelty and who despised wealth and pleasure. I shall never forget our brief exchange when I smiled and asked him, "You cannot read. How can you conduct investigations?"

Quite unperturbed, he replied, "Legend confers on the sacred griffon the ability to distinguish between good and evil. It can neither read nor write, and yet it recognizes the truth."

Decapitated: Those three years of merciless repression. Bloodshed wiped away bloodshed; crime assassinated crime.

I summoned the prosecutor Lai Jun Chen to a private audience. He prostrated himself before me and then stood a few paces from me, upright and motionless. His face was magnificently chiseled; he would have been a beautiful man if there had been a hint of color in his ashen cheeks, if his face had been animated, and if his eyes had looked on this life with any warmth.

I showed him scrolls of denunciations.

"Zhou Xing, Suo Yuan Li, Fu Yu Yi, and Wang Hong Yi are dead; you alone are alive. There are just as many accusations leveled at you: corruption, buying favors, attempts to seize power—how dare you disobey the law?"

His face remained marble-like and his voice devoid of emotion as he replied, "Zhou Xing and Suo Yuan Li were anonymous scholars. When Your Majesty discovered their talents, they were able to make careers for themselves as magistrates, and this position meant they could take their revenge on the rich and the powerful. As for Fu Yu Yi and Wang Hong Yi, they both came from the lower depths of the Empire. They used flattery and intrigue to achieve their ends. Your Majesty likes unusual talents, their pride at the recognition you granted them outweighed their gratitude: They exploited their independence to build a separate network of power, and that is how they came to nurture the evil ambition of challenging Your Majesty's strength. I was condemned to death and kept in a dungeon when Your Majesty heard my cry and gave me the opportunity to live and serve her. Ever since that day, I have sworn myself to my sovereign, body and soul. The real Lai Jun Chen was already dead. The one who prostrates himself at Your Majesty's feet is another man, a creature who lives only to follow her orders and only by her will. The day that he ceases to be of use to her will be the day he returns to the shades. The officials understand the powerful ties I have to the sovereign; they are afraid of my intransigent devotion. That is why I have frequently been attacked by their paid assassins, and when their attempts at murder fail, they slander me. They want to be rid of me by whatever means they can, to weaken Your Majesty."

I looked Lai Jun Chen in the eye for a long time. Other judges harbored anger, hatred, and perversion, but this prosecutor fascinated me with his coldness and his calm. The judges' ferocity had served their own longings for power, and that was why I had them killed once they had served my ends. But Lai Jun Chen's ferocity knew no vanity; this man who was once condemned to death was probably the greatest torturer of all time. He carried the Abyss within him, the Eternal Fire, Hell itself. He wanted neither to conquer nor to subdue. He was a destructive force—both chilling and blazing—offered to me by the gods.

I threw the denunciations into a brazier.

"I shall give you your life once again. You are now master of the Court at the Gate of Magnificent Landscape. I want no more persecutions and torture. Men apply hatred in response to hatred; my dynasty shall apply compassion."

I was careful not to admit that this magnanimity was calculated. By leaving the most feared and loathed magistrate in his position, I was implying to officials that I had ceased to fight, but was by no means disarmed.

Lai Jun Chen prostrated himself before me. His voice was still echoing around the room as he backed out: "May my sullied existence allow Your Majesty to remain immaculate."

MY DAY BEGAN at three in the morning, summer and winter. Every other day I received the Salutation of my officials at daybreak. After the prostrations and the ceremonial wish for ten thousand years of my reign, some presented reports, and others received my instructions. At the end of the audience, the officials went to their respective ministries, and I moved to my private room to read political files and discuss them with Great Ministers.

On the intervening days, I remained in my bed chamber until dawn when I received the prostrations of the overseeing eunuchs and the lady governesses who presented me with accounts, bills, plans for forthcoming banquets, lists of birthday gifts, embroidery designs for official costumes, and requests for promotions and punishments. As Emperor of China, I was also my own empress.

In the afternoons, after a brief siesta, I would be taken by litter to the Pavilion of Treaties and Interviews. I would sit behind a curtain of purple gauze, although I might remove this for those I knew well. Poets and calligraphers, Taoists and monks, merchants and peasants prostrated themselves at my feet: Each of them came to me with a complaint, a piece of advice, or some new knowledge. Thanks to the things they told me, I traveled to distant towns, witnessed foreign customs, learned of alliances and rivalries between neighboring kingdoms, and ensured my armies remained loyal even in the furthest limits of the desert. With poets I talked of rhymes and language; monks interpreted the sutras they brought back from India after braving a thousand dangers; geographers suggested building new roads and canals; astrologers spoke to me of the stars.

251

On some days at the end of the afternoon, I would go for a long ride through the Imperial Park on one of my horses. The thought of this period of escape brightened my mood from the moment I awoke. The vermilion glow of the setting sun tinted the tops of the trees and turned the River Luo into a ribbon embroidered with golden waves. A retinue of animals followed me: dogs, leopards, giraffes, and elephants. There were many men to dispute the honor of leading my steed by the bridle: my nephews the kings; Lai Jun Chen, the magistrate; and the Great Ministers. It was when I was inspired by the melancholy calm of these rides that I improvised my most beautiful poems.

Deep in the forest, eunuchs would free thousands of birds: blackbirds, orioles, skylarks, and thrushes launching themselves into the skies. Their song, an exuberant hymn to life full of virtuoso trills, moved me to tears. The more I was surrounded, the more I was alone. Dusk was falling. It would soon be everlasting night.

ONE MOMENT OF bliss followed another, and time wrapped itself around me like an endless thread tightening its stranglehold. From the depths of my opaque cocoon, I was expecting a miracle: never to grow old.

My lovemaking with Scribe of Loyalty was losing its intensity. At first his vigorous body and well-defined muscles had been like an unfulfilled fantasy, then a vague dream. As the years went by, his virile youth became disturbing.

My lover was thirty, and I sixty-nine. Like other wealthy debauched monks, he had bought houses for his mistresses in the commoners' town outside the Forbidden City. His many wives dripped with jewels and lived off my generosity through him. The one he liked best was a young girl of sixteen bought for a jug of pearls in a brothel. She could make love to him for hours on end without tiring. Their cries of ecstasy had even carried to the depths of my gynaeceum where I struggled with my jealousy and despair.

Scribe of Loyalty came to the Palace less and less. Once a month, on the night of the full moon, he would caress me and spill his seed on me as a peasant sows his field. His every move was precise and attentive; he performed his duties as a favorite like an official carrying out a laborious task. In the darkness I could still read his pity, his resignation, and his indifference. Scribe of Loyalty no longer loved me. I no longer afforded him any pleasure.

I developed a profound loathing for my own body, this Future Buddha's body which was said to be sacred and indestructible. The baths, massages, and unguents could no longer stop this flesh from slackening and crumpling. I hid my resentment toward my young lover who shattered the myth every time he undressed me.

I was obsessed by hygiene: I forced him to undergo medical examinations and to be washed from head to toe before he came to my bed. In spite of the soaps and the vigorous scrubbing by my serving women, he still gave off a smell of earthly debauchery, underlining the irony of my decrepitude. His member had trawled through the town; his dirty hands had delved in other orifices; his tongue had licked fresh, pungent young skin. Every time I took him in my arms, I exposed myself to his gaze, to being compared.

One night, I exploded angrily, and he dared to reply: "Majesty, I know you have me followed and that your spies have been sold into my houses as slaves. You spy on my every coupling; you follow my life with the ferocity of a lioness. But you have never tried to look into my heart. Have you ever thought that it is you who drives me into other women's arms?"

"Little Treasure," I sneered, using his original name. "All these years, I have never forbidden you from finding pleasure elsewhere when I could have demanded your complete faithfulness. Imperial concubines are shut away in the gynaeceum, but I have allowed you to run free. That is the greatest proof of affection an emperor can give. Instead of showing gratitude, you abuse my patience. Now you dare accuse me of driving you into other women's arms! What do you mean by this? Am I so very old and hideous?"

"Faithfulness, yes, let us talk of that," he said furiously. "Has Your Majesty herself been faithful? If you had told me at the very start that, as sovereign, you had the right to every pleasure, then I would have been forced to accept that in silence. But you claimed that I was the only man in your life. You prided yourself on your faithfulness and found some glorious virtue in the fact that you did not have ten thousand beautiful men in your Inner Palace. Can you explain to me then why you enter into relationships based on intellect and affection with your ministers, your magistrates, and your generals? That particular love, which has no physical element and is forbidden between master and servant, is so much more intense than mere copulation. You love Judge Lai Jun Chen! I only have to see you with him to know that you marvel at his coldness and that you guard his life jealously even though the whole Empire wishes him dead. You exiled Great Chancellor Li Zhao De because your ministers urged you to, but soon you will call him back to Court as if nothing had happened. If that is not love, what other word is there to explain it? There is also the Great Secretary Ji Xu, who holds your horse's bridle and who can make you laugh so readily. Two years ago, like a loving wife stitching a war uniform for her husband heading off to the front, you gave each of your delegated governors an official tunic sewn by the serving women in your gynaeceum. You claimed you yourself embroidered the words "firm, supple, calm, ardent" on the back of these garments. Majesty, do you realize that some of these coarse creatures sleep with those tunics folded neatly beside their pillows, that others have laid them on altars and converse with them as if they were divinities? When you receive the candidates for the final imperial test; when you sit behind your gauze curtain and interrogate them in your deep, kindly voice; when you seduce budding ministers with your humor and erudition, you sew the seeds of love in their hearts, and those seeds will grow into blossoming trees whose fruits you can harvest. And after this great succession of men, there is me: a pitiful vagrant, a monk whom you forbid to take any part in politics! I am your weakness, your sickness, the shame that you keep hidden. There are plenty of humble girls who appreciate my kindness and venerate me, but Your Majesty is a cruel goddess who neglects me and destroys me! She offers her attentions to her subjects—men, women, young, and old—all of them beloved in her heart. She therefore saves herself from becoming attached to any single man; she manages her feelings so that she can never be disappointed. Her eyes never truly look at men; they are fixed on the skies. Her hand gives, takes away, pardons, kills . . . and I, Scribe of Loyalty, I live in the mire, struggling with contempt and longing. I am an object of slander and ridicule. Your ministers hate me, and the kings believe I manipulate you with a giant phallus! And yet you receive me only by night like a thief, and you turn me away when I want to make love to you!"

I had not realized that Scribe of Loyalty could feel jealousy, and his admission filled me with joy. I would have liked to ask his forgiveness and to admit that I was ashamed to let him touch my tired, old skin. I would have liked to reveal to him the secret that I kept hidden: I despaired as I grew old. My heart was calling out for his help, but my pride made me respond with a sigh: "What can I do to improve your standing? The Temple of Ten Thousand Elements has brought you wealth and notoriety. Twice I have appointed you commander of my imperial armies to fight the Tibetans, and I have given you the glorious title of Great General of the Invincible Defense and that of Lord of the Kingdom of Liang. But, as you are unable to rise early, you never attend the morning salutation. How do you expect to earn the Court's respect if you do not respect its constraints and discipline?"

"Majesty," Scribe of Loyalty interrupted me, "you know very well that I am not interested in power. If you care for me, if you love me, I ask just one thing of you: give me status. Marry me! Name me your Imperial Husband!"

I was so astonished by what I heard that I could find no words to reply. An emperor's wife received the Empress's Seal, but could a female emperor raise a man to the position of Imperial Husband? If an empress were considered to be the mother of the Empire and the most perfect incarnation of feminine virtue, would an imperial husband be the father of the Empire and master of all men? If Scribe of Loyalty received prostrations from the Court and the veneration of an entire people, would he not foster a desire to reign, would he not be tempted to usurp power? The people would never tolerate the image of a former drug peddler to be associated with me. How could I renounce the tomb of my glorious late husband, Celestial Emperor, Sovereign Lordly Ancestor, and lie down in the grave of an ordinary man?

My voice became hard and surly as if I were addressing a minister: "This may be what you dream of, but it is impossible."

"Majesty," he insisted, "you have encouraged widows to remarry; you have scorned tradition and created new laws. You have just inaugurated a dynasty and ascended to the throne. An Emperor has an Empress, four wives, nine Concubines, nine Elegant Ones, nine Beauties, nine Talented Ones, twenty-seven Forests of Treasure, twenty-seven Imperial Serving Women, twenty-seven Gatherers, and a huge Inner Palace to satisfy his desires. And you have just one lover whom you have forced to become a monk and who has become a laughing stock for the entire world! Majesty, you need to take just one more step to be equal to a man. Marry me! I will abandon my freedom."

"It is late. I have to rise at dawn. We must sleep."

"Majesty, just one word. Do you want me as a husband?"

My heart felt the chill of a strange premonition. Instead of replying I turned my back to him. He shook me and wept as he held me in his arms. Half way through the night, he sat up with a start, leapt to the ground, and disappeared.

While I sat on my raised throne the following morning, I was distracted. During the Celebration of the Double Sun, my nephew Piety presented me with a petition of five thousand signatures in which State officials and common people begged me to take the title of Sacred Emperor who Turns the Golden Wheel. All this glory was now my enemy: I was a divine sovereign, Master of the World, but I was losing my hair, my teeth, and my strength like any lowly creature. The Sacred Emperor

who kept time and the fortunes of this world turning was also a prisoner of the wheel that would ultimately lead to downfall. Life, like love,
strengthens and betrays, soothes and punishes. I was a usurper. I had
stolen a crown, an epoch, a transient illusion.

SCRIBE OF LOYALTY was sulking and avoiding me. He paid no attention to my summons and lay low in his monastery.

In the arms of the imperial doctor Shen Nan Qiu, I found the confidence of which Scribe of Loyalty had robbed me. His body was docile,
discreet; it soothed my anxieties and eased my troubles. The news
spread through the Forbidden City, and the Court made no effort to
hide its joy in seeing the monk losing my favor. The dignitaries who,
only the day before, had been proud to call themselves his friends were
now eager to speak ill of him. It seems that Scribe of Loyalty, the Lord
of the Kingdom of Liang, Great General of the Left of the Invincible
Defense, thought of himself as a founding force in my dynasty and
chose to play the role of master in the Monastery of the White Horse.
He fortified its walls and recruited thousands of young monks who
were experts in martial arts. The clash of bamboo poles and war cries
rang out all day long: this was Scribe of Loyalty having fun training his
soldier-monks. When he came out of his temple and went into the city,
he surrounded himself with the most beautiful and vigorous of his disciples. His horse would be decked in a harness of gold set with gems,
and around him he would have a troop of young monks carrying the
rod of iron and the long saber, marching in time. When they came
across Taoists and devout followers of other religions, on a nod from
their master, they would attack them, shaving their heads and forcing
them to convert to Buddhism. It was not long before the prosecutor Lai
Jun Chen, who loathed my lover, begged me to charge him for abduct-
ing and sequestering women, for forming an illegal army, and for attempting to usurp power.

Scribe of Loyalty came before me only when he had been beseeched
through three imperial summons accompanied by my handwritten or-

ders. I felt my stomach contract when he came into the room: I had not seen him for three months and had forgotten how beautiful he was. He stood head and shoulders above the other men and walked with a swagger like the heroes of ancient mythology. When he prostrated himself, I noticed that his face was thinner and that his forehead bore the mark of melancholy. I was overwhelmed by emotion: Scribe of Loyalty was suffering!

I indulged him by offering him a seat. Then I asked him gently about his life, and he answered me in brief sentences. I caressed him in my mind. His eyes lingered neither on my face, which had been smoothed of all wrinkles by the latest unguent concocted by the doctor Shen Nan Qiu, nor on the very open neckline of my gown. He seemed to look through me and stare glumly at the screen behind my seat. Our love was damned: the forty years that lay between us were drawing us slowly but inexorably to a tragic conclusion. But, at my age, I had no time for tears. He was the one my desire had chosen!

I would have liked to tell him that Shen Nan Qiu had never had permission to penetrate me. The fifty year-old had served me as a sleeping draft and a bed-warmer. The affair had been a game, just to have revenge for Scribe of Loyalty's infidelities, to make him jealous. I would have liked to tell him that I was disappointed by my sons and felt that my grandchildren were strangers, that my nephews could think of nothing but taking my place on the throne, and that he alone—he, Little Treasure, fished out of the mysterious river of destiny—brought light into my life. I was prepared to offer him a flock of young women to keep him close to me as he had been before, like an exuberant talkative child.

I was unable to put all this in words and was afraid that he would blackmail me; instead I spoke of the accusations leveled at him. First he paled, then he sneered: "So it is true then, what they say about the doctor Shen Nan Qiu. If you want to be rid of me, nothing could be easier. If you hand me over to Lai Jun Chen, I will tell him everything without being tortured: your obsessions, your fears, your weaknesses, your secret fantasies. You would do better to have me killed straight away!"

Seeing that he had flushed scarlet in his indignation, I smiled.

"I am showing you these denunciations only to tell you that I am prepared to forgive you. Don't you see that, without my protection, you will be trailed by the judges like a hare hounded by hunting dogs. In your few years in the Forbidden City you made very few friends and a good many enemies. What would you be without me?"

He stared at me, and his eyes glowed with a dark fire.

"Why do you toy with me? You must choose between the doctor and the monk. Just one word: do you wish to marry me?"

My heart turned to ice, and the smile froze on my face. I delivered a prepared speech: "I still have not appointed the successor to the throne in Court. If, in such a situation, I were to marry, if I were to confer the first imperial title on one man, my actions would create confusion."

"Majesty," he cried, throwing himself at me and almost suffocating me, "I love you. I want you to be my wife; I want to call you Heaven-light; I want to be joined to you in life and in death! Yes, I will renounce the title of husband; I spit on recognition. Let us be married in secret, here, now; we shall take Heaven and Earth as our witnesses. Swear to me that you are mine."

How could I believe that such a young and beautiful man could love an old woman so passionately? Was he hoping to manipulate me? Was he willing to usurp the throne? I pushed him: "The insolence! Kneel before your sovereign!"

Scribe of Loyalty froze and collapsed at my feet, and I spoke slowly and deliberately: "Leave and never come back!"

He smacked his forehead heavily against the ground and then ran off. When his silhouette was reduced to a blur and then disappeared between the gates of my palace, I was devastated.

The gods had not invented love for an emperor.

* * *

I WAS HAUNTED by Scribe of Loyalty's sadness. I could not forgive myself for hurting him. By breaking off with him, I had deprived myself of happiness and of my remedy for immortality. I drove the doctor Shen Nan Qiu from my palace to lock myself away with my pain.

News of my lover reached me: The master monk was sowing terror in Luoyang. His disciples trawled the streets all day picking fights. They broke down the doors of foreign temples and destroyed their unfamiliar idols. For Buddha's anniversary celebrations, the monk secretly arranged to have a pond dug out in front of his monastery. He stood up on a stage in public and cut his own thigh, then he unveiled the huge hole filled with the blood of an ox he had had slaughtered the day before. Claiming that it was his own blood, he said he would commission a divine portrait of me in this crimson paint.

Word of his clashes echoed through the Court. Some said he had gone mad; others called for him to be punished. His cries of despair tore me apart, but I brushed aside my own weakness by asking the judges to disarm his monastery. Delighted to be free to attack the imperial favorite, the Court raised an army and surrounded the estate. The monks were surprised and surrendered immediately. They were chained, thrown into prison, and then exiled. After a brief morning in custody, Scribe of Loyalty received my edict granting him grace and was freed from prison. He headed for the Palace and asked to speak with me, but I refused.

One night two months later, I woke with a start. There was an acrid smell in my pavilion. I asked for the door to be opened: Outside the sky was lit up like a brazier and seemed to be rippling. A column of smoke rose up from the Temple of Ten Thousand Elements where clusters of giant flames were blooming like monstrous flowers and spitting out showers of sparks.

Gentleness ran to me in tears. "Majesty, it's the temple. Heaven is angry!"

My eunuchs arrived with a litter. They wanted to take me to a palace beside the river, but I refused to move.

Swarms of birds wheeled in the darkness screeching in fear. In the courtyard outside women fell to their knees, joined their hands and recited prayers. The fires rose up and dropped back down in time to their chanting. I was overwhelmed by a dark premonition and stood rooted to the spot. The macabre dance of the flames fell on my retinas, beneath the vault of my head, within my bleeding soul.

My ministers were silent during the morning salutation the following day. They feared my rage, but what they feared most was that the blaze might have been a warning from Heaven, a harbinger of imminent catastrophe. To calm the mood of anxiety spreading through the Empire, I decided to sacrifice myself. I published an imperial edict in which I asked my people and officials to lay the blame on me. Libations were made in the Eternal Temple. Taking the Ancestors as my witnesses, I prayed that the punishment of the gods might be visited on me alone.

I decided to have the Temple of Ten Thousand Elements rebuilt, and Scribe of Loyalty was appointed to oversee the work. But the master monk seemed to take a long time to come and thank me for this appointment. Gripped with indescribable anguish, I cancelled my evening ride and waited for him. A few days later, I was told that a beggar child claimed to have a message for me from Scribe of Loyalty. I received him. The boy was so awestruck that he shook from head to toe and could not answer my questions. I nevertheless managed to tear a crumpled letter from his hand. The paper seemed unbearably fine to me. My heart felt heavy in my breast, and my body froze under the effects of an unspeakable fear. I took a long time unfolding that piece of rice paper. My lover's terrible handwriting leapt off the page at me: "Heavenlight, you shall never grow old. Tonight I shall be your sacrifice to Heaven."

Near the Southern Gate of the Forbidden City, tens of thousands of workmen were toiling to evacuate melted bronze statues, charred wood, and ashes that were still glowing hot. One official reading through the Sacred Writings found a verse which said that the bodhisattva Maitreya had become Buddha of the Future after sacrificing himself by fire. This reading triggered a new religious fervor and restored hope among the people.

The world was borne on a wave of renewed enthusiasm that I pretended to share. As I watched the new temple reaching toward the skies, taller and more sumptuous than its predecessor, I saw Little Treasure's smile, red on white. I sometimes dreamed of him, this man whose imposing statue was now silhouetted against the sky. With his phallus in my belly, he would lean over me and say, "Heavenlight, you misunderstood me."

I had not realized that he loved me. I had thought he was acting out of self-interested ambition. I had been afraid he would rob me of my throne.

I had destroyed my own immortal remedy.

Had I become a senile tyrant?

FOR MY BIRTHDAY I ordered that feasts be offered to the people in every town for a period of nine days. Within the Palace I summoned only members of my family and a few favorite ministers to a banquet set up in the Pavilion of Flying Snow.

That evening I missed Scribe of Loyalty's voice. The night had not come yet, and snowflakes fell against the window, gray forms wriggling down on a translucent screen. I sat with pride in the heart of the palace, with my back to the north, looking southward. Serving women stood behind me holding round or square fans on long handles, symbols of my imperial splendor; Gentleness and my Court ladies brought ink, paper, flowers, incense, handkerchiefs, and vases. They were all dressed as men. My son and his twenty children were lined up on my right, on the eastern side. His large family still seemed tiny compared to my thirteen nephews and the spreading mass of scores of great nephews and great nieces in the opposite wing. Further away from me, closer to the door, I had put my relations from my mother's family and the ministers, indistinct silhouettes merging in the candlelight.

I had had the year of my birth erased from every register in the Forbidden City: No one knew how old I was, but this was a bitter secret that filled me with piercing melancholy. When the Empire paid homage to my eternal youth, I pretended I too believed in it.

The Emperor of China had just turned seventy, a figure that terrified me. The Ancients said that, at the age of seventy, certainty opens the door to wisdom. Yet, on that evening, watching the sun set and the light fade, my doubts flooded in with the darkness.

My dynasty still did not have a legitimate heir. I was torn between a son who bore the blood of the overthrown dynasty and a nephew descended from a brother I had loathed. My gaze came to rest on Miracle to my right. Music meant nothing to him, and here, at this jubilant gathering, he drank incessantly and concentrated on his food. His drawn features afforded a glimpse of the weariness and boredom in his soul. Since he had reached adulthood, I had never seen him smile or express anger. Miracle was an aesthete with no ideals. Life flowed through his body like an unruffled river. He never made any decisions, never voiced an opinion. He was shut away in his own world pervaded by the purity of calligraphy and the voluptuous delights offered by his concubines, and he bowed to every current. Recently yet another group of conspirators had made use of his ambiguous status. When they were arrested by Lai Jun Chen, they claimed that Miracle had given them orders to reinstate the Tang dynasty. The prosecutor urged me to punish the unworthy prince, but I was satisfied with merely moving him to a guarded residence. I really could not exile the last of my four sons!

I caught the eye of his wife, Lady Liu, who had been Empress for a few years. I had never liked her round face with its thin lips. I stared at her. Her gaze wavered, and she looked away.

The two county princes, Happy Success and Prosperous Inheritance, rose to their feet behind her and threw themselves at my feet. They asked for my permission to dance. How old were these boys? I did not know. With their crimson lips and pink cheeks, they had the proud bearing of children of high birth. On their invitation, the little princesses stepped forward, bowed to me, and began to play various musical instruments. The boys imitated adults' solemn movements and swirled their sleeves, singing: "Ten thousand springs for the Sacred Emperor, the ownership of ten thousand kingdoms."

They twirled with their arms in the air like butterflies struggling in a rainstorm. These innocent creatures could not know that they would be struck down by misfortune. Before the banquet, a serving woman had come to denounce their mothers to me. Lady Liu and the Favorite Duo had set up an occult altar in a secret alcove within their palace. With their evil incantations, they had called forth the souls of my two rivals, the deposed Empress Wang and the disgraced concubine Xiao, and had ordered them to destroy me. Anyone who practiced sorcery was condemned to death by law, but I would not give Lai Jun Chen the pleasure of spreading a family scandal. That evening, neither Lady Liu nor the Favorite Duo, who was sitting in the shadows, would return home. My eunuchs had received orders to keep them back at the end of the meal. They would help them to commit suicide.

I could almost hear the orphans weeping, but I felt no pity. The following day an imperial decree would order my grandsons to abandon their residences and come to live in an enclosed wing of my palace. By holding his heirs hostage, I would find it easier to watch over Miracle, whom I could not punish.

The princes stepped back, and my nephew Piety came forward. He prostrated himself energetically and called loudly for me to have ten thousand years of good health. He had barely returned to his seat when the musicians began to play the *Melody of Long Life.* The doors of the Palace were drawn open, and one hundred dancing girls streamed onto the vermillion carpet of silk and wool threaded with gold. They wore black scholars' caps, mauve tunics lined with yellow, emerald colored belts, and gray trains, and they performed a dance devised for my birthday by Piety.

My eldest nephew sat in the half light smiling and clapping in time to the music. He was now over fifty and had a curly beard, thick eyebrows, a hooked nose, and eyes that blazed with ambition—a curious mixture of features inherited from my Father and the latter's first wife who had some Tatar blood. Everything about my son Miracle and my nephew Piety was different. The first, an imperial prince, had grown up surrounded by silk and velvet; the second, son of my commoner brother who had been scorned and exiled, had lived in contempt and poverty. Miracle had been given the title of king when he was four years old; Piety had become king when he was fifty. Miracle, the fervent Buddhist, refused to kill game; Piety, the cannibal, beheaded his enemies without a moment's hesitation. Miracle, the poet, felt only distaste for command; Piety, the banished, longed for revenge.

My nephews' rise had shadowed my sons' fall. Ever since Splendor's death, Wisdom's suicide, and Future's exile, Piety—now head of the Wu clan—had adapted to his good fortune and done everything he could to improve his position. He may have looked coarse, but he did understand the subtleties of human relations. He had defended my legitimacy, he had supported the magistrates in their persecution of the conspirators, and he had organized the personality cult surrounding me. When my own sons had tried to revolt against my authority, he had urged officials to sign the petition calling for my accession. It was also him, with his feverish imagination, who had invented all the emphatic titles that the Court was so eager to give me.

The blood of a wood merchant flowed in our veins. Piety, who was not unlike me, had inherited from Father an infallible calculating mind. The very day after my coronation, he had set to work on having himself recognized as heir to the throne. The fact that my sons were descended from the overthrown household did, indeed, throw some doubt over the legitimacy of my reign. If Miracle came to the throne, he would reinstate his father's dynasty. If Piety, my nephew, were appointed as successor, he would more likely ensure the eternal sovereignty of our Wu clan.

Opinion was divided in Court. Some of the ministers saw my reign as a glorious extension of my husband's; these were men who consented to grant me their loyalty so long as my son Miracle continued to represent a moral guarantee for the future. But there were countless young officials united behind Piety and my nephews, determined to replace the former dynasty's dignitaries. They called for a break with the past and insisted we have a radical and bloody revolution.

That evening, once again, I looked back and forth between my son and my nephew. I had no strong ties of affection with either of them. Both were yoked to me by blood. I was hurt by Miracle's indifference and put on my guard by Piety's ardor. If Miracle were Emperor after my death, he would probably remember the mother who had brought him into the world whereas, if Piety were sovereign, he would surely be eager to honor his father, the brother I loathed, and his mother, the sister-in-law I despised. Even if I had forgiven the Wu clan for humiliating my mother and assassinating Little Sister, my nephews would always remember the period of exile that had robbed them of their youth. Even though I had brought our ancestors into the Eternal Temple, even though I had handed out provincial kingdoms to my nephews and the seals of county princes to their sons, this generosity was only a display of reconciliation. The clan had been both my torturer and my victim. The magnificence of the present could not erase the past, the Wu village with its small dark rooms. There was only a self-interested kind of solidarity between my nephews and myself. They gave me political leverage, and I held their future in my hands.

GENTLENESS WOKE ME from my reverie. The music was growing louder, bonze bells were ringing, and thousands of birds were singing. The dancing girls knelt on the ground and then flipped over backward, their faces disappearing in a ripple of sleeves. A giant peony opened up one petal at a time, and in the heart of this great flower, I read the characters, "Ten thousand years to the Sacred Emperor." I ordered for a glass of wine to be taken to Piety to congratulate him for his creation. Proud and gratified, he prostrated himself toward me and downed the entire glass. Miracle sat facing him, his bored expression unchanged.

Not far from him, Spirit, my eldest brother's son, suppressed a grimace and forced himself to smile at his cousin.

Spirit was beautiful, elegant, and cultured; he was the one successful incarnation in a clan bent on raising its status to extraordinary heights. Where Piety was still rigid and unrefined as a peasant, Spirit—who was five years younger than him—was from a more highly evolved strain, comprising subtlety and an urbane ambiguity. Piety was as inflexible as Spirit was amenable. The first was like an attacking chariot storming forwards; the second could navigate every kind of current, could insert himself through every closed door. The more demonstrations of loyalty Piety laid on, the less I trusted him. Spirit kept to his cousin's shadow, but he showed me genuine adulation. While he urged Piety to supplant Miracle, he knew how to tackle my son, who the officials no longer dared approach. He slipped easily from one camp to the other, and he strove to reconcile my ministers with the clan by acting as my secret messenger. The more impatient Piety was to oust Miracle from the Eastern Palace and take up residence there himself; the more adroitly Spirit carried out his work. His maneuvering had not escaped my attention. Spirit also wanted the title of Supreme Son and was waiting patiently for the outcome of this insoluble conflict: The two cousins would kill each other, and he would then present himself as the ideal candidate.

The Princess of Eternal Peace was sitting close to Spirit, but she seemed distracted. With her oval face, wide forehead, and full mouth, her slender, well-muscled body and her haughty, energetic bearing, she was disturbingly like me in my youth. Given that her ancestors, grandfathers, father, mother, and brothers had all been Emperor, my only daughter wore her name, Moon, with glory. My large family of descendants paled in comparison to her luminous presence, they were the insignificant stars in my darkness. I had renounced the affection of my sons long ago and concentrated all my maternal passions on her. She was erudite, intelligent, and blessed with a scope for politics that was lacking in the male members of both clans. But this princess would never be heir to the throne: The ministers would not let her reign; her brothers and cousins would join forces to supplant her; the people would see her accession as a usurping of power and would rise up in revolt on the smallest sign from one of the princes. Moon was sentimental, tortured, hesitant, and fragile. She could advise, but she would never subdue. Too much power would have killed her.

I had given her an income equivalent to that of a king. I had chosen a life for her devoted to the arts and to love; I had hoped her life would be full of pure, crystalline joy to make the immortals jealous. But terrible suffering—that epidemic that ignored the crimson walls of the Palace, which invited itself into the homes of rich and poor alike and which struck down beggars just as readily as princes—had succeeded in reaching Moon in her jade cocoon.

At the age of thirteen, my daughter conceived a violent passion for Xue Shao, whom she had met while walking beside the River Luo. To fulfill her desires, I ordered the young aristocrat to repudiate his legitimate wife, and I offered them the most lavish wedding in history. But prince consorts have hearts as capricious as imperial princesses: Having been forcibly married, Xue Shao remained attached to the memory of his first wife who had chosen to commit suicide rather than be abandoned. He had treated Moon with respectful contempt. Moon was accepted and rejected, feared and loathed by her husband's family, and she had hidden her pain from me until the day I discovered that this unworthy son-in-law was involved in a conspiracy.

Xue Shao was executed; Moon lost her failed source of happiness. I urged her to remarry, and she fell in love with my nephew Tranquility who was also a married man. The cousin, astonished by this unexpected good fortune, did not wait to be begged. He dismissed his wife and loved Moon with religious fervor. But she was haunted by the memory of Xue Shao: The imperial princess preferred an impossible love to the adoration she was offered. Very soon after they were married, she betrayed her husband in the arms of a guards officer.

I despaired at my daughter's turbulent emotions. When she chose

Tranquility, I thought the gods had showed me the path of hope: Marriages between my nephews and my children would knit together the two clans, both tributaries of the same river. But the failure of this exemplary marriage only increased hostilities.

Filial love cost me endless waiting, much disappointment, and considerable pain. I kept the succession unclear to maintain the balance: My nephews continued to live in hope, and my ministers continued to obey me, while I woke a little more tired every morning. The crown, which conferred power on me, was not enough to alter the course of the stars, the cycle of the seasons, or the hearts of men.

After his wife and his concubine had been executed and his sons had been captured, Miracle became a ghost. Moon changed her lover, and Tranquility drowned his sorrows in alcohol. My nephews pursued their fight for my favor. None of them was interested in the people, the land or the splendor of the Empire. None of them knew anything of self-abnegation and the sacrifices of being sovereign.

I envied all those who saw their lives stretching to infinity in generations to come. I searched in vain for the future of my dynasty.

TWELVE

The seasons came and went. In springtime, the skies were filled with peach rose, pear white, grenadine orange, and magnolia mauve. In the autumn, the wounded leaves of the maples and the bloody tears of the persimmon trees showered over the city. I lived in the most beautiful palace in the most beautiful city in the world. I was surrounded by indolent calligraphers and sensuous poetesses draped in muslin and silk. I owned the world's best chargers, so swift they struck flying swallows as they galloped. I commanded warrior and spiritual princes, philosopher and strategist ministers. I was adored by an entire nation of passionate, hardworking people. But these triumphs, this grandeur—the apotheosis of earthly achievement—no longer moved me.

Beauty is not happiness. The secret flavor that wet my appetite had disappeared. The inner light that gives people their soul, the city its color, the rain its sweet melancholy, and the monotone days their serenity—that light had been extinguished.

I lost my faithful companions Ruby and Emerald that year. Despite her perseverance, the Princess of Gold proved unable to seduce Time. Death interrupted her futile gabbling and juvenile laughter. Her perfume dissipated; her name was no longer whispered. The very day after her burial, she was forgotten.

I could not bear anyone to use the words "old" or "tired," and I exiled every official who dared advise me to retire. I flew into a rage whenever my ministers broached the subject of the succession. "I am not senile yet," I would reply coolly to anyone who tried to imply that I must appoint a Supreme Son. I would wake with new aches and pains and go to bed with a little more despair. The world may well have recognized me as a goddess, but I was no less human for it. My slide into decline proved that my fate would be as miserable as a commoner's: I was condemned to die.

The accusations leveled at Miracle began to accumulate, but I could not make up my mind to eliminate the last of my sons. My nephew Piety made one appeal after another: His impatient ambition was almost usurpation in itself. My nights were haunted by terrible nightmares. Sometimes I would see Piety crowned, exterminating Miracle, Moon, and Future. All my grandchildren whose legitimacy challenged his were reduced to bloodied flesh and severed heads borne aloft on iron pikes. Sometimes I saw Miracle as emperor, weak and easily influenced, becoming a puppet to his concubines and eunuchs. As a powerless sovereign, an impotent lord, he would be besieged by Future coming out of exile at the head of a rebellious army and demanding his birthright. The Forbidden City would burn; my nephews would revolt. Piety would ascend to the throne only to be supplanted by Spirit, and he in turn would be assassinated by some other power. The Empire would shatter into a thousand rival kingdoms. Armies of mercenaries would trample the fields, burn villages, massacre the population, and ransack towns. Luoyang, Long Peace, Jinzhou, Bingzhou, and Yangzhou would be strewn with corpses and reduced to ruins and cemeteries. I would wake with my forehead covered with sweat. Peace on Earth was fragile, and prosperity precarious. Every dynasty was destined to perish.

At night my bed was frozen. As I lay in the darkness, I knew that the music I missed was the music of love. How I longed for that blissful drug that could allow me to escape from my desperate aloneness! I would sometimes dream of a silhouette, a smile, a combination of Little Phoenix and Little Treasure. This stranger would heal my anguished soul, and I would forget the tragedy of being an emperor without a successor. The bitter solace would vanish when I woke. I had not known how to love, and now it was too late.

The precious flavor had been wasted; the light had dimmed. I would occasionally savor a boy or a young girl, sent to me secretly by the eunuchs to fortify me. Not one of them could save me from the river in which I was slowly drowning. My flesh was weary, my heart impervious. I was turning into a deep sea monster, guardian of an illusory world.

GRIM DAYS ALTERNATED with moments of exultant happiness. Determined to conquer my mood, I threw myself into extensive building projects. The excitement on the huge construction sites drowned my despair. Thousand year-old trees groaned and crashed to the ground, furnaces taller than the hills blazed, and the streams of red-hot bronze set the sky alight. The constant din of hammering and the hiss of metal plunged into water reverberated around the four corners of the kingdom.

The workmen's skills meant I could realize the most outlandish dreams. The ramparts were fortified and built up all round the Imperial Capital. The avenues were widened to accommodate nine giant tripods, monsters molded out of 560,000 jins[20] of bronze and decorated in bas-relief with landscapes from our nine regions. They were drawn by 100,000 soldiers and countless oxen and imperial elephants and taken to the foot of the new Temple of Ten Thousand Elements. A celestial temple was built behind the sacred sanctuary, standing two stories taller than it. This new temple housed the largest Buddha in the world, big enough to sit ten people on just one toenail. The imperial path was adorned with seven gold statues: the Wheel, the Elephant, the Celestial

[20] One jin is equal to a half kilo.

Girl, the Winged Horse, the Pearl of Intelligence, and the Divine Servants. By the Southern Gate of the Forbidden City stood the Celestial Pivot.[21] This extraordinary monument, offered by three barbarian kings, conversed with the clouds, and overlooked the entire city from its dizzying height. It was a column of bronze covered with magical inscriptions, sacred drawings, and celebratory poems, and at its highest point, four golden dragons reared up to the sky bearing the Pearl of Fire that lit up the Empire with its eternal flames.

After endless reshuffling, I succeeded in putting together a well-proportioned government where strengths balanced out weaknesses in a harmonious structure. I gave my steadfast ministers complete freedom to reprimand wrongdoers and suggest changes. My nephew kings ensured my authority went unchallenged. The prosecutor Lai Jun Chen and his collaborators terrified the disloyal. I granted closely supervised autonomy to the provinces. Our social hierarchy was consolidated: Every caste had its own symbols, its constraints and privileges. But gone were the intransigent segregation and the fatal lack of social mobility. Every eventuality was permitted. Every talent must be allowed to flourish.

The equitable statutes of the former regime were respected, and ancient rites and forgotten traditions were unearthed and restored. I had created a new culture while respecting the continuity of dynasties. With the favor granted to me by the gods, the Empire's prosperity was like a galloping charger: Controlling it was now just a question of balance, breathing, and concentration.

I had a burning desire to realize my husband's unfulfilled dream, to perform the Sanctification of Heaven at the top of Mount Song. I was impatient to be the unique woman in the world who leads the supreme ceremony awarded to the greatest sovereign. The preparations soothed away the boredom that gnawed at me constantly. I raised the imperial

---

[21] According the Annals, 250,000 kilograms of bronze and 1,650,000 kilograms of iron were melted down to make this monument.

parade, accompanied by my Court and our foreign vassals. The procession was wider than the River Luo and filled entire plains and valleys. As I observed the rites of purification, I felt a weight lift from my body and my spirits. Despite my seventy-one years, I reached the snowy peak of Mount Song. After carrying out the libations, I dismissed my attendants and stood alone in the sacred enclosure at the very top of an altar-hill built as a sequence of terraces in five different colors of Earth. There prostrated, I recited the prayers of invocation.

Somewhere in the distance, musicians were striking their bronze bells and their sounding stones. The peak was shrouded by the wind and snow. In the darkness, I searched in vain for a light, a sign from the Supreme Being. I could see nothing. The god was deaf to my prayers. He who turned the wheel of destiny knew that I had falsified the stone with the inscription "Divine Mother, who graces the earth, through her, let the Emperor's reign prosper" and thrown it into Luo River. He knew that I had dictated to the monk, Clarity of Law, the passage concerning a Celestial Daughter called Purity of Heavenlight when he was translating the Sutra of the Great Cloud. I had fashioned the divine will to take the reigns from men's hands. But God had not appointed a woman to rule the world. I was just a usurper, and this was why I had no heir!

I wept in silence. Suddenly, the sun sprang out of the darkness and poured out a thin stream of red that swelled to tumbling waves in an ocean of mist. In those brightly colored undulating clouds, I could see celestial horses galloping toward me. Suddenly the miracle I had waited for all my life came to pass: The glowing disc of the sun drew closer, grew larger and larger like a silk sheet unfurling, then it filled space in its entirety. Its countless rays were like sharpened arrows hurtling toward my flesh, and the pain as they burned me became the sweetest pleasure. God was there; God appeared to me! With my forehead to the ground and my eyes closed, I let his incandescence embrace me bodily. I did not have time to ask him whether I was his beloved daughter, nor what death was, nor who would be my heir. I forgot to beg his protection for my dynasty or my people. I forgot my dream of an eternal reign. The questions that had always tormented me ebbed away. I was burning. I was turning into a ball of fire revolving slowly on itself. I could feel myself dissolving in a sea of light. I suddenly saw my own body prostrating itself at the top of a mountain, surrounded by the snow. I saw the world below, beneath the clouds, in the depths of the abyss.

Rivers scour through the earth and run toward the ocean. The snows fall, and trees cover themselves with leaves. Palaces crumble, paths disappear, wheat sprouts up and transforms deserts into fields. God is the source of all movement, inexhaustible life, eternal energy. God had made me and sent me here to demonstrate his might: He creates and destroys, erases and renews. Even at the heights to which I had risen, I remained dust in the palm of his hand.

THE JOURNEY BACK to Luoyang was gloomy. I lay huddled in fur coats inside my carriage surrounded by fires crackling in braziers, but still shivering with cold. The strength was being drawn out of me like an ebbing tide. My ears were filled with a buzzing sound. My eyesight became hazy, and I ordered my officials to write their political reports in larger characters. Once I had dictated the commemorative hymn that would be engraved on the stela erected at the top of Mount Song, I accepted the idea of dying.

One evening the prosecutor Lai Jun Chen asked to speak to me in secret. He was brought to the palace along an underground passageway. As he threw himself at my feet, I noticed a feverish red flush on his pale cheeks. His wolf-like eyes glowed with something akin to joy. My wildcats seemed to have picked up the scent of blood on him; they roared and paced agitatedly. The judge was surrounded by dogs and leopards, but he showed no fear. He took from his sleeve a scroll of paper and held it aloft in both his hands to offer it to me. I unrolled it in the candlelight to reveal a diagram in which the First Magistrate had traced the networks of conspirators from the time of Wu Ji, Shang Guan Yi, and

Pei Yan right up to the present. There were hundreds of names, all written in large characters and connected to form a tree whose branches reached as far as provincial governments and the encampments of those who had been banished. Every enemy of the State was inscribed there: The dead were ringed with red ink, the exiled with blue, and prisoners in green, and there were black circles hovering threateningly around those who were still free. At the very end of the scroll, I found Miracle, Moon, Future, Piety, and Spirit.

Lai Jun Chen's voice quavered slightly. Miracle, the Emperor who had resigned; Future, the deposed emperor; Piety, the King of Wei; Spirit, the King of Liang; Moon, the Princess of Eternal Peace; and her husband, Tranquility, the King of Jian Chang were secretly planning a coup and preparing to share the kingdom between them.

"Lord Lai," I sighed, "I have taken note of your observations. You may leave."

"Majesty," he said, edging forward on his knees, "the King of Wei has been restless the whole time you have delayed appointing an heir. He is weary of waiting; he is preparing to resort to force and will call on his cousins who command your guards regiments. The Princess of Eternal Peace is secretly scheming to establish an agreement between her brothers and her husband's clan. Majesty, the time has come, an uprising in the Court is imminent!"

"Let me think!" I said, silencing the prosecutor with a wave. He disappeared through the partition. Lai Jun Chen had an acute sense of smell like an animal, which meant that he could identify the ideas that people were harboring and the longings they themselves had not yet formulated. While other judges were happy simply examining the facts, he projected himself into the future. The plot he was imagining was one I had already lived in my nightmares. Men's strengths go hand in hand with their weaknesses. That is why there is no such thing as an invincible warrior, and why heroes die.

Two days later during the morning audience Piety, King of Wei, asked to speak. His powerful voice reverberated around the hall: He charged the magistrate Lai Jun Chen with corruption, exploiting his influential position, and attempting to usurp power. My Great Ministers and my nephews Spirit and Tranquility stepped forward and unanimously upheld his charges. In keeping with Palace codes, Lai Jun Chen had risen from his seat and prostrated himself as soon as his name was mentioned. I was surprised by this violent attack and remained silent. Someone had betrayed the prosecutor by warning the King of Wei, who had responded with an adroit riposte: Piety had pointed the finger at Lai Jun Chen for the crimes of which he himself was accused. The entire government had joined him and was declaring war on the most feared man in the Empire. How was it that the prosecutor, who saw plots in every direction, had been unaware of this one, like a soothsayer blind to his own fate?

I silenced my own irritation while my ministers pressed me for a response, and Lai Jun Chen asked to speak. Either I would hand the magistrate over to the Court, or I would let him explain himself. He would denounce the conspiracy: With one hundred members of both my families in prison or condemned to death, I would become the laughing stock of the entire world. I would be the senile emperor sinking the very ship on which she sails. What authority would I have left to reign? Who would be heir to the throne? Piety had played his part very cleverly. On the chessboard of the Forbidden City, he had just checkmated his opponent. I did not grant the judge the right to defend himself, but pretended to be furious and ordered that his cap and official's tablet be removed and that he be thrown in prison.

A wave of hatred rippled through the Court. I created a special court made up of high-ranking magistrates and Great Ministers, and while they were deliberating the charges brought against the accused man, the kings and dignitaries and the Princess of Eternal Peace filed past me begging me to apply the law. A stack of thirty scrolls, listing 1,500 charges, was laid before me. A petition bearing hundreds of signatures was brought to me. The entire Court was asking for this torturer to be put to death. Ten years earlier, I would have firmly defended Lai Jun

Chen. But now my soul, which had embraced God himself, was weary of human quarrels, and my policies were restricted to engineering compromises. A sovereign is never entirely master of his kingdom. I was constrained to abandon thoughts of exiling him and to concede that he should be put to death.

The wind picked up, and the mountains whispered. Migratory birds crossed the sky with anguished cries. The chrysanthemums in the Imperial Park exhaled their bitter fragrance and dropped their petals into the River Luo. I watched the moon wax: It would soon be the mid-autumn full moon, the date set by the ancestors for public executions.

The night before the fateful day, I tossed and turned in bed before falling asleep. In my dreams, I climbed up to the observatory. The Forbidden City at my feet steeped in shadows, like a cemetery where the red lanterns of night watchmen on their rounds danced like will-o'-the-wisps.

All of a sudden someone stepped out of the darkness and threw himself to the ground.

"I have come to prostrate myself at your feet one last time," Lai Jun Chen told me, his voice echoing as if from the depths of a well and his iron chains rattling. "Before leaving this world, I wanted to tell you that all the accusations are false. I have never betrayed Your Majesty's trust."

"Lord Lai, you made only one mistake: You criticized my family."

"Majesty, they are plotting against you!"

"I am tired. I no longer have the strength to unravel all this hatred and to cause bloodshed. In a kingdom everyone except the king is a conspirator. There is always an intelligent way of making peace with enemies. Why did you not realize that? Why have you forced me to sacrifice you?"

"Majesty," he said, prostrating himself, "I am not yet beheaded. So long as there is breath left in me, I shall fight for you. Majesty, you must choose! Either you shall reign for ten thousand years, or the Zhou dynasty will be overthrown, and you will be betrayed for all eternity!"

"Lord Lai," I cried despairingly, "look at my hands; look at my face.

I'm growing old; I'm going to die! What does glory mean to me now or the dynasty!"

"You are wrong, Majesty; you are a goddess who will live as long as the River Luo flows and Mount Song stands!"

"I am a mere mortal in this existence. I too shall end up in the Yellow Earth, like all the other emperors resting in their tombs. While I am alive, I am Master of the World. Once I die I shall have only the narrow confines of a coffin! Lord Lai, leave me. Our families are a congenital illness. Mine is my infirmity. I did not choose it; the gods imposed it on me. I am condemned to disappear along with my dynasty."

A sob wracked the man whom I believed to be incapable of emotion. His weeping was the strangled howl of a dying animal.

"How can I leave Your Majesty alone in this world! How can you fight everyone alone? Majesty, I beg you, let me live; let me defend you!"

My heart contracted, and my voice shook as I said, "Leave!"

"Majesty," he said, wiping his tears, "your wish is my command. For you, I shall go to my death. May my sovereign be granted ten thousand years of happiness! May the Sacred Emperor be granted ten thousand years of good health!"

The wind lifted, and the judge disappeared. I was woken by a needling pain. The glow of nightlights danced on the walls of the Palace, like dying fireflies. I asked for Gentleness to be woken, and she played the zither until dawn.

The following day I hosted the annual banquet held in celebration of the moon. Dancing girls on the stage swirled their long sleeves. My son, my daughter, and my nephews took turns offering me wine. I waved them back to their seats. Up on my throne, I served myself and got drunk. I contemplated the heavenly mirror in its full and perfect splendor. In the middle of its silvery surface, there were darker patches that made its luminosity seem all the more pure and mysterious. Judge Lai Jun Chen had been the impurity that had accompanied me in my solitude. His head would already have rolled to the ground, and his body would have been handed to the crowd to trample on it in their fury. I had lanced an infection. I had stripped myself of my last weapon.

I stood alone at the top of the world. Before me and behind me, there was now only emptiness and infinity.

THE REGIMENTS OF the imperial guard were posted along every avenue, and the inhabitants of Luoyang received orders to stay at home with their doors and windows closed. I stepped into the golden carriage to join Moon, who was celebrating her thirtieth spring. The imperial procession filed through the streets for hours on end.

Hills covered in blossoming plum trees undulated around a frozen lake, and crimson galleries snaked through the snow. The residence of the Princess of Eternal Peace was a palace of jade and crystal. Fires crackled in braziers, and rare dishes appeared in a heady succession. This banquet marking the reconciliation between emperor and her family brought together every powerful figure in the Empire. The great men in magnificent finery were soon drunk, constantly raising their glasses to toast the omnipotent princess and to wish her a thousand years of happiness. A dais had been set up for me at the far end of the room, and perched on my throne, I was bored as usual.

A rustling sound woke me from my snoozing; I opened my heavy eyelids and saw a silhouette in the doorway. Whoever it was prostrated themselves and came toward me through the turmoil of the banquet, a slender boat plying through a lotus field. The figure drew closer and revealed itself to be an extraordinary beauty: Now I could make out the square tips of his shoes and the flowing movements of his tunic with its long sleeves. His oval face was lightly powdered, and he had dark slanting eyes. There was something familiar about this stranger!

He prostrated himself again, then took a bamboo flute from his belt and brought it to his lips with his eyes still modestly lowered. When he blew into the instrument the world suddenly stopped buzzing around me, the winter faded away, and spring spread its wings. Flowers bloomed between his arpeggios, and I saw swallows flying overhead. A great plain of green meadows embraced me in its cool, fresh grasses. A hill wreathed in mist appeared on the horizon. A pathway zigzagged through fields of sorghum toward the top of the hill where there was a stela covered with inscriptions. Then the vision melted away. The youth bowed to me once more and backed away respectfully before disappearing. I looked at the emptiness he had left, speechless and terrified.

I called Gentleness and asked her the musician's name. She told me that he was called Prosperity and was a descendant of Zhang Xing Cheng, a minister in the Department of Punishments during Emperor Eternal Ancestor's reign. She added that my daughter, Moon, was hoping to find a position for him at the Court.

That night I was haunted by the boy's pale face and pink lips. A year earlier, as I returned from Mount Song, I had secretly met with a Taoist monk who claimed he had lived a thousand years and could see a thousand years of the future. I remembered his enigmatic prediction: "The end will come when the Celestial Prince plays his bamboo flute."

Prosperity had come, the end was beginning. A bamboo flute was guiding me through the darkness to the mouth of the labyrinth. It had all been written.

The very next day I sent a message to Moon, and that evening the princess sent her lover to the Inner Palace and offered him to me.

HOLDING PROSPERITY IN my arms, I realized I was no longer the same woman, no longer ashamed of my old age or filled with self-loathing. The despair had vanished. This coming together of two bodies had been inscribed in the *Book of the Earth*. Prosperity was a present from God. He was bringing me new life even as he announced my death.

When the Mistress of the World, Emperor of the Zhou dynasty, quivered to a man's rhythms once more Tai Mountain crumbled, the Yellow Sea boiled, wild animals roared in the forest, and the whole universe shivered with joy and amazement. It was a long time since I had had an official favorite, and the Court was bowled over by the news.

Urged on by my Great Ministers, the imperial doctors recommended that I should be examined immediately, and they forbade violent orgasms that might prove fatal. Their eager concern amused me. From the very first night with my new lover, I knew that my pleasure was no longer the physical contractions. In my dotage, death's mystic light was blinding me. My erotic pleasure was almost a breathing exercise, an elation that lay along the torturous path of caresses on my skin. It was a dreamlike pilgrimage toward the kingdom of the immortals.

A month later, for my entertainment and to ensure that he was no longer the only man in the gynaeceum attracting jealousy, Prosperity brought his elder brother Simplicity to my bed. The boy was eighteen. Their fresh faces, their soft skin, and their exquisite smell of crisp green leaves overwhelmed me. I had been neither a good mother nor a good lover. The Zhang brothers were my last chance to savor the joys of ordinary women. They were my last rays of sunlight before the ultimate sunset.

I gave them the most beautiful things in my possession. Sumptuous palaces had been raised for them close to the Forbidden City. Their stables were filled with the rarest chargers, gifts from kings in the west. Imperial peonies bloomed in their beautiful gardens where little boats glided over serpentine lakes, and cranes danced under canopies edged with gold bells. I gave noble titles to their mother and brothers, and all five boys from the family now had honorable positions. I indulged their faults in a way I never had my husband, and I was tender with them as I never had been with Scribe of Loyalty. I had stopped questioning my every move and forbidding myself pleasures. I had given up worrying about betrayal and usurpation. Simplicity and Prosperity's delicate virility erased memories of the presumptuous phallus of man. I was no longer an assailed female, a conquered land. The love that I had always thought of as a theft was offered as a soothing balm.

Spring spread its fragrance. Swallows flew back to the eaves of the Palace. With the first mild breeze, the willows flowered. Soon their downy, silvered catkins were fluttering. The court ladies fixed colored kites to lengths of red string and made them dance in the sky. Waking became a delicious treat. The eunuchs congratulated me on my glowing good health so frequently that I felt young again. Where I had lost a tooth, a new one was growing: This miracle flooded me with childish joy. My frugal soul had been seduced by pomp and splendor. My thrifty mind stopped counting the cost. I gave sumptuous banquets and let the Zhang brothers organize extravagant shows with fireworks, animals, and acrobats from the western kingdoms.

Death was no longer an ice-cold bed, a fatal boredom. I wanted to leave this world in a whirlwind of celebrations. Politics were no longer a priority. Like a peasant who has worked hard all his life and resolves to enjoy his accumulated wealth, I decided to appoint an heir. I had to choose between my nephew and my son. The problems were still the same, but I felt less anxious when I confronted that tangle of hopes and frustrations. I was determined to be done with it. The ministers dared to give me frank advice, "Years ago the Emperor Eternal Ancestor braved the wind and the rain, and bared his life to the blade of the sword. He himself led his troops into battle to overcome disorder in this world. He founded the Tang Dynasty so that he could hand it on to his descendants. Before he died, the Emperor Lordly Ancestor entrusted his sons to you so that you might make great sovereigns of them. If Your Majesty now chooses to offer the throne to strangers, her actions would betray his wishes! Which is the more intimate connection, between a mother and her son or between a mother and her nephew? If Your Majesty appoints her son as successor, she shall still be receiving offerings in the Temple of Ancestors in ten thousand years' time. If Your Majesty appoints her nephew . . . your servants have never heard of a nephew building a temple to honor his aunt!"

Lai Jun Chen was no longer there to pick out the dark plans for restoration beneath these words. Without his hissing comments, I myself was less susceptible to doubt. Granted, the imperial banners bore my colors, I had altered the calendar and the Empire venerated my ancestors as the founding sovereigns . . . but my husband's Tang Dynasty lived on through his descendants and through me. Heaven's wishes were more powerful than my own. I could not devour my own children so I decided my dynasty should not be the cause of radical revolution, no blood should flow. The forces of destiny had unarmed me for such was the destiny of the Empire. Piety the despot and Miracle the power-less emperor would see their claims brushed aside. I would call Future back from exile. This unworthy son had neglected his principle respon-sibility. His fourteen years banished from the Court might have put some polish on his flippancy. Now that his youth was buried in the wild mountains, he would come to me with no hint of arrogance.

AT THE BEGINNING of the first year in the era of the Divine Calen-dar[22] my third son returned from the distant region in the south. At forty, the chubby, jovial prince had become a thin, stooped man with a graying beard. When he threw himself at my feet calling me "Mother" and "Majesty," my eyes filled with tears. It was like hearing Splendor's voice, and Wisdom's, the echoes of their cries as tiny babies. I remem-bered the polo matches, the noisy celebrations with all four of my sons fighting for the golden goblet in my husband's hand.

The past was a hurricane blasting through my dreams. How strange, how sad, to be receiving grandchildren—flesh of my flesh—who were strangers and already head and shoulders taller than me! Some had fea-tures vaguely like mine, others were like the Emperor Lordly Ancestor or their grandfather the Emperor Eternal Ancestor. Peaceful Joy, the daughter who was born on the road to exile, delivered into her father's tunic, had grown into a princess whose beauty was mysterious and proud. Fourteen—the age at which I had come to the Imperial City for the first time. And this young girl who grew up in the wilds of the countryside like Heavenlight, was she too reeling and disorientated?

When he heard that his eldest brother had returned, Miracle was ea-ger to offer him his title as Imperial Descendant. He made the request

---

[22] A.D. 698

three times in writing. In the ninth month of that year I appointed Future as Supreme Son and his eldest son, Progress, as Supreme Grandson. At the same time I pronounced a Great Amnesty and gave banquets for the people. All the pomp of the celebrations was interrupted by Spirit weeping in grief: Piety had just died! He had been struck down as his father had been sixty years earlier.

General jubilation became imperial mourning. Laughter and congratulations turned to tears and lamentations. My nephew's body went into the belly of Mount Mang. He would rest in an underground palace with funeral treasures fit for a powerful king who could so easily have been emperor. The entire Court and all of Luoyang was there to witness his journey toward Heaven. My nephew kings and my great nephew county princes wept, and their tears devastated me. I had just dashed their hopes for the future. The defeated were now open to reprisals from their victorious rivals.

I appointed Spirit as head of the Wu clan and first officiator in worshipping our ancestors, well aware that this subtle, learned man would succeed in endearing himself to the heir. To protect my clan from the possible revenge of the Tang princes, I arranged countless marriages between my granddaughters and great nephews, and ensured that my great nieces ruled in my grandsons' households and gave them descendants. In order to calm the inevitable rivalry, I summoned Future, Miracle, Moon, Spirit, and all of their children to the Temple of Ten Thousand Elements. I stood facing the Altar of Heaven, the Altar of the Emperors of the Five Orientations, and the Altar of Ancestors. I asked my highest Court dignitaries to bear witness, and I ordered my descendants to swear on their lives to serve the dynasty together like the left arm and the right arm of one body. Their oath that they would never quarrel was inscribed on an iron blade and laid in the heart of the sanctuary.

HAVING EMERGED TRIUMPHANT from the succession crisis and free of the prosecutor Lai Jun Chen, the Court was ready to follow me to inaugurate a new era. On my way to Mount Song, I had discovered the River of Rocks, and beside it I commissioned the Palace of Solar Breath. The skilled workmen transformed the deep valley into an extraordinary garden of marvels. Pavilions with turquoise roofs blended into the luxuriant forests. Birds flew in and out of open windows and doors. Waterfalls cascaded inside pavilions built with the trunks of trees. Fish like long, translucent arrows swam beneath the crystalline floor. I kept beehives and herds of sheep. I liked watching Simplicity and Prosperity coming toward me through the huge magnolia woods, their tunics and wide sleeves flying in the wind as they brought me a chick, a fawn, or a butterfly. After two years of research, the bonze Hu Chao offered me the Immortal Remedy.

The pills he gave me warmed my entrails and made my body feel light. My hearing and eyesight improved. The world became limpid: Its waters began to whisper, bees no longer buzzed in silent abstract words. Soon I could even pick out the yawn of a leopard, the sighing of the trees, or even of the wind as it blew across the valley. Everyday I rediscovered forgotten sounds, and I listened delightedly to the creak of a shutter as it was lifted or the sneeze of a little eunuch who believed I was still deaf. To thank the gods and demonstrate my humility I renounced the title of Emperor who Holds the Mandate of Heaven and Turns the Golden Wheel. I entrusted the monk Hu Chao with a golden blade engraved with my prayer to all the gods in the universe. He toiled all the way to the summit of Mount Song and pushed it into a crack in the rock.

I set off with my lovers, sons, nephews, and ministers, on my boats decorated with dragons and phoenixes. We were an elegant gathering, all rustling silks and brocades, as we made our progress down the River of Rocks, passing cliffs where waterfalls languidly stroked the rusts and emeralds of lichens and mosses. The young princes plucked at musical instruments and the princesses danced, fan in hand. Great ministers served as cup bearers while I judged a poetry competition between my lovers, my nephews, and my sons.

The alchemy of Hu Chao's pills gave me new energy: I undertook my last mission on this lowly earth—pacifying the murderous conflict between Buddhism, Taoism, and Confucianism. My dynasty would recognize these three doctrines as three pillars of Chinese thought. Any quarrels or confrontations between their adherents would be punishable by death. Gods, immortals, Buddhas, spirits, Heaven and Earth would all be considered so many different manifestations of the one God, the source of multiple divinities. In my Imperial Park there were pavilions all along the River Luo, linked by brightly colored galleries. Geese, cranes, and storks flew through the soft red twilight along the reed-lined banks. That was where I set up the Academy of Sacred Cranes, where I asked Simplicity and Prosperity to compile the great encyclopedia *The Pearls of the Three Sects*. With the help of illustrious scholars, they produced 1,300 volumes in which they gathered every tract on Buddhism, Taoism, and Confucianism. I succeeded in proving—from the way they used the same words to spread different convictions—that the three religions had the same veins through which the one and only source of Wonderment flowed.

IN THE FIRST year of the era of the Foot of Buddha[23], on the day we celebrated the Feast of the Moon, I hosted a banquet for 3,000 people in the Forbidden City. Lanterns and glasses full of wine floated along the city's rivers. Lamps of jade and crystal sparkled in the trees. Acrobats vaulted through the starry sky leaving trails of pale flames behind them. Tatar dancing girls with masked faces and bare midriffs undulated between the river banks and the firework displays and snatched improvised poems from my guests' hands. Sitting there watching those cheery, drunken faces, those dancing eyes, and smiling lips, and lulled by the hubbub of music, I succumbed to the sweetest sleep.

I was suddenly woken by a scuffle at a table in the distance. I sent my eunuchs off hastily for an explanation. My great nephew, the King of

[23] A.D. 701

Wei, who was married to the Princess of Eternal Plenty, had just argued over a game with his cousin and brother-in-law, the Supreme Grandson. I called the two troublemakers over—one had a torn tunic, the other had blood trickling from his head. My last illusion was now shattered, and my anger soon found loose tongues willing to explain: The King of Wei, Piety's eldest son, had accused his cousin's family of assassinating his father. The Supreme Grandson had responded by saying that Piety had been an ungrateful intriguer. With alcohol fueling his hatred, my great nephew—who would have been the Supreme Grandson if his father had been appointed heir—vented his anger on the boy who had robbed him of his future. The two cousins who were brothers-in-law had insulted each other and come to blows. Their indignation unleashed ancient resentments. Great nephews and grandsons from both sides of my family had fought violently.

I trembled with shame and disappointment, but I did not want to spread any scandal. I silenced the servants, sent the two young princes back to their seats, and called for a deafening piece of music from the drums and mouth organs. I did not summon my two families to the Temple of Ten Thousand Elements until half a moon-phase later. I ordered the princes and princesses to kneel and asked for the iron blade, on which their oath of unity was carved, to be taken from his golden casket. There, before the Altar of Heaven, the Altar of the Emperors of the Five Orientations, and the Altar of Ancestors, I decreed that the law must be applied.

The King of Wei and the Supreme Grandson removed their brocade coats and their caps with jade pins. Wearing their simple white tunics and with their hair loose about their shoulders, they prostrated themselves at my feet, bowed to their parents, and went to hang themselves in a wing of the sanctuary. Silence reigned. I stared into space watching motes of dust dancing. Then I heard the sharp sound of two wooden stools being overturned. The first wife of my son and heir let out a gasp; she had just lost her only male child. Behind her, the Princess of Eternal Plenty—sister and wife to the dead men—passed out. Three days later Gentleness told me that this poor granddaughter had lost her child in the seventh month and had died bathed in blood. She was barely eighteen.

The Supreme Grandson and the King of Wei had both dreamed of bearing the crown one day. But the crown had struck them both down.

I gradually broke away from that accursed family and turned toward the soothing smiles of the Zhang brothers. When I listened to Prosperity playing his bamboo flute, I forgot the gaping wound in my entrails.

On my way to the Palace of Solar Breath, I had visited a misty hillside and followed a sinuous path through fields of sorghum. At the end of the path I found a simple, rustic temple dedicated to a prince from the venerable Zhou dynasty, a distant ancestor of mine. He had become immortal by means of purification exercises and had broken away from the honors and cares of the earthly world to join the skies, borne on the back of a white crane. When I was sad, when I lost all hope, I would picture that scene. My serving women would set up lacquered tables, young eunuchs would hold quivering silk parasols, Court ladies would spread out the paper and prepare the ink, Gentleness would hold her calligraphy brush, and with my hands behind my back, I would dictate the hymn of the Celestial Prince.

The wind billows through my long sleeves. The sun strokes my face. The sorghum leaves rustle, creating endless murmuring waves. Not one bird sings, even the grasshoppers are silent. The ephemeral is a reflection of the eternal.

The Celestial Prince blows into his bamboo flute, announcing the End and the Beginning.

THİRTEEN

Why does the body shrivel and dry when the soul, this fathomless voice, still longs to flourish? Why did anyone invent mirrors to glorify and assassinate women? Why should I, Emperor of the Zhou Dynasty, Master of the World, a Divinity on Earth, be obsessed with my ephemeral form? And why should I, who knew celestial beauty, still strive so desperately to look after my earthly face? Why did I choose this torture when I aspired to deliverance?

I asked to be woken when it was still dark. While the Forbidden City slept, my eunuch hairdresser would subject me to his excruciating routine: He positioned a stag's horn wrapped in hair on the top of my head, then he took my own hair, one strand at a time, and drew it into that gleaming black topknot. The horn was a symbol of virility and was meant to impart its tonic properties to me. My scalp was pulled so tight that it smoothed my forehead, temples and cheeks. Once this impression had been successfully created, my makeup women would apply four layers of unguents and powder to my face before drawing in new features for me. A wide strip of fabric wrapped round my waist supported my back, which ached from the weight of the topknot and the ornamentations on it. I had stiff collars on my tunics to hide my wrinkled neck and my slumped bosom, and long sleeves to cover my liver-spotted hands with their gnarled, reddened joints. The Court marveled at my eternal youth, and I accepted their praise with a bitter smile.

How could I dupe myself? I was worn down by frequent intestinal complaints. My strength was slipping away like water from a cupped hand. I walked more slowly, grew short of breath more easily, forgot people's names or important dates, and Gentleness acted as my memory. I had difficulty heaving myself onto my charger. My doctors first forbade me from cantering, then from riding altogether. I would suddenly be gripped by violent rages and then would be despondent for days on end. Without a horse, I had no energy or enthusiasm. I was no longer myself.

On some days, then, as dusk fell over the Imperial Park, I would ask to be taken to the top of a hill, and I would sit out on the terrace of a pavilion. On a sign from me my eunuchs would raise flags, and Earth would tremble as hundreds of horses surged out of the forest and stampeded around a track at the foot of the hill. I watched, fascinated, their every muscle was tense, their manes streamed in the wind. My most able young horsewomen would stand on their saddles and perform acrobatic displays. Their supple movements, so perfectly attuned to the rhythm of the gallop, lifted me out of my motionless body. On the distant horizon, night closed in like a rising tide, eating away at my life a little at a time, the races and the battles, the turmoil and the rage.

My friends and mistresses had disappeared! Every month the government presented me with a list of the dead, and I recognized the names of exiled enemies, retired servants, poets, and monks. They had all closed their doors, leaving me in a world where—sunbeam by sunbeam—their light was dimming.

The hillside would succumb to the darkness and my servants would light lanterns and braziers. Somewhere musicians played. My world had shrunk to the confines of that tiny pavilion. Candles lit the faces in the frescoes that would line my tomb: Gentleness, seen in profile with her pensive brow, holding a writing case in her hand. Behind her, Court ladies and serving women all painted according to traditional codes, perfectly proportioned and with a melancholy beauty. In the background, little eunuchs in brown tunics and black lacquered linen caps merged into the balustrades. The moon, pinned close to a window, lit various minutely drawn objects: an incense-burner, a bonsai tree, a long-handled round fan, a curly-coated puppy, a bowl, a teapot. The group of women looked like a great cluster of peonies, standing facing Simplicity in Tatar dress with tight sleeves. They did not look at each other, but into space, at absence, at the dead woman. In the distance Prosperity's graceful silhouette was outlined beneath a clump of bamboo, drawing serene notes from his flute.

ONE NIGHT THE town of Long Peace appeared to me in a dream. The gates and archers' towers of its Forbidden City loomed through golden clouds. Flocks of birds circled over its crimson walls. Its avenues filled with cherry and wild orange blossom had the outdated charm of an abandoned concubine. Overcome by a pain I could not name, I woke.

All of Luoyang trembled and the order was given: My Court and dignitaries packed up the furniture, the tableware, and the animals. The Southern Gate opened, and the city reverberated to horses' whinnying and my soldiers' rhythmic marching. I sat in my carriage of gold, led by two hundred coachmen, and hurried toward the past. The Emperor of China was traveling to Heavenlight. I was fleeing Luoyang, where the sun was about to set, in order to reach the sunrise in Long Peace.

The smell of meadows seeped through the pearl-edged brocade door hangings. Soon my sleep was haunted by the breath of the Yellow Earth and the slow music of its rivers. Memories of a former life came back to me in snatches: I was in a carriage heading for Long Peace, huddled in my seat weeping, my stomach knotted with fear. I missed Mother and Little Sister. Why did I have to grow up?

I sat up with a start, thinking I could hear thunder. Thousands of voices were chanting, "Ten thousand years to the Sacred Emperor, ten thousand years to the Sacred Emperor, millions of years of health and happiness to the Sacred Emperor of the Celestial Mandate and the Golden Wheel!" Through the window of my carriage, I could see endless horsemen with stirrups of gold and silver, countless crimson banners fluttering in the wind and bristling arms plying forward. Prosperity was riding close by and he called out, "Long Peace is not far now! I can see the crenellated ramparts." He broke off to draw level with me again. "Majesty," he went on, "the people have come out of the city to greet you. Men, women, children, the elderly, all prostrated along the way with their foreheads in the dust." A moment later he added, "Majesty, the whole city is at your feet. The people are weeping with joy and asking for your blessing. Majesty, here is the avenue of the Scarlet Bird. Ah, Majesty, the Imperial City!"

My eyes filled with tears. I suddenly remembered a smell from the past, familiar figures forgotten for half a century. Their high foreheads, their distant eyes, their slow, precise footsteps: serving women and governesses from the Palace who had come to greet the new Talented One.

I was so young then and I am now so old!

The door hangings were drawn apart. Great ministers prostrated themselves and asked me to alight. I decreed the Great Remission and the beginning of a new era, the Era of Long Peace, in homage to the city that had been awaiting my return for twenty years. I made offerings and ceremony of prayers to my august parents, to the Emperor Lordly Forebear, the Emperor Eternal Ancestor, and to my husband, the Emperor Lordly Ancestor. Leaning on my cane, I walked slowly through the Forbidden City, followed by Gentleness, Simplicity, and Prosperity. I could see my sister sitting before her bronze mirror with her gold flasks of perfume. I stroked the yellowed scrolls of silk on which the Delicate Concubine Xu had written her poems. I stood in quiet contemplation in the pavilion where the Gracious Wife had lain naked in the scarlet glow of the setting sun. I envied all these women I saw before me, their beauty still intact. Life has its revenge of life. Untimely death is the secret of eternal youth.

After the fevered excitement of the first months, I was overwhelmed with exhaustion and my hands started to shake violently. My calligraphy, always a source of such pride, became tortured scribbling. I sometimes tripped when there was nothing in my way. I saw a succession of doctors and was deluged with their diagnoses: unhinged winds, warring hot and cold elements, internal disorders. Some prescribed herb teas, baths, ointments, whereas others would have me bled, counsel acupuncture, and breathing exercises. The morning salutation was a challenge that I renewed daily. I should get out of bed, walk, get into a carriage, and endure the difficult journey to the Outer Court.

But I myself had found the best remedy against old age: never stop working, continue to invent. Amid the affairs of state and celebrations, I forgot the trembling of my body. I set up the military Imperial Competition and I myself corrected the papers on strategy and arbitrated the tournaments. I received ambassadors from Japan who, after a thirty-three-year hiatus, had crossed the boiling seas once more to prostrate themselves before the sovereign of the Celestial Empire. I sent my son Miracle to command my forces in war against the Tatars who had rebelled once again in the northwest. I arranged a marriage between a princess and a Tibetan king. When the King of Sinra died, I quickly sent an emissary to help his younger brother take the throne. The judicial mistakes made in the days of the torturer-prosecutors were corrected and the condemned rehabilitated. I reclassified the books in the Imperial Library. My nephew Spirit oversaw a hundred archivists and scholars compiling the annals of the overthrown Tang Dynasty.

TWO YEARS HAD passed since I left Luoyang when a terrible winter cold confined me to bed. It took me longer than usual to recover; I had to suspend the morning salutation for a month. Even when I was well again, I could no longer walk without help. I was horrified by this deterioration, convinced that I had fallen prey to the evil spirits of my rivals. Fifty years after their death, the Empress Wang and the Splendid Wife had surged suddenly in my dreams, accusing me of having ordered the murder of my own daughter. I hastily fled Long Peace.

Luoyang welcomed me with acclamation and tears.

THE COURT WAS like a merciless mirror, reflecting my decline: The Supreme Son grew more stooped every day—so much waiting for the crown had turned him into an old man. Moon was nearly forty, and she was a grandmother herself. The kings, my nephews, who were still involved in endless intriguing, had to dye the hair black at their temples, and their foreheads were ravaged with creases. The great voice among my ministers had fallen silent: The chancellor Di Ren Jie had died. The government had lost its soul and I my right hand man.

The Empire continued to flourish, although I had less energy to bear the weight of prosperity. My judgment had slowed, and it took me twice as long to study a dossier. I was no longer a wizard of solutions. I secretly longed to retire, leaving Luoyang with my lovers. I dreamed of spending my last days in the Palace of Solar Breath far away from earthly matters: In the spring, there would be the cruise along the River of Rocks; in the summer, open-air concerts; in the autumn, poetry competitions would be washed down with chrysanthemum wine; in winter, my palace would be surrounded by snow, and puppets would act out plays that I had written.

I accepted when the Court offered the Zhang brothers the title of Great Lord, but refused my children's hypocritical suggestion that they be raised to the rank of kings. Favorites should be kept far from the circle of power. But my rigorous attitude failed to reassure my anxious ministers. Some leagued against the two brothers and queued before me, trying to convince me of their ambition. I took note and made no comment. I left my government to its worrying. I left my sons, daughter, and nephews to their hateful jealousy. I left my favorites to pursue their pleasures in torment. My loneliness was bleaker than ever. Paralyzed by fear and despair, I watched my eightieth birthday draw nearer and nearer.

How could I abandon my empire, my lovers, and my descendants? How could I leave Luoyang, its peonies, canals, and bewitching loveliness? How could I exchange the comfort of my bed for a coffin, my sumptuous palace for an underground chamber? How could I close my eyes, stop hearing, or let myself forget? How could I stop breathing, stop existing? What would my next life be? Would I be a beggar having been a sovereign? Would I change into a bird to fly away from the very pinnacle of humanity or into a stone thrown down from the summit having fulfilled my destiny?

I called exorcists to my palace. Monks in monasteries recited purifying sutras and prayers in my name. I offered up my sacred veins to leeches, my divine scalp to the acupuncturists' silver needles. I braved snakebites and suffered in hot mud and iced baths. There were brief periods of improvement, occasional miracles, but evil continued to make its progress through my body. I could no longer walk; two sturdy serving women carried me in a litter. My words became confused and Gentleness served as my interpreter. The most simple tasks and gestures became personal battles. Something stronger than my own will was triumphing over me. The gods punish men in their arrogance and pride. Little Phoenix, so indolent and offhand, had ended his days in a morass of pain. I who had held the reins of my destiny so firmly, I who had commanded the greatest Empire beneath the skies, was robbed of authority over my own flesh.

Every day I lost a little more control over myself. My deterioration bewildered the high-ranking dignitaries so accustomed to my energetic authority. There was talk of the Supreme Son and his wife growing impatient, of my nephews adjusting their strategies, of more and more courtiers abandoning Simplicity and Prosperity to join the heir's camp. Terrified by the slander, my favorites sought more privilege and fortune to insure their future.

The internal conflicts that had been kept secret burst out into the open one day. The prosecutors from the Lodge of Purification opened the hostilities by accusing Prosperity's and Simplicity's three brothers of corruption. My lovers rested their heads on my pillow, sobbing, and pleading their family's innocence. The ensuing investigation attracted further complaints: more and more people came forward as witnesses with various forms of proof. I was unable to act against the rulings I myself had imposed and was forced to exile the guilty parties to distant provinces. But I also banished two of my eminent ministers who had lead the hostilities against Prosperity and Simplicity. These judges were insisting—on the grounds that the law saw all close relations of condemned men as guilty of a comparable crime—that my favorites be stripped of their positions and their nobility. I had to be very wily to extricate myself from the situation. Under my instructions, Great Minister Yang Si Jian stood up indignantly, exclaiming, "The Lords Zhang have helped ensure the Emperor's longevity, and for this the Empire is deeply indebted to them. They are, therefore, protected from crimes committed by their relations."

A few months later, the prosecutors made the charges again, issuing a writ against Prosperity for annexing good farmland so that he could extend his residence. Once again I had to negotiate with the government, and the young man was punished with a fine.

Prosperity lay weeping in the gynaeceum, tears rolling down his lovely face, transparent droplets, morning dew on a pale peony. When he was tormented and distressed, he was even more intoxicatingly beautiful. I secretly relished his charms as he wept, and I forgot to scold him for his lack of judgment. I promised I would remove his enemies from power—just to see him smile.

The world did not know that Prosperity's idleness meant as little to me as the government's obsessive tendency to see him as a challenge to the Supreme Son. I wanted to be done with it, and I was afraid of dying. I was making preparations for my final hour, and all the while hoping for another outcome. I concentrated what little strength I had left on fighting the terror every night before I fell asleep. One day I should never awake.

THE TEMPERATURE HAD plummeted in Luoyang, and autumn rains had turned to winter snow. The sky never cleared and was heavy as a sheet of iron. The roads became impassable and travel along the rivers had been stopped. Cut off from the world, the Capital began to deplete its reserves. I ordered for the imperial grain stores to be opened to save the poor, and for blankets to be handed out to vagrants.

The city was struck by an epidemic. Despite its deep ditches, high crimson walls and closed gates, the plague penetrated the Inner City. Nothing could hold it back, neither the medicinal herbs I had burned, nor their thick smoke that hung in every room, nor the monks' prayers and conjurations against the spirits spreading this sickness. Along with many of my officials, I succumbed to a violent fever. I lay in bed in the Pavilion of Gathered Immortals and lost all notion of time.

Shadows danced against the walls; sobbing and murmuring came to me as distant waves. I was wandering through the dark, murky corridors of a world with only two seasons: winter, which turned me to ice, and summer, which grilled me in the sun. All of a sudden I stepped over the horizon and saw a lilac-colored sky dotted with mysterious twinkling. A moment later I realized I was seeing my embroidered velvet bed-hangings. I summoned my strength to turn my head to one side. In the lamplight I saw Simplicity and Prosperity sleeping on the bare floor, huddled together like two lost, frightened children. My heart beat with fierce emotion and images came back to me: I remembered Prosperity soothing my burning brow with ice-cold cloths, and Simplicity cradling me in his arms to feed me. I looked at their beautiful, pale faces and thought of their future, which was no longer a future. A son's Court would take revenge on his mother's favorites. All the pomp and wealth of the present would be their downfall. In the glory they enjoyed today was inscribed the punishment they would suffer tomorrow.

Outside the wind rattled through the bells hanging under the eaves, and their mournful tinkling made my pavilion seem even more dismal.

What season is it? Am I still alive? Have I already stepped into eternity, and are my two lovers—lying huddled and motionless—two bodies sacrificed in my name, two souls imprisoned in my tomb?

THE MOON WAXED and waned. The powerful infusions prescribed by my doctors quelled the burning fever in my body but upset my inner balance, and I was struck down with violent stomach cramps. Every morning the heir and my ministers would prostrate themselves before the gates of my palace, but I would send them away. I did not want them to see my ravaged face, my ashen complexion, or my withered body. I was not yet dead; my son would have to wait.

Like a silk worm curled in its opaque cocoon, I was wrapped in my lovers' tender care: Simplicity pushing back his crimson sleeves, revealing the plum-colored lining, to bathe me; Prosperity weeping as he wiped my bed sores with a green handkerchief; Simplicity's cheeks glowing from the dancing flames as he stood over the oven boiling my medicinal infusion; Prosperity's cherry red lips blowing on a bowl of hot soup with a coriander leaf floating in it; Simplicity's fine fingers plucking the seven horizontal strings of a zither; Prosperity, a vertical silhouette in the doorway, playing his bamboo flute.

My body slowly recovered its equilibrium, my appetite returned, and I was able to speak again. Now that I was out of danger, Prosperity and Simplicity went back to live in their residences outside the Forbidden City. The first night they did not sleep at the foot of my bed, I could not sleep. I was jealous, imagining Simplicity kissing a beautiful courtesan, and Prosperity, already drunk, letting himself be undressed.

From my bed, I began dealing with affairs of State again. Reports from my judges accused the Zhang brothers of harboring dark plans to usurp power. They claimed that a physiognomist had identified the features of an emperor in Prosperity's face and that, having been told this, the young man had commissioned a temple in the province of Ding, choosing the site to favor his imperial destiny.

The prosecutors gathered by the door to my bedchamber, clamoring for the immediate arrest of the alleged culprit. Prosperity knelt beside my bed, so overwhelmed with tears that he could not speak. I eventually handed him over to them under the condition that the interrogation took place within the walls of my palace.

Eunuchs shuttled backward and forward to keep me abreast of the trial. I soon learned that Prosperity had refused to answer any questions but, in a rush of courage, had started insulting the Great Ministers and magistrates. The overseer Song Jing was furious and called for his instruments of torture.

Gentleness was sent immediately to announce my imperial clemency, and Prosperity was carried back by a eunuch, bathed in his own blood. This boy who cried so easily did not shed one tear; he prostrated himself to thank me and passed out. My lovers took up residence in my palace and, for fear of being arrested or assassinated, they no longer left that closed world. I had succeeded in keeping them by my side.

The pains and ills vanished from my body one after another. The Zhang brothers' attentions had been more effective that any medicine. I started getting out of bed and forced myself to take a few steps. The year was drawing to a close; as one cycle ended, hope for a new beginning dawned. From within my palace, I granted the world the Great Imperial Remission: With the exception of rebel leaders, everyone who had been condemned for participating in conspiracies against my authority was pardoned. I dictated a proclamation changing the Era of Long Peace into the Era of the Divine Dragon. May the dragon's squally breath blazing to the very skies give me the strength to defy death!

In the south, spring had already set light to the River Long. Another moon phase and it would reach the Sacred Capital: The River Luo would thaw, the sun would disperse the clouds. I would reach that miraculous pinnacle of longevity: My eightieth birthday would be a triumphant celebration. The peonies in the Imperial Park would bloom once more, and my eunuch gardeners would bring me new varieties—green, mauve, black, pearly, gold. . . .

I would live.

THE SNOW DANCED and swirled, cedar-wood crackled in bronze braziers. I only had to cough for my serving women to light their candles hastily and bring me hot tea. In that first year of the Era of the Divine Dragon, on the twenty-second day of the first moon, I was happy to wake. I looked up at the ceiling and down the scarlet pillars, and my eyes came to rest on a huge branch of plum blossom that Prosperity had brought me. I urged my hairdresser and makeup women to hurry and finish their torture. Then I put on a saffron-colored tunic with a dark, inky lining, and a purple brocade coat lined with crimson. I lay on my bed and made sure that one end of my sash trailed along the floor; it was painted with mountains in winter and frozen rivers, birds flying over naked trees, a deep cave where the goddesses of water played a game of go.

A eunuch prostrated himself at the door, and I heard him informing one of my Court ladies that Prosperity and Simplicity had just left their pavilions and were heading for mine. I pictured my lovers' progress: They were coming down the steps freshly swept by their serving women; they were stepping onto a little path, a covered gallery where branches laden with snow were like beams of crystal and rafters of diamonds. Prosperity was wearing a light red coat lined with sable and was followed by a page carrying an umbrella of pine-colored oiled cloth. Simplicity was walking behind his younger brother, wrapped in a cape of white damask woven with silver thread and lined with silver fox fur, and on his head he had only his white tiger-skin hat pulled down over his ears. His wide sleeves swished through the snowflakes making them flutter nervously about him before falling into his footprints in the snow.

That morning, as I looked in the mirror, I saw a hint of pink had returned to my cheeks. My body was alive with new energy. I felt like braving the cold to scatter corn for the sparrows and squirrels. It would be a long day: I was expecting my ministers who would be discussing the construction of a new road to facilitate deliveries of supplies to the Capital.

Gentleness was late. Had she caught a cold? I sent a serving woman for news of her. Simplicity and Prosperity had still not arrived. Had they stopped off somewhere? I asked a governess to tell them to hurry.

She had only opened the door a fraction when I saw the points and crests of helmets looming forward through flurries of snow. Men in breastplates had climbed the steps and pushed past the serving women who tried to stop their intrusion. They came into my room and prostrated themselves before my bed with a clattering of weapons.

The powerful smell of leather and metal damp with snow swept over me. I stared at them, wide-eyed. There was a long silence.

"What's going on?" I eventually managed to say, "Is there a revolt in the Palace?"

Great Chancellor Zhang Jian Zhi stepped forward. He was a scholarly man in his seventies, and he had put his battledress over his Court robes. His white beard, which he usually combed so carefully, was now a knotted mass. The usual gentleness and humility in his face had vanished, and his glittering eyes revealed all the cruelty and determination of someone who has just committed a crime. He unclenched his jaw, "The Zhang brothers held Your Majesty hostage a long time. The enemies of the Empire have now been eliminated. Your Majesty is out of danger . . ."

My head swam. The inevitable had happened: Simplicity and Prosperity should not have lived; it was written in the book of their destiny. I had never known why I loved them, and I now realized that their disturbing beauty had been sculpted by death. Eight years had passed, and every exquisite day spent in their company had been a petal they tore from their own flesh and laid on my altar.

A pain wrenched my chest, but I controlled my trembling. I looked slowly over those ashen faces and picked out Li Zhan, Lieutenant General of the Guard of the Right.

"I have heaped honors and wealth on you and your father," I told him: "Why are you here today?"

He kept his eyes lowered, stayed silent and impassive.

Then I turned to Great Secretary Cui Yuan Wei, "While others owe their promotion to ministerial recommendations, you alone have been trained under my supervision throughout your career. What are you doing here? Are you not ashamed of what you have done?"

He backed away on his knees and prostrated himself, keeping his head to the floor.

"Future, there is no point in hiding. I can see that you are here too, to 'reassure' me. Now that the usurpers are dead, you may go back to your palace!"

He paled, struck his head against the ground, and headed for the door. The Magistrate Huan Yan Fan caught hold of his sleeve and cried, "Majesty, the Supreme Son must not return to his palace! Long ago the Emperor Lordly Ancestor entrusted his education to you, but he is a grown man now. It is the wish of the heavens and of your people that you should hand over power to him now!"

"Who is so insolent that he speaks for the imperial heir?" I asked. "Remove him!"

Future tore himself from his servant's grasp and fled.

"Majesty," said Great Minister Zhang Jian Zhi, prostrating himself again, "the Supreme Son is ready to reign. Please trust in him!"

"The Supreme Son has left. Why are you still here?" I said, turning my back to them. Without the Heir, the conspirators were quickly discouraged and withdrew one by one. I could hear Court ladies weeping, and the serving women I had sent to find Simplicity's and Prosperity's bodies returned: The entrance to my pavilion was guarded by soldiers and no one could leave. I learned that Gentleness would not be coming—it was she who had opened the door of my palace to the insurgents.

Filled with extraordinary energy, I rose to my feet. The Sacred Emperor who held the Celestial Mandate and the Golden Wheel would open every closed door. She would find her lovers' bodies and bury them with her own hands.

As I stepped out of my palace, the North Wind pierced right through me. I who had outwitted every plot, how had I not foreseen this one? Had I been reduced to this? I felt overwhelmingly faint and coughed until I spat blood. The soldiers' gleaming lances became stars scattered across the night sky.

Ministers slash the still-twitching bodies. Soldiers throw the corpses onto a carriage and abandon them by a river. Snow falls, clouds of furious butterflies. Snow brushes over the black peonies of gaping wounds. Snow melts into open eyes, empty holes drinking in the sky. Crows spread their wings and hop down from the trees, cawing. Lean wolves and jackals come out of the woods, bellies brushing through the powdery snow. Pointed beaks lacerate those purple faces, and bloodied jaws delve through the exposed entrails. A starving fox circles round the carcasses then lunges, snatching Prosperity's sexual organ before fleeing across the plain.

I was woken by the sound of my soul screaming.

In that overheated room with its glowing braziers, the feeble crying of my serving women was punctuated only by my own rasping breath. A fever burned in my chest but my limbs were icy cold. The pain spreading through my body only aggravated my unbearable suffering. With the shutters closed and curtains lowered, I did not know whether it was day or night. The flames projected shadows on the walls, and I thought I could see Prosperity's silhouette among them. It was all a nightmare! The Zhang brothers would wake me from this anguished sleep, slipping under the covers with me. With their cool skin against mine, we would wait and see dawn break: The windows would open and the light would wash away the painful memories.

A man started speaking. Startled, I turned toward him and recognized Great Chancellor Zhang Jian Zhi kneeling beside my bed. His words dug deep into my ears. His very presence reminded me there had been a massacre. It was all over: Simplicity and Prosperity were dead!

The wicked traitor tried in vain to justify his actions and to persuade me to sign a decree of abdication. His droning monologue was maddening; I did not even know how long he had been there, worrying at me. Seeing that I remained silent and unmoved, he withdrew, and my nephew Spirit took over trying to make me understand how serious the situation was. Even he had betrayed me!

Eventually my daughter Moon appeared. She talked about my health and how I needed to rest. She said that an empire could not survive without a master, and that the time had come to hand over the reins of power. Her words made perfect sense; they reminded me of Mother: Just like her, my daughter had never understood me.

I interrupted her explanations: I would sign my abdication if she gave the Zhang brothers a decent burial in a monastery on Mount Mang.

"I have carried this crown to save the Palace from discord and to delay the fall of the world. Ambitious men have urged your brother on, and he is now claiming it as his. I shall give it to him!"

Moon left with the document on which I had put my seal and my thumbprint. The silence rekindled my pain. I closed my eyes and could picture a troop of soldiers marching; I could hear the clatter of their weapons, their officers shouting, their feet stamping. Simplicity and Prosperity are running away through the snow. Simplicity's face is suddenly twisted, his eyes roll back; he totters and falls. Prosperity carries on running toward my pavilion. He has lost his shoes, he trips over the bodies of serving women, crying "Majesty, help me!" An arrow carves through the air and strikes him in the middle of his forehead. His body freezes, his pupils dilate. He opens his mouth to give a silent wail and falls to his knees. A bright, frothy trickle of blood runs down between his eyes and over his nose. His face becomes so transparent that I read his last interrupted thought, his shattered poetry and evaporating breath.

Simplicity and Prosperity were dead. The last music in my life had fallen silent. What did anything else matter to me?

FUTURE ASCENDED TO the throne and gave me the title of August Emperor of Celestial Law. To distance me from my followers, the Court ousted me from the Forbidden City and set me up in a summer palace on the southern bank of the River Luo, to the west of the city. Every five days, the New Empress and Princess Moon would come to my door for news of my health, accompanied by Gentleness who now worked for my son and had been raised to the rank of Delicate Concubine. Every ten days, Future and his high dignitaries would raise an imperial cortège, and he would come to offer me his respectful salutation. The Court longed for me to die. All this artificial commotion was just play acting, to fool the people and the history books.

Despite the orders sent out to cut me off from the world, information filtered through those high, well-guarded walls. The Zhang brothers' clan had been decimated. Officials and artists known to be their friends had been beheaded. There were countless heads displayed outside the Southern Gate of the Forbidden City, exposed to the abuse of passersby. The Empress, who wanted to start everything afresh, had driven out three thousand palace servants and Court ladies.

The activities of the Forbidden City no longer affected me. The anguish of my grief had stripped me of my vanity as if casting off unnecessary garbs. I was reduced to skin and bone, but I would not succumb. My will to triumph had come back with new vigor. As I lay on my bed, drawing each painful breath through my mouth, I decided to stop shedding tears over my fate and to accept the will of Heaven with my eyes open.

Future brought an end to the Zhou Dynasty I had inaugurated, closed the Sacred Temple of Ten Thousand Elements and expelled my ancestors from the Eternal Temple. The Empire bore the name Tang once more. The ministries went back to their former names, and banners and official tunics returned to the colors of old. The Court abolished the writing I had invented, and Luoyang was demoted, conceding its precedence as Capital to Long Peace. The world I had built was annihilated and I barely suffered from this appalling waste. The children I brought into the world, the ministers I trained and Gentleness who I set free had all betrayed me. But I was not haunted by the agonies of betrayal. I had not followed prosecutor Lai Jun Chen's advice and had not exterminated my two families. I had not had Gentleness killed when told of her secret liaison with the woman who had become Empress. My indulgence was not a mistake, it was a renouncement. Just as beauty begins to fade the moment it blossoms, so I had already accepted that my Zhou Dynasty was the briefest episode in the great dream of History.

Yesterday Master of the World, today a humiliated prisoner, captive in my own paralyzed body, confronting the final trial of my existence. I did not loathe Zhang Jian Zhi and his followers who had snatched power from a sovereign weakened by old age. I forgave the heir his cowardice, taking the crown from his dying mother. I understood the choices my nephews had made as they struggled to stay on top of the churning waves. All those people had to carry on with their fears and efforts, and I no longer needed a mirror or a seal. I had freed myself from all that posturing; I was relieved of my burden.

Spring came once more. Prosperity and Simplicity would not see the peonies flower and the swallows return. My heart was at peace. The Court hoped that I would die but I was breathing. Defying illness, opening my eyes, throwing myself into life every morning were my duties. I had to finish writing in my mind the book of my life.

The frustration of an heir who had waited too long turned into the dissipation of an emperor too eager to enjoy his power. Future was permanently drunk, reeling from one party to another. Zhang Jian Zhi and Spirit vied for power in the Outer Court, and in the Inner Court the Empress Wei found a formidable rival in Moon, appointed by her brother as the Great Imperial Protector. Both women interfered with political decisions and fought to influence the weak sovereign.

Officials were already secretly regretting the end of my reign. Messages from them reached me, stitched into belts worn by my eunuchs. Too late! My body was still in this world, but my spirit had already left. One night, Spirit was let into my bedchamber. He threw himself at the foot of my bed and shed copious tears. This wily nephew had changed his tune: He promised to free me and to avenge Simplicity's and Prosperity's deaths. He tried in vain to obtain my signature authorizing him to overthrow Future. I watched him pityingly: I refused to give my dying name to another massacre. My lovers' assassination would not be avenged; the Zhou dynasty would die with me. No more blood would flow in my lifetime. The Empire would not descend into chaos.

The news and messages dried up: My faithful eunuchs had in turn been driven out of the Palace, and I was now watched over by cold, aloof women. I was seen by a succession of imperial doctors. They too were new faces and, instead of curing me, their prescriptions weakened me.

From then on I refused every remedy, and the Court had to accept that their revelries must wait a little longer: So long as I was alive, I acted as a stern conscience, a pitiless mirror for them. My serving women no longer helped me change position; they had probably been given orders to let my flesh rot. Suppurating wounds gnawed at me day and night. My hair and nails kept on growing. The women filled my room with budding flowers and baskets of fruit to smother the fetid smell of their crime. The Emperor and his Court had stopped their salutations; Moon and Gentleness no longer came to see me. They wanted to kill me by forgetting me.

A rainstorm battered the peach blossom, and summer was upon us. A mysterious vitality within me still refused to capitulate. My pavilion was full of life: Simplicity and Prosperity, dressed in white lilac tunics and gazing at me dreamily, filled the air with their exquisite perfume; Mother leaned on her cane and described the marvels of the Pure World of Buddha; Little Phoenix rushed in and out, my celestial husband was always eager to set off on some journey. Ships with their sails ballooning in the wind navigated across my face and sailed off onto the ocean.

Then hundreds, thousands of horses made the floorboards thrum, galloping across my room with their hectic manes flying.

My ecstatic smile converted the women watching over me. They saw a golden light radiating from my body, and they prostrated themselves at my feet, venerating me feverishly. When they had washed me, fed me, and arranged my hair, I had my bed moved over to a window. Robins, magpies, crested parrots, and peacocks pecked at the garden where the irises had wilted and the orchids were shyly opening their buds. A wide path snaked through thickets of bamboo, its paving stones untouched by visitors' feet for many months and covered in damp moss. I watched the lotus flowers blooming in the middle of a pond, aware I was seeing them flower for the last time.

I bid good-bye to the autumn as it left forever, then winter held me in its grip. Snow fell from the sky. I remembered the same time the previous year, watching Simplicity and Prosperity throwing snowballs at my court ladies. Their laughter and shouts still echoed but their silhouettes had already blended into the withered trees. Simplicity and Prosperity were gone. I did not know what had happened to my women. The silent falling of those white flowers had strung a net between the earth and the sky, where the living frolicked and played.

In the first year of the Era of the Divine Dragon,[24] on the night of the twenty-fifth day of the eleventh moon, the snow stopped. Prosperity appeared beside my bed. He prostrated himself and then played his bamboo flute. Pearls of crystal streamed around me. The moon turned into a silvery river carrying me off in its glittering currents. I saw jade palaces in the skies, misty plains, and fields of light!

The following morning I asked for my topknot and makeup to be done as soon as the sun was up. Wearing my most beautiful jewels and dressed in a flame-colored tunic over a dazzling white gown, I dictated the epitaph that should be engraved on my funeral stela to be erected beside my husband's.

[24] A.D. 705

I would reveal the beauty of the Zhou dynasty to any man who stopped before my tomb. He would learn of its prosperous towns, swift horses, deep forests, and magical rivers. He would admire the way the arts flourished and would praise the glory of its poetry. I described my pride in adoring the gods, venerating the ancestors, subduing men's struggles, sanctifying Heaven, and reigning in the Temple of Clarity. I drew a portrait of myself as a humble sovereign, bowing to the will of one true God, the source of all divinities. The end would be the beginning; the ephemeral would become the infinite. My trials over, I would return to the skies.

At dawn the next day, the silence in my bedchamber was broken by the sound of horns and drums. Other sounds—horses whinnying and men shouting—were carried to me on the wind: Future and his Court were beating through the imperial forest.

Banners cracked in the wind. Leopards and hunting dogs ran ahead of the horses as stags fled through the undergrowth. Branches drew closer, whipping the intruders' faces, then parted. Snow heaped on the tops of trees collapsed and fell in a fine powder. Breathing more labored. Heart beating, fit to burst. Suddenly, there was a lake, a block of ice, a mirror on eternity.

In a single leap, my soul broke away from my body and launched itself into the sky.

THE SERVING WOMEN beat their breasts and wept, and a posse of soldiers galloped off to inform the sovereign. Bronze bells were sounded, and prayers went up from every monastery. Stunned and saddened, weaving women abandoned their looms, merchants their ledgers, and peasants their toils. The people tore their clothes, untied their topknots, and wailed lamentations. Music, laughter, and bright colors vanished from Chinese soil overnight. Horses were stripped of their ornate saddles; men wrapped themselves in hemp tunics held with belts of woven straw. Galley warships raised white sails, and mourning flags flew over every rampart.

The Court altered my will. In keeping with "my last wish," the sovereign withdrew the title of emperor and gave me the posthumous title of August Empress of Celestial Law. After lengthy debate, Zhang Jian Zhi and his adherents gave in to officials determined to respect my wish to return to Long Peace and be interred with my husband.

The Palace undertook the twenty-seven funeral ceremonies: calling upon my soul, bathing, clothing, making offerings, the invocation, and laying me in my coffin. Meanwhile, officers from the Department of Funerals went to Mount Liang and carried out ritual libations to appease my husband's spirit before opening up the passage to his burial chamber. The frescoes were repainted, false chambers and the true burial chamber were redecorated, and tri-colored ceramic sculptures representing animals, slaves, and houses embellished the underground corridors.

The work was finished by the time spring came round again. The imperial soothsayers chose the day of the fifth full moon for my departure: my coffin, an interlocking set of four sarcophaguses in lacquered wood, silver, gold, and jade, and hundreds of vases, pots, and jugs filled with ice were all arranged on a carriage drawn by one thousand soldiers. With no jewelry, makeup, or fine brocade, wearing simple white linen, the sovereign, kings, princesses, and dignitaries climbed into their carriages and followed my body as it made its slow progress with majestic dignity.

The road was covered in yellow sand, and it snaked across the Central Plain. The sun rose. The moon set. People came from the four corners of the Empire to lay funeral offerings made of paper and gold leaf: palaces, horses, servants, money, all the way to Long Peace. In the evening, after I had passed, they set light to these gifts, turning them into thousands of pillars of smoke reaching for the stars.

Mount Liang, my tomb, loomed up on the horizon. Two hillocks had been built at the mouth of the tomb with two archers' towers to drive away demons. The gates of the Sacred City opened to reveal its palaces, temples, and pagodas. The stone statues of horses, griffons, ministers, and lions passed beside me as my hearse rumbled up the Imperial Way. Two huge stelas stood out against the sky. One had shimmering inscriptions filled with powdered gold: my eulogy for my husband's reign. The other was smooth as a mirror, waiting for my words intended for men of the future.

The sun withdrew from the horizon. The sky shrank and then vanished. There in the mouth of the mountain, the wind from the shades flattened the torch flames. In the frescoes along the walls, the great imperial parade marched toward the light, and I descended into eternal darkness.

The torches lit up a huge chamber in which trunks containing my clothes, jewels, paintings, and calligraphy had already been arranged. The workmen had respected my will and had added portraits of Scribe of Loyalty, Simplicity, and Prosperity—disguised as eunuchs—to the frescoes on the walls. On the ceilings my animals and serving women were already enjoying the carefree life of the other world.

The coffin was put onto a white marble catafalque up on an alabaster stage decorated with scenes of rejoicing.

The officiators recited the final prayers, then withdrew.

A deafening roar made the whole mountain tremble.

The door of rock closed.

The Gates of Heaven opened.

313

FOURTEEN

The Empire venerated me as the wife and mother of Tang Dynasty sovereigns. Future destroyed the epitaph I had prepared for my stela and decided to replace it with a commemorative text dedicated to an empress and not an emperor. Ministers and princes argued over every turn of phrase. The different stages of my life were disturbing for these men who had to deny me and cover me with praise at the same time. Spring left and came again. The Court dignitaries could not agree on terms to describe my reign, so my stela remained a virgin surface, smooth of any inscription. It was forgotten.

Future could not identify his allies from his enemies within the Palace. In the gynaeceum, Empress Wei wanted to follow in my footsteps, with Gentleness to back her. She had her brother and cousin appointed to the government and took to sitting to the left of the Emperor during the morning audience. She sided with Spirit against Great Chancellor Zhang Jian Zhi and exiled the septuagenarian minister.

The heir, who was the son of an imperial concubine, saw that his position was threatened and decided to ensure his future by means of force. One night, leading a troop of high officials and lieutenants of the guard, he assassinated Spirit, forced his way into the Forbidden City, and called for the Empress's head. She fled to the Northern Gate and the imperial regiments arrived in time to save her. The insurgents beat a retreat, and, during their flight, the rebel prince had his head sliced off by a soldier.

The Emperor appointed his third son as successor. Unable to wait any longer, Empress Wei poisoned her husband and pronounced herself Regent. Only five years after his accession Future left the world. He was only fifty-five.

While the new empress's family and followers maneuvered to cope with another Supreme Empress, two of my family decided to defend their lineage: Moon, the Princess of Eternal Peace, and Miracle, the former emperor. On a dark night twenty days after Future's death, Miracle's third son, Prosperous Heritage, led his army through the gates of the Forbidden City. The Supreme Empress Wei and the Delicate Concubine, Gentleness, were sleeping embraced until they perished under the rebels' sabers.

Moon took the initiative, insisting Future's son should abdicate, and she urged Miracle to take the throne. This prince who had never wanted to reign was now constrained by history to become Emperor for the second time. Now it was up to the High Princess of Eternal Peace, Great Imperial Protector Moon to vie for influence over the sovereign with her nephew Prosperous Heritage, now appointed Supreme Son. When Miracle abdicated two years later, it took the new sovereign only one day to kill all of Moon's adherents and to compel her to hang herself in her palace.

Six years after my death, everyone who had tried to overthrow my dynasty had met with a violent death. Convinced that I had put an evil spell over the Court, Prosperous Heritage sent sorcerers to my Funeral City. My stela with no inscription stood on the side of Mount Liang, at the foot of my tomb, looking down over the Central Plain. The sorcerers spilled human blood round the monument. Their black magic, which combined telluric powers with furious demons, was meant to hasten my vengeful soul to hell. But still I haunted the Empire. Even though Prosperous Heritage condemned every male member of my Wu clan to death, my blood flowed through his own veins. He was a blossoming branch, and I was the tree.

The Empire never returned to its once insolent prosperity. The century drew to a close, and the Tang dynasty declined. The Tatar invasions eroded the land as stealthily as time itself, annihilating green fields and flourishing towns. The Empire shattered into five kingdoms, then each of them perished in turn. Long Peace and Luoyang were now little more than ruins. The imperial tombs and princely sepulchers were desecrated. Hordes of peasants now wandered the country pillaging. My palaces had been burned. The bronze of the Celestial Pillar had been melted down long since to make weapons.

Time passed. The wheel of fortune turned. Skills vanished in the flames of war, and men no longer knew how to build palaces tall enough to touch the clouds. The Tatars streamed in from the deserts and the steppes, one dynasty followed another. Women abandoned the arts and bound their feet. Emperors continued with the Mandarin competitions I had instigated and still used the Urn of Truth I invented. But I had become a symbol of a corrupt woman. The Annals told how I had strangled my daughter so that I could ascribe the crime to Empress Wang. Misogynistic historians accused me of poisoning my son Splendor who contested my authority. Novelists invented a life of debauchery for me, attributing their own fantasies to me. With passing time, the truth became unclear, and the lies took root.

Other women reigned behind the purple gauze of the curtain. Other women governed the Empire but not one found a dynasty. Other emperors undertook the pilgrimage to the Sacred Mountains, but not one witnessed a celestial revelation.

Eternity runs on. Ivy crawls up over the walls, and the frescoes fade. Wooden pillars are gnawed away by worms and rot under the lichen.

Why do some things cross through the curtain of time? Why do some places resist erosion and decline? Why should one name, one jewel, one vase moor up in a distant century, stray vessels finally finding a harbor?

All the trees have now been cut down in the region where the Palace of Solar Breath once sprawled. Glass phials cast their gloomy reflections in the dark underground galleries. Workmen streaming with inky, black sweat operate machines to extract energy from the darkness. Some say they have seen women in muslin dresses, trailing their long silk sleeves, slipping in and out of those walls of black crystal. They claim to have heard laughter, tinkling bells, a bamboo flute between the mechanical drumming.

One thousand three hundred years later, floods have poured earth and stones into the River of Rocks. The emerald cliffs have become piles of black rock. The poems that I had engraved can still be seen on two rock faces—almost illegible. Peasants confirm that when the moon is full and the sky is clear, when the wind whispers through the wheat fields, you can still see boats dripping with gold and bristling with scarlet banners navigating to a concert of sumptuous music.

My mountain tomb has watched civil wars and foreign invasions. It has resisted extremes of frost, heat, and torrential rain. All that remains of my discredited name and my forgotten dynasty is my stela. Men come to visit it in the vain hope of finding some answer to their questions. It is flat and smooth, reaching for the skies but naked. Some see this lack of any inscription as a symbol of my humility: I wanted to give men the opportunity to inscribe it with their blame or their praise. Others interpret it as an expression of overweening pride from a woman who became emperor: No one can comment on my destiny.

God robbed me of a legacy to make me timeless, to spread my soul over the entire earth:

I am the peony blushing red, the swaying tree, the whispering wind
I am the steep path leading pilgrims to the gates of heaven
I am in words, in protests, in tears

I am a burn which purifies, a pain with the power to transform
I travel through the seasons, I shine like a star
I am Man's melancholy smile
I am the Mountain's indulgent smile
I am the enigmatic smile of He who turns the Wheel of Eternity

ACKNOWLEDGMENTS

Thanks to Jacqueline Favero, Lucinda Karter, Solène Chabanais, Judith Regan, Anna Bliss, Samuel Jamier, and Adriana Hunter.

READING GROUP GUIDE

Introduction

Empress, a new novel by critically acclaimed author Shan Sa (winner of the Goncourt Prize for *The Girl Who Played Go*), explores the extraordinary life of one of China's most extraordinary rulers. Sa's latest novel brings seventh century China—and its controversial, intriguing sovereign, Empress Wu—vividly and daringly to life.

The history books tell us that Empress Wu, born into the noble and wealthy Wu clan, rose from her station as a diplomat's daughter to that of imperial concubine at age thirteen. When the emperor died, she married his imperial heir, eliminated (by execution) her rivals for his affection, sired imperial sons, ruthlessly deposed them when she could not influence them, and eventually became the first female ruler of China. Sa's *Empress*, however, gives us a slightly different version of this story.

Within *Empress*, the much-maligned ruler is given a voice, and a chance to tell the narrative of her life and prosperous reign from her own perspective. In *Empress*, she is intelligent and cunning, strong and determined—retaining many of the qualities historians have ascribed to her over the years. The difference between Sa's tale and the one perpetuated by the history books, however, is the humanity that Sa instills in her heroine. Through Sa's pen, Empress Wu becomes a complicated individual, at times fiercely ambitious and, at others, frighteningly vulnerable. She is as capable of deep compassion as she is of unflinching cruelty, a stunning and clever mix of reason and passion.

With her meticulously researched *Empress*, Sa raises the bar for historical fiction. Here is the memoir denied Empress Wu by the men who destroyed her writings; within these pages is the poetry she championed. Here, Sa connects us with the past while providing a model for our future.

Discussion Questions

1. *Empress* begins with Heavenlight's poetic description of her time spent in the womb. Discuss the description in this novel's first chapter: Was this a surprising perspective? Was it believable? How did it set the tone for the rest of the book?

2. The death of Heavenlight's father is a large blow—to her family's economic and social status, as well as to her emotional and psychological state. In what ways does her father's death foreshadow particular events in her adult life, and how did his death impact her

future relationships with men, especially? In what ways did her father's humble background affect her decisions as a sovereign of China?

3. When Heavenlight leaves her father's family to go to the Imperial City to become a concubine of the emperor, she is fourteen. Discuss the point at which you feel she transforms from adolescent girl to adult—what events inside the gynaeceum are the most significant? Discuss the ways in which sexuality and gender both limit, and aid, Heavenlight's rise among the ranks of the imperial concubines.

4. Early in her life, Heavenlight's love of horses and riding earns her the attention of the Gracious Wife and the friendship and admiration of Little Phoenix. Later, she sees her time spent riding as a symbol of her attraction to heaven and her general distaste for all things earthly. What else does this activity suggest about her character? Does the animal symbolize any other aspect of her life and/or reign? What other examples of symbolism do you find in the book?

5. Historians portray the Empress Wu as ruthlessly ambitious, depicting her as a social climber and a cold-hearted mother and wife. Discuss Little Phoenix's seduction of Heavenlight: In what ways do we see her resist his advances initially, and why does her rejection of him appear earnest and genuine? Consider her elimination of Empress Wang and the Resplendent Wife—the history books accuse her of killing her own baby girl in order to frame the current Empress and gain the Emperor's sympathy. How does Sa retell this story in Heavenlight's favor? Which version of the tale seems most feasible?

6. Heavenlight's relationship with her family is contentious and complicated, at best—particularly with the females in her clan. Describe her interactions with these women: her mother, Little Sister; her elder sister, Purity; and Purity's daughter, Harmony. What did you think about Heavenlight's use of Purity with regards to Little Phoenix—how accepting were you of this incestuous relationship, and with Little Phoenix's infatuation with Harmony? What did these relationships convey about Heavenlight's emotional life, and about her ambition? How responsible was Little Phoenix for the discord between Heavenlight, Purity, and Harmony? Discuss the extent to which Purity's and Harmony's names are ironic.

7. Conversely, now consider Heavenlight's relationships with the males in her clan, and the men who advise her and officiate in her court. In what ways is she ahead of her time in her dealings with them? Compare her relationships with her father's family before she becomes Empress with those afterward, particularly toward the end of her reign. Also discuss her dynamic with Little Phoenix, in matters of state and in matters of the heart. In what does she remain deferential or subordinate?

8. Eventually Heavenlight is called a "mother" of China by her people, but her relationships with her children are vulnerable and based almost solely on the power each lends (or detracts from) her. Do we ever see her come close to regret for the way she has raised them?

Does she fail them, or do they fail her? Compare her relationships with her sons to that with her daughter, Moon, especially.

9. Consider the role of the Buddhist monastery, and of Buddhism in general, in Heavenlight's life. Compare the time she spent in a monastery as a child with the time she spent in one as a nun, before she married Little Phoenix. Compare her attitude toward her mother's religious dedication with her own attitude after her husband's death: What motivated her change of heart? Did you see it as authentic and sincere? Were there times when you questioned her motivation for building temples or going on spiritual journeys?

10. Discuss the role(s) that sensuality and sexuality play in Heavenlight's life, and in seventh-century Chinese culture, using Heavenlight's interaction with the following as examples: Gracious Wife, Little Phoenix, Gentleness, Little Treasure, and Prosperity and Simplicity. Discuss, in particular, the ways in which love and passion transcend gender and age. In what ways does seventh-century Chinese sexuality seem both modern and antiquated?

11. How does Heavenlight bring political and social change to China during her reign? Discuss the extent of her improvements, and evaluate the ramifications of such institutions as the Urn of Truth and the Temple of Clarity. In what way(s) did this near-autocratic ruler make China more democratic? Also discuss the extent to which her male successors undo her hard work and destroy her legacy. What about Heavenlight's ethics and ideals make her a ruler ahead of her time?

12. Discuss Sa's poetic prose style and the extent to which it suits the tone and content of the book. What does her choice of first person narration allow her to show the reader (instead of simply telling)? How would this book be different written in the third person? Or, from the point of view of another character? Would it be as successful? How thoroughly does Sa develop Heavenlight's character, and are there any drawbacks to the way she portrays the empress?

13. *Empress* is a work of fiction based on a particular segment of Chinese history. How well does Sa portray China in the seventh century? Does the reader's lack of knowledge about this particular time and place in history impede his or her comprehension of the book? How smoothly does Sa integrate historical fact with her imaginative prose? Are the few footnotes distracting or helpful? How much does your knowledge that the Empress Wu really existed affect your impression and acceptance of the novel?

A Discussion with Shan Sa

1. How did you arrive at the decision to write a book about the Empress Wu? How much research and preparation did you have to complete before you could begin writing the book? Did any of the "factual" information you came across ever impede your ability to fictionalize her life, or take liberties with certain historical elements?

Empress is the encounter of two Chinese women, myself and Empress Wu. I came to Paris in 1990 at the age of seventeen. Coming from post–Cultural Revolution China to Paris, this city of luxury and lust, I felt the shock and suffering that my heroine experienced when she entered life in the Forbidden City.

The historical research took three years, and I made several trips to China to explore the regions where the Empress had lived. Before I started writing, I created a film set in my mind. I visualized the palaces before placing the people there.

2. Your writing has been translated into several languages. Are there differences between your international audiences, and their reception of your novels? Do you work in conjunction with your translators? Do you ever write in more than one language?

My novels have been translated into twenty-eight languages. Every country reads my books through their own past, their own culture, their own current reality. For example, Greeks ask me about fate, the Spanish ask me about revolt, the Poles about nostalgia for communism.

I go over the Chinese and English translations very carefully, since I speak these languages and I want to give my readers the most beautiful prose possible. In China, I have published poems and essays in Chinese. After French and Chinese, I am tempted to write in English someday.

3. Besides being an award-winning novelist, you're also a celebrated painter who studied with the enigmatic French artist, Balthus. How has your background in visual arts influenced your writing? What necessitated your need to express yourself in a written language, as opposed to visual images? Was the transition from painter to writer an easy one, or have you been able to maintain both "hats" simultaneously?

Painting is great practice for the mental eye. I learned to frame scenes, put surroundings in perspective, and describe characters' gestures and expressions in detail—anger, joy, regret, melancholy, jealousy. . . . Art is a whole. Painting enhances my writing.

4. What are you working on now? Are you painting or writing? What can we expect to see from you in the near future?

I have published a new historical novel, *Alexander and Alestria*. My paintings are being exhibited in the Marlborough Gallery in Monaco. I'm also busy working on the film adaptation of my previous novel, *The Girl Who Played Go*.